THREE BREATHTAKING WOMEN—ABDUCTED . . . ENSLAVED . . . BORNE TOWARD THEIR FATES . . .

THE WIFE: Before her abduction, Marilu had loved and honored her husband, the gallant don Gonzalo, Marques de Clavijo. Her stately, flawless body and radiant beauty had been his alone in wedlock. Now she was to be concubine to a Moorish stranger. With horror she contemplated her rape, her state of sin, the fires of hell. . . .

THE WIDOW: Zoraya, darkly beautiful and audacious, had mourned her beloved husband for twelve months, keeping herself chaste in his memory. Now she was to be slave to one called the Black Vizier. In spite of herself, her body quickened at the thought. So it was with mixed feelings that she was borne toward her fate. . . .

THE VIRGIN: A ravishing, innocent girl, fair-haired Conchita was of a strict religious upbringing, sheltered by her father. Little did he know that, even now, his darling, wrenched brutally from her bedchamber, stood indentured before a young Moorish prince. Conchita knew she should be terrified, and yet, she was anxious to know a man's touch. . . .

THE RAPTURES OF LOVE

Jackson Reed

PYRAMID BOOKS  NEW YORK

THE RAPTURES OF LOVE

A PYRAMID BOOK

Pyramid edition published October 1976

Library of Congress Catalog Card Number: 76–29171

Printed in the United States of America

Pyramid Books are published by Pyramid Publications (Harcourt Brace Jovanovich, Inc.). Its trademarks, consisting of the word "Pyramid" and the portrayal of a pyramid, are registered in the United States Patent Office.

PYRAMID PUBLICATIONS
(Harcourt Brace Jovanovich, Inc.)
757 Third Avenue
New York, New York 10017, U.S.A.

To the memory of Mary Crayg

CONTENTS

PART I

THE ABDUCTION

CHAPTER 1

What is this world's delight?
Lightning that mocks the night—
Brief even as bright!
Such is the raid by night;
Plunder, then take to flight,
Or, if God wills it, fight—
Glory the soldier's right!

Conchado y Bello

The carriage, its curtains tightly closed, careened from side to side as it sped at breakneck speed down the road to Córdoba. Two horses, flecked with foam, strained at their harnesses as they pulled the heavy vehicle behind them, while two other horses, hitched to the carriage by their halters, galloped in the rear. On one side rode a huge man wrapped from head to foot in a white burnous and silken *haik* that covered his head, leaving only his eyes showing, although from time to time the flowing burnous opened in the wind, revealing a rich green and gold brocade robe that showed him to be a person of rank and importance. On the other side of the carriage, two soldiers clad in light chain mail, similarly covered by a flowing white burnous, galloped alongside, each with a lead horse hitched to the cantle of his saddle. The riders held their bridles Arab-fashion, in both hands, never rising by so much as a hair's breadth from their saddles as their bodies rose and fell in unison with the smooth motion of their steeds.

Within the carriage, three women in torn cotton

gowns, covered by long silken capes, huddled together as they were jostled from side to side with every bump in the road. Although disheveled and red-eyed from crying, they were women of unusual beauty. The one in the center, her two wrists manacled to the wrist of her companion on either side, was fair-skinned, with long flowing hair that, even in the dim light of the curtained coach, glittered like burnished gold, while her eyes were of a blue so blue they were almost violet. On her right, there sat, still sobbing and obviously frightened, a girl of perhaps fifteen or sixteen summers, smaller than the young woman in the center but so like her in complexion, hair, and the extreme blueness of her eyes, that they might well have been sisters. The woman on her left, perhaps the oldest of the three though certainly not more than twenty-five, presented a sharp contrast to the other two. Of a smooth olive complexion, with jet-black hair that hung in a thick braid over her left shoulder, and hazel eyes that sparkled through her tears, she was unmistakably Spanish and just as surely a native of southern Spain—Andalucía.

It was the year of our Lord one thousand and ninety-one. Three quarters of the Spanish peninsula was governed by the Moors—by Berbers from North Africa; and, by Arabs from Syria, the Yemen, and elsewhere. These were the conquerors who had occupied Spain for nearly four hundred years, and blended their blood with that of the native Iberians and the former conquerors, Romans and Visigoths, to form a new civilization and a new empire that they called al-Andaluz, in Spanish Andalucía or Vandalucía, the land of the Vandals.

For sixty years Andalucía had been in a state of turmoil. The former Caliphate of Córdoba that had governed practically all of Spain except a narrow strip of northernmost Galicia, Asturias and Viscaya—

the last the land of the unconquerable Basques—had split up into more than a dozen warring kingdoms: Sevilla, Badajoz, Valencia, Zaragoza, and others.

Taking advantage of the dissension among these petty Moorish kings, Alfonso VI, King of León and Castilla, had carried forward the Reconquest of Spain, his victorious armies opposing the Sword of Islam with the Cross of Jesus and the Banner of St. James. The Spanish heartland of León and Castilla, and all Galicia, were solidly Christian. Only seven years earlier, the great city of Toledo had been captured by Alfonso from the Moors—or the Saracens, as they were known in Spain, from the name of a small Bedouin tribe in northern Arabia. Christian Spain now extended as far south as the Guadiana River, with outposts extending as far as Pozoblanco, some fourteen leagues further south. Most of the kingdoms of Andalucía, while still independent, paid tribute to his Most Christian Majesty, who assumed the title of Emperor of Spain.

Separating Moorish and Christian Spain were the Spanish Marches, the vaguely defined military frontiers that fluctuated back and forth with the fortunes of war. Into and across these borders, the Saracens, waiting only for the gleam of the planet Venus in the skies to ensure them victory, would gallop, scimitar in hand, to strike a sudden and devastating blow at some Christian village or military encampment. Like the Bedouin *ghazzia* of Arabia, these forays were undertaken chiefly for the glory and excitement of a raid in the night, for the proof of courage and virility they afforded; and only secondarily for the loot—treasure, horses, and women—that were the booty of a successful raid. If they could escape unscathed, so much the better; but, if there was opposition, the enemy were slain without quarter. Of course, the Christian Spaniards retaliated in kind and, with their Arabian steeds, were as fast to strike, as quick to escape, and as ruthless in slaughter as their Saracen opponents.

The cavalcade on the road to Córdoba—the curtained carriage and some fifty riders, preceding and following, each with a lead horse behind, in most cases bearing a young girl tied to the saddle—was the outcome of just such a Saracen raid. The Moors had struck the town of El Viso, some forty leagues south of Toledo, at dead of night. Quickly they had ransacked the largest mansions of that mountain town, and decamped with their loot: small bags of gold and precious stones, some forty girls, and three score Arabian horses, most of which had undoubtedly been stolen from the Saracens on some prior Christian foray.

The three women in the carriage were a special prize chosen by the *kahraman*, the majordomo and chief eunuch of the Grand Vizier of the Kingdom of Sevilla and Córdoba, for his master and the two other chiefs of the Saracen forces. They were guarded by the burly figure of the majordomo himself as well as by the troops.

The cavalcade galloped across the dusty Pedroches plateau, huge strange-shaped granite boulders on every side and scarcely any vegetation other than the stunted holm oaks and holly oaks that covered the landscape. Some two leagues south of El Viso, after more than an hour of furious riding, they drew to a halt at the post garrison of Alcaracejos.

The chief eunuch opened the door of the coach and peeked in. The three women, exhausted, were sound asleep or at least appeared to be. He drew back the curtains a few inches, for they were now safe in Moslem territory, and opened the windows, for it was stifling in the coach, even though the June sun had barely risen in the dawn.

As he closed the carriage door quietly, the women

stirred and soon were fully awake from the noise and commotion of changing horses and from shouted orders given by the captain of the raiders to the sergeant of the frontier garrison.

"Fresh horses for the coach and cavalry, and send back two score of these captured mounts to Córdoba after they have been watered, fed and rested.

"If any Spanish troops come in pursuit, send a courier to warn us, and fight them off as best you can."

"Yes, Captain," answered the sergeant. "It will be done."

The captain knew there was little danger of immediate pursuit from the small garrison at El Viso to deep within the Andalusian territory, but he thanked the sergeant for his speed in providing remounts, and gave orders for his men to get some refreshment and be ready to leave in ten minutes.

Meanwhile, the three women, wide awake now but still feigning sleep, listened eagerly as the chief eunuch gave instructions to two younger men who had ridden up. They were dressed in the same fashion as the chief eunuch and were at least as burly. They listened respectfully to the words of their chief.

"The woman in the center is for the Grand Vizier. She's a Galician, as you can see, named Marilú, the wife of the Marqués de Clavijo."

Turning to the more swarthy of the other eunuchs, he added: "The black-haired one is for the Black Vizier; she's the widow of the Conde de Ayala and is the owner of the big palace on the side of the hill where we found all three women. Her name is Zoraya.

"As for the other one, the little blond," he went on, turning to the other eunuch, "she's for Prince al-Mamun and is a cousin or a niece of Marilú. Her name is Conchita. And I can assure you that, unless my nose for maidenheads has played me false, she is *virgo intacta*, which is the way your master likes them. . . . Although I can't see why, as he loses no time in robbing them of the very virginity that he seems to prize so highly.

"Guard these women carefully," he continued, "and draw the curtains closed. If the captain or his men should gaze upon them, it will so inflame them they will be unable to gallop on their mounts without injuring themselves, and Allah knows we have enough eunuchs in Medina al-Zahra already."

The two men nodded and peeked inside the carriage where the women were still apparently dozing. They drew the curtains and closed the carriage doors, then hastily remounted their fresh steeds as the column got under way.

Once again, the cavalcade set forth at a gallop, although at a more moderate clip than in the first leg of their flight from El Viso. Fortunately, the carriage was of solid construction, built of Spanish oak with huge, spoked wheels. The old Roman highway, maintained and improved by the Moors, was as level and smooth as any in all Europe. No lesser vehicle could have stood the pounding and jolting to which the carriage and its occupants had been subjected during the first leg of the journey. The Saracens themselves never used either wagons or carriages but, from frequent raids, they had learned to handle the heavy vehicles as expertly as the Spaniards and could cover as much as fifteen to twenty leagues at a gallop—fifty to sixty miles—from sun-up to sun-down, with post changes every two or three leagues.

Left to themselves, and bouncing along inside the coach, the three women discussed what they had heard. A sharp jolt caused them all to lurch violently to one side.

"Goodness," shrieked Zoraya, "that Jehu of a coachman certainly drives furiously!"

"Well, at least we know what's going to happen to us," said Marilú, "no better, no worse than what I expected, from the moment that big fat eunuch burst into my bedchamber before sunrise this morning."

"The Grand Vizier must be ben-Zaydun, who is the chief general of King al-Mutamid," interjected Zoraya, "but I wonder what he's doing up in Medina al-Zahra. Medina al-Zahra is just a league or so from Córdoba—it used to be the Caliph's palace and is supposed to be the most beautiful in the world. And ben-Zaydun is said to be a wonderful person, tall, handsome and *simpático*. So, at least you'll be all right, Marilú."

"And you, Conchita, will be with the Prince who is Governor of Córdoba, young, good looking, and, if he is as virile as his father, the King of Sevilla, you couldn't wish for anyone better prepared to initiate you into the art of love."

At that, the poor distraught Conchita burst into tears again and snuggled close to Marilú, who tried to comfort her as best she could, keeping up the conversation so as to distract her young cousin from her fears: "What about you, Zoraya? They said the 'Black Vizier'. Is he really black—a Berber from North Africa, or a Senegalese, one of those horrid people who massacred so many Spaniards at the Battle of Azagal? I'm worried about you, my dear."

"I don't know whether he's black or brown or what," answered Zoraya, "I only hope that they call him the 'Black Vizier' because of the color of his skin and not because he is as black-hearted as those Berbers and Senegalese you speak of. The only vizier I've ever heard of in the Kingdom of Sevilla, besides the Grand Vizier ben-Zaydun, is ben-Bakr who is descended from the first Caliph of Islam, the successor of Mohammed. If he's black, it's because he's also supposed to be descended from the Queen of Sheba and from Abyssinian royalty. Anyway, if it's a sin to have a lover—and I don't see why it should be when we are captured slaves and can't help ourselves—I don't see what difference it makes whether he's black or white or brown. So please don't worry on my account, my darling."

But, of course, the three women *were* worried and frightened. And all three, as good Christians, were horrified at the thought of living in sin and not only in sin, but with an Infidel. Excommunication on earth, and the fires of Hell after death, were prospects too real to be lightly disregarded.

To keep up her spirits, and particularly to bolster the spirits of poor Conchita, whom she had known only for two days but whom she had come to love as a younger sister, Zoraya kept on talking. She told them what she knew of life in Moslem Spain, drawing on her own experience as a child in Cádiz and, later, as a married woman in Toledo and in El Viso. The luxury of Moslem life—the baths, the rich clothes, the fine foods, the music, dancing, and entertainment—she contrasted with the crude, almost barbarous state of existence in Christian Spain.

"And," she continued, "I can tell you that when you are first brought in, as a Christian slave, to meet your lord and master, you must kneel down like an Arab at prayer and kiss the ground between your stretched-out hands."

She tried to illustrate, but couldn't with one hand manacled to that of Marilú.

"Furthermore, when your lord and master asks you to do anything, it is a command, and you must answer: 'To hear is to obey,' or 'Hearkening and obedience', or else 'With love and gladness.'"

Marilú and Conchita smiled at this, their first smiles

since the terror of their abduction only a few hours earlier. Then each withdrew into her own thoughts.

It all seemed so unreal, thought Marilú. That she, María Luisa Andrade de Araujo, should be subjected to such an indignity, such a tragedy, seemed impossible to believe. Only a month ago she had left her two beautiful daughters, aged three and four, with her mother in Betanzos, the family seat in Galicia. She had joined her husband, the gallant and romantic don Gonzalo, Marqués de Clavijo, in Toledo where King Alfonso VI had established his court some six years earlier. The *Marqués* was a general in the King's army, and constantly off on one foray or another; and the King having a notoriously wandering eye, much to the dismay of his poor French Queen Constance, don Gonzalo had sent Marilú down to El Viso a fortnight ago to stay with the widow of his old comrade in arms Conde de Ayala, who had died in the previous year in the King's service.

There, in a beautiful Moorish palace, with a breath-taking view of the Pedroches valley—hence the name, El Viso, the outlook—she met Zoraya, perhaps the most beautiful woman she had ever known. They formed an instant friendship. From Zoraya she had learned much about the elegant life of Moslem Spain, for El Viso, although now the southernmost outpost of the Emperor Alfonso's empire, was a Moorish town in every sense, a favorite summer resort of the wealthy and noble families of Toledo, which lay just forty-five leagues to the north. And, with Alfonso's armies everywhere victorious, and all the kings of Andalucía paying tribute to his Kingdom of León and Castilla, there seemed to be no danger from the Saracens. Above all, there was no danger in quiet El Viso from the King, who had cuckolded half his courtiers in Toledo.

And here she was, the Marquesa de Clavijo, handcuffed in this coach with two of her dearest friends, and headed at frightening speed to be the slave and concubine of the Grand Vizier of the King of Sevilla!

Conchita's thoughts wandered back to the long trip she had made a scant two months ago, from her home in Puentedeume to the court at Toledo. She had accompanied her widowed father, the Conde de Andrade, who had been summoned by the King to discuss plans for the rebuilding of Galicia which still bore traces of the ravages of the Saracens nearly a century ago. And then, she recalled, her father had said that Toledo was not a safe place for a young girl of fifteen, for reasons which she had not fully understood, and they had moved to Santa Eufemia, a long day's journey south, where a priest whom her father had known in Galicia had been established as Abbot of the newly founded Monastery of Santa Eufemia.

There, certain events that she tried hard to forget, but which still troubled and excited her, had caused her father to send her, with her duenna, to join her cousin, Marilú, in the palace of the Condesa de Ayala—the most beautiful and luxurious residence she had ever seen, a sharp contrast to the rugged fortress castles of her native Galicia.

And, only two days later, she had been rudely awakened and abducted from her bedchamber by that huge man who was now galloping somewhere outside the heavily curtained coach. The thought of being carried as a slave to a Prince, a man of exceptional virility, as Zoraya had intimated, both troubled and excited her, and she tried to erase from her mind the horrible events in Santa Eufemia that had caused her father to send her to El Viso.

Zoraya was troubled, not so much for herself as for that darling girl, Conchita, and for Marilú, whom she had come to love as a sister. As for herself, she had been brought up in Cádiz as a *Mozarab,* Christian by religion, but indistinguishable from her Arab acquaintances in costume, customs, education, and philosophy of life.

She was a fatalist. What will be, will be. If it be the will of God—and in her mind she said "the will of Allah"—that she become the slave of the Black Vizier, so be it. There was nothing she could do about it, certainly not now, handcuffed as she was in the coach and garded by three eunuchs and Lord knows how many soldiers.

She had been deeply in love with her husband and, even though childless, had lived happily with him for ten years, first in León, and later in Toledo and the mansion at El Viso. But her twelve months' widowhood was almost over and she remembered St. Paul's admonition: "It is better to marry than to burn." Certainly, she burned to be married again, and was at no loss for suitors. But now, what would be, would be.

The carriage again drew to a halt, this time at Puerto Calatraveño, outside a small frontier fort. The chief eunuch opened the door: "We shall be here for fifteen minutes. I am going to get you some silk scarves to cover your hair and faces and then, if you wish, I shall have some food and refreshments brought to you in the coach."

His voice was pleasant, his manner respectful, and his tone solicitous, and the three women were reassured by his presence—a sharp contrast from the night before, when he had forceably seized each of them in turn from their beds, clad only in the sheerest of cotton gowns, thrown them their traveling cloaks, handcuffed them, and rushed them down the stairs to the waiting carriage. They realized, of course, that in a raid, Saracen style, there was no time for the amenities, that the faster the raiders got on with their business of looting, the less chance there was of resistance and of wholesale slaughter.

After the chief eunuch brought the scarves they were served bowls of hot soup with wooden spoons, delicately perfumed cold sherbets of milk of almonds to drink, *patés* of cold chicken, pastries filled with chopped squab and almond paste, and a large basket of pears, peaches and cherries. The stop would certainly take far more than the fifteen minutes the eunuch had mentioned, and the three passengers in the carriage were not surprised to overhear the captain discussing the matter with the chief eunuch.

"You see," the captain was saying, "my men are anxious to get back to Medina al-Zahra as fast as possible with the loot they gathered at El Viso, and I might say I feel the same way. We have barely covered three leagues since morning, and at the rate this coach is going, with post changes practically every hour, we shan't arrive until after sundown."

"I suppose you do all want to bed your booty," replied the eunuch, "and, while I do not share your sentiments, I can understand them. We're safe in Moorish territory now; why don't you just leave me a squad of men with a seargeant—those who have not taken such perishable loot—and the rest of you ride on ahead as fast as you wish."

"With joy and gladness," replied the captain, delighted, "and I think I'll give my men a half hour right now to inspect their cargo in the field, while I do the same in the officers' lounge."

Orders were quickly given and greeted by loud cheers as the soldiers dispersed into the underbrush with their prizes while the captain entered the garrison arm in arm with as comely a wench as one was likely to see in all of Andalucía. The air was soon filled with shrieks.

Zoraya drew the curtain aside, and there, not ten

paces away, the three women saw one of the sergeants with a buxom and struggling girl in his arms, his trousers down and her blouse wide open.

"My," said Zoraya, staring at what the three women could not help but see.

Conchita blushed from head to foot, but no less eagerly watched a scene which she had often imagined but never before seen. The sergeant twined his legs around the girl and in an instant they tumbled onto the grass, the sergeant on top, the girl's skirts high up over her thighs.

Gasps and moans came from the underbrush, the couple now practically hidden from view. Zoraya drew the curtain closed again, and the three women snuggled close.

A few moments later, Marilú shook herself and murmured, "I don't think I want any more food right now."

"Nor I either," said Conchita.

Zoraya nodded her head in acquiescence.

Marilú summoned the chief eunuch and said they were through eating. He took the food and plates away, leaving the basket of fruit, and a jug of the almond beverage with three metal cups, to relieve the tedium of the voyage.

"Señor *nazir,*" he said to the sergeant, "we are ready to leave now, if you are."

A moment later, they were on their way, the carriage accompanied by the three eunuchs, the *nazir*, and a squad of eight soldiers, one of them bearing a red and white pennon on a lance. The garrison was soon left far behind as the small cavalcade took off in a cloud of dust.

A half hour later, the carriage was overtaken by the captain and his remaining four squads, each with a sergeant and its varicolored pennon, and the company guidon fluttering in the wind. They passed the coach and its escorts at a full gallop, but not before the three ladies noted through the half-drawn curtains that the soldiers' captives were no longer tied to the saddles of the lead horses but were seated close behind their captors on the horses' cruppers, their arms tightly entwined around their masters' waists, while the lead horses, tied to the cantles, galloped along behind, saddled but riderless.

Steadily on, the smaller cavalcade galloped, fording two small streams, changing horses at Campo, and again at Clavellina. By this time, the three women, utterly exhausted after over ten hours of travel, were sound asleep. They entered Córdoba through the Amir gate, where the horses were forced to slow down to a trot. A few minutes later, they left the city through the Djawz gate, but it was not until they drew up at the outer gate of Medina al-Zahra that the ladies drowsily stirred and vaguely returned to consciousness as they became aware of stopping and starting again at yet another gate, the entrance to the palace itself.

There they were taken by the chief eunuch down a long passageway to a dungeon, dimly lit with oil lamps in sconces on the walls. The iron door to the dungeon closed behind them, and they could hear the lock turn and the eunuch's footsteps in the hall as he left, presumably to report his arrival.

A few minutes later, the door was unlocked and opened. There entered a woman, no longer young, but handsome and beautifully robed, accompanied by two younger women, one carrying several cushions, and the other a tray and small table with bowls, a jug, and silver cups.

"I am Nardjis," said the older woman in a voice so sweet and gentle that the three prisoners could not but be reassured. "You are now in the palace of the Grand Vizier, and I am here to serve you. I'm sorry I cannot remove your manacles, but the eunuch who brought you here has the keys. He will return shortly. Meanwhile, pray be seated."

One of the younger women placed the cushions on a stone bench against the wall, the only furniture in the dungeon, aside from a large leather mattress in one corner of the room.

"And do have some of this hot soup and wine," she added, as the other young woman placed the small table in front of them, with the tray on top. "I'll help you," she said to Marilú, whose two hands were handcuffed to those of her companions but who was still able, with some difficulty, to manage the wooden soup spoon and the winecups.

"And don't be worried. You will find that the Prince and the two viziers, whose slaves you now are, are men of great charm and understanding, virile but gentle. You must have no fear; it is one of those burdens that we women must suffer. Tonight you will sleep undisturbed, for you are very weary and dusty from your long journey, but tomorrow the three of us will be here to attend to you."

The three captives thanked Nardjis and her two companions profusely, and meanwhile finished up the soup which was hot and thick and nourishing. It revived their bodies and spirits, so weary after the long travail and fears of the past twelve hours.

"And drink your wine; you will find it soothing and it will help you sleep," insisted Nardjis.

This they did, and almost immediately dropped off into a sound sleep.

"That wine certainly acts quickly," whispered one of the younger women, as she helped her two companions steady the three captives, swaying drunkenly on the bench. "I wish the chief eunuch and the other two eunuchs would hurry back and take them out of this horrible dungeon."

CHAPTER 2

Marilú opened her eyes drowsily. She stretched and arched her back, cat-like, as she always did on waking. Where was she? A bed so large, so soft yet firm, like none she had ever experienced, the dim half-light through curtained windows at ceiling height far above the floor, the scent of delicate perfumes in the air, women's voices talking, laughing somewhere in the distance—all these things impinged on her consciousness as she stirred in bed.

A dim form, a woman clad in a long robe, glided softly out of the room. Marilú closed her eyes and tried to piece together the events of the previous day—the abduction, the long and wearisome ride, the dungeon, the lovely woman who had given her and her companions a bowl of soup and a cup of wine. That was it—the wine; there must have been some drug in it, hashish or something, because she could remember nothing further.

The heavy draperies at one end of the room were pushed aside, and a woman, vaguely familiar, entered, while two young women pulled cords that drew back the curtains covering the clerestory windows. The sun shone in through a lacework of lattices and colored glass panes, and the room suddenly became bright.

"I am Nardjis. Do you remember me?"

The soft, sweet voice brought back instant recollection.

"Yes, I do. You gave us soup and wine in the dungeon last night; there must have been something in the wine that made me sleep."

Marilú glanced around—a small room, about twenty feet square, the walls of rose and white marble studded with silver, the floor of black and white marble squares covered with a square Persian rug of beige and rose, high latticed clerestory windows on two sides, the ceiling elaborately carved in blue, red, green and gold, and two doorways between marble columns on the other two sides, with heavy, rose and gold silk draperies closing the room off completely from the adjoining rooms. Bronze sconces on the walls held glass lamps which, however, were not lit. The only furniture consisted of two white marble benches on the two sides of the room, but four bronze stags with gleaming green eyes stood in the four corners. The bed was nothing but a thick leather mattress covered with a felt rug and fine cotton sheets, and may have been placed there temporarily for her use, as it did not seem to go with the bare yet rich appearance of the room.

"Where am I? Where are Conchita and Zoraya? Are they all right? What time is it?" The questions came fast and furious.

Nardjis smiled. "True; there was a form of hashish in the wine. You were exhausted, frightened; I gave it to you as a sedative so that you could sleep and rest—it will have no after-effects. Your friends are safe. They were carried off by the two eunuchs at the same time that the chief eunuch of the palace carried you here on his shoulder.

"Your little blond friend—Conchita is it?—was taken to the summer apartment of Prince al-Mamun, and Zoraya was taken to the apartment of the Vizier ben Bakr. Both apartments are connected with this part of the palace by corridors so that you are all practically in the same place, although in separate buildings, each completely private. For you know that a harem is a sacred place, not to be entered by anyone except the master of the house and his wives, concubines, eunuchs and maid servants.

"And where are we?" She continued rhetorically. "We're in the private apartments of what used to be the Caliph's palace in Medina al-Zahra. I'll tell you more about the palace, and show you around, some other time. This room is the vestibule of the *hammam*—the bath—and we shall give you a bath immediately to wash away the dirt and grime of your journey, and to wash away your cares and fears.

"But first," and Nardjis nodded to one of the two young women, "let me give you a glass of sherbet—it will refresh you."

One of the serving women came forward with a small table, the other with a brass tray on which she carried a pale blue crystal jug and two crystal goblets. Resting the tray on the table, the girl poured a small amount of the beverage into one of the goblets and drank it, then filled the other goblet to the brim and offered it to Marilú.

"This is Ourda," said Nardjis to Marilú and then turning to the girl, "From now on, you will be the handmaiden of Doña María Luisa Andrade de Araujo, the Marquesa de Clavijo, while you, Shamsi," turning to the other girl, "will stay with me, although you will take turns with Ourda from time to time to make sure that the *Marquesa* always has what she needs."

Marilú acknowledged the introductions graciously, and the two girls expressed their pleasure shyly and sweetly.

"Ourda sipped the sherbet to show you that the drink has not been poisoned," explained Nardjis, "and there's no hashish in it this time, I can assure you. It's ginger and rose petals."

Marilú sipped it. It was delicious—icy cold, almost frozen, and the most refreshing drink she had ever tasted. "Thank you, it's lovely," she murmured.

"Let's go into the *hammam*," said Nardjis as she led Marilú through the draperied doorway.

"If you've never had a Moorish bath, you will enjoy it. This is the disrobing and dressing room."

And they entered a much larger room, again with latticed clerestory windows, in this case of clear glass, high above the floor and extending the full length of the room on both sides. A large chandelier, holding some two score crystal lamps, was suspended from the ceiling of translucent alabaster. This room was also marble, of various colors, studded with silver and surmounted by a broad frieze of blue, green, red and gilt marble elaborately carved in floral and geometrical designs and Arabic lettering. Like the vestibule, this room had four glass-eyed bronze beasts—dogs this time—in the four corners, and high marble-columned doorways, one leading from the vestibule and two at the far end. The doorways were completely closed off with draperies of gold brocade with elaborate designs woven into the fabric.

The floor was again of black and white squares almost entirely covered by a large rug of Esparto grass. Two marble benches stood between large bronze and gilt coffers, one of which was open, disclosing an array of slippers, cotton robes and other accessories. In front of the benches were several small Persian rugs, matching the blue, red, green and gold of the frieze, while on all sides of the room, between the marble columns, were a number of ancient Roman statues of white marble. From the floor there appeared to come a current of warm air.

"There are lead pipes and channels of hot water running beneath all the floors of the *hammam*," explained Nardjis. "In the next room, you will find it even warmer, and in the last room it will be just about as hot as you can stand it."

The two women disrobed, or rather were disrobed by the two young attendants who had discarded their own outer garments and wore nothing but thin cotton trousers tied around the waist with a drawstring—that, and silver anklets and bracelets. Marilú looked at their slim young figures and thought that they could not have been more than fourteen or fifteen years of age.

She had nothing to be ashamed of in her own figure—her waist almost as small as that of the two young girls, her breasts full but firm and uptilted, her hips broad and buttocks well rounded, her thighs and legs slim and shapely, her neck long and graceful, her posture erect, her navel deep and smooth and *mons veneris* prominent, tufts of light brown hair in her armpits and growing luxuriantly at the crotch, while her long golden blond hair, disheveled though it was, hung in a graceful, wavy curl over her shoulder.

Nardjis glanced at her admiringly, while Marilú could see that Nardjis herself was slim and erect, her hair jet black—perhaps forty years old, she judged. Nardjis must have been beautiful when young. The attendants handed the two women cotton gowns and slippers, and they went into the next room.

"This room is what the Roman colonizers of Spain would call the *tepidarium*," said Nardjis, "although the Moorish bath is more luxuriant than the Roman, and our soaps and perfumes of finer quality."

"Soap? For the bath?" asked Marilú. The only soap with which she was familiar was a soft, messy mixture of goat tallow and wood ashes that was harsh and caustic and could be used only for scrubbing clothes.

"Yes, you will see," answered Nardjis. "It is made by Arabs in Italy, but I expect we shall soon be making it in Andalucía as we have plenty of olive oil here, and the perfumes for it come chiefly from the Yemen in southern Arabia."

The room was long and narrow, all of varicolored marble, with the same blue, red, green and gold marble frieze, and clear clerestory windows, that Marilú had noticed in the dressing room. The bronze animals in the four corners were magnificent prancing Arabian horses. The ceiling, studded with silver stars, was made of thin, translucent marble slabs, varying in color from blue to beige to rosy pink—the colors of a glorious sunset, thought Marilú, as she looked around the room in wonderment. The floor was of white marble, channelled to drain off any splashing water; and, between the channels, it was covered with runners of Esparto grass rugs.

Dozens of sconces on the walls held glass lamps. Against one wall were two large marble basins carved in the form of scallop shells. And in front of each shell stood a long, wide, white marble bench. There were containers next to the basins holding sponges, wash clothes, and what looked like pieces of ivory that Marilú soon learned were cakes of hard soap such as she had never seen before.

The room was delightfully warm, but not hot, and the air was delicately perfumed with a fragrance that Marilú recalled but could not identify. So she asked Nardjis, who replied: "It is narcissus, one of my favorite flowers, and I thought you might like it. We shall use a different perfume for the bath this evening when the Vizier returns from Córdoba, as men cannot stand the fragrance of narcissus."

The attendants had the two ladies sit down on the marble benches, their heads over the basins, while they washed and rinsed their hair again and again with soap and clear warm water. To Marilú's delight and amazement, the soap made a foamy lather, fragrant and soothing.

Following the shampoo, Ourda clipped and then gently shaved the tufts of hair under Marilú's armpits, while Shamis shaved the armpits and calves of her mistress where the black hairs marred the smooth olive of her skin. In Marilú's case, the soft blond fuzz on her arms and legs was almost invisible, or at most gave a shining lustre to the unblemished rosy whiteness of her limbs.

This done, the two young girls led their charges though a connecting door to an adjoining room almost identical to the *tepidarium*, with a star-spangled ceiling, two shell-shaped basins and two marble benches. There were large masonry cauldrons in the four corners of the room filled with water, boiling and bubbling and flooding the room with steam. In front of each cauldron stood a rampant lion of bronze with terrifying red glass eyes. In the center of the room, side by side, and facing the benches, were two small pools, each with a flight of steps leading down into the water. The bottoms and sides of the pools were of blue tile and the rims were covered with Arabic inscriptions and adorned with gold and silver. On the three sides of each pool facing the steps were three small golden animals spouting liquid from their mouths—in one pool frogs, the other swans.

"This is the *calidarium*, the steam room," whispered Nardjis.

The two attendants, soaked to the skin, their petti-trousers clinging revealingly to their slim legs, asked Nardjis and Marilú to recline on the marble benches, on which they proceeded to lave, soap, scrub and rinse them. This done, the two young girls led the ladies to one of the pools, tested the water, and held them by the hand as they descended the five marble steps. There they sat, submerged to their necks in water slightly above body temperature, but gradually made hotter and hotter with the flow of hot water from one of the three spouting frogs. From the mouth of the center frog dripped a small stream of narcissus-scented liquid. The third frog gushed forth cold water whenever the bath became too hot.

The two women sat, their eyes half closed, for half an hour, while Marilú felt every last bit of tension drain from her body.

Still submerged in the bath, they were served a light lunch placed on trays at the side of the pools—tiny, fresh shrimp in oil and vinegar, delicately seasoned pastry tarts garnished with *quenelles* of finely chopped chicken, flaky pastries sweetened with boiled honey, chopped pine nuts and rose petals, a basket of fresh figs and pomegranates, and tall crystal goblets of icy cold water scented with orange blossoms.

Thoroughly relaxed, they were next led to the pool of the three swans. Marilú gave a shrill scream as a shock of icy-cold water touched her ankles. The other three laughed, but drew her into the pool until she was in water up to her neck. They remained only a moment, the two girls helping their mistresses to make a hurried exit up the steps, whereupon they were vigorously rubbed dry with huge Turkish towels. The shock of the cold water, following the relaxation of the hot bath, brought an exhilarating glow to Marilú's body from head to toe, and a rosy pink shone through the creamy whiteness of her skin.

Then Nardjis and Marilú returned to the benches which, meanwhile, had been carefully dried. They were massaged and rubbed with fragrant oils, thumped and pounded from the back of the neck to the small of the back, down to their buttocks, thighs and calves, then, lying on their backs, they were massaged from forehead to ankles, and, finally, their feet were kneaded and rubbed until at last every muscle in their bodies was relaxed and rejuvenated, and the perfumed oils had been totally absorbed into their glowing skins.

Ourda and Shamsi gave their mistresses long gowns made of Turkish toweling, and they themselves hastily washed their hands, dried themselves, and donned fresh garments, virtually identical.

Another door in the *calidarium* led them back into the dressing room, and Marilú could now see that the two bathing rooms were side by side, connected with each other, and connected with the dressing room through the two doors on its side. Ourda then led Marilú into a private dressing closet.

Marilú looked at the girl. This was the first time she had been alone with her, and she found her charming, and as pretty a child as she had ever seen. Like a young Zoraya, she thought—jet black hair, cut short and tied with a small black silk bow, sparkling eyes of hazel hue, firm breasts, small but well developed for her age, the tiniest of waists, the slimmest of arms and legs, and dainty hands and feet, a tempting morsel, Marilú thought, for any man. The child was clothed in a costume that revealed more than it concealed—a flimsy white silken blouse, baggy silk pantaloons that reached from her waist to her ankles, and a bright red sash that left her navel bare, altogether a charming spectacle.

"Ourda is a pretty name. Does it mean anything?" Marilú remarked.

"Thank you. Yes, Ourda is a rose. And Shamsi's name means 'my sunshine' while Lady Nardjis's name means 'jonquil'. They are all nicknames, of course, but we are never known by any other name, and I don't even know Lady Nardjis's full name. Although I do know that she is a very grand lady, that she took care of the Vizier ben-Zaydun when he was a child, and was the lady-in-waiting of his wife, Zohra.

"She has been a widow for many years, and is in

charge of all the women in the *seraglio*—Shamsi and me, the dancing girls and concubines, and more than one hundred slaves and servants. Lady Nardjis is wonderful, so kind and sympathetic, and yet so strict with all of us. We are very lucky to have her as our mistress, and not be bossed around by a dozen wives as in most households.

"The Grand Vizier only had one wife, Zohra, and she was a lovely person."

Here Ourda burst out crying, and Marilú took her in her arms to comfort her. She soon dried her tears, and they rejoined Nardjis and Shamsi in the dressing room.

"My, you two have been gone a long time," smiled Nardjis. "But it makes no difference; we shan't take long with the make-up this time, as we two shall be alone together until evening. This evening, though, before the Grand Vizier returns, you will know how really complete a beauty treatment can be in Andalucía."

Just then, they could hear a cock crow somewhere outside the windows. "Oh, it is still early morning," exclaimed Marilú. "I had no idea of the time, but I had thought it was much later in the day."

"It *is* much later in the day—an hour or so after midday, I should say. You slept late this morning. But in Andalucía, the cocks crow all day long, not just in the morning. They say that the roosters are just like the men in Andalucía, and that they want to impress their harem with their virility, so they crow and perform their marital duties from sunup to sunset. The men are worse though. With them, it is all night long as well!"

Shamsi and Ourda gave the ladies some powdered walnut bark, and Ourda showed Marilú how to rub her teeth and gums with it until the teeth were gleaming white and the gums and lips a rosy red.

They then rinsed their mouths with perfumed water and were given scented gum arabic to chew so that their breath would remain fragrant for hours. Meanwhile, the girls were busy drying their mistresses' hair and, after rubbing in a few drops of perfumed oil, brushing it vigourously with ivory brushes.

"You might do my hair in the usual style," said Nardjis, "but I think you should leave the *Marquesa's* hair long, in the northern fashion."

Lady Nardjis's jet-black hair was short, and Shamsi brushed it up in curls, leaving her forehead and the nape of the neck bare, although a tiny curl was allowed to drop in front of each ear, close to the cheek. She looked most attractive, with two small pearl earrings to enhance the beauty of her ears.

"This is the style of coiffure that we have used in Andalucía ever since it was introduced to Spain by the Persian, Ziryab, nearly two hundred and seventy years ago," Nardjis remarked.

"It is a great nuisance. Everything that Ziryab thought was proper, we still have to do. Everything he disapproved of simply is *not* done—at least in society. I admit he was a wonderful musician and it is said that he knew ten thousand songs that he brought with him when he fled from the Caliph's court in Baghdad. And I admit that he introduced all kinds of new musical instruments, and delicious new foods, and even the proper way to serve a meal in courses instead of having it all heaped on the table at once.

"He trained dancing girls and started beauty parlors and schools to teach young girls like Shamsi and Ourda to take care of our hair and faces and bodies. I suppose he *did* bring civilization to al-Andaluz, but it does seem strange, almost three centuries later, we must all change from bright clothes to white clothes and back again precisely on the dates he prescribed, that we must use crystal goblets and ceramic dishes instead of the gold plates and cups we used to use, just because he thought gold and silver were too ostentatious. In fact, there is scarcely a thing we do here in the palace that is not done exactly as Ziryab thought proper.

"But the Emir Abd ar-Rahman II made him the arbiter of elegance, and none of us dares do anything differently. I guess I'll have to confess I like it that way. I don't mind obeying a man; I always have. But I don't like having to obey a dead man whom you can't even wheedle to make you do what you yourself really want to do. Oh, well!"

During all this time, Ourda had been vigourously brushing Marilú's long wavy hair, and finally parted it in the center with an ivory comb and draped it in two soft coils over her shoulders and covering her breasts. It looked lovely, thought Marilú, as she looked in the long-handled silver mirror that Ourda handed her—shinier and cleaner than she had ever had it before, and it gleamed like pure gold in the sunlight that filtered through the alabaster ceiling and shone resplendent through the windows.

"It is a beautiful summery day," said Nardjis, "so we shall take our walk and *siesta* together in the garden, and shan't have to wear veils."

They were quickly dressed by the two girls in cool thin cotton robes reaching to their ankles, with a cotton blouse and baggy pantaloons beneath. Comfortable, soft silken slippers with chamois sole, and little dome-shaped red velvet caps fringed with pearls, completed their outfits. The two ladies left the room arm in arm, leaving Ourda and Shamsi, smiling and bowing, to tidy up.

"This way," said Nardjis, as she led the way up a flight of stairs and down a long covered corridor, across a shaded patio, into another room, and out onto a marble balcony, then down a long flight of stone steps onto a terrace, and out into the garden. Marilú was amazed at the beauty of all she saw, so luxurious in comparison with her husband's and her father's simple castles in Galicia, and even compared to the elegant mansion in which she had stayed with Zoraya in El Viso, up to now the most beautiful house she had ever seen. But this palace—it passed all description in beauty and luxury!

"We shan't have nearly enough time for me to show you around the palace today," said Nardjis, reading Marilú's mind, "but we can talk together in the garden and I'll tell you all about Medina al-Zahra and everything else you wish to know." And she gave Marilú's arm an affectionate squeeze which Marilú reciprocated.

They came to an ancient Roman arch beyond which stretched a vista of incredible beauty. The keystone of the arch, which in former days may have borne the proud Roman inscription "S.P.Q.R.", was inscribed with Arabic characters in the classic *Kufic* style.

Nardjis translated: "Here the wicked cease from troubling and the weary are at rest."

Passing through the bronze gate, they walked along a shaded gravel path between groves of frankincense, acacia, and fruit trees—pomegranate, peach, orange and lemon—the citrus trees in full bloom, the pomegranate with only a few blossoms still clinging to the branches. Beneath the trees were clumps of jasmine, violets, narcissus and other flowers. The air was heavy with perfume, and the sound of gurgling water came to them from a brook of which they caught glimpses through the willows that fringed its bank.

"It is a paradise!" exclaimed Marilú.

"It is indeed! The Koran, you know, describes Paradise as a shaded, leafy garden, full of pomegranates and palms, and refreshed by running water and a gushing fountain. The blessed dead take their repose there, in separate pavilions, reclining on raised couches, and surrounded by ever-virgin houris with large dark eyes and teeth like pearls. Goblets of the choicest wine, never full and never empty, are always at hand, cushions laid out and carpets spread, and everything is there that is needed to delight the senses of the faithful.

Then, changing the subject: "Now tell me what you want to know."

"Well, you say you are going to show me the palace some other time, so tell me all about the Grand Vizier, for I understand that I am to be his slave. Who is he? What is he like? Will he be cruel to me? Will he insist on having his pleasure with me? I'm frightened, you know, because I am a married woman and have never been unfaithful."

"I thought that would be uppermost in your mind, but I can assure you that you will never find him cruel. And, as for your marriage vows, it can be no sin to break them when you are a slave and have no choice—except to take your own life, which would be an even greater sin. Well, I'll try to tell you as much as I can about the Grand Vizier. I have known him since he was a baby and I was a little girl of six who took care of him in his father's house."

They approached the pavilion—a delicately constructed bronze and iron gazebo, open on all sides, yet so covered with climbing roses in full bloom, and other bushes, as to be completely secluded. In fact, it was not visible until the two had circled a fountain that shot a jet of clear water twenty feet into the air that cascaded into a white marble pool, surrounded by four bronze lions from whose open mouths there spouted four small streams of water.

Shamsi and Ourda were in the pavilion, arranging cushions on which their mistresses could either sit or recline. There was a tray between them, on which were two glass goblets and a large earthenware jug, moist with the liquid that seeped through the side and whose evaporation would keep the contents cool.

"You may leave us now," said Nardjis. "We have many things to talk about, and you must take your *siestas* too, to be fresh for the evening."

"Well, now," she continued, as the two girls walked away down the garden path, arm in arm. "Let's begin at the beginning. The Grand Vizier—his name is Ahmad abd ar-Ra'uf ben Zaydun. But only his most intimate relatives and friends call him Ahmad. He is generally known as ben Zaydun, or by the title of Grand Vizier. That's not his full name, either his full name, which lists his father, his grandfather, his tribe and his origin, is so long you would never remember it.

"He is the son of abu al-Walid Ahmad ibn Zaydun, may he rest in peace, who died just twenty years ago, the greatest poet of all al-Andaluz. The Zayduns are from the noble *banu* Makhzum, one of the tribes that made up the *Quraysh*, the group of aristocrats who ruled over Mecca at the time of the birth of the Prophet, upon whom be the blessings and benediction of God.

"The vizier's father, ibn Zaydun, was imprisoned and then banished because of his love for Walládah, the daughter of the former Caliph al-Mustakfi Mohammed III. Walládah was herself a poetess, the Sappho of Spain. Her house was the meeting place of all the great wits and wise men and poets of Andalucía, and it was there that ibn Zaydun, who was only seventeen at the time, first met her and became passionately enamoured. Ben-Zaydun is the fruit of their love.

"Ibn-Zaydun's most famous book of poems, *The Divan*, had many verses extolling the beauty and intelligence of Walládah, and the beauty of these gardens of Medina al-Zahra. One of the poems that he wrote to Walládah when he first fell in love with her goes:

> We were two secrets
> Hidden in the heart of Night,
> 'til that prying hussy Dawn
> Revealed us with her rosy light.

"That's charming," Marilú interjected. "What happened to ibn-Zaydun after his exile?"

"Well, you see the caliphate no longer existed. It came to an end before the child ben-Zaydun was born. There was no reason for the King of Sevilla and Córdoba to hold a grudge, so ibn-Zaydun was pardoned, and King al-Mutadid named him *dhu-al wizaratyn*—Vizier of the Sword and of the Pen. I was an orphan, and had been taken in by Walládah's mother as an infant, and later became Walládah's lady in waiting. So I came to live at the house of ibn-Zaydun to take care of the baby until he was eight years old, when I married and went to live in Sevilla. When my husband died five years ago, I became lady in waiting to the Grand Vizier's wife, Zohra.

"Ahmad ben-Zaydun grew up to be one of the handsomest young men I have ever seen. He is nearly forty years old now, tall, straight, bronzed by the sun, with a ginger-colored beard and hair that is only beginning to turn gray around the temples. His eyes are hazel and so piercing that one feels transfixed by them—yet they can be kind and thoughtful, and I feel that, if he had not been so occupied with war and fighting, he might have been a poet like his father and mother. He is the greatest soldier in all al-Andaluz, the *Amir* or Commander-in-Chief of all the armies of King al-Mutamid, who is the son of al-Mutadid."

"If he is Commander-in-Chief," asked Marilú, "does

that mean he lives in Sevilla? And, if so, how is it that he is in Medina al-Zahra?"

"Well, you see, Córdoba is the northern outpost of Andalucía and, although the Kingdom of Sevilla must pay tribute to your King Alfonso, the fighting still goes on, and the commander-in-chief must be near Córdoba. Medina-al-Zahra is only a league away and is the palace and town built by the great Caliph Abd ar-Rahman one hundred fifty years ago. The Grand Vizier goes to Córdoba practically every day, but he lives here and so did his wife and children until six months ago."

Here Nardjis suppressed a sob, and took a sip of the ice-cold drink beside her, then continued: "His wife and all his children were slaughtered in a Spanish border raid last winter while the Grand Vizier was in Córdoba. He returned just in time to prevent the Spaniards from burning the palace. He and his troops pursued the raiders and killed every last one, then allowed them to be given a Christian burial, while his own dear ones, and the score of slain Arabs who had fought valiantly to protect them, were interred below in the cemetery of Medina al-Zahra.

"I was on the lower terrace at the time—you will see it tomorrow—with the women of the household, the dancing girls, concubines, musicians, and other slaves, so we were saved from slaughter. Ben-Zaydun has entertained himself with these girls, but he is a very lonesome and unhappy man and plans a pilgrimage to Mecca as soon as the fighting in Andalucía comes to an end. He has never had, nor wanted to have, more than one wife, true to the principles laid down by the scholar, Ibn-Hazim, and quite unlike most of his correligionists. He has had and enjoyed many concubines, of course, as becomes a man, but he and his wife were too much in love with one another for him ever to seek another wife while she lived."

"And what about my cousin Conchita and Zoraya? Where are they?" asked Marilú, purposely changing the subject, for she could see that it was too harrowing for Nardjis to continue talking about ben-Zaydun, for whom she herself was already beginning to feel, if not affection, at least sympathy and perhaps tenderness.

She realized that, at least in this instance, the Saracens had been more merciful in abducting her and her companions than had her fellow Christians in murdering the wife and children of the Grand Vizier.

"I've been awfully self-centered, thinking only of myself, when I've been treated with such kindness, and not worrying about my companions who may be in I don't know what terrible straits. But I've been so bewildered by the terrible events of yesterday, and by all the strange and wonderful things I've seen today, that I just don't seem to be myself."

"That's only natural," answered Nardjis, "and I can reassure you at once. Your companions are in no more dire straits than you—slaves, of course, and no doubt this evening they will submit to the wishes of their lords and masters. . . . But, after all, that is a woman's lot and you may be sure they are in good hands.

"Conchita, she's the little blond, isn't she?"

"Yes, she's my first cousin, and I was supposed to have taken care of her. What's happened to her?"

"She is now the slave of Prince al-Mamun. He is Governor of Córdoba, and son of King Mohammed II of Sevilla, who is known as the poet King. They are said to be descended from the Lakhmid kings who ruled in al-Hirah in Arabia as far back as three hundred years before the birth of the Prophet, upon whom be the benediction of God. The first of their clan in Spain came here two hundred years ago as an officer in the Syrian army from Damascus, and they have been high in the government of Andalucía ever since, both under the Caliphs and now as kings of Sevilla.

"Prince al-Mamun has his residence in the old palace, the Alcázar, in Córdoba, but a fortnight ago he sent his wife, Princess Zayda, and their children to the Castle of Almodóvar del Río, between here and Sevilla, for safety. The castle is the strongest in all al-Andaluz—impregnable because it is perched on a hill whose sides are as steep as the pyramids of Egypt. No engines of war, no attacking army can approach it.

So now the Prince lives in the summer residence here in Medina al-Zahra, which is in a wing of the palace of the Grand Vizier, although entirely separate and secluded, with its own harem, garden and grounds. That is where your cousin is now, and I am sure she has been made comfortable and treated with loving care, as befits the new concubine of Prince al-Mamun."

"A concubine!" exclaimed Marilú. "I can't bear to think of it. She is so young and innocent—a virgin. And a devout Catholic. She must be tortured by the thought of confession, that is, if she is ever allowed to go to confession again. Ay! My poor dear Conchita!"

"We must all lose our innocence, you know. It's true that she may be frightened at the thought of it, but I'm sure your cousin, if she's anything like the other girls I've known—including myself—will not be at all unhappy after a while. In fact, I'm told that the Prince is quite a womanizer and, with his wife away, and his concubines in Córdoba, he should be able to devote all his attention to Conchita. I'm sure she will be happy.

"You know, we women always cry at weddings, but it's not because weddings are a tragedy. So don't worry, my dear. The Prince is young—just twenty-two—handsome, although, in my opinion, not as handsome as the Grand Vizier who is nearly twice his age. But then, of course, I'm prejudiced."

"And what of Zoraya?" asked Marilú. "We overheard the chief eunuch say she would be the slave of the Black Vizier. Who is he? Is he really black—a Berber or a Senegalese?"

"No, my dear, he's not black—swarthy yes, but certainly not black, and he is neither Berber nor Senegalese. In fact, the Vizier ben Bakr comes of an even more distinguished ancestry than either the Prince or the Grand Vizier. The *banu* Bakr, the Bakr clan, was one of the most aristocratic of Arab tribes. They were Christians, but were among the first to embrace Islam. An ancestor of the Vizier ben Bakr was Abu Bakr, the father of Aisha, the child wife of the Prophet; Abu Bakr became the Prophet's successor, the first Caliph. It is he who collated all the *ayats* and *suras*, the verses and chapters of the Koran, which are the sayings of the Prophet of blessed memory, and he put them in the numerical order we use today.

"The Black Vizier is also descended from King Solomon and his beloved Balkis, the Queen of Sheba—we call it Saba—a city in Southern Arabia. It was a Sabean king, descended from Balkis, who founded the Kingdom of Habashat—you call it Abyssinia; the Bible calls it the Land of Cush—a thousand years before the birth of Christ. In some centuries the Arabs ruled over Abyssinia, in some the Abyssinians invaded and ruled over southern Arabia, while at other times both were a satrapy of Persia. Their great castle in al-Yaman, in southern Arabia, was the tallest building ever built by man since the tower of Babel. It was twenty stories high, each story ten cubits in height—two hundred cubits, or nearly four hundred feet. At each cornerstone stood a brazen lion which roared with the wind, and the lion has remained ever since as the symbol of the Himyarites.

"Because of the many mixtures of blood in that dynasty, and because the people of South Arabia are darker than the people of Damascus and northern Arabia, the Ka'id ben Bakr is known by the troops as the Black Vizier. In fact, because of his Abyssinian ancestry, and despite his descent from the first Caliph, he is considered by some to be a *mawla,* a Moslem who is not of pure Arab descent.

"And as for your friend, Zoraya, I am certain she is, or will be, very content indeed. Ben Bakr is a man of magnificent physique, a giant in every way, and the Condesa looks to me like a woman who would appreciate virility. She is in a secluded wing of the Palace with the *Ka'id* ben Bakr, just like the Prince and Conchita. The *Ka'id* has his wives and family in Sevilla.

Marilú thanked Nardjis for her reassurances about Conchita and Zoraya although she could not help but be apprehensive at what might lie in store for her and her companions.

"Let's take our *siesta* now," said Nardjis. "Ourda or Shamsi will awaken us in time for your preparations for this evening, and it will do you good and relieve your anxieties to get a little sleep."

Lulled by the gentle breeze that blew through the roses, the gurling fountain, the rustling leaves, and the cooing of turtle doves, the two women were soon fast asleep on their cushioned bed, their arms twined around one another in affectionate embrace.

CHAPTER 3

It seemed only a moment later—although by the sun in the heavens Marilú could see that it was already late afternoon—that the soft voice of Shamsi woke the two women from their slumber: "It is the hour for the *hammam,* my ladies. I'm sorry to disturb you."

Ourda and Shamsi were standing at the arched entrance of the gazebo. They had brought light cotton robes for their mistresses against the cool of the afternoon, and were busy gathering up the cushions and the tray of refreshments. The four women walked back along the garden path to the palace, which looked even more beautiful in the twilight. The sun, low in the sky, shed an aura of light behind the many towers and spires, while the deep shadows in the foreground emphasized the beauty of the variegated marble columns, and the intricately carved round and horseshoe and clover-leaf arches of the façade.

They entered the *seraglio* through the same doors they had used before, and walked along the corridor, and down the stairs, to the vestibule of the *hammam.* The oil lamps were lit now, although it seemed hardly necessary as the sunlight still shone, although less dazzlingly, through the high windows.

Nardjis gave instructions to Ourda: "It will not be necessary to shampoo us this time. And, after the bath, you will give the *Marquesa* only a gentle sensuous massage—you know how—instead of pounding and thumping. And, for this first night, Ourda, do not use *kohl* on the lashes and lids. Leave the hair loose around the shoulders as it is now. Your mistress must be a lovely fair-haired Galician—her own true self, not a *Mozárabe* or an Arab. You understand?"

Then, turning to Shamsi, she added: "You will make me up as though for a banquet, for the chief eunuch and I shall accompany the *Marquesa* when we present her to the Grand Vizier. And thank you both, my dears."

The two girls bound their mistresses' hair tightly in turbans of Turkish toweling, then helped them disrobe in the dressing room which was agleam with the glow of some forty oil lamps in the great crystal chandelier suspended from the ceiling. They then handed the two ladies the heavy white Turkish towel robes similar to those used earlier in the day, while they themselves, naked from the waist up, donned the gauzy pantaloons they had worn while bathing their mistresses that morning. They passed through the *tepidarium*, where the girls picked up the soap, wash cloths and sponges, and went directly to the *calidarium* with its two pools of clear water.

The many sconces, with their gleaming crystal lamps, shed a soft refulgence over the marble walls and benches, and were reflected a hundred fold in the twin pools. Marilú noted that the scent that perfumed the air was not narcissus this time, but what seemed to be a combination of violet and jasmine, sensuous but not cloying.

The soaping, rinsing, and soaking in the bath were not greatly different from that of the morning, but gentler. Then too, the girls were careful not to let the two white-turbaned heads get wet in the twin pools of hot and icy water. A pretty sight they were indeed, the two ladies, one so fair and smooth of skin, the other a soft brunette, both turbaned, and immersed up to their necks in steaming water, while their two attendants, slim and graceful as nymphs, hovered around the pools, collecting wash cloths, soaps, sponges, and tiny flasks of scent.

Finally, they were through with their hot and cold baths, and back in the *tepidarium*, where the girls rubbed their mistresses dry with huge Turkish towels. To Marilú's surprise, Nardjis and Shamsi left directly for the dressing room, leaving Ourda and Marilú alone. Ourda covered one of the marble benches with a large cushion and asked Marilú to lie down on it, face down. Ourda then placed a few drops of fragrant oil in her palms and started to massage the back of Marilú's neck, gently but firmly, and well up behind the ears and beyond the hairline. Slowly moving down to the two hollows of the shoulders, Ourda's fingers pressed gently around the shoulders, and down the arms from shoulders to wrists, then back again under the armpits and softly around to the breasts.

Marilú felt a delicious sensation, exciting yet soothing, from one end of her body to the other. The wandering fingers moved back to her neck, then down her spine, rubbing and massaging, to the small of her back, then moulded and squeezed the roundness of the buttocks and hips, almost but not quite to the secret place that snuggled against the cushion. Back to the buttocks the fingers wandered, ever kneading and moulding the soft skin and tensing muscles, down the thighs, exploring the soft inside as well as their outer contours, down the calves to the ankles and feet.

Unresisting and almost hypnotized, Marilú allowed Ourda to turn her over on her back. The young girl, from time to time renewing the perfumed oil in her palms, bent low over her mistress as she recommenced the gentle massage, beginning with the neck, reaching up behind the ears, down into the hollows of the shoulders, under the shoulders and almost, but not quite, to the breasts.

The massage over, Marilú allowed herself to be taken back to the *calidarium* and sponged off with icy cold water, then doused with rose water, and vigourously rubbed dry again with a Turkish towel and massaged lightly with the scented oil. With that, they moved into the dressing room where Shamsi had almost finished with the elaborate preparation of her mistress.

"My! you two have been a long time with the massage," exclaimed Nardjis. "But it makes no difference; your simple make-up will only take a few minutes, while mine is a long process and I'm not nearly through."

Shamsi was in the process of applying the finishing touches of a salve made of powdered antimony—*kohl*—to Nardjis's eyelids and lashes. The jet-black brows had already been plucked to a smooth contour, the hair brushed neat and tight, but curling at the ends, well up on Nardjis's brow, leaving the nape of the neck and forehead bare; and the procedure was almost at an end. Nardjis's teeth were gleaming, and her lips and gums a vivid red from the powdered walnut bark that she had rubbed into them while Shamsi had brushed her hair. The *maquillage* finished, Shamsi gave her mistress an admiring look, then handed her the mirror for her approval.

"You can put my earrings on after I am dressed, my dear."

"Yes, my lady," and Shamsi handed her mistress the filmy white blouse and equally filmy white pantaloons that would be her undergarments, then the short green and gold jacket, brocaded trousers, red silk sash and golden slippers that completed the outfit, finishing with golden anklets and bracelets and dangling pearl and gold earrings, and a miniscule red velvet cap circled with jewels. A thin voile veil covered but did not conceal her hair and mouth.

"You are simply beautiful," exclaimed Marilú, delighted. And it was indeed hard to believe that Lady Nardjis, with her slim, straight figure and face free of wrinkles, was two score years and five.

Meanwhile, Ourda had been busily brushing her mistress's golden locks, and arranging them in two long, wavy coils, parted in the center and hanging loosely around the shoulders and over the rosy breasts. During the brushing, Marilú briskly rubbed her teeth, gums and lips with the powdered walnut bark and, after rinsing her hands, she was ready for the undergarment that Ourda handed her—a gossamer pair of silken white pantaloons. To wear over these, she was given another pair of baggy pantaloons, heavy with gold brocade at the seams, but of sheerest rosy voile between, so that they covered but by no means concealed her slim legs and thighs and well-rounded hips.

"This is your *sarawil*," explained Ourda.

Marilú noted that the drawstrings of the two pantaloons were tied in a single bowknot, so that a simple tug at one end would release them both simultaneously. The jacket, like the pantaloons, was of rose-colored voile with heavy gold brocade seams, while a deeper rose satin sash completed the costume, leaving her waist and navel bare. Ourda fastened golden earrings to Marilú's ears, and gently placed two gold brocaded slippers over her mistress's bare toes.

"Put on the *khalkhal* and half a dozen *asāwir*," instructed Nardjis, and Ourda fastened a golden anklet to Marilú's left ankle, and slipped three golden bracelets over each arm—symbols of slavery, Marilú thought, but beautiful.

Nardjis showed Marilú how to adjust the veil so that she could eat easily without removing it, and cautioned her that the meal would be both enormous and delicious, but that she should eat and drink sparingly, adding with a smile? "When you feel you would like other entertainment, more amusing than eating or singing, you drop the veil—thus. That will be the signal. And don't be frightened, my darling. You look simply beautiful—ravishing, and you will find the Grand Vizier all that I have told you. Good luck. My heart goes with you, my dear. And now it is time for us to leave."

As the two women left the *hammam*, followed by their handmaidens, who were charmingly arrayed in waist-revealing jackets and pantaloons, they were joined by the chief eunuch, magnificent in red, yellow and green satin and brocade with a huge, pearl-studded scimitar in his sash. Together, they proceeded down the corridor, the chief eunuch leading the way, Nardjis and Marilú side by side, and the two girls bringing up the rear—like a bridal processsion going to meet the groom, thought Marilú, and she felt as nervous as any bride.

"We are about to enter the Salon of the Caliphs," whispered Nardjis. "At the far end, behind the Grand Vizier, is the alcove, the bedroom. You will kneel when I present you to the Vizier."

They came into a huge square room, breath-taking in its magnificence. In the center was a large green marble pool that seemed to be full of shining silver, irridescent with the light of hundreds of candles in sconces on every wall, and reflecting an enormous, glistening pearl, egg-shaped and over two inches in diameter, suspended over the pool by a delicate golden circlet and three golden chains hanging from the ceiling. The ceiling itself was of varicolored translucent slabs of marble, framed in intricately carved beams of gold. Just below the ceiling, and extending around the room without interruption, was a broad frieze of creamy white marble, elaborately carved into a filigree of foliage, geometric designs, and cursive Arabic script.

The walls were of many-colored marble encased in sculptured golden borders, and draped with gorgeous woven tapestries. The four walls were punctuated by eight magnificent doorways, two on each side, each standing between thirty foot piers of colored marble and crystal, surmounted by a horseshoe arch. The doors themselves—each with two wings—were of gold and blackest ebony, but were half concealed by gold and silver draperies, except for the door through which the women and the chief eunuch had entered, which was flung wide open, the draperies drawn aside. Between the doorways were twelve other pairs of arched marble and crystal columns, three on each side of the room, that encased an equal number of windows made of a delicate lacework of carved wood, between whose interstices were panes of blue, red, green and gold stained glass in floral and geometrical designs. The windows reached nearly to the floor, and almost as high as the doorways.

The columns, forty in all, with their horseshoe arches, formed a colonnade within the room, surmounted by the entablature of the pierced marble frieze. On the floor were four large Persian rugs around the four sides of the octagonal center pool. Between the rugs, one could see the marble floor, laid in black and white squares with glistening mosaic borders in blue, red, green and gold.

Marilú's eyes could not take it all in at once, particularly as her whole attention was riveted on the Grand Vizier himself who sat regally on a pile of silken cushions, with two silk-clad slave girls kneeling on either side. A bronzed and handsome man with thick reddish brown hair and beard, slightly graying at the sides, a long aquiline nose, and a deep barrel of a chest, the Vizier was garbed in a heavy green silk robe, rich with gold brocade. He wore slippers of silver brocade, and a turban of green and gold, surmounted by a clasp or brooch of emeralds and pearls. His costume was completed with golden earrings and a gold bracelet on his left wrist. A small curved dagger in a scabbord, rich with emeralds, rubies and pearls, was tucked in a silken scarf around his waist.

Marilú recalled dimly that the Arabs were descended from Ishmael, the son of Abraham and of the Egyptian slave girl, Hagar, whom Abraham bedded because his own wife, Sarah, was barren. And she remembered that God had said of Ishmael: "And he will be a wild man; his hand will be against every man, and every man's hand against him." She shuddered, and wondered whether the curse of Ishmael had descended upon the handsome and manifestly civilized personage she saw before her—he certainly didn't look like a wild man, she thought.

The chief eunuch passed the silver pool, followed by four women. As he approached the Grand Vizier, he salaamed deeply and stood aside.

Lady Nardjis stepped forward, make a deep salaam, and gravely announced: "Your Excellency, Doña María Luisa Andrade de Araujo, Marquesa de Clavijo, your humble slave."

Marilú knelt gracefully, touching her forehead to the floor between her two outstretched hands, as she had been taught by Zoraya, and awaited the command of the Grand Vizier. He stood up, and Marilú noted admiringly his towering height and regal posture.

She heard a deep baritone voice: "You may arise, my dear," and, as she stood up, the Grand Vizier, with an ingratiating smile, extended his hand to hers and motioned to her to sit down beside him. Marilú could see that he was by no means displeased at his first impression and, as for her, she thought she had never seen so handsome, distinguished, and gracious a personage.

"Let us see what we can provide for our refreshment and entertainment," and the Vizier clapped his hands.

The door at the far end of the room, beside the one through which Marilú had entered, opened. In a trice there appeared a bevy of slave girls bearing small tables elaborately inlaid with ebony, ivory, mother-of-pearl, and tortoise shell, and large brass and silver trays piled high with jugs and goblets and covered dishes that they placed beside the cushions in front of the Grand Vizier and Marilú. The chief eunuch, Lady Nardjis and the two girls retired to the far end of the room, bowing deeply as they withdrew, while the four slave girls in attendance on the Grand Vizier joined with their companions in setting up the tables and refreshments.

Two of the girls proffered golden basins filled with warm water, bedecked with rose petals, to the Vizier and Marilú. They rinsed their hands and dried them on small towels which the slave girls immediately whisked away. Another girl filled three crystal goblets with clear white wine from a crystal jug, sipped from one of the goblets, and offered the other two to the Vizier and to Marilú.

The former raised his glass, looked Marilú full in the eye, and toasted: "To your happiness, my dear."

"And to yours, my lord and master," she responded, blushing at her boldness.

A large silver and brass platter of cold *hors d'oeuvres* was set before them—tiny shrimp, prawns, anchovy, *patés* of chicken liver, and thin slices of spicy sausage. As they nibbled on these, Marilú, warmed by the wine, and even more by the gracious smile and manners of her host, plucked up courage to ask:

"Aren't you Moslems forbidden to drink wine? That is what I had always heard in Galicia."

The Vizier smiled: "It is true that there are passages in the *Sunnah* which would seem to prohibit the drinking of wine, and certain Moslem sects are total abstainers.

"On the other hand, the Koran—and that is the word of the Prophet himself, upon whom be the benediction of God—tells us that in Paradise there are rivers of wine to delight those who are privileged to quaff it. And Paul of Tarsus tells his son to drink a little wine for thy stomach's sake and thine often infirmities, while Jesus changed water to wine at Cana. So, surely, wine cannot be forbidden to us. But you will find that we are quite abstemious; we in Andalucía drink no distilled liquors, other than an occasional tiny goblet of liqueur, and we partake of wine only in moderation. With these next courses, for example, we shall drink only water, or sherbets. Does that answer your question?"

Marilú nodded in assent as the serving maid took away the first platter and placed a bowl of steaming soup on each of their small tables, together with prettily carved spoons of ebony. She noted that her host partook only sparingly of either the soup or of the first course and, remembering Nardjis's warning, she decided to do likewise, commenting: "Everything is so delicious that I am tempted to eat down to the last morsel, but I am afraid that, if I do, I shall not have room for what is yet to come."

And she was glad she had made that decision, for the maids now served them large bowls of a fragrant stew with smaller bowls of saffron rice and some sort of preserve. The aroma of both the rice and stew was something she had never known before, and, when she tasted them, she exclaimed delightedly: "This is marvellous! What is it? It is simply delicious!"

"The rice is flavored with saffron from the stamens of crocuses which we cultivate and gather here in Andalucía; the stew is of chicken, spiced with *kari* that we get from southern India and Ceylon; the preserves are made of mangos and spices from Persia. You know we derive our foods, our customs, every aspect of our way of life, from all parts of the Moslem world—India, Persia, Arabia, Egypt, the Maghrib, Greece, Italy, al-Andaluz—bringing the best from everywhere. It is our aim to make Spain—I wish it were all Spain—as close to a Paradise on earth as it is possible for man to make it. . . . But you had best drink as you eat, for you will find that the *kari* and the chutney—the preserves—are quite pungent and call for some refreshment."

Marilú's tongue and palate were burning pleasantly with the hot foods, so she sipped from the crystal goblet beside her—deliciously icy water perfumed with rose petals. "Everything is so delightful," she enthused, "I've never had anything like it before."

"I trust you will find all the entertainments this evening delightful, and such as you have never experienced before."

Marilú wondered whether the Grand Vizier had intended a *double entendre* or not. His eyes, piercing yet tender, followed her every movement and seemed to penetrate her to the core—not that it would take much piercing to penetrate through her flimsy garments. He seemed obviously pleased by what he saw.

The curry course, like the soup, had been served with finely carved wooden spoons—fortunately, Marilú thought, because everything else was eaten with her fingers, and she had tried to be dainty, not soiling either her hands or her veil.

The curry and rice bowls were taken away, and replaced by a large platter on a table between the two of them, the platter being laden with small tarts garnished with steaming hot chicken *quenelles*, piping hot pastries filled with finely chopped duck mixed with almond paste, and other dainties. These were not difficult to manage without soiling the fingers, and Marilú tasted one of each.

That course was followed by another—perhaps the most delicious of all, and Marilú hoped it would be the last or at least the last of the main courses of the banquet—a baby lamb, which one of the serving girls carved before them. Marilú asked for only a tiny piece of the deliciously browned and crisp outside meat, and a small morsel of the juicy and tender meat within. She thought she had never eaten anything so perfect, and it was piping hot—much more sensible than in Galicia where everything was put on the table at once, and was cold before one could reach the end of the meal. She wiped her fingers daintily on the napkin that covered her knees.

After the lamb came a platter of cheeses and crisp toasted bread. The white wine was replaced with a light red claret that gleamed in the crystal goblets, and proved the perfect accompaniment to the cheese. As the cheese course was served, the sounds of music—girls' voices, lutes, guitars, and other instruments—came from behind a screen at the far end of the room, behind the silvery pool. Was the screen there before? Marilú couldn't remember. It may have been brought in later, with the same silent service with which the slave girls, moving gracefully, quickly, and noiselessly, had served them with one course after another throughout the evening.

Marilú was beginning to feel uncomfortably full, although she had barely sampled each of the courses laid before her. She noted that the Grand Vizier had been almost equally abstemious in his eating. But she could not resist the next course—tiny *beignets* fried in oil and dipped in scented boiling honey that formed a crisp and pully crust over the fritter. Although every course had been a delight to her palate, she breathed a sigh of relief when she saw the maids clear away the dessert and replace it with a pannier of fresh, ripe figs and grapes, that she knew marked the end of the meal.

The Vizier noticed the sigh and understood its meaning: "Had enough, my dear."

"Oh, my yes. It was all so delicious, but I just can't eat any more."

The slave girls brought them each a silver basin of warm water with a slice of lemon floating in the center. They washed, and dried their hands on dainty towels, and rinsed their mouths with violet scented water—the final touch, thought Marilú, that emphasized the refinement of Moorish ways compared to the crude manners to which she was accustomed in her native Galicia.

The Grand Vizier clapped his hands. Everything was cleared away, tables and all, except for fresh goblets of scented water and two panniers of grapes. The Vizier motioned for Marilú to move closer to him, which she did, not reluctantly, as they rearranged the cushions so they could sit up comfortably for the next stage of the evening's entertainment.

The music became louder, and in pranced two troupes of dancing girls, each astride a tiny *papier maché* horse—or, rather, the horses were suspended by silken cords from the shoulders of the dancers, their own slim legs showing underneath, while little stuffed silk legs dangled in the stirrups. One squad of eight girls, clad in golden helmets with golden coats of mail, and mounted on black horses, circled one side of the marble pool in the center of the room, and brandished their red and white lances menacingly at their opponents. The other squad, similarly attired, but all in silver, with green and white lances, and green scarves and pennons, circled the other side of the pool. They charged at one another in mock combat, advancing and retreating in time with the music, with first one squad fleeing from the enemy, and then the other, the wounded reeling and dropping to the floor, then miraculously recovering to engage in combat once again.

The spectacle was so entrancing, so amusing, that Marilú let forth peals of laughter as the combatants pirouetted gaily and fiercely around the room.

"What a lovely laugh you have, my dear," exclaimed the Grand Vizier, "so sweet and bell-like—such laughter as I have not heard since childhood. It makes you even lovelier than I had thought, and I must say that your pink and golden, blue-eyed charms had not escaped me. Go on and laugh, my sweet, and let us enjoy the show."

Her laughter was contagious, and the Vizier, up to that point so grave and almost silent, joined in heartily. For the first time, Marilú felt at ease, delighted to be there, delighted to be with the Grand Vizier, and enjoying herself without restraint. The dancers' legs twinkled provocatively beneath their steeds and, when they fell to the floor which they did again and again, they left little to the imagination.

"It is all so amusing—like children romping," said Marilú to her companion, "and yet I can see that they are by no means children—so voluptuous and yet so gay. It makes love look like fun. And that's the way it is and ought to be," she added, surprised at her own boldness.

"Yes, that's the way it is and ought to be—sometimes, not always. For love can be gay, and fun as you call it, but at times it can be deeper, more serious, even anguishing, filling the whole mind, body and soul with an ecstasy that no other joy can provide. And we can enjoy both kinds of love, just as we can enjoy the gay dance music they are playing now, and at other times be enthralled by grander music that seems to fill your very soul with rapture. The important thing in love is the ecstasy. Perfection in love calls for the union of so many forces, not only the purely sensual aspects, but affection, the sharing of rapture and delight as well. And that is true, regardless of whether the union of forces is gay and fun, or deep and voluptuous. . . . But I did not mean to be so serious, my sweet. Let's enjoy the music and the dancing."

By that time, the green and silver warriors had vanquished their foes in a final assault, and they marched their forlorn prisoners to where the Grand Vizier and his companion sat. One of the victors handed Marilú two small pennons, one red, one green, as trophies of the combat, and the Vizier turned to her: "What is your verdict? Shall the gold and red soldiers be slain?"

"By no means! I think they are all lovely, delightful—let them be pardoned."

"With that the vanquished, so forlorn and drooping, perked up at once, and vanquished and victors pranced off gaily, arm in arm, amid peals of laughter from Marilú and her companion.

The music changed from *allegro* to a more seductive rhythm, a sort of fandango, but in six-eight time. A young girl came out from behind the screen, tiny, but erect and proud. She was lovely, Marilú thought—something like Zoraya but more *petite* and far more made-up, her raven black hair parted sleek and shining in the center, then gathered tightly into a large coil at back, with two spit-curls in front of her ears which sported large golden earrings. Her brows were plucked in two large arcs, meeting in the center; her eyelids and lashes were black with *kohl*, her lips red—surely with some unguent, Marilú thought, and not just reddened with the walnut bark that she and Nardjis had used.

Her fingernails and toenails were brightly henna'd, and glistened as she threw her arms into the air with abandon, her many bracelets jingling in time with the music. Her skin was as smooth as a child's, and a soft seductive brunette, from her forehead and shell-like ears to the tips of her graceful arms and whirling legs.

This was indeed the high-breasted virgin, wondrous fair, with black lashes and langourous look, told of by the poets—a model of beauty, comeliness, symmetry, and perfect loveliness, who walked with the grace of a gazelle which panteth for a cooling stream.

The dancer's garments seemed to consist of nothing but flowing veils in ever-changing colors of reds and yellows and blues, that give the impression that her body was enveloped in flames as she whirled around, closer and closer to her audience. Around and around she danced, sometimes slowly with seductive gestures, sometimes a whirl of rapid movement. Her arms and hands, her hips and legs, seemed things alive, provocatively alive and in constant movement.

Marilú sat entranced, and so, she noted, was the Grand Vizier, who followed very movement, every beat of the music, with fascination.

The music changed. Slower and more seductive now, and in three-quarter time. The dancer flung off her veils, which fluttered to the floor. Clad now only in the briefest of gossamer-thin jackets which revealed her firm, full, red-tipped breasts, and in equally thin pantaloons topped by the narrowest of silken scarves, that left her navel bare and scarcely covered what was left to hide, the dancer stood almost motionless before the two watchers who now sat close together, their arms unconsciously twined round each other. The music became slower and slower, in soft and sensuous rhythm, while the dancer, her legs close together, softly undulated her body, from calves to thighs, to hips, to breasts, her head ever erect, her arms moving in snake-like patterns, upward, downward, sideways, subtly caressing her sleek body with every movement.

The music changed again, became faster and faster. The dancer's body and limbs moved in time, and her belly became a living thing, moving around and around, up and down, from side to side, smoothly, then convulsively, as her hips and thighs twitched in a kind of ecstasy, and her breasts hardened with rapture.

Marilú could stand it no longer. The bewildering events of the day, the warm baths, the massage, the spicy foods and wine, the music and the dancing horses, above all the presence of the strong and handsome man by her side, his arm around her waist—overcame her. She felt her breasts swell, her lips parted, and she swayed dizzily with the music. She looked toward her partner, equally entranced, and quickly she tore the veil from her face.

The Vizier clapped his hands—twice. In an instant, the dancer, together with the girl musicians, ran toward the screen and disappeared behind the far doorway to the left. A score of slave girls instantly extinguished the hundreds of candles, leaving only a faint oil lamp gleaming in a sconce in front of the alcove behind Marilú and the Vizier. The chief eunuch closed the heavy draperies over the two far doorways, the only ones that had been open that evening, bowed deeply, and closed the doors behind him with a thud. It had all taken only a few seconds. Marilú and the Grand Vizier were alone in the great hall—alone and overcome with desire.

Marilú could feel the warm hands of her companion groping gently but firmly at her breasts. He doffed his turban and threw it on the floor. His robe came open and Marilú could see with fascination his hairy chest and great manroot, erect and ready. She raised her face to his and, as his lips approached hers in passionate embrace, she felt him deftly place one of the cushions beneath her heaving hips, while he bore her slowly down upon her back.

The ecstasy seemed to last for hours, never stopping, and growing more and more intense, as she moaned and panted beneath his bulk—then came a sudden avalanche of passion as she felt herself filled to bursting.

The two relaxed, all tension gone, but did not separate as his eager mouth found hers again, and their tongues became living spears, darting in and out of one another's mouths, exploring fiercely. Gasping for breath, Marilú drew her mouth from that of her paramour, the two still tightly conjoined below. "You are wonderful, wonderful," she sighed, "I have never known such rapture."

"And you, sweetest one, are all that I hoped for. Let us be still, still, still now—joined together and never moving. If you so much as move, I swear the ecstasy will begin again. Be still, my darling!"

Marilú could feel him inside her, soft and tender, but still throbbing and pulsating. "But it is you who are moving," she cried, "I can feel you in me. Why are you never still?"

"It is you who are kissing me, kissing me with your so tender lips down there, I can't stand it any longer."

And Marilú felt him inside her swelling larger and larger, and the whole rapturous struggle began anew.

"My God! my God!" she gasped. "Good God! it doesn't stop. It comes again and again. It won't stop, my darling. It is coming over me wave after wave. *Por Dios!* Oh, my love, my love, it just won't stop." And she moaned and gasped until, at long last, they lay, panting and exhausted, in each other's arms.

"Oh, my dear, my lord and master, my beloved Ahmad," and for the first time she dared use his given name, "I never knew love could be like this!"

"It was sweet, indeed, my own dear Marilú. I never realized there could be such passion in one so young, so fair," and he fondled her golden locks, now disheveled on the cushions. "You know we never did retire to the alcove as we are supposed to do, and our bed waits for us there, all fresh and soft."

The two of them arose from the cushions, still swaying and dizzy. They walked arm in arm toward the alcove which was enclosed with heavy golden draperies.

"I think I'll go and freshen up," said Marilú.

"And I too."

They parted in the alcove, Marilú through the small door at the right, the Vizier to the left. An oil lamp was burning and Marilú saw, not without surprise, a young girl who could have been Ourda's twin, waiting for her, reclining on a small divan.

"Oh, I am sorry; I had dozed off," said the child. "Ourda couldn't be here tonight, but I hope you will let me wait on you. My name is Bahar. Poor Ourda is sound asleep; she was completely exhausted."

Then Bahar whispered to her shyly, "I can only give you a sponge bath here, but you will find it quite refreshing. Then with your permission, I shall retire through the back door, and tomorrow morning you can use the *hammam* where Ourda will meet you."

They moved to the other side of a partition and found themselves in a small square room with marble walls and a marble floor carved out in the form of a large basin. There Marilú stood naked, while the girl, drawing water from a shell-shaped washbowl on the wall, sponged her, soaped her, and rinsed her off in rose perfumed water, then dried her briskly with a large Turkish towel. Marilú lay down on the small divan while the child rubbed her from head to toe with scented oil that was soon absorbed into the skin. She brushed Marilú's hair until it glowed again, and handed her a fresh cool cotton nightgown, and a long silk robe and slippers.

"You can use these to go to the *hammam* tomorrow morning. There is a jug of ice-cold water beside your bed, and a goblet. Will there be anything else you want, my lady?" Bahar asked.

"Nothing at all, my dear. You run along and get some rest." And the child slipped out the rear door of the room while Marilú rejoined the Vizier, also freshly bathed and perfumed, and reclining on the bed, waiting for her.

The bed was a large wooden frame, raised high above the floor. Piled high with mattresses and pillows, and covered with velvet brocade and fine cotton sheets, the bed looked comfortable, as indeed it proved to be. A heavy coverlet lay at the foot, but was not needed, as the night was cool but not uncomfortably so.

"Let's go to sleep, my love," said the Vizier. "You must be exhausted after your long journey from El Viso, and the long day today, while I am weary from a hard day's work in Córdoba. But if you want me at any time during the night you will find that I am always ready and eager to serve you."

"Goodness!" thought Marilú, after all the times he has had me already! And never once withdrawing! What a man!" He caressed her hair, kissed her chastely on the forehead, and then—she was so sweet and lovely—he fondled her neck, her breasts, which he pressed and cupped in both his hands. Marilú caressed and kissed his face and neck, then joined her mouth to his, her tongue exploring to discover new, secret places it had not found before. His hands slipped lower, and she thrilled with exquisite delight.

"Thou art all fair, my love," he murmured, "there is no spot in thee. Thy lips are like a thread of scarlet, and thy speech is comely."

And his lips again sought hers while his tongue devoured what it could find in the deep recesses of her mouth. "Thy two breasts are like two young roes that are twins, which feed among the lilies," and he placed his lips first on one then the other, caressing them with his tongue.

"How much better is thy love than wine! and the smell of thy ointments than all spices! Thy lips drop with honey as the honeycomb, honey and milk are under thy tongue, and the smell of thy garments is like the smell of Lebanon. A garden enclosed is my sister, my spouse, a spring shut up, a fountain sealed. A fountain of gardens, a well of living waters, and streams from Lebanon."

And his strong hand slipped down into her garden, where eager fingers sought and probed, then entered deep within and were watered with streams from Lebanon.

The probings and caresses within her most secret parts roused Marilú to a pitch of passion of which she had never dreamed herself capable. But, torturing herself by holding in and prolonging the pleasure, she responded in kind, for she recognized the passages her paramour had quoted from Solomon, and she recited: "Let him kiss me with the kisses of his mouth: for thy love is better than wine. A bundle of myrrh is my well-beloved unto me; he shall lie all night betwixt my breasts. His left hand is under my head, and his right hand doth embrace me."

Suiting the action to the words of his beloved, the Grand Vizier tenderly took Marilú within his arms, and whispered: "I am come into my garden my sister, my spouse: I have gathered my myrrh with my spice; I have eaten my honeycomb with my honey; I have drunk my wine with my milk . . . yea, drink abundantly, O beloved."

And they both drank deep, with mouths and tongues, with manroot and secret places, again and again, as passionately as before, but far more tenderly. At last, the two, panting and exhausted, lay side by side within one another's arms.

"Don't leave me now," whispered the Vizier. "There is no need to. I want to feel you and smell you next to me—the smell of a wonderful woman, with no fresh perfumes—until morning."

"And I don't want to leave you, my beloved. Let us just go to sleep together as we are, naked beside one another, and let us dream happy dreams that couldn't possibly be as happy as the ecstasy we have just known. Good night, my love."

"Good night, my darling Marilú." And they both dropped off into an untroubled sleep, from then until sunrise.

CHAPTER 4

At dawn, a beam of sunlight shone through the roof and eastern windows of the great salon, and past the open curtains of the alcove. The Grand Vizier stirred, awoke, drew the draperies closed so as not to awaken his sleeping paramour who lay stretched out at full length, naked on the bed. He gazed fondly at the sleeping form—so lovely, her golden hair disheveled on the pillow, her eyelids closed, lips slightly parted in an expression of utter bliss and contentment. He bent over and planted a soft kiss on her forehead, thinking to leave at once for the business of the day which awaited him in Córdoba.

Marilú stirred drowsily. Without opening her eyes, she stretched her limbs and arched her back sinuously—like a more than lovely panther, thought the Vizier, as he looked at her in fascination. She opened her eyes, and at once flung her arms round his neck, drawing him to her bosom. Not at all reluctantly, they recommenced their games of love, as ardently and even more fondly than on the previous eve, ending in an explosion of unrestrained and mutual passion.

"O, you wonderful, wonderful man! I never dreamed that it could be anything like this. You must never, never leave me, my dearest, my Ahmad!"

"I must leave you now, my sweetest love. I have to be in Córdoba all day, but I shall see you again this evening. You go to sleep again; I'll draw the curtains, and when you wake, my darling, Nardjis will take care of you until I return. Good-bye, my sweet." And the Vizier kissed her gently on her two closed eyelids, leaving hastily lest he be tempted again to prolong their night of love.

It was another two hours before Marilú awoke again. She rose, put on the nightgown and robe that had been flung in disarray on the floor, and tiptoed to the curtains in her new slippers. Peeking out, she saw Ourda, bright and smiling, waiting for her. She embraced the child, and they went hand in hand to the *hammam.*

Disrobing took but a moment, and they passed to the *tepidarium,* where they found Nardjis already partly through the ritual of the bath, with Shamsi busily soaping her mistress's gleaming body.

They greeted one another affectionately. "Don't kiss me," shrieked Nardjis, "You'll get your mouth full of soap. I have much to tell you, but let's wait until we're soaking in the hot baths together. The girls can leave us, and we can talk to our hearts' content."

"And I've so much to tell you too! The Grand Vizier—he's just everything you told me, and so much more. I'm so happy, and I can't wait to get to the baths and tell you."

Ourda soon finished soaping, scrubbing, and rinsing her mistress, and they joined Nardjis who was luxuriating in the steaming pool.

"May I join you?" asked Marilú.

"I don't see why not. Come on in. And run away, girls, and bring us something to eat."

"Wait until Shamsi and Ourda come back with our breakfast," protested Nardjis, "and then, after they leave us alone, we can gossip as much as we wish."

The girls returned in a moment and placed two trays at the poolside, each with some fresh fruit, several tiny, flaky crescent-shaped rolls and preserves, a steaming pot of clear liquid, a bowl of sugar, and a cup.

"What is this drink?" asked Marilú, "it's delicious,

and just hits the spot. It's something like the tea we make in Galicia from linden or mint or camomile, but this is better."

"It's a tea that comes from China, I think, but we get it from Persia. It's good, and refreshing. But let me tell you—I saw the Vizier this morning, and I have never seen him so happy. You were brought here as a slave, you know, and I'm sure he had never thought of you as anything but one of his *jawari*—concubines, you know, perhaps a favorite one, but still only a concubine. You know that the Arabs are especially fond of the golden-haired girls they capture in Galicia or Vizcaya, but they are brought here as *jawari*—slaves and concubines.

"But now, the Vizier acts and talks as though you were his wife, or at least someone whom he wants to marry as soon as possible—his very dearest and only bride. I've never seen such a change in a man, and I've known Ahmad since he was a little boy.

"He wants me to take you all around Medina al-Zahra and meet him one day in Córdoba. And when he can, he wants to come back here for lunch and a *siesta* with you. He has asked me to take you to the Mosques here and in Córdoba, and tell you something of Islam, of our people, our ways of life, our religion. And that sounds like marriage to me—not just a bed-fellow. And I'm so happy, too, my dear sweet Marilú, for his sake and for yours."

"And I wanted to tell you about the Grand Vizier," replied Marilú. "He is a wonderful, wonderful man—so strong, gentle, kind and wise, and oh, so virile. I'm in love, and if he wants to marry me, I'll be so happy, and if he doesn't I'll be happy too—just so long as I'm with him. Oh, Nardjis, I do love him so."

Nardjis rang a small silver bell to summon the two girls, who tripped back smilingly, and, after a brisk

... the icy pool, they proceeded to dry their ...tresses vigorously.

"We shall want to wrap up," said Nardjis to Ourda and Shamsi, "as we shall be going down into the town. But we shan't wear our *haiks* until later, as I first want to show the *Marquesa* around the palace. We'll do that alone, but when we go to the market and Mosque, you two girls will accompany us, and ask the chief eunuch if either he or one of his eunuchs would please go with us. Also, please ask the *hammam* mistress to come here."

A heavy-set, rather more than middle-aged woman appeared almost immediately, and bowed deeply. "Your wishes, my lady?"

"When we return this afternoon, we shall wish to have a steam bath and, after that, a Turkish massage. And then the usual. Thank you very much."

The *hammam* mistress bowed again to both ladies. "To hear is to obey." And, still curtseying, she left the room as quietly as she had entered.

The girls dressed the two women in long tunics of rich materials that covered them from their necks to their ankles, leaving them wrapped like mummies—perhaps elegantly from the Moslem point of view, but completely shapeless.

"We have to dress this way to go into town," explained Nardjis. "Mohammed, may Allah bless him, said that if an Arab sees even the contours of a woman's figure, he becomes so aroused that, even if he is in the middle of prayer—and no Arab can be more occupied than that—no woman is safe from his desires. So, when we go into town, we shall cover our hair and faces, all but the eyes, and wear an outer tunic just as long as this. Now, let me show you around the palace.

"I think we should begin with the patio at the entrance," she continued. "You will see the gates later, as we go down to the market place.

"The city of Medina al-Zahra was built a hundred and fifty years ago by the greatest of the Caliphs of al-Andaluz, Abd ar-Rahman III, for his favorite concubine, Zahra—Medina means city, you know. He wanted it to be more magnificent than the palace that Haroun al-Rashid had built in Baghdad a hundred years earlier. And it is, but it is also more beautiful—a jewel, compared with which the old palace in Córdoba, the *Alcázar,* is just a huge pile of architecture."

They walked down a corridor flanked by marble columns of various colors and shapes—simple, fluted, corkscrew—topped by round and horseshoe and clover-leaf arches, each one different from its neighbor. "The rose, pink and green marble comes from Damascus, or from Tunis—Sfax and Carthage," explained Nardjis, "the white mostly from Tarragona and Almería in Spain, and there is veined onyx from Granada, but much of the marble you will see in the palace, including the black marble, comes from Byzantium, Italy, and the Gallic kingdoms beyond the Pyrenees—gifts from the sovereigns of all those countries to the great Caliph."

They came to a great iron gate, in an archway of blue and yellow porcelain. "This is the *bab as-Sudda—bab* means gate—the gate of the palace itself."

Beyond it stretched a vast esplanade at the far end of which they could see another gate, huge, but dwarfed by the distance. "That is the *bab al-Akba,* the gate not only to the palace grounds but to the whole City of Medina al-Zahra. We shall see it when we go to Córdoba. The field in front of you is the *place d'armes,* the drill field, but it serves also as a *court d'honneur* where visiting dignitaries in the days of the Caliphs used to arrive with all their entourage and were greeted by the Grand Vizier.

"But there has been no Caliph in Spain for fifty

years," continued Nardjis, "and the King of Sevilla has his palace in that city. And Córdoba, once the capital of all Andalucía, has become just a vassal of Sevilla. And Medina al-Zahra is now no more than the temporary residence of the Grand Vizier.

"But let me show you the patio that visitors first entered in the days of the Caliphs, after they had dismounted from their horses or carriages and passed through the *bab as-Sudda* gate."

The spacious patio they now entered was enclosed in a colonnade of arches supporting a red-tiled roof. It was fringed with fragrant orange and lemon trees in full bloom, and carefully tended flower beds laid out in geometrical designs and filled with daffodils, jonquils, tulips, rose bushes, and numerous other flowers. In the center, surrounded by a flagstone terrace, was a huge gilt bronze fountain that sent a single jet of water fifty feet into the air, while a dozen lesser jets spouted water six feet high, all tumbling noisily down into a large bronze and gold basin elaborately carved with figures in bas-relief—dancing nymphs or goddesses in Grecian tunics, armies of men in Byzantine armor, engaged in mortal combat, on foot, on horseback, or standing tall in chariots.

"This is beautiful," exclaimed Marilú. "I have never seen so lovely a fountain. But I thought that Moslems were not allowed to make statues, or even paintings, of animals or human beings. Yet there seem to be animal statues all over the palace, and here there are all those wonderful sculptures of dancing nymphs and warriors."

"If you think this is lovely, wait until you see the fountain in the *seraglio*," answered Nardjis. "This fountain comes from Byzantium, the other from Damascus. And the Koran does not forbid pictures and graven images. We consider that the prohibition in the Bible, 'thou shalt not make any graven image, or any likeness of any thing in heaven, on earth. or in water' was because some of the Hebrews, the ungodly, used to make graven images and worship them. We would not dare to make or have any images of Allah or of Abraham, Jesus or Mohammed, may his soul be blessed by Allah, nor of any other of God's prophets—that would be sacrilege. But these sculptures, and the others you have seen and will see, are quite innocent, and you will admit they are beautiful."

"They are indeed," answered Marilú.

"Perhaps before we go any further," continued Nardjis, "I should explain to you that the palace is divided into three parts, entirely separate. This patio is the entrance to the halls of state, the reception halls where the Caliph used to receive kings and ambassadors from foreign lands, and governors from other parts of his empire. That part of the palace includes many rooms which we shall not have time to visit—it would take a week to see all the rooms of the palace—but the most important rooms are the one to which distinguished guests would first be brought when they left this patio, and the Salon of the Caliphs, sometimes called the Hall of the Ambassadors, that you saw last night.

"The second part of the palace is the *Mexuar*, the public halls where every Monday the Caliph used to hear the petitions of the people, and where he or one of the *qadis*, the judges, would administer justice. It is closed off now, and anyway it is not very interesting. The *qadis* still come here every Monday to hear the petitions of the people of Medina al-Zahra but the important cases are heard by the Prince who is Governor in Córdoba, or by the King in Sevilla.

"The third part of the palace, the most important for us, is the *seraglio*, separated from the Salon of the Caliphs by doors which were open last night but are generally locked in the daytime. They are made of massive bronze and iron, although faced with ebony and gold, and, with the draperies, they ensure the absolute privacy and quiet of the *seraglio*—and also of the Salon of the Caliphs when it is used, as it was last night, for private entertainment. Only the chief eunuch has the keys.

"Part of the *seraglio,* but completely separate from it, are the two wings which I told you that Conchita and Zoraya are living in; they were built for occasional visits by the sons of the Caliph, with their harems. We cannot visit that part of the palace, for harems are always kept strictly apart. The very word, *harim,* means a sacred or inviolable place.

"Then I should explain," she continued, "that, just as the palace is divided into three parts, so also is the City of Medina al-Zahra. The City was built on one of the foothills of the *Sierra Morena.* The water that you have seen in the gardens, the fountains, the *hammam* and elsewhere, is brought from the *Sierra* in an aqueduct that then goes on to Córdoba, a little more than a league from here. The aqueduct is three leagues in length-ten miles—and the water is the clearest, freshest in all al-Anduluz this side of the *Sierra Nevada* at Granada.

"When the Caliph built Medina al-Zahra, he had the hill landscaped into three terraces, each entirely separate, but connected by flights of stairs. The palace is on the topmost terrace. When we went into the garden yesterday, we descended to the second terrace, and each terrace is surrounded by a stone wall—a fortress. The bottom terrace—the Great Mosque, the City, the market-place, and all the houses—is protected by the most massive wall of all, practically impregnable to assault, they tell me. I hope so.

"We shall visit the market-place and Mosque, and

see the garden again. But you cannot hope to see all of it, as much of the garden terrace, the *Generalife*, is forest, a game preserve with hundreds of deer, wild boars, hares, pheasants, quail, and other game. All together, Medina al-Zahra extends over a mile from East to West, and two-thirds as far from North to South, so you see we could not possibly see it all on foot."

"My, it *is* enormous," commented Marilú.

They left the patio and entered a long, rectangular room, large but not nearly so large as the Salon of the Caliphs that Marilú had seen the night before. A fine bronze and gilt doorway at each end gave access to the room, while the sunlight filtered through six large windows, three on each side. The walls, up to ten feet high, were of mosaic—blue, red and green, but chiefly gold—depicting various scenes, rural and urban. These mosaic murals were framed by tiles, forming intricate geometric designs. The ceiling was elaborately carved in brilliant colors; the floor was of marble, covered, except for the border, by a single huge Persian rug in soft, pastel colors. But what chiefly struck Marilú's attention was the twenty foot frieze of marble, carved with Arabic inscriptions, above the mosaics and tiles, that ran around the entire room, interrupted only by a latticework grill over the doorway at the far end.

"This is the reception room through which all visiting diplomats and monarchs passed before seeing the Caliph in the Hall of Ambassadors. It is called the *Sala de la Baraka*—the Room of the Blessings—because of all the inscriptions from the *Koran* in *Kufic* characters. The latticework grill at the far end covers a passageway from the *harim*, through which the wives and concubines of the Caliph could see all the visitors without being seen—that is why you call that kind of lattice a '*celosía*'—a jealousy."

The two women passed through the other door into

the Hall of the Ambassadors, using only the small door within the huge door that would have been too heavy for them to move alone.

"My, it's warm in here," exclaimed Marilú, "It was so pleasant and cool last night."

"Yes. The heating is shut off in the summer time. All they have to do is shut off the flow of hot water through the pipes beneath the floor, and, of course, the braziers are never used in the summer. But it gets rather warm during the course of the day, so each night, or in the day if the Grand Vizier is going to use the room, it is cooled with big blocks of ice right outside the room, and slaves fan cool air over the ice and through those ventilators you see all around the room. The same is true of many of the other rooms of the palace, but only while the rooms are in use, as we have to conserve our supply of ice to last all summer—for sherbets and ices and cold water as well as for air-conditioning. We can only get a new supply of ice in the winter from the high peaks of the *Sierra Morena*. We are not as fortunate as the King of Granada who can get ice all year round from the *Sierra Nevada*."

They walked together across the great hall, which looked only vaguely familiar, in part because with all the curtains closed, it was illuminated by the rays of sunlight through the ceiling, instead of the enchanting gleam of hundreds of twinkling candles, but chiefly because, the night before, Marilú had been too entranced and overcome by the music, the dancing, the food and, above all, the Grand Vizier, that she had not had time to appreciate all the marvels of the room itself.

"Let's go through the Hall of the Ambassadors quickly," said Nardjis. "You will be able to see it better one day when the draperies are opened," and she headed toward the two doors at the far end. "We shall go through the same alcove you used last night. The other door leads to an almost identical alcove but, as the Vizier never had more than one wife, he used it only for his bouts with the dancing girls, and it would not be proper for you to see it. There are scores of other bedrooms upstairs, but none of them are in use. Both of these two alcoves lead to the same patio, which I would like you to see—the patio al-Muniz."

They crossed through the bedroom, out to a small vestibule, and then through a large glass door to the patio. It was much smaller than the other patio, but charming, bordered with flowering trees and blooming flower beds laid out in geometrical designs. The center was paved with gravel, divided by flagstone walks. In the very center stood a green marble fountain spraying five jets of water into the air. The fountain's basin was surrounded by twelve small statues of ruddy gold, encrusted with pearls and precious stones—on one side, a lion, a stag, and a crocodile; opposite, an eagle and a dragon; and, on the two ends, a dove, falcon, duck, hen, cock, kite, and vulture. From the mouths of each of these precious creatures there issued a stream of water, joining with the water of the five central fountains to form a pool in which swam a dozen or so gold fish with waving, frond-like tails. Nardjis explained that the fountain came from Damascus, but that the statues had been made in Córdoba.

"It is a jewel," exclaimed Marilú, just as you told me it would be. I don't think I have ever seen anything so lovely."

She examined and admired each of the gold statues in turn. "Why every one is a gem. It is all too perfect to be true. No wonder the Caliphs were so happy here!"

"They had much pleasure here, it is true," replied

Nardjis, "and Zahra, and all the lovely ladies of the palace who followed her, must have had many hours of enjoyment here. But, do you know that when the great Caliph, Abd ar-Rahman III, was an old man, he looked back on his life and said that in all his years he had enjoyed only fourteen completely happy days?"

"I can't believe it. He was a pessimist, I'm sure. Anyway, I'd much rather be here with the Grand Vizier than with any sad-faced Caliph. Imagine—fourteen happy days! I bet he's not even happy in Paradise," she added with a snort.

Nardjis smiled. "Let's go out on that balcony, where we can get a good view of the other two terraces." And they walked through the colonnade of marble pillars and arches that bounded the far side of the patio, and on to a broad balcony from which they had a magnificent vista of the *Sierra Morena* mountains stretching out far into the distance. Snuggled beneath them was the great park, and the City of Medina al-Zahra itself, far below on the nethermost terrace.

"I see what you mean," said Marilú. "We saw only a small part of the garden yesterday. We could spend a week there and never visit the same spot twice. And I can see the forest over to the right. The city is much larger that I had thought. The Mosque looks like another palace and just as beautiful as this, with all its spires and domes, and the tall tower beside it. It *is* a Paradise!"

"The garden is all on this side," Nardjis went on, "but most of the forest extends around to the other side of the terrace, facing Córdoba. Most of the people in the town live on the other side, so you can see only a small part of the city—the Mosque, and only a part of the marketplace where we shall go after lunch. That is the Guadalquivir River curving around the Mosque. It goes on in that direction to Sevilla and the ocean. In the other direction, it curls around Medina al-Zahra, and on to Córdoba and beyond."

As she spoke, Shamsi and Ourda, and three other girls whom Marilú did not know, emerged from the patio bearing tables and trays piled with refreshments. "I had asked them to serve us out here on the balcony at noon. We shall hear the call for prayer in just a few minutes."

"We say prayers seven times a day, sometimes eight," Marilú remarked. "How often do Moslems say their prayers?"

"The formal prayers, the *Salah*, come five times a day, but we recite the *fatihah* to ourselves twenty times a day," Nardjis answered. "That is like the Lord's prayer that Jesus taught us, but, of course, all our prayers must be in Arabic."

Just then, they could see, but not hear, the *muezzin* calling the faithful to prayer, and the six Moslem women laved their faces and their arms up to the elbow, in the brass basins that the girls had brought, then wiped their feet and ankles.

"You can perform the *wazu* ablution too," whispered Nardjis, "the Koran instructs us to do it before prayer, and the water won't hurt Christians. And you can kneel with us, facing East; if you will point just a fraction of a degree further north, you will be facing Jerusalem and Bethlehem instead of Mecca, and no one will know the difference."

"You're teasing me, Nardjis. Of course I'll wash and kneel, and with reverence too." And she performed the *wazu* ablution, then knelt beside Nardjis and the other women, and recited to herself the sext, for the sixth hour of the day.

Inwardly, Marilú resolved that, whenever she was awake, she would try to remember to say her matins, primes, tierces, sexts, nones, vespers and complins. Whenever her Moslem friends recited their *salah* prayers, it would remind her. And she would say the Lord's prayer to herself twenty times a day whenever they recited the *fatihah.* Nor would she forget an unspoken grace before each meal, nor silent vigils if she woke at night.

These resolutions relieved her conscience which had not ceased to be troubled by all that had happened to her, and by all that she had done, since her captivity.

They remained kneeling until Lady Nardjis gave the signal to rise. Marilú and Nardjis then seated themselves on hassocks high enough for them to look through the balustrade and get a view of the Guadalquivir below, glittering like silver in the sunlight. Meanwhile, the girls arranged the tables and refreshments. "We shall be not more than half an hour," Nardjis told Ourda, "so you two be ready to go with us."

"To hear is to obey, my lady. The chief eunuch says he will be delighted to accompany us."

"I am so glad," Nardjis told Marilú. "I always feel so safe with Masrur, and he is a very intelligent and cultivated person. I suppose he must have frightened you out of your wits when he abducted you, but he is really very gentle—gentle to us, but terrifying to strangers."

There was an inscription on the balustrade. Nardjis translated: "Surely, amid delights shall the righteous dwell." She explained: "It is from the *Koran,* and refers to Paradise, but it *is* appropriate, isn't it?"

Marilú nodded in agreement, and the ladies soon finished their light collation: *quiches* of smooth, delicate cheese, pears and peaches, some tasty nougat full of almonds, and steaming cups of tea. "I remember you liked the Chinese tea," Nardjis remarked, "and it is so refreshing, whether one is about to go for a walk, or returning all hot and dusty."

Then Ourda and Shamsi helped them on with the *haiks* they were to wear on their trip into town. Shapeless as they were already, with the tunics they had donned that morning, they looked like two rolls of carpet, slightly pointed at each end. The white silk tunics covered them from head to ankles, leaving only a slit for the eyes. On top of their *haiks,* they wore cone-shaped hats of green velvet.

"I feel like a butterfly going *into* a cocoon," thought Marilú; "oh, well, I'll come *out* of this cocoon some time and be a butterfly again!"

CHAPTER 5

Masrur, the chief eunuch, met the four women in the entrance patio. He bowed low as they approached. He was a handsome man, huge of bulk, and clean shaven, which gave him an appearance of softness, quite unlike that which Marilú had remembered ffom their first meeting. Richly attired in many-colored silks and brocades, he wore a huge scimitar, its scabbord and hilt encrusted with jewels. His robe was open from his neck almost down to his navel, disclosing an almost hairless chest. On his head perched a high silk turban, Baghdad style.

"Greetings, my ladies. I am at your command. And may I have leave to address you as *Marquesa*," he said as he turned toward Marilú. "I beg you to call me Masrur, as we shall be seeing much of one another, I trust, from this time forth. . . . And please do not be frightened of me. I am your slave, hearkening and obeying."

His voice was friendly and gentle, and Marilú warmed to him at once. He led them through the *bab as-Sudda* gate. Outside stood the carriage—the same one that had borne Marilú and her friends in captivity to Medina al-Zahra. But what a difference! Polished until it fairly glowed in its black and gold finery, the coach was now drawn by four jet-black horses with gold encrusted harness. On the left lead horse a postilion sat proudly, clad in green and gold silk. A coachman, seated on the broad front seat, held the horses in check, while two footmen waited at the carriage door. All four men were similarly attired, and all bowed deeply as the ladies approached.

"We are not accustomed to using carriages in Andalucía," Masrur remarked, "but you will find this Spanish carriage comfortable for your trip down to the Mosque. It is far too long to walk, and you are not attired for riding horseback."

The footmen helped the four women into the coach. Masrur jumped up onto the front seat, beside the coachman, while the two footmen clambered onto the high seat in the rear. In a moment, they were trotting briskly across the *place d'armes* and down a road that skirted the palace grounds, then down to the second terrace through the park, and on to the lowest level, beside the great Mosque, a scant two miles in all, but down a steep incline that would have been difficult to descend on foot, and even more tedious to ascend.

"We shall visit the Mosque first," said Nardjis, "it will be crowded soon, at the next call for prayer. Let's go inside now; we can see the outside later before we go to the market-place."

The four women, accompanied by the chief eunuch, who gave instructions to the coachman to await them in the square facing the Mosque, walked through the gate, entering a spacious patio, over forty cubits—eighty feet—on each side. The patio was paved with wine-colored marble and was bordered with flowering orange and lemon trees. In the center stood a bronze fountain, spouting twelve streams of water into a large marble basin. Marilú followed the example of her companions and washed her face and her arms up to the elbows. An attendant handed them towels to dry their hands and faces and wipe their feet; he then bowed deeply as Masrur handed him a small gratuity.

They skirted a square marble tower standing forty

cubits high beside the Mosque, and entered through the main door. Facing them were five naves, separated by four rows of marble columns, no two alike. As they walked down the center nave, thirty cubits long, Marilú could see that the columns formed ten cross-aisles, thirty-six columns in all. The floor was of black and white marble squares, partly covered with criss-crossed runners of Esparto grass. The walls were brilliant with gold and silver mosaics, framed by tiles in many colors, and pierced with windows and doors on every side, excepting on the side facing them, which was of solid marble, intricately carved.

As they approached that end of the Mosque, Nardjis whispered to Marilú: "Ahead of us is the place of the *Mihrab,* the niche which shows the direction we must face for prayer—the East, toward Mecca."

They entered a broad, white marble platform enclosed within a bronze railing. Straight ahead was the *Mihrab,* an eight-sided enclosure of carved white marble topped by a large fluted shell. Within and around were prayer rugs—"for cleanliness and the purity of the place of prayer," whispered Nardjis.

Masrur, Shamsi, and Ourda started to prostrate themselves in prayer, but Nardjis signalled to them to follow her. She led them all through a smaller bronze-railed enclosure to another enclosure at the side, almost identical to the first.

"The Muezzin has just started for the tower to call the faithful to prayer; if we pray in the public enclosure, we shall be caught in the crowd, and it will take us an hour to escape." She explained to Marilú: "This is the private oratory of the Caliphs. It is now used by the Grand Vizier and his family—and we are the only family he has," she added sadly.

The floor was covered with precious silk carpets, more beautiful than any Marilú had seen, even in the palace itself. They knelt in prayer, Nardjis reciting the *fatihah* in hushed tones, while Marilú whispered the Lord's prayer, and prayed for her friends, Conchita and Zoraya. As they knelt, they heard the voice of the *Muezzin* from the tower calling the hour. The Mosque filled with people, coming from the doors on every side, cramming every nook and cranny up to the *Mihrab* itself, and pressing against the railing that enclosed Nardjis and her companions. The crowd, seeing the Chief Eunuch in his splendid apparel, knew that they were of the household of the Grand Vizier.

"For every person you see in here," whispered Nardjis, "there are a dozen more outside, all kneeling and facing Mecca. In a few minutes the *imam* will give a sermon—a *khutbah* based on the Koran—and everyone will stand up in row after row. Then he will lead us all in prayer."

The murmur of thousands of hushed voices filled the place, and Marilú felt that she was being carried on myriad waves of prayer to the very feet of the Lord. The distinctions of creed were forgotten in the midst of these multitudes, all worshipping the same God, and kneeling to pay him reverence. There came over her an undefinable sensation of religious ecstasy that she could not express in words, and that she had experienced only rarely in the course of her religious life: once, when praying at the shrine of St. James in Compostela; again at her marriage; and later at the baptism of her two children at Betanzos.

These thoughts troubled her beyond measure, and she felt the tears running down her cheeks. She had not ceased to love her husband, nor, of course, her children, yet she knew that she was drawn to the Grand Vizier by a force too strong to resist, and she could not in her heart feel that it was lust alone. It must be love. Why couldn't she love two men? Solomon and many of the great prophets of the Lord had more than one wife, and loved them all. Why wasn't it right for her to love both her husband and the Grand Vizier at the same time?

If only she had someone to confess to—why not confess directly to God without the intercession of a priest? She did so, pouring out her soul in wordless confession, and praying for guidance. The answer came, and Marilú knew deep within her that the answer came from her heart, her soul, her conscience, and her God: She must never cease to love her husband to whom she was wed in holy matrimony, and if he were still alive, and if ever she had an opportunity to go back to him, she must do so without hesitation. Meanwhile, she was a slave to the Grand Vizier and forced to obey his commands. If she could do so with love and gladness, if she loved him with all her heart —and she did,—that was no sin, but God's will. If it were not God's will, it would not be happening, for God was everywhere, all-seeing, all-knowing, and all-powerful. Her prayer had been answered; her conscience was clear; and she rose dry-eyed and happy when Nardjis nudged her to signal that the time of prayer was over. The five of them left the Great Mosque through a private exit on the Eastern side, just to the right of the prayer niche of the Caliphs.

"We can see the exterior of the Mosque now," Nardjis advised, and they walked around the south side of the building overlooking the Guadalquivir. Crowds of people poured out from every door.

Thin lines of the faithful piled out in all directions, mingling, merging, separating, as they headed for their various destinations. How neat and clean they all were—such a contrast to the crowds in any other city that she had known. Medina al-Zahra must be a privileged place—no poor, at least no one abjectly poor, and no beggars. She must ask Nardjis about that. She turned to look at the Mosque.

It was indescribably beautiful, lovelier, in fact, than the palace itself—more compact, and obviously it had all been built at one time according to a single plan; it had not just grown, like the palace, over a span of forty years.

As they walked away from the Great Mosque, Marilú could see and appreciate its perfect proportions—the great, rounded domes of shining gold, the four delicate spires of colored marble, extending forty cubits high, the solid, square tower of the *Muezzin* equally high, with its four windows facing the four directions of the compass so that the call to prayer could be heard by all—the contrast of massive bulk and fairy lightness all combined in wondrous harmony.

"Would you shepherd us through the market-place, now," Nardjis asked Masrur.

"To hear is to obey, my lady. But my four lambs must keep together, and not stray from the flock, for it is crowded in the market."

And so it was. Thousands of people walked in all directions, hustling, bustling, jostling, stopping to gossip, to bargain at the hundreds of shops that lined the narrow streets. People, donkeys, horses, and dogs mingled together. In some stalls, great bolts of beautiful cottons, woolens, gorgeous silks, satins, velvets, and rich brocades were piled high. The place was a bedlam, voices pitched high, dogs barking, children laughing or crying—an exciting and never-ending confusion of sights and sounds. Marilú was enthralled.

"Who are those women with rosaries over there?" Marilú asked Nardjis. "They don't look like Christians."

"They're either Sufis—a mystic Moslem cult of ascetics—or else Byzantine Christians. Those with the crosses are certainly Christians. The rosaries were introduced from India—prayer beads, you know."

"Who are those serious-looking men in turbans," Marilú then asked.

"Lawyers. . . . And that other group over there in the yellow skullcaps are Jews."

Some people wore red or green skullcaps, others high turbans of raw silk, still others, men and women, wore conical velvet hats like their own, or brocade or felt toques. Everything was strange and fascinating.

"What is that group of people over there, all in white, but not just white *haiks* like ours?"

"They are in mourning," answered Nardjis. "We wear white in memory of the departed. The poet, al-Husri, has written:

In Andaluz, the tunics white
Mean mourning for the dead.
So I lament my long-dead youth
With white hairs on my head.

"That's charming!" exclaimed Marilú, "Andalucía is certainly the land for poetry. Even the King—everyone—seems to be a poet. But white doesn't seem to be appropriate for mourning; I should think it would be black."

"No. When a person dies, all color leaves his cheeks. When you think of a ghost, it is white. It's all what you're used to. But the white costume for mourning is very different from the white *haiks* we are wearing. And in a few days, all of us will be wearing white instead of colored silks. That's something else that Ziryab introduced to Spain—white must be worn from mid-June to the end of September. No one would dare disobey that rule; it's just not done. And it looks very gay after all the brilliant colors of winter. You'll see."

They passed other stalls selling jewelry. "The most precious gems are kept inside; what you see are only the cheaper things—gold bracelets, anklets, bangles. Would you like me to buy you anything?"

"Thank you, my dear, but there is nothing that I want."

Soon they entered the market itself. There was food of all kinds in a profusion and variety that Marilú had never seen before: meats, fruits, vegetables, fish. The fish markets in Galicia are better, she thought, but everything else here is marvellous. They came to the flower stalls. At one, there were some red roses of a beauty and perfection that Marilú had never seen.

"There is one thing that I wish you would buy for me, Nardjis, if you would—a red rose, a red rose that I would like to give to the Grand Vizier tonight."

"Very well. And I have just the vase for it at the palace—a long, slender crystal one from Damascus that will hold just a single rose, no more. . . . Do you know what a red rose means?"

"I do indeed. That's why I want it. Besides it is so beautiful. And I do want to give Ahmad something from me."

She selected one of the roses, a deep red, not yet in full bloom but of perfect shape. The saleswoman wrapped the stem in a damp cloth. Masrur offered to carry it, but Marilú would not surrender the precious gift.

"I think we might go back to the carriage now, and see the rest of the city by driving around," Nardjis said. "It is a very large city, and I don't want to tire you."

The chief eunuch stepped to the edge of the crowd and summoned the carriage with an imperious gesture. The coachman, footmen and postillion sprang to their places, and in a moment the carriage had crossed the square and drawn to a stop before them.

The footmen, attentive and polite, helped the women into their places, and in a trice they were trotting briskly across the square.

"Not so quickly," exclaimed Nardjis. "We want to see everything—the baths, the university, the school, the main library, Masrur's house, the house I live in, all the mansions—everything, and then back to the palace."

The coach slowed down to a walk. Its windows were open wide, the curtains drawn back, so the four passengers had a splendid view of everything.

"That is the public bath-house," and Nardjis pointed to a huge and beautiful building in Moorish style. It is just as fine as the *hammam* at the palace so far as the facilities are concerned, although, of course, not so exquisitely decorated. And it is far larger. It can accommodate over a hundred people at a time—over three hundred if you include the people lolling in the steam baths, and the steam baths are the most popular feature. People spend hours there. Of course, every house has its own bathing facilities too—anything from a simple copper basin to a *pila*, a little pool, or even a *hammam* in the larger palaces."

They passed the library, the school, the university, all of which Nardjis pointed out. "There are other schools too, and the children's playgrounds," Nardjis commented, as they drove along a beautiful park and esplanade near the river, "but we can't see everything."

They came to a large marble palace with two fountains in front of it. "That's where I usually live," said Nardjis, "when I'm not staying in the *seraglio* as I am now."

"But it's so big," commented Marilú.

"Oh, but I have so many women living with me—Shamsi and Ourda and all their friends, the musicians, dancing girls, all of the women except the servants who live in the palace—it is a women's hostel, and has to be big to accommodate everyone. But Masrur's palace is much finer—one of the best in Medina al-Zahra. There it is over there."

They passed a gem of a building, smaller than the women's hostel but, thought Marilú, almost as beautiful as the Caliph's palace itself. There were a number of other fine houses along the same avenue, and Nardjis pointed to them as they went by. They belonged to wealthy merchants.

"But where are the slums?" asked Marilú. "Where do the poor people live?"

"The poorer people live in those smaller houses down the side streets, but there really aren't any slums in Medina al-Zahra, no really impoverished people such as you would find in any other city of Spain and I suppose elsewhere in the world. You see, Medina al-Zahra is a made city, founded by the Caliph for his favorite and for the court. It didn't just grow, like other cities, and it hasn't had time to rot and decay. I suppose it will, some day, and that in time, like Ninevah and Tyre, it will cease to be. . . . There, I think we had best return to the palace," and she called out to Masrur to do so.

"It has been a wonderful trip," said Marilú, clutching her red rose to her as the carriage rolled along at a brisker pace. "The whole city is amazing. I don't see how the Caliphs could do it, in the lifetimes of just two men. I don't see how they could afford it."

"The Caliph, Marilú,—the great Abd ar-Rahman at least, was probably the richest man who ever lived, richer than Solomon or Caesar. His income from taxes alone was over six million gold dinars a year—that's nearly thirty tons of gold. And, besides that, any lands or money that were captured during his wars and raids belonged to the Caliph, and one-fifth of all other booty.

"And, in Abd ar-Rahman's time, he also received tribute from foreign kings and from the Christians and Jews in Andalucía. So you see, he had lots of money, and we are told that he used to spend one-third of it on the army, one third went into the royal treasury, and one-third on Medina al-Zahra and other royal buildings."

"Goodness! I didn't know there was that much money in all the world. I guess one can do a lot of building with thirty tons of gold a year."

The carriage rolled into the palace grounds. The footmen jumped to the ground, extended their arms to the ladies, and Nardjis and Marilú thanked them all, and especially the chief eunuch, for a fascinating tóur.

CHAPTER 6

The four women went through the patio, down the corridor, and into the *hammam.*

"We shall be wearing our full robes this evening, Shamsi," said Nardjis. Turning to Marilú, she added: "This will be your first steam bath and Turkish massage. I think you will like them, and you will find them restful, as we have had no time for a *siesta* today. The Grand Vizier almost always has that treatment after his return from Córdoba."

They passed directly from the disrobing room to the *calidarium.* Billows of steam greeted them as Ourda opened the door. "It is hot in here," exclaimed Marilú. "The floors almost burn my feet."

"You would not be able to stand them if it were not for the grass carpets. When we get to the other end of the room—we can't see a thing through this steam—you will see that the benches are covered with wood. Don't touch any of the marble—walls, benches or anything."

The two girls led them by the hand to the far end of the room. There, in front of one of the steaming cauldrons, were two large marble benches covered with wooden lattice-work. Marilú could barely make out, through the steam, two huge, muscular women, clad only in baggy cotton pantaloons that clung to their massive thighs.

The women bowed deeply and one of them said: "We are here to serve you, my ladies."

"Thank you. We shall sleep. Wake us in half an hour for the massage." Turning to Ourda and Shamsi,

Nardjis added: "You two can meet us after the massage, and soap us here in the *calidarium.*"

The two girls left with a curtsey, and Nardjis and Marilú lay down on the two benches. "Close your eyes, my dear; you will fall asleep in no time."

They lay on their stomachs, stretched out at full length, their heads facing to the side, cradled on one arm. Tired from the exertions of a long day, and warmed by the steam which seemed to increase in heat minute by minute, they fell fast asleep almost immediately.

Some time later—to Marilú it seemed eons later—they were awakened from their nap by the two *masseuses.*

Marilú then felt two strong arms massaging her back as it had never been massaged before. Kneading, squeezing, rubbing, and pounding until Marilú thought every bone in her body would break, the *masseuse* worked on her for what seemed an eternity. Marilú was limp, every muscle relaxed, when the woman gently lifted her in two strong arms and turned her over on her back. The kneading and rubbing commenced again, the pounding this time being confined to the thighs, shoulders and upper arms—"thank goodness," thought Marilú, "or I wouldn't have a whole bone in my body."

The two masseuses bowed out of the room as Shamsi and Ourda entered and began to soap and scrub their steaming bodies as the four cauldrons in the corners of the room ceased to boil, and the steam gradually dispersed, leaving only a faint haze in the room.

"You are truly clean, now," said Nardjis. "The steam and the massage have cleansed every last bit of dirt and oil out of your pores and, when our bath is over, you will find yourself more relaxed and invigorated than if you had had an hour's *siesta.*"

The girls rinsed their mistresses with warm water, led them to the hot pool to luxuriate for another fifteen minutes and then, after a quick plunge in the cold water, dried them vigorously, and took them to the *tepidarium* for the final touches. The girls' deft fingers, smoothly rubbing the perfumed oils into the skin from neck to feet, felt like gentle zephyrs after the heavy-handed massage by the two Amazons.

"You can leave us now, after you have brushed our hair," said Nardjis. "We shall want to be alone and rest while you get our clothes and makeup ready."

"Just a moment," interrupted Marilú. "Do you think it would be all right if I were made up in Moslem fashion? I shan't be as beautiful as you were last night, Nardjis, because I don't have your lovely black hair, but I should like to try it if you think the Grand Vizier won't mind."

"Very well. I was sure you would want to do that, one of these days, just out of curiosity. We shan't cut your hair short like mine, but Ourda knows how to coil it on top of your head so that it will give the same effect. And I am sure you will be beautiful, regardless of how you are made up.

The girls left, and Nardjis whispered: "Now I'll tell you why I wanted to be alone with you. I want to help you to acquire mastery over certain arts of love that only Moslem women know. You mustn't be embarrassed or shocked, because it is most important. And, when you have learned these secrets, it will give you and the Grand Vizier a happiness more intense than any you have ever experienced."

"I don't see how anything could be more wonderful than the pleasures I have already enjoyed," said Marilú, "but please instruct me. It sounds mysterious—and fascinating. I shan't be embarrassed with just the two of us here."

"Let me first ask you, dear. If I were to put my

finger up into your most secret places, do you think that you could hold it tight, so that I could hardly get it out again?"

"Yes, I think so. I would just close my thighs tight, and hold your whole hand so that you'd have to pull pretty hard to get your finger out—but what in the world for?"

"Well, dear," Nardjis laughed, "if you always keep your legs close together, you will never need the secrets I'm going to tell you—and you will miss a great many pleasures. But what I want to teach you is to be able to hold on tight while your legs are far apart.

"And I'll tell you why. Right now, the Grand Vizier is so infatuated with you—I really should say, so in love with you—that you will not need any further arts to keep him infatuated. But some day the honeymoon will be over. It may be more than one moon, perhaps many months—I think it will be. But if you want the honeymoon to be perpetual, for him always to prefer you to any other woman, you will have to learn the secrets that Moslem women learn from childhood.

"If you can hold onto my finger tight, with your thighs apart—and of course, I am not thinking of fingers—you will find that your lover will be enraptured. He will feel himself held in your grasp from one end to the other; his period of arousal will be prolonged beyond anything you would have thought possible. And when you can stand it no longer and release your grasp, you will both come to a climax together, after enjoying the most excruciating bliss that human beings can experience. You will be in seventh heaven!"

"Excruciating seems a strange word for bliss," said Marilú, "but you are right. Even the bliss I have enjoyed thus far has been excruciating, a combination of turture and ecstasy—and it's wonderful! So tell me more."

"I can tell you this: If you fail to learn this art, the day will come when the Grand Vizier will find some dancing girl, perhaps from Baghdad or Damascus, who will hold him tight, and he will begin to think that she is more passionate, more loving than you. He will even begin to wonder whether you are not merely a beautiful blond—beautiful but cold—and he will seek his satisfaction in some warm and passionate Moslem girl. We call such a person, who is adept in the art, a *kabbázah*—one who holds.

"But, if you master the art, he will never leave you—your beauty, your intelligence, your close companionship, your love, will give you every advantage over any stranger, no matter how young and lovely she may be. And the secret is so simple—although it will take you months to learn the art."

"You see, there are muscles that can be squeezed together. And at the very entrance there is a strong muscle that you can contract just as easily as you can contract your lips to a pout, and much more strongly. But I have been practicing that art since I was eleven or twelve years old—since I first became a woman, when my nurse taught me how. Your muscles have never been used, and there is no strength in them. Worse than that, you don't even know how to make them contract. But you are young enough to learn. The method is simple but the learning is difficult."

"What must I do?"

And Nardjis proceeded to give Marilú the precise instructions necessary to master the art of *Kabbázah.*

"Now if you will do that, say twenty times, whenever you have a moment to spare during the day, that will strengthen the muscles. At first, nothing will happen. It may be months before you even begin to feel the slightest tightening of your muscles. You will even start to think that it is useless, that your muscles must be completely atrophied, and will not function. And then one day—perhaps months from now—you will begin to feel a slight twinge, the barest flicker of a contraction and, once that has happened, once you learn where the muscles are and how to control them, the exercising will come easy, and you will make more progress in a week than you had made before in a month. And the final success will come when you no longer have to think about it; you will grasp what you have to grasp as naturally as a baby's fingers grasp his mother's breast. You will be a *kabbázah!*"

"I shall try so hard," said Marilú. "I don't care how difficult it is to learn, I simply must, and I *will* learn! It means so much to me, I simply have to learn immediately—in weeks. I cant wait until it happens—until I'm a real *kabbázah.* And thank you, Nardjis, ever and ever so much!"

Then, with apparent irrelevance, she asked: "That Moorish dancing girl we saw last night—where is she?"

Nardjis burst out laughing. "You needn't worry about her. She is lovely and she is young. But the Grand Vizier had no eyes for anyone but you last night, and by the time his eyes do begin to wander, that dancing girl will be long forgotten.

"It is other dancing girls, and other singers, yet to come, whom you must worry about, and by that time, you may yourself be a *kabbázah* and need not fear any rivals, no matter how young and how seductive they are. You have an incentive, at least, to keep you hard at work, for I can tell you that it will be a tedious and unrewarding processs until you acquire the knack. . . . And now let's go to the dressing room where Shamsi and Ourda are waiting for us."

They went out to the adjoining room, arm in arm. Their little attendants were waiting for them there.

"Use violet fragrances this evening, Ourda," instructed Nardjis. "It will please the Grand Vizier. And for me" she added, turning to Shamsi, "the hyacinth. It must not compete with, yet it must not clash with, the violet."

Ourda helped her mistress on with the gossamer undergarments—blouse and baggy pantaloons—similar to those Marilú had worn the previous evening. She then brushed her hair, applying a few drops of oil, and brushing until it gleamed like burnished gold. She braided the long tresses into two coils, which she intertwined in a knot at the back of the head, leaving the nape of the neck and ears bare. A few wayward strands were touched with egg white and pressed into two curls, like question marks, in front of each ear. Ourda then rubbed and scrubbed Marilú's teeth, gums and lips with *souak*—powdered walnut bark—until the teeth glistened like pearls between the red, red lips.

"Please close your eyes," Ourda requested, "while I apply the *kohl*."

Deftly the girl rimmed both lower and upper lids and lashes with the black unguent. "Do you think I should do the eyebrows too?" she asked Nardjis who was being similarly attended to on the adjoining bench.

"Yes. You will have to. The blond eyebrows are almost invisible over the *kohl*-blacked eyes."

Ourda plucked a few straying hairs, and then blackened the brows, extending the line of *kohl* until the two eyebrows met in the center.

"No," advised Nardjis. "That's too much—just the eyebrows themselves. The heavy black line does not go well with the blond hair above."

Ourda carefully erased the line between the brows with a touch of oil, stood back to admire the effect, retouched the brows, and applied just the barest trace of rosy powder to the cheeks. Then, with a small brush, she tinted Marilú's toenails and fingernails with henna.

"Just a moment now, before I give you the mirror. I want to fasten the earrings so that you can see the full effect."

Adjusting the two golden rings, each with a single blue sapphire, Ourda stepped back to admire the effect. "You are simply beautiful!," she exclaimed. "Let me hold the glass; the henna hasn't dried yet. . . . Look, Lady Nardjis, isn't she lovely with this *maquillage* and *coiffure*?"

Nardjis and Shamsi turned their heads to see, the latter letting out a little gasp of sheer delight.

"Perfect," Nardjis said, "you are ravishing in that Andalucían make-up. It is most becoming. . . . But," she added in an afterthought, "I really prefer you just as you really are—a lovely, blond *Gallega*, without the *kohn* or henna, and with your long golden tresses draped over your shoulders.

"Don't be disappointed, my dear, if the Grand Vizier tells you he likes you better as a *Gallega*. He will be pleased that you have made this effort to please him, and he is bound to find you ravishingly beautiful. You are. But to him, your blond Galician loveliness is exotic and alluring, and he may prefer it. Then again, he may not. And he will love you for having adopted the ways of his beloved Andalucía."

She turned to the two handmaidens. "We shall be wearing the heavy silken robes tonight, you know, and the opaque veils. The *sha'ir* will be in the great hall this evening.

"The *sha'ir*," Nardjis explained to Marilú, "is a minstrel. He will be reciting a long poem, probably an ode on some historic subject—a *maqamah*. He may even sing parts of it but, in any event, he will have a lute to accompany some passages of the poem. It will be a poem that he composed himself, of course, and I am sure you will find it highly dramatic and very moving. . . . But, as there will be a man present, we cannot wear the revealing garments we wore yesterday evening, nor can Shamsi and Ourda, or any of the other attendants."

It occurred to Marilú for the first time that, on the previous evening, aside from the Grand Vizier and the eunuchs, there had not been a single man present in the Salon of the Caliphs, nor had they passed any in the corridors. "But shall I be able to understand the *maqamah?*" she asked.

"Oh, yes. It will be in *Romance,* you know—in the Mozarabic Spanish vernacular. There is hardly any Arabic spoken in Andalucía nowadays, aside from prayers, and, even though people write with Arabic or Hebrew letters, what they are writing is nearly always *Romance.*"

The two girls gave their mistresses soft, silver brocaded slippers, then helped them to adjust the long silk robes that reached from the neck to the ankles. Although the garments effectively concealed every curve of the body, they were by no means unattractive. In fact, the rich, embroidered green velvet robes—Marilú's gold-embroidered, Nardjis's silver—were quite becoming. They rippled in graceful folds as the ladies walked about the room. The girls adjusted the little, round, green caps, Marilú's fringed with a circlet of blue sapphires, Nadjis's with pearls and diamonds. Silken veils, one golden, the other silver, completed their attire. Ourda and Shamsi hastily donned similar robes and caps of bright red and gold, which made them look impudently pert and ridiculously overdressed for their age.

The four women trouped out of the room, to be met at the door by the chief eunuch, smiling and bowing. "Your Ladyship is entrancing this evening," he said to Marilú, noting approvingly her Andalucían attire and *maquillage.* "A true *muwallid!* And you too, Lady Nardjis, are lovely, as always."

"A *muwallid* is a Christian convert to Islam," explained Nardjis, "but Masrur means it as an expression of admiration. He is referring to your looks and not to your religion, for I know that you Christians regard *muwallids* as renegades."

The four women entered the grand salon preceded by Masrur, Marilú with some trepidation as to how the Grand Vizier would react to her changed appearance. As they skirted the central pool, and bowed low, the Grand Vizier arose and went to meet them. He stopped for a moment in brief amazement.

"My dear, you are simply beautiful tonight—too lovely for words! No, perhaps there are words for your loveliness—a poem that my father, ibn Zaydun, wrote for his beloved Walládah, my mother, may their souls rest in peace:

When you're away,
The world's awry;
The days are gray
When you're not nigh.

But when you're near,
The darkest night
Turns bright and clear
With radiant light!

"Oh, thank you, thank you!" exclaimed Marilú, blushing. "I shall always remember and treasure that lovely poem. But I don't deserve it—really. . . . I've brought you this rose from Medina al-Zahra," she added shyly, "and Lady Nardjis gave me this crystal vase for it. I *did* want to give you something. I hope you don't mind."

"On the contrary, it *is* lovely, and I shall treasure it. It reminds me of you, in a way. Thank you, my love."

Nardjis, Masrur, and the two girls bowed low, and withdrew to the far side of the salon, as they had done the night before, while the Grand Vizier fondly escorted Marilú back to the pile of cushions against the wall. A bevy of serving girls trouped through the door at the far end, and placed tables between them piled high with green olives in brine, ripe olives in oil, marinated sardines, tiny shrimps, and other *hors d'oeuvres*. They partook of these viands and sipped the cool white wine, in blissful silence, having no need of words to express their pleasure at being together.

The *hors d'oeuvres* were followed by a plate of braised lambs' hearts and crisply fried slices of eggplant, then by a roast duck, beautifully browned in a delicious sauce, followed by a platter of honey tarts perfumed with vanilla and stuffed with almonds and pistachios. The Grand Vizier explained that they were dining lightly that evening; otherwise, the food would sit heavily on their stomachs during the stirring passages of the *maqamah* that he said would follow.

The maids cleared away the tables and trays, brought bowels of hot water and rose petals to wash their hands, and towels to dry them, then small bonbons of gum arabic to chew to perfume their breath. They left a large basket, piled high with fruit, a jug of ice-cold sherbet, and two crystal goblets. The Grand Vizier signalled to the *kahraman*, Lady Nardjis, and the two girls to sit beside them to hear the *maqamah* that, quite evidently, was to be a rare treat, more noteworthy than the dancing girls of the previous evening. The screen had been moved to the rear, and the musicians sat in front of it, silent, eagerly awaiting the event of the evening.

"I trust you won't be offended by the theme of the

maqamah tonight," the Grand Vizier remarked to Marilú. "I have asked for an historic ode tonight and, of course, it will portray history as we Moslems see it. Not that it will make the Christian generals less noble and heroic than they are—there would be little glory in the victories of Islam if our enemies were cowards—but that you will find the virtues of the Arabs perhaps magnified out of due proportion. The alternative to an historic epic would be a long poem of romantic love and, frankly, I am rather sick of those.

"The *juglares*—the troubadours—of Spain nowadays write only of courtly love, and they have adopted the convention that true love, to be truly true, must have three attributes: First, it must emphasize the power of love to improve and to enoble to protagonists—I have no quarrel with that. Second, the lover must place his beloved on a pedestal. to admire her from afar and to make her slightest wish his supreme command—I prefer a mutal embrace on one level, and have no desire to put my arms around a pedestal with my beloved perched far above me. And, finally, they hold that the ideal of love, romantic love, is an intense and passionate desire that must never be allowed to attain fulfillment. I don't think much of Platonic love; I prefer the Ovidian.

"As the theme of the poem will be historical, our minstrel will use an old-fashioned parchment-bellied lute to evoke the spirit of the past, instead of the modern all-wooden lute that you may have seen. Here he comes!"

The *juglar* entered the room at the far end, a tall, erect man of rather more than middle age, his full beard and long, flowing hair more white than black. His jacket was of soft, natural chamois, open at the neck. He wore leather breeches, and sandals laced from the ankles to just above the calf, in lieu of the conventional baggy pantaloons. Over his shoulders he carried a lute of strange appearance. He walked slowly, gravely, around the pool in the center of the room and bowed low before the Grand Vizier and his guests. Then, removing his lute from his shoulder, he seated himself on a large leather hassock just in front of his audience.

Fixing his eyes upon the Grand Vizier and Marilú, the minstrel announced in resonant tones: "This is the ode of Abd ar-Rahman al-Khahlifa al-Nasir li-Din Allah Amir al-muminin, Caliph and Victorious Champion of the Religion of Allah and Commander of the Faithful." He strummed a few chords on his lute to denote the commencement of the *maqamah.*

I sing of the sword of the Prophet,
of warriors brave and glorious,
Of the greatest Caliph of Islam—
But only God is victorious!

The *sha-ir* again plucked his lute to focus the attention of his audience, then changed to a more sonorous, unrhymed meter for his epic recital.

The story of Islam's glory under the great Caliph, and his battles against his enemies, told by the minstrel in his deep and resonant voice, stirred his audience to such a pitch that their hearts rose and sank with every triumph and every disaster as though they themselves were there to share in the thrill of victory and the heartbreak of defeat. The vivid narrative was followed by a crescendo of chords on the minstrel's lute that carried the listeners to an ever higher pitch of emotion, until the Grand Vizier, Marilú and all the others were flushed and panting, hanging breathless on every word and note.

Then, solemnly, the *sha-ir* declaimed: "*Wa-la ghalib illa Allah*"—"Only God is victorious!" And he told of the decline of the Caliphate, and of the usurper, Mohammed ibn-abi-Amir, a humble-scrivener who became the lover of the Caliph al-Hakam's widow, a beautiful golden-haired Basque, Aurora, and then how this scrivener rose to become Royal Chamberlain—the *Hajib*—with royal powers and prerogatives; how he then confined the new Caliph Hisham II, a boy of twelve, as a prisoner in his own palace; and how, after a triumphant invasion of North Africa, the usurper assumed the title of al-Mansur bi-Allah—Conqueror by the aid of Allah. And he described how al-Mansur, or Almanzor, as the Christian Spaniards called him, sailed with his fleet up the Douro River from Porto, then marched with his army inland to Iria Flavia de Compostela which he razed to the ground, after looting all its treasures, leaving not one stone standing upon another, destroying the great church of Saint James and sparing only the tomb of the Apostle; and how he devastated all the western towns of Galicia from Iria Flavia to Coruña, capturing the Monasteries of San Cosme and San Damián, and the fortress of San Payo.

Marilú shuddered as she heard the dread name of Almanzor, for she knew that her beloved city of Iria Flavia de Compostela had not yet recovered from the destruction wreaked by the Saracens nearly a hundred years ago. But so thrilled was she by the poetry and the music of the minstrel that she listened entranced to the recital, and was breathless at the account of the successive victories of the Conqueror.

The bard then brought forth from his lute a sonorous chord like rolling thunder, coming closer and louder, and rising to a crescendo of sound that made his listeners feel that the whole world was crashing down around them. And he told of the fall of the Caliphate, of the imprisonment of the last Caliph Hisham III by the rebellious leaders of the community of Córdoba, and his death in a vaulted dungeon beside the Great Mosque of Córdoba, half-frozen, half-stifled in the fetid air, in pitch darkness, and how he finally starved to death, clutching his infant daughter to his bosom to keep her warm, and giving her his last morsel of bread.

Lady Nardjis was reduced to tears by this tragic tale, and Marilú and the others were sobbing audibly as the minstrel played his lute in tones so doleful that his listeners felt he was plucking at their very heart-strings.

The bard went on to describe the events following the fall of the Caliphate; the division of Andalucía into many petty kingdoms, each ruled by a so-called *taifa,* partisan king, and of the disintegration of the Islamic Empire in Spain; the rise of Christian Spain under Ferdinand and Alfonso; and the invasion of the barbarians from Africa under ibn-Tashfin. His poem ended in a note of starkest tragedy, the story of the fall of the Umayyad dynasty, from the incomparable glory of the great Abd ar-Rahman to the shattering of all his dreams for the welfare of his beloved al-Andaluz.

Not an eye was dry as the minstrel concluded, with a sob in his throat:

> *Behold, how the mighty have fallen,*
> *Abd ar-Rahman great and glorious,*
> Wa-la ghalib illa Allah—
> *God alone remains victorious!*

CHAPTER 7

The minstrel stood up gravely, slung his lute over his shoulder, and bowed deeply. The Grand Vizier, and Marilú as well, were too overcome with emotion to express their thanks for his elocution. Instead, they both acknowledged the perfection of the performance by bowing, and wordlessly thanking the *juglar* through their tears. The bard bowed, walked backward five paces, bowed again, turned around and slowly walked toward the exit.

The Vizier recovered his calm, clapped his hands twice, and the eunuchs and musicians quickly extinguished the gleaming candles around the room, leaving it in total darkness save for the faint glow of the oil lamp at the entrance to the alcove behind the Vizier and Marilú. The women gathered up their musical instruments, two of the eunuchs removed the screen, the great doors were closed silently and the draperies drawn, and Marilú and the Vizier were left alone in the semi-darkness.

Marilú rose from the pile of cushions, dropped her veil and at the same time loosened the heavy robe which enveloped her from neck to ankles. As she stood there, swaying slightly, overcome by a feeling of faintness after the emotions induced by the *maqamah,* the Vizier picked her up in his strong arms and carried her to the alcove.

He laid her warm and trembling body gently upon the bed, drew the outer drapes at the doorway, closed the massive doors and approached the bed. As he contemplated the graceful figure of his beloved, naked except for the sheerest of blouses open at the neck, and equally gossamer baggy pantaloons, their drawstring untied, he placed his turban on the floor and loosed and discarded his enfolding silken robe.

Marilú watched eagerly, as she noted with a glance the great manroot pointed stiffly toward the ceiling knowing yet not knowing what was yet to come. Her lips parted in ecstasy and she half panted, half whispered: "Come! come to me, my beloved! come quickly, come!"

The Vizier gathered her in his arms and, placing one hand under her head while the other curled around her waist and embraced her breast, he drew her panting mouth to his. Their lips met, their tongues probed deeply, exploring every secret, hidden part, as though there yet were secrets unrevealed in the previous night's love-making. Her breasts titillated against his, then were crushed in a hot embrace as the Vizier bore her down backwards on the bed and deftly placed her legs over his shoulders. Her thighs were now crushed against his breast as her calves encircled his neck, the feet meeting and clasping in fond embrace. Her arms encircled, then caressed and fondled the heaving form on top of her. And then—rapturously—she felt the great manroot penetrate her most intimate being.

Never had they been closer together, never had the full length of her thighs and calves touched so much of her beloved, while her arms fondled and hugged him around the waist, the neck, the shoulders, his great heaving thighs. Their mouths were sometimes joined together, their tongues mutually exploring, while from time to time he would wrench his mouth loose from hers and plant it deliciously deep within the crevices of her neck and shoulders. They heaved and twisted in mutual ecstasy—then, with a convulsive explosion, came the climax and she was inundated with a giant spurt of warm flowing pleasure that seemed to penetrate her very being.

"Oh, God!" she murmured as they lay exhausted side by side, wrapped in each other's arms, "What ecstasy! What rapture! What a man you are!"

"My love! my love! So beautiful, so passionate, so dear to me!"

Their endearments, the softness yet fierceness of their accents, led to further caressing. He gently fondled her breasts, her neck, her waist, until, silently, the four hands met as each grasped the other's most secret places. He drew her to him, side by side, her left leg beneath his waist and thighs, her right leg above and clasped around his body. Again he penetrated deep within her, and again and again he thrust his pelvis into her while she weaved her hips wildly in rhythm or in counterpoint to his. She came to climax, ecstatically, overwhelmingly—and still he thrust and thrust, his manroot never slackening, never softening.

Without withdrawing, or stopping even for an instant the pounding of his body, he turned her over full upon her back, and thrust and churned until she gasped with pain and pleasure. "My God! My God! It won't stop! It won't stop, my dearest! It comes again and again. Oh, God, make it stop! No don't, don't ever stop! Oh, my God! My love!" she gasped.

And then it came—a mutual climax that overwhelmed them in a cataract of love. And once again, they lay exhausted in panting embrace.

"How can you do it?" she whispered fondly. "How can you keep it up, and do it again and again, without ever slackening? It's wonderful, oh, it's wonderful!"

He explained to her the art of *imsak*, of a man retaining himself to the utmost limit, which reminded her that she must practice and learn to perfection the art that Nardjis had taught her.

"Let me just stay here in your arms, my love," she asked. "I just want to stay with you for a while, to feel close to you, and talk with you, before I go and freshen up."

"Of course you may, my dear. You seem troubled. Is it the *maqamah*, or is it something else that is worrying you?"

'No. It's chiefly that I just want to be with you a little longer. But, of course, the *maqamah* did excite and disturb me deeply—I have never heard anything like it before, so eloquent, so moving. And then, too, I am worried about my little cousin, Conchita. She must be terribly frightened—a virgin. And poor Zoraya—with the Black Vizier. Dear Lady Nardjis tried to reassure me, but I can't help feeling worried."

"Well, then you may cease your worries, my love. Your little cousin, I am sure, is very happy with Prince al-Mamun. He is quite a man, and she could hardly lose her maidenhood under more expert hands or with greater enjoyment. It is true that he is of a restless nature; his own wife is very beautiful and very demanding, and he has many concubines in Córdoba and in Sevilla. But little Conchita has no rival here in Medina al-Zahra so far as I know; her troubles, if any, are for the future, and you know, the Bible tells us: 'Take no thought for the morrow. Sufficient unto the day is the evil thereof. Consider the lilies of the field, they toil not, neither do they spin, yet Solomon in all his glory was not arrayed like one of these.' "

Marilú smiled, and the Grand Vizier continued: "And, as for Zoraya I'm afraid you are unduly worried merely because the Vizier ben Bakr is called the 'Black Vizier.' You know, the Shunamite maiden whom Solomon loved when he said 'thou art black but thou art beautiful' was not a negress, but an Arab of the Kedar tribe. The mother of Abd ar-Rahman I was a Berber slave, and men spoke of her as 'black'—la *negrita*. She may have had some negro blood, from Senegal, perhaps. Most Berbers do—and most southern Arabs too, from the Abyssinian invasions—but neither she, nor the Shunamite maiden, nor ben Bakr, are black or negro. Ben Bakr's complexion is not much darker than mine, and mine is merely tanned by the sun and wind, as you know from having seen the rest of my body. Ben Bakr is not black, but what you northerners would call '*moreno*'—Moorish, brunette.

"And, anyway, we Moslems have no feeling about the color of a man's—or woman's—skin, one way or the other. The only reason we look down on the negroes from Senegal or the Congo or Upper Nile is not that they are negro, but that they are savages. And, I suppose, because we Moslems, I must admit, are the great slave traders of the world. We buy them as slaves from their enemies, or from treacherous friends of their own tribe, in Africa, and we trade and sell them throughout the world. And it is a despicable, but human trait for men to despise those whom they wrong—in an attempt to justify their own misdeeds.

"So don't worry about your friend, Zoraya. You may be sure that she is quite contented with her lot. The Black Vizier is himself, as Nardjis may have told you, descended from Solomon and Balkis, the Queen of Saba, and of nobler blood than mine. His ancestors, the Sabeans, are descended from Shem like the Hebrews, and from Ham like the Egyptians, and are hence of the same race as we Ishmaelites. And his family were converted to Islam from Christianity in the time of the Prophet, upon whom be the benediction of God.

"So your friend need not fear him on the ground of

religion any more than on the ground of race. His people are people of the Book, believing in one God, the same God whom you worship.

"It is seven centuries since the Sabeans worshipped the sun goddess, the moon god, and their great god, Ashtar, whom the Sidonians worshipped as the goddess Astarte, the Canaanites as Ashtoreth, and the Iraqi as Ishtar. The vizier ben Bakr is no pagan, and if he, and all we Moslems, still await the coming of the star Venus as a favorable omen for our *ghazzias* and wars, it is not because we think that that planet, *An-najm*, is the embodiment of Astarte, but because we believe that it is an omen sent to us by Allah. So, set your mind at rest, my love. Ben Bakr is one with me in race and religion, and my own most trusted companion in arms. Zoraya will find him wholly delightful as her companion."

Marilú smiled again. "Perhaps I'm not really worried. Perhaps I just wanted to be with you a little longer, to have you talk with me. I've never known a man as learned as you, not even my father who is considered a scholar.... But I must leave you now and freshen up before my maid believes I am never coming to the bath."

As the Grand Vizier gazed at her, her hair disheveled the *kohl* smeared down her cheeks, but still beautiful despite it all, he said softly: "You know, my dear, when I said that you were beautiful made up as a *Muwallid*, I was not deceiving you. You are and were, but I still love you best as a blond *Gallega*. So, if you want merely to wash off all that make-up, instead of taking the time to have it reapplied, please do so. I like you best just as yourself, with your golden hair hanging down your shoulders, and I would prefer it if you were always that way—or nearly always, changing into a *Muwallid* only when you wish to excite me by being gloriously different. I'll see you soon, my sweet."

She left, thinking how thoughtful he had been. If he had shown the slightest dismay when first he saw her made up in Moslem fashion, it would have killed her, she thought. How kind of him, how loving—and what a wonderful man!

Marilú was met outside the door by a smiling Shamsi whose smile turned quickly to a look of dismay as she saw her mistress disheveled, her hair in a tangle of knots, and the black *kohl* from her brows and lids smeared all over her forehead and cheeks. "My, it will take an hour at least, my lady, to get you tidied up, and made up again as Ourda made you up for this evening."

"Don't bother, then,"said Marilú. "Do you think you can get the *kohl* off, and brush my hair straight? I've decided I want to be a *Gallega* again, with no make-up, and my hair over my shoulders."

"That will be much easier and faster," and she handed Marilú a small ball of scented gum arabic. "If you will chew on this while I am finishing your *toilette,* it will perfume and freshen your breath. I think you'll like it." Then, with a small towel soaked in perfumed oil, Shamsi removed every trace of antimony from her mistress's face, brushed and combed the long hair until every tangle was out. She then wrapped a towel turban-fashion over Marilú's head and said she would prepare a hot bath.

When Marilú was ready, Shamsi used a faintly scented, clear liquid to remove the henna from her mistress's finger and toe nails, and sponged her from forehead to toes, then soaped her well, sponged and rinsed again and, finally, dried her with a large towel, rubbing until the skin glowed rosy red.

"It will only take a few minutes now, *Marquesa,*" said Shamsi as she massaged Marilú's body with gardenia-scented oil. "This perfume will go better, I think, than the violet, which was suited to your Moslem make-up.... If I had to apply that make-up again, it would take at least another hour."

"Goodness! I wouldn't want to wait that long," exclaimed Marilú, adding, lest she shock her young companion, "I'm so sleepy."

Shamsi smiled, "Oh, yes, milady; it is late."

She removed the turbaned towel, and brushed her mistress's long locks until they fairly gleamed, then draped them in two graceful, wavy coils over Marilú's shoulders. "There—you are yourself again, and oh so lovely. I trust you won't think me rude, milady, but I really think you are more beautiful that way.... But I do hope you will let me make you up sometimes in Moslem style; it is such fun making you up in different ways and you are so lovely in every fashion."

She handed Marilú a fresh, sheer cotton gown and stepped back to admire her handiwork. The transformation was complete—from dark-eyed *Muwallid* to clear-eyed *Gallega*, as different as day from night, and just as difficult to decide which might be more beautiful.

Shamsi, with Marilú's assent, left by the rear door while Marilú stepped out, confident in her renewed natural beauty, to rejoin her paramour.

"Oh, my sweetness," whispered the Grand Vizier, "you are truly lovely. Come and snuggle beside me and, if you wish, go to sleep in my arms."

"No, my dearest, I am too full of love to sleep. I want to tease you tonight, as you teased me last night, until neither you nor I can stand it any longer. Please let me ... please, my love. You are so strong, I can't do it unless you let me.

"And do you know what I'd like to do," she whispered, as she lay down beside her beloved, "I'd like to take you by force as you take me. I want to ride you as you have ridden me, to have you under me panting, as I was under you, gasping for breath. . . . But, of course, you'd have to let me do it, you'd have to pretend I was taking you in spite of your struggles. Because you're so much stronger than I. Would you let me? Please."

The Vizier seemed dismayed for a moment at least, then explained: "I can't, my love, I really can't. You know, we Arabs have been taught from childhood that it is shameful for a man to lie beneath, and to have a woman bestride him—we mock any man who allows such an indignity as effeminate. But we are told too that it is harmful to our health, that it weakens a man's virility, and that a woman's fluids pouring into his body will rob it of all vitality."

Then, seeing Marilú's disappointment, he stopped to reconsider: "I guess, after all, that the latter can't be true, that it must just be an old wives' tale. The Moslems and Hindus in India do it, and in fact it is said to be their favorite way. Yet, certainly, the Indians are by no means impotent. And now that I think of it, Mars was said to have enjoyed Venus most when she bestrode him, and he could lie on his back and fondle her two lovely breasts while she rode him up and down like a rider on a rampant stallion.

"I guess it could be fun—exciting fun," he added thoughtfully as he played with the idea for the first time. "But not tonight. I'll have to think it over. After all, we've been schooled for so long to think it shameful, that I just can't change my mind so quickly. Not tonight, my love . . . I promise I'll let you do it sometime, but not now . . . and you mustn't breathe a word of it to Lady Nardjis or anyone. They'd think that I had let you make me somewhat less than a man. We'll try it, but it must be our own secret . . . our own secret pleasure, just for you and me alone.

"But I shall grant your other wish; I'll let you tease

me—fondle and caress and tease me—and I shan't resist. Until I can stand it no more, and then I can't promise what the consequences may be—something terrifying, I'm sure, terrifying and wonderful, so I'm warning you."

Marilú laughed: "I'm not afraid of you, you big bully. Now you lie right there while I have my will with you," and she proceeded to stroke his hair gently while he lay flat on his back wondering when and where and how she would attack—her "teasing," as she called it.

Marilú snuggled close, still stroking his hair with one hand while with the other she gently stroked his cheeks. She bent over his face and kissed his eyes, being careful not to give the slightest impression that she had any intention of mounting him, for she understood the reasons for his misgivings and was determined to respect them—at least for this night.

She transferred her lips from his eyes to the deep recesses where his neck met his powerful shoulders. With open lips and the tip of her moist tongue, she strayed around his neck from one side to the other, noting with pleasure how this powerful man beside her shuddered with delight at every kiss. Her own being responded to the pleasure she was giving her lover, and she could feel her breasts swell as they brushed against his chest.

"Careful now," she thought, "I mustn't get too excited or I shan't be able to prolong the pleasure, and keep on teasing him to desperation, as I want to do."

Her lips just brushed his mouth, not giving him time to insert his tongue as he yearned to. She stroked the rippling muscles in his shoulders and arms, down to the wrists, then back again to his chest, at the same time kissing, kissing, kissing with parted lips and tongue, his neck, his chest, his navel, and down to where she could feel the hair between his legs brushing against her chin. Then quickly, violently, she planted her mouth on his, plunged her tongue deep within his eager mouth and probed and explored the warm recesses she knew so well. Meanwhile her hands gently, roughly, stroked his neck and head, while her breasts hardened again as they grazed his chest. She knew that he, as well as she, could feel her nipples expand in tantalizing contact with his own.

He attempted to seize her head in his hands and insert his tongue between her lips, but she drew brusquely away while her hands wandered down his body to his waist, to his navel. She felt her wrist struck sharply by his rising manroot, but swiftly withdrew her hands and let them slide down to his hips, his thighs, his calves. Then, slowly, they wandered back along the inside of his legs, up to his thighs again and then beyond, where her fingers gently touched the base of his manhood. They passed gently, tantalizingly, along the full length of that most virile member, to the very tip.

Her fingers caressed their prey with soft, kisslike strokes. The great manroot stiffened and expanded to what seemed an enormous length, and she could feel her own thighs moist with expectation. Suddenly, she could stand it no longer and grasped the rampant member with both hands, moaning and breathing heavily as she did so.

The Vizier groaned, then seized her violently by the shoulders and turned her over while Marilú's eager hands hastened to insert their prize into her straining body. The two, joined into one, strained and twisted and heaved, their hips now gyrating, now plunging and rearing in ecstatic embrace. They moaned and gasped and panted in the violence of their movements, and then it came again—like an avalanche, gathering speed and intensity to an unbearable, overwhelming climax, and then—again and again and again—Marilú felt wave after wave of ecstasy shake every fiber of her being.

The lovers fell back exhausted, side by side, arm in arm.

"Oh, you are wonderful, Ahmad, my dear," sighed Marilú, her eyes closed in utter contentment.

And then, suddenly, as the Grand Vizier's hands caressed her breasts, and she could feel them swell under his touch, she sobbed: "Take me again, my darling."

"Kneel down," he ordered brusquely. "Kneel down as you did when first you saw me, on your knees, in a position of prayer, with your arms outstretched before you, and your forehead between them, touching the mattress."

Marilú did as she was told and then, as he came up behind her and encircled her breast with his arms, she feared for a moment that she was about to endure what she had always been taught to regard as an abomination. Submissive, she steeled herself for the worst, and then—oh, utter bliss—she felt him enter her flower from behind, and start thrusting, thrusting, thrusting . . .

She said forbidden words to herself again and again, as the Vizier's great manroot probed secret parts and places deep within her that she had never known existed. She moaned and screamed with pain and delight as her lover groaned and gasped above her, grasping and caressing her breasts, and pushing, pushing deeper and deeper into her vital parts. And then, at last, after what seemed an eternity of bliss, it came, and again she was inundated with a flood of heavenly contentment.

They sank down into the bed, side by side, their arms around one another in blissful exhaustion. "Oh, Ahmad, it was wonderful—and I was so terribly frightened. Let me kiss you, you marvelous man."

Her lips touched his, gently at first, then, as their mutual passions mounted, violently and crushingly. Their tongues wrestled with one another for victory, with first one than the other expelling its rival from the mouth and entering triumphantly, lasciviously, into the not unwilling mouth of its vanquished foe. The Grand Vizier threw Marilú onto her back, lifted her legs above her until her knees pressed against her ears, but imprisoning her legs this time with his arms so that they extended straight out behind her head instead of falling over his shoulders.

And then it began again.

Her lover pressed down closer, crushing her thighs and breasts under his as he sought and found her eager, open mouth, and they joined in a kiss of passion that seemed to have no end. He came, and she came, almost simultaneously, and then in an ebb tide of relief and exhaustion, they sank back on the bed again, side by side.

"I love you," she sighed blissfully, and kissed her lover's eyes. "Let me sleep now, my dearest one—let me sleep and dream once more of you."

"Sleep, my sweetest one, and let us dream together." He kissed her eyelids, and they both dropped off into a sound, untroubled sleep.

CHAPTER 8

The morning sunlight filtered through the curtains of the clerestory window, bathing the small alcove in soft and still dim light. The Grand Vizier stirred uneasily, then, like a soldier, awoke immediately. He sensed an unwonted but not unpleasant feeling of tension in his loins, the source of which was not hard to discover.

Marilú, still sound asleep, and on her side, facing her bed companion, held firmly grasped in her right hand that part of him which she treasured most. As he became aware of this sweet imprisonment, his member, already tumescent, stiffened sharply. Marilú stirred and, her eyes still closed, she stretched sinuously in the bed, arching her back, extending her limbs with catlike grace, but never relinquishing her hold on him. The Vizier watched in fascination, his senses aroused still more by the voluptuous movements of his paramour.

Marilú opened her eyes, uttered a soft squeal of delight, and whispered: "Come into me, my love."

The Vizier moved over on top of her, while Marilú inserted him gratefully between her moist and pulsating nether lips. Again they groaned and gasped in frenzied passion. The two strove valiantly in exquisite pain and pleasure until at last, in transport of delight, they fell back wholly exhausted and content.

"I must leave you now, my love. Close your eyes again and sleep." The Vizier gently kissed the two closed eyelids and tip-toed out of the room.

It was broad daylight when Marilú again awoke and, as she donned her robe, she found Ourda waiting to lead her to the *hamman* for her morning bath. As she bathed, Lady Nardjis, already fully dressed, stuck her head through the door of the *calidarium*. "What would you like to do today," she asked.

"I don't quite know," Marilú responded. "I feel ill at ease, but I don't know why. Could we go for a long walk, perhaps through the garden, perhaps down to the lowest terrace—I'd like to walk until I'm completely exhausted. Perhaps that would help."

"A good idea. The day is cool and sunny, and we can walk down to my house. You can meet the musicians and see their instruments." Nardjis turned to Shamsi who was close behind her mistress: "We shall need our town clothes and walking boots, and please ask Masrur to send one of his *eunuchs* to accompany us. And a carriage to meet us at my house in town, at four o'clock. We shall have a bite to eat in the dressing room as soon as the *Marquesa* has finished her bath."

"To hear is to obey," said Shamsi, and departed immediately.

Ourda finished the preparations of her mistress while Lady Nardjis waited in the dressing room. Marilú did not seem disposed to chat.

"Homesickness," thought Nardjis, so the two women remained in silence as their attendants helped them don the long robes they would wear for their walk into town. The girls fitted them with soft suede boots that came above their ankles. Marilú noted that the soles were hard leather, which would protect them from the stones and gravel.

While they dressed, two attendants brought small tables into the dressing room, and trays piled high with food.

"You girls may sit down on that bench," said Lady

Nardjis, turning to Ourda and Shamsi, "and join us for lunch."

"With joy and gladness, my lady," the two girls said, almost in unison.

The luncheon was a light one, according to Andaluz standards—a small roast patridge for each, fried eggplant, bread, stewed rhubarb, and iced sherbet flavored with orange blossoms.

Luncheon over, the four women walked upstairs, and down the corridor, where they were met by a young and handsome eunuch whom Nardjis introduced as Ibrahim. Not as tall or stout as *Masrur*, Ibrahim nonetheless looked a doughty opponent and adequate protection for the ladies. He bowed low, and followed at a discreet distance as the women went out on the balcony, through the iron gate, and down the long flight of steps that led to the garden on the middle terrace of Medina al-Zahra.

They took a different path from that which they had followed on their first excursion. The plants and flowers and stately shade trees were different from those Marilú had noted on her first visit, but just as beautifully laid out. In some places the flowers and ferns were arranged in formal beds, in others in seemingly natural disarray. Everywhere, a rippling brook crossed or followed the shady path, its gurgling rivalling the cooing of the turtle doves that flew in and out of the trees or preceded them, two by two, on the gravel walk. Everywhere too, the fragrance of narcissus or jasmine, rose or privet, assailed them.

Marilú, however, seemed unconscious of all this beauty, quiet and preoccupied. Lady Nardjis knew better than to disturb her thoughts with idle conversation, so the two walked in silence. Suddenly, Marilú gave a scream of delight as they came across a little clump of furze, bright with yellow blossoms. She stooped low, and picked one of the flowers while a tear dropped down her cheek.

"Think nothing of it, Nardjis," she sighed. "It's just the *morriña*—the homesickness that we *Gallegos* feel when we are far from home. And this *toxo* flower brings back memories of far away and long ago. I'll be better soon, now that I have this little weed to comfort me. But the *morriña* is a terrible feeling. It brings back all the tears we have ever shed since childhood, all the joys and all the sorrows, and makes me long for home, for Galicia that I may never see again. You must excuse me."

"That's all right," Nardjis reassured her. "We are all moody at times, and even the sweetest memories are sad when they are only memories. And I suppose that even the saddest memories are sweet when they remind us of happier days."

They walked arm in arm, followed by the eunuch and the two girls, along the shaded perfumed paths, to another iron gate through which they passed. A second long flight of stairs took them down the ramparts that protected the middle terrace, and on to the lowest terrace at a point almost directly opposite the mansion that Marilú had admired the day before.

They crossed the road and Ibrahim pulled the bell rope that hung through an aperture in the gold and ebony door of the palace. It was answered almost immediately by a young woman who greeted Lady Nardjis and her guest with a warm smile and the deepest of bows: "Welcome home, my ladies, I am at your service."

The eunuch bowed: "I shall await you in the garden, my ladies, ready to hear and to obey your commands."

Nardjis whispered a few words of instruction to the young woman at the door, and she and Marilú, accompanied as always by Shamsi and Ourda, walked across a spacious patio to a large salon that was obviously the music room as one end was crowded with musical instruments of every description, resting against the silken cushions that were strewn on the floor. They were joined shortly by some forty women, who bowed deeply as they greeted Lady Nardjis, and were introduced one by one to Marilú.

Most of the musicians were older than Marilú had expected, although there were several who could not have been more than fifteen or sixteen years of age. Nardjis introduced the oldest of the group, who seemed to be the directress, as a former companion of hers at the music school, explaining that many of the students at the school were ladies of the court who would learn to play or sing but would not go on to become professional musicians.

"Most of these instruments are now made in Sevilla," explained the directress. "The King, al-Mutamid, you know, is not just a patron of the arts, but is himself a poet and one of the finest singers and lutanists of al-Andaluz. Bahar, my dear, would you show the *Marquesa* your lute, and play a few chords so that she will recognize it when she hears it in the orchestra."

One of the women came forward with a large, pear-shaped, wooden instrument whose strings were drawn tightly along the long neck that bent sharply downward at the end. She sat gracefully on a large cushion in front of Nardjis and Marilú, and plucked the strings with a tortoise shell plectrum.

"That is the Persian lute, the *al-ud,* that you call *laúd* in *Romance.*

"Some of us strike the strings with our fingers instead of a plectrum. This is one of the instruments that the great Ziryab introduced to Andalucía from Persia. Before that, we Arabs only had the old-fashioned lute, the *mizhar,*" and the directress motioned to one of the musicians to show and play a heavier, cruder instrument with a skin stretched over its belly like a drumhead. The music was sonorous, and less delicate and varied than that of the wooden-bellied *al-ud* which, Nardjis told Marilú, was the favorite of all musical instruments, although the viol, too, she said, had its devotees.

The musicians showed and played in turn many of the other instruments that the directress said had been introduced to Andalucía by the Persian Ziryab when he was exiled from the court of Haroun al-Rashid in Baghdad: the Persian flute or *nay*, with six holes and a mouthpiece at one end—the directress explained that the *nay* had practically replaced the old *qasabah* which they also showed and played; a flageolet, like the *nay*, but smaller; the *duff*, a square tambourine; the *mizmah* or oboe, a wooden double-reed pipe that played treble to a deep-voiced, eight-foot bassoon, also with a double reed; the *mizafah* or psaltery, a ten-string instrument something like a dulcimer, which they also played, striking the strings with two small hammers, making the music resound from its trapezoidal, almost triangular sound-box; the *buq*, a straight brass horn; the *tabl* or drum; the *sunuj* or castanets; and a small Persian violin. Then they showed and played the viol—one with five strings, another with seven, both played with a small bow; a ten-string harp that they played with both hands, and a four-string half-harp that they played with one; the Moorish three-string rebec with its tiny bow; a timbrel or kettledrum, and several *tabirah* or tabors, one nearly four feet tall, the others shorter; a four-string mandolin; bagpipes—one large, and a small one that Marilú recognized as a Galician *gaita;* a wooden, single-reed clarinet; a straight brass trumpet and a Roman tuba made of heavy bronze; cymbals—one pair with jingles around the edge like a tambourine;

and then the various kinds of guitars; an oval-shaped Moorish guitar, a modern, woman-waisted, six-stringed, Roman guitar, and . . .

"A *bandurria!*" exclaimed Marilú in delight as she saw a stubby, three-stringed guitar with no frets on its short neck. "May I play it?"

And, when its owner, a smiling young girl of her own age, handed the instrument to Marilú, she played on it a nostalgic Galician melody, her eyes half closed in dreamy rapture.

"I'd love to play it tonight for the Grand Vizier, and sing him a song of Galicia. May I?" and she addressed her question indiscriminately to the young musician, the directress and to Nardjis.

The musician smilingly nodded her acquiescence, pleased that her instrument should have found such favor, and recognizing Marilú's expertise as superior to her own."

"I know that the Grand Vizier will be exchanted to hear you sing and play," said Nardjis, "and I shall ask his permission before supper this evening. In fact, I know he will be so curious and eager to hear you sing that your suppper tonight may be a hasty one, so let us have a little light refreshment while these good people entertain us."

Turning to Ourda and Shamsi, Nardjis added: "You two may leave us now, and have a bite to eat with your friends." The girls bowed and slipped out of the room.

Nardjis and Marilú were served sherbets and cakes while the directress conducted the orchestra in a series of light but hauntingly melodic pieces, undoubtedly of Moslem and probably of Persian origin, thought Marilú. After expressing their enthusiastic appreciation of the entertainment, Lady Nardjis and Marilú took their leave of the directress and the members of the orchestra.

"Would you like to see the rest of the house?" asked Nardjis.

"I would indeed," answered Marilú, and Nardjis led her to her own apartment at the other end of the patio, overlooking a small but beautifully cultivated garden where they could espy Ibrahim lolling contentedly beside a goldfish pond while Shamsi and Ourda plied him with sweetmeats and sherbets, serving him with as as much deference as if he were the Grand Vizier himself. Or almost, for Marilú and Nardjis, unobserved behind an arras, watched with amusement as thhe two girls, who had shed their long town capes and were clad only in thin silk blouses and pantaloons, practiced their wiles on one whom they supposed to be immune to feminine charms.

They sipped and nibbled daintily from the refreshments they offered to their new master, and Marilú noted that each time one of them placed a tray on his lap she would let her hands graze, as if by accident, below the tray, while her companion would find some excuse for encircling Ibrahim's neck and shoulders with her arms from behind, proffering him a napkin or seizing some dainty from the tray.

Closer and closer the two mischievous nymphs hovered around the eunuch, their young breasts grazing his cheeks, their slim legs brushing against his thighs, their arms and hands touching his neck, his waist, and close to his private parts, as they brushed off an invisible crumb or tried to tempt him with some especially dainty cake. In mock alarm, they evaded his protesting arms, until finally the poor eunuch, teased to distraction, seized Shamsi in his powerful arms and carried her like a baby to the shelter of a small pavilion where they were hidden from view. Ourda ran after them and, just as they disappeared into the pavilion, grasped the eunuch around the waist and pulled the string to his pantaloons.

Marilú gasped, but Nardjis whispered "Ibrahim can do them no harm, but he will teach those two a lesson that they will not forget. And, between you and me, they will enjoy it. Because you know that a eunuch, although he is castrated and cannot impregnate them, is sometimes still a man, and in many cases can give, and take, much pleasure. Not enough to impair their virginity, but enough to give them plenty of excitement. And Ibrahim is strong enough and young enough to handle the two of them."

The laughs and screams that came from within the pavilion confirmed Nardjis's predictions, and Marilú felt a tremor in her limbs as she thought of the more potent pleasures that she could look forward to this evening. She must decide what song to beguile her lord and master with, and must be sure that she remembered every verse and every inflection of the words and music.

"We had best be going back now if you are to have time for your *siesta*," said Nardjis. "I have ordered the carriage to be here to take us to the palace, as it is a much harder walk up the hill and the two flights of stairs than it was coming down."

The directress and musicians bade them goodbye at the door, and soon the five of them were being carried at a brisk trot up the steep road to the palace. On the way, Marilú, silent with her thoughts, the guitar in her lap, concentrated on an old Galician folksong she had sung and played so often and with which she now planned to regale her lover this evening. She found to her satisfaction that she had not forgotten a single verse or cadence, and she rehearsed in her mind the quick fingering of the strings and every gesture and expression of her face and body that would accompany her singing. So intent was she in her reverie that it was almost like waking from a dream when the coach drew to a stop before the palace gate.

"Sleep with the angels, my dear," Nardjis whispered to her, "You must be at your best, and you will need the *siesta*."

Marilú smiled her acknowledgement, and after doffing her traveling costume, was soon sound asleep for a restful hour, just enough to wipe out the sad nostalgia of the *morriña* but not enough to leave her logy on awakening. Ourda was there to escort her to the *hammam*, from which she emerged nearly two hours later, clear-eyed, relaxed and refreshed—the epitome of *Gallega* loveliness. A long tunic of transparent voile covered but by no means concealed her gossamer silk blouse and pantaloons, and the still lovelier charms beneath.

Nardjis had excused herself some fifteen minutes earlier, and returned, nodding her head affirmatively in answer to the question in Marilú's eyes: "Of course, he wants to hear you. I think he is burning with curiosity . . . and with love. I'll hand you your *bandurria* after the meal, and Ourda will draw up a hassock for you."

Together they walked down the corridor to the Salon of the Caliphs. The great doors swung open, *Masrur* bowing them welcome, a eunuch on either side. Again the Grand Vizier rose to greet them, smiling, his eyes riveted on Marilú.

"I have never seen you lovelier, my sweet," he exclaimed as the women bowed before him.

Offering his arm to Marilú, he allowed her to slip her arm through his, and together they took their places on the cushions. The serving maids swarmed round them with tables, trays, finger bowls and viands. Course followed course—a bisque of river shrimp, fillets from the back of a hare in rich gravy, a spiced roast capon, crisp fried eggplant, bread, white wine, pistachio and hazelnut tarts rich with honey, figs, pears and peaches, all washed down with icy cold, delicately perfumed sherbets.

The two diners partook but sparingly of these rich and tempting viands, and almost before Marilú knew it, the Grand Vizier clapped his hands; the tables, dishes and glasses were cleared away in a trice; and two serving maids approached with basins of warm water and serviettes for their hands. The troup of women musicians filed in and took their places on cushions in front of the screen at the far end of the room—to hear, not to participate, in the performance.

"And now, my dear, I understand you have a special treat for me this evening," the Vizier whispered in Marilú's ear.

Nardjis approached with the guitar and handed it to Marilú who arose to receive it. Nardjis then withdrew as Ourda slid a large leather hassock to the center of the floor. Marilú beamed a radiant smile at the Grand Vizier and bowed deeply, trying hard to appear calm, although inwardly she was nervous as a child at first communion. The Vizier had eyes for nothing in the room but her, and he leaned eagerly forward on his cushions.

All eyes focussed on the young minstrel as she stood facing the Vizier, guitar in hand, and announced hesitatingly at first, but gaining courage as she spoke, that she would sing a song of her native Galicia in the Galician dialect which she hoped they would understand.

She bowed again and sat gracefully upon the hassock, the guitar in her lap. The fingers of her left hand flew like darting swallows as she pressed the strings up and down and the neck of the instrument, while with the fingers of her right hand and a tortoise-shell plectrum, she brushed the strings with amazing speed and dexterity.

Although the *guitar* was small and devoid of frets, her skill was such that she drew from its three strings sounds as sweet and varied as most musicians could achieve from the many-stringed lute. The combined use of the plectrum between her thumb and forefinger, with the remaining three fingers brushing the strings directly, gave the effect of two instruments played simultaneously.

The faces of her audience was rapt in attention as the music filled the room, her overture developing the varied themes and moods that she would use in the various movements of her song.

Ending her overture with a flourish of flying fingers, Marilú rose from her seat, placed one foot upon the hassock, and accompanied herself on the *guitar* as she opened her mouth to sing. Her voice was a full soprano, bell-like in its clarity, yet rich and resonant. Such a voice, the Vizier thought, as angels might have, singing in Heaven—yet, he reflected, it was not wholly angelic, for there was a sensuousness, a femininity in her tones that aroused far from angelic thoughts in his mind. Heavenly thoughts, but not of angels.

Standing there, her long golden tresses flying around her neck and shoulders, her blue eyes sparkling, her teeth shining, her figure and her movements lithe, graceful and appealing, her expression varying from the most radiant of smiles to the most rueful of countenances, from the liveliest of moods to the most passionate, the most nostalgic, the saddest, the happiest, carrying her audience with her, entranced, as she changed from one mood to another, it would have been difficult to say which was more beautiful, the singer or the song, the music or the musician.

She sang of Galicia, its mountains and valleys, verdant with grasses and herbs and mosses, white-flecked with sheep, colored like the rainbow with red and yellow and scarlet and pink and purple blossoms, bathed in the morning dew and mist or brilliant in the sunlight. She sang of the rippling brooks that streamed down Galicia's mountainsides, of the cascades and torrents and fast-flowing rivers, of the still waters of the fjords or *rías* that so forked Galicia's coasts that it would be hard to tell whether the land was stretching out into the sea with a hundred grasping fingers or whether the ocean was reaching far into Galicia's vitals with its long tidal arms. She sang of the towering pines, the venerable oaks, the weeping willows, and the mighty chestnut trees, that dotted the Galician plains and mountainsides. She sang of sights seen only in Galicia—the *hórreos,* those granite corn cribs perched high on granite posts, with a granite cross at one end and a sculptured granite urn at the other; and of the tall, slim granite posts that formed the arbors on which the rich purple grapes hung in luscious bunches trellised high above the ground. She sang of hard-working farmers, of the shepherds and their dogs, of the fishermen who drew from Galicia's seas and *rías* and *ríos* so rich a harvest of fish and clams and oysters and lobsters and crabs and crayfish, and swimming and crawling creatures of every variety; and of the great mussel barges with their thick ropes hanging down into the salty waters of the *rías,* covered from one end to the other with pearly, purple mussels.

But, above all, she sang of the poignant homesickness of the *Gallegos,* the *Morriña,* with all its longing, all its bitterness, its sweet and haunting, plaintive and mysterious sadness, its heartwarming and heartbreaking memories of far away and long ago. There was a lump in her throat, a tear in her eye, as she came to the end of her song, and there was not a dry eye in her audience, who followed her every change of mood and tempo as an orchestra follows the baton of its director. But she ended with a glorious crescendo of heavenly sound from her guitar, her head lifted, chin pointed defiantly forward, her hair streaming down her back, her bosom high and heaving with emotion, and a smile, as lovely as a rainbow after a storm, illuminating her face as she stood there erect, her arms raised above her head, the guitar in her left hand pointing to the ceiling.

Marilú bowed as her audience—Masrur Zud and his eunuchs, Nardjis, Ourda, the serving girls and the musicians, and, above all, the Grand Vizier himself—burst into wild applause, with shouts of *w'Allah!* Oh God! *olé!* They seemed transported with delight as they wept and sighed and shouted, and Marilú witnessed for the first time the state of exaltation and ecstasy—the *sihro halal* or white magic of the Arabs—of which Nardjis had told her. She herself was flushed and excited from her emotion and success, and delighted that the Grand Vizier was so manifestly pleased with her efforts.

Suddenly he clapped his hands, and the great hall was cleared and silent in an instant, the oil lamps snuffed out, the massive doors closed, and the Grand Vizier and Marilú were left alone in the semi-darkness. He rose and embraced Marilú with pride and passion, wrenching the guitar from her hand and placing it upon the hassock. She could feel his breast heaving as they walked quickly to the alcove, their arms twined round each other, their bodies close together.

As though reluctant to loosen his grasp even for a moment, he backed her against the wall of the bedroom and flung off his robe and turban as she pulled the drawstring of her pantaloons. As she encircled his neck and breast with eager arms, their mouths and tongues meeting in passionate embrace, she could feel the Vizier lift her legs and wrap them around his waist, and then—oh, heavenly rapture!—he penetrated into her very vitals. She tightened her legs around his waist, leaving his arms and hers free for the most voluptous caresses while, her back pressed against the wall, he lunged and thrust deep inside her, deeper and deeper. Suddenly, with a wild and furious thrust the Vizier pressed Marilú with such intensity that she felt surely his manroot would penetrate her very body and leave her nailed to the wall.

She could contain herself no longer. "My God! O God! I'm dying! You're killing me! O my God!" And with a convulsive shudder, her legs still tight around his waist, her arms pressing him close to her heaving breast, her tongue almost as deep within his mouth as his manroot was within her nether lips, she shuddered in a final ecstasy, overwhelming and rapturous.

Slowly, lovingly, the Vizier untwined her legs from his waist, but did not cease to embrace her as he pushed her toward the bed and laid her down beside him, arm in arm.

"Oh, Ahmad, Ahmad, you're wonderful," she moaned as she snuggled close to him, her head nested upon his breast, he flat on his back, his arms around her.

"And, Marilú, my darling, my light of love, you too are wonderful—more than I deserve, more than I ever expected. To think that you came here captured, as a slave, and now it is you who have captured and enslaved me so completely. You're wonderful, my dear."

So they lay in each other's arms, relaxed and wholly satisfied. But the close contact soon awakened fresh desires, and Marilú pressed close to her paramour, felt herself pressed hard by his stiffening member. Her breasts and nipples swelled, her lips parted, and a tremor seized her limbs as she moaned and gasped in expectant ecstasy. Roughly he seized her, turned her over on her back and began anew.

"O God!" she moaned, "it won't stop! It won't stop. My God! O my God! My God!"

She writhed and wriggled, grasping him ever closer to her. The heaving and pushing, the groaning and moaning and gasping seemed to last for an eternity, and then a hot volcano of passion shook them both and overwhelmed them in a mad upheaval of burning rapture.

They lay again in one another's arms, panting and sighing. And soon they were sound asleep, full of contentment.

CHAPTER 9

Marilú slept uneasily throughout the night, her dreams troubled by recurring pangs of nostalgia, heightened by the subject of her song—home and Galicia—that served to intensify her homesickness.

The Vizier rose at sunrise without disturbing her. Looking at his companion indulgently, noting the young innocence of her smiling countenance, and recalling the catlike grace with which she stretched her back and limbs each morning on awakening, he thought to himself: "What a lovely, wonderful cat she is!" He departed noiselessly, closing the arras so that not a ray of light would disturb her dreams.

When Marilú woke, Nardjis as well as Ourda was there to greet her, the latter bearing a tray with hot tea.

"Good morning," Nardjis smiled. "Drink this and then let us go to the *hammam* immediately. You must look your best, for the Grand Vizier will be coming back for lunch and a *siesta,* and this will be the first time he has ever seen you by daylight. He has a special entertainment in store for you, and we are not to breathe a word of it."

Excited, Marilú sipped the hot tea, then together she and Nardjis hastened to the *hammam,* where they were met by Shamsi who had gathered together the silken garments they were to wear after the bath. As Marilú neither wore nor needed make-up, the procedure was the same as usual, except that she was given powdered walnut bark to massage her teeth to sparkling pearls and her lips and gums to rosy brightness—a treatment previously used only for the evening.

She was a picture of delight as she and Nardjis walked out on the terrace overlooking the garden, the sun shining on and through her hair and bringing out the rich golden hues and shining nuances in the wavy tresses. At the same moment that they, with Shamsi and Ourda, entered the terrace, the Grand Vizier made his appearance through another door. Smiling, he approached his beloved and, as he struggled to find words to express his admiration of her radiant beauty in the dazzling sunlight, the voice of the *muezzin* reached them. They knelt together for the noonday prayer, assailed as they were by wandering thoughts and hot desires.

At the conclusion, the Vizier tendered Marilú his arm. "You are an angel, my beloved, and the sun has given you a halo of light," he whispered.

Marilú smiled and pressed close to him as they walked toward the door. "I'm afraid my thoughts are hardly those of an angel, my love. But you are so handsome, and so strong. I've never seen you by daylight before, and you look so grand and wonderful."

They entered the Salon of the Caliphs together, followed by others. Against the wall, between the two doors to the terrace, Marilú noticed a large table she had never seen before. "Why, this must be a chess set," she exclaimed. "I've never seen one like it. It's so beautiful—marvellous! And much too big to play with."

The table, six feet square, was of ebony, encrusted with gold, the squares of ebony and ivory separated by fine lines of yellow gold. The chessmen, of white and red ivory, studded with rubies and diamonds, were extraordinary, the soldiers a foot high, the other pieces taller, with the king towering over them by at least six inches.

"Let me look at them," asked Marilú, "they are so

different from the chessmen I play with at home, and now I think I am beginning to understand why our chessmen are made in such funny shapes—called 'king' and 'vizier' and so forth, when they certainly don't look any thing like kings and viziers, but just strange pieces of stone."

"You play chess, a man's game?" asked the Grand Vizier in some astonishment.

"Yes, my lord. My father taught it to me and we used to play together nearly every evening. I have no brothers, and I suppose that is why Father taught me to play. I don't know any other woman in Galicia who plays the game."

"We shall play tonight, and I think you will find the pieces we play with are very much like your own. This set was given to the Caliph Abd ar-Rahman III by the Shah of Persia, may they rest in peace. It is the most beautiful I have ever seen. In those days, the pieces were moved from square to square by two servants, as the Caliph or his opponent commanded. They would be too heavy for you to lift easily."

Marilú picked up the red king with two hands and examined it curiously. "It *is* heavy!"

"The game, you know, was invented in India, although we Arabs got it from Persia," explained the Grand Vizier. "That is why the king—they called it the rajah or shah—is seated on a howdah on top of an elephant. His eyes are closed in meditation. That is supposed to show his strength and greatness."

The king had a large diamond in his turban; the elephant on which he sat had a smaller one in its forehead; while the golden howdah and a gold blanket under it were studded with pearls. All the pieces were elaborately and realistically carved, and Marilú noticed that, while the red and white pieces were practically identical, the red all had a diamond as a distinguishing mark—even the soldiers—while the white had rubies. "Now I see why our king looks something like a chair; it is just the howdah. And our vizier is just a smaller chair."

The vizier on the board in front of them was almost identical to the king, but smaller and less elaborately decorated, adorned and bejewelled.

"We call the king the 'shah' after the Persian word," said the Grand Vizier, "and the vizier is the '*firzan*' meaning 'wise.' I think that may be the origin of the word 'vizier.' I hope so anyway. And you know that the *firzan*, like a good vizier, never moves more than one square away from his sovereign."

On each side of the king and vizier were elephants, each with a single diamond or ruby in its forehead. The Grand Vizier continued; "This is the *alfil*. In Arabic, *al-fil* means 'the elephant.'

"I never knew what *alfil* meant," interjected Marilú. "I thought it was a peculiar word, but now I understand why our *alfil* looks like a lump of stone with two pointed breasts in front. They must represent the tusks of the elephant."

Next to the *alfiles*, on prancing horses, were archers, their bows drawn and arrows pointing fiercely toward their foes. The Grand Vizier continued his exposition: "Although these pieces are the archers, we call them *caballos*—horses—or, in Arabic, *faras*. In the pieces we play with nowadays, and I suppose in yours, it is just a little cylinder, rounded at the top, and you must have wondered why you called them 'horses.' Sometimes we Arabs call them 'camels.'

"The rook we use today is just a small cylinder with a few dents on top that are meant to represent the castellations on the top of the tower. *Rukhkh* means 'tower' in Arabic, and, in the Caliph's chess set, you can see that it is a tower mounted on a war chariot, the strongest piece of all on the battlefield.

"You call these pieces '*peones*'—pawns," he went on,

"but they are not meant to be laborers, but foot soldiers—*Baidaq* in Arabic—for the whole game of chess is the game of war. That is why in Persian arabic they say '*Shah mat*,' the Shah is dead, and we say 'check'—*xaque*—meaning 'Remove, O King!' and 'mate' —*mate*—which means 'kill!' It is war to the death! And tonight, my beloved, we two shall fight a war to the death."

"If I can die in your arms, my master, I shall ask for nothing better." Marilú gave her paramour a radiant smile, and together they walked past the silver pool to the cushions at the end of the great salon.

As the serving maids brought in the various tables, trays and dishes—cold *hors d'oeuvres*, grilled roast lamb spiced with cumin, rice flavored with finely sliced white truffles, pancakes with butter and honey, and the inevitable fruits and sherbets—the Grand Vizier continued his discourse on the game of chess, Marilú listening in rapt attention.

"The game," he said, was invented centuries ago by a Hindu sage, named Sissa, for the amusement of his sovereign, King Shihrham. The rajah was so delighted that he offered to give Sissa any reward he wished—lands, palaces, jewels, gold, women, whatever he wanted. Sissa, a mathematician, said that, as his only reward, he would gladly accept some grains of wheat—one grain on the first square, two on the second, four on the third, and so fourth, doubling the number on each successive square. The rajah protested that this was too small a reward for such a great invention, but when the sage pointed out to him that two multiplied to the sixty-fourth power would mean more grains of wheat than could be grown in India in a century, the king was amazed.

"Far from being angry with his wise man, however, the rajah admired his cleverness, and it is said that the two played chess together until the old man died.

And this is why," the Grand Vizier went on, "we call the squares 'granaries'—*halaynda*—or 'houses'—*casas* or *beit.*

"I was fortunate to have as my teacher the great mathematician of Córdoba, abu-al-Hakam Amr al-Karmani. He died when I was only sixteen, but he played with me every week and each time—he always beat me—he made me tell him where I had made my mistake. And the next time, before we started a new game, I had to set up the chess board again at the point where I had made the error, and we would start from there. Sometimes I managed to tie him on those replays, and occasionally—very rarely—I would beat him, but there was no doubt that he was the master and I the pupil.

"You know, many Arabs—like the Indians—are great mathematicians. We brought trigonometry, algebra, and analytical geometry to Andalucía, going far beyond anything that Euclid or the other Greeks had dreamed of. The Romans never could master mathematics—with their Roman numerals, they could hardly be expected to. But we brought in the Arabic numerals which are now used all over Spain, and introduced the zero, which the Greeks and Romans had never thought of.

"The greatest mathematician in the world today is Abu al-fath Umar ibn-Ibrahim al-Khayyami, sometimes known as Omar Khayyam. He invented a new calendar with an error of only one day in five thousand years. The calendar invented by Sosigenes for Julius Caesar has an error of nearly one day every century. Al-Khayyami has also written some rather scandalous, blasphemous verse, but he will be remembered by the world as an astronomer and mathematician, not as a versifier.

"And chess is not the only game we have brought to Spain, for you know that the playing cards you use were introduced here from Arabia. But let us go on to the entertainment I had planned for you," and the Vizier clapped his hands sharply.

The tables, trays, and viands were quickly cleared away, and, even as this routine proceeded, Marilú felt the whole room start revolving.

She gripped the Vizier's arm and noted, beside the silver pool, two young eunuchs with wooden paddles dipping them into the silver center, which seemed to become liquid and blazing with light as they stirred it. The bright sunlight was streaming through the translucent marble ceiling and through the intricate carvings of the broad marble frieze circling the room below it, and particularly through the blue, red, green and gold stained glass of the windows. The rays bounced back and forth on the shimmering silver ripples in the pool, on the many colored walls and columns, and on the glistening mosaics bordering the marble floor.

The gold and silver on the doorways, draperies and walls sent forth lightning gleams that bounded and rebounded from every niche and angle. The great pearl, as large as an orange, suspended over the pool by its three golden chains, had come to life and turned into living fire, shooting its opalescent rays back into the pool of liquid silver, and round and round the room.

As the two eunuchs paddled the quivering silver with increasing force, the kaleidoscope of darting lights and colors took on increasing brilliance and velocity. The room revolved upon its axis, and the axis itself moved back and forth in rhythm with the pendulum of the fiery pearl that seemed to have become the controlling spirit of the *seraglio*, casting its magic spell over everything in the room and even over the Grand Vizier himself whose every jewel, in turban, robe, sandals and rings, gleamed in ever-changing and dazzling display.

"I'm getting dizzy," Marilú cried, swaying giddily as she tightened her grasp on the Grand Vizier's wrist, "please stop it." and she raised her free arm to her head to steady it, dislodging the veil which fluttered to the floor.

The Vizier clapped his hands again. The eunuchs ceased their paddling and, almost instantly, the shimmering silver had returned to its solid shining state, the kaleidoscope of flickering lights came to rest, and the room, as if by magic, ceased to revolve. At the same time, the eunuchs and other attendants disappeared, leaving the Grand Vizier and Marilú alone in the room. The Vizier rose and helped Marilú to her feet. She shook her head as if to clear away the giddy feeling, and burst out laughing.

"I was so dizzy and frightened," she said, clinging tightly to her companion, her arm around his waist. "It seemed that I was under some magic spell. I just can't believe it. But I'm fine now—full, and affectionate—and if I fall down, it won't be dizziness, but just for you."

They walked quickly to the alcove, their arms around each other's waist. The Grand Vizier whispered softly: "My poor little lamb, so dizzy with that trick of lights I played on you."

"I'm not a poor little lamb, but a very happy sheep who will follow you gladly wherever you go, and you're my great and glorious ram who mounts me so often and pushes me so hard."

"Well, if I am a ram," replied the Vizier, "I'll mount you like a ram. Down on your hands and knees, my little ewe lamp—there, on the soft carpet."

Marilú complied willingly, first loosing her blouse and the drawstring to her pantaloons. Her lover, turban and robe cast aside, bestrode her from behind, fondling her pendant breasts with both his hands. Like a ram he pushed and pushed while she rotated convulsively against his navel. Then, to make the close contact even closer, he shifted his hands from her breasts to under her arms and clasped her shoulders from below, pulling her willing body toward him until she was crushed against his churning body. The two of them moaned and groaned with joy and pain.

"Oh, my love! my love!" she screamed, "Good God! Don't! Please don't do it any more! I can't stand it! No! Don't Stop. Please don't stop! Do it again! Do it again! O God!" And Marilú groaned as she came again and again in wave after wave of ecstasy.

And then, with a final convulsive push, the great ram filled her full to bursting. They stayed there blissfully coupled together, panting and moaning, until the Vizier gently took Marilú in his arms and lifted her into bed beside him. "That was hardly what one would call a *siesta*," he whispered.

Later, they woke refreshed and again eager. Somehow or other, snuggling face to face against him, Marilú had managed to get her left leg under his right arm, so that the Vizier took her in that way, lifting her other leg over his left shoulder. Side by side, neither one wholly on top nor wholly beneath, they heaved and groaned, her breasts crushed, her pelvis churning, while all the while he pressed and pushed and then, suddenly and with a mighty groan, he shuddered. This in turn triggered a quick reaction, and Marilú, moaning and groaning, experienced ecstasy upon ecstasy, finally relapsing into a blissful state of utter and delightful contentment.

Then, parted, but still side by side in each other's arms, Marilú asked: "Tell me about the pool. It was quicksilver, wasn't it? I've been told they mine quicksilver in Andalucía, but I've never seen it before."

"Yes, the pool is quicksilver. They don't actually mine quicksilver, but cinnabar, which is a dark red mineral that is used to make vermillion paints, and also to make quicksilver, which is sometimes called mercury after the Greek god who was so fast on his feet.

"This isn't the only palace to have a pool of mercury, but it is the only one where the play of reflected lights is so marvellous that the room seems to go round and round. There was the palace of Khumara Wayh in Egypt, built by the Sultan Ahmad ibn-Tulun two hundred years ago, that had a pool of mercury. The sultan used to have large leather cushions placed in the pool, moored by silken cords to silver columns all around it. Mercury is a very heavy metal, you know,—a liquid metal heavier than gold—so the cushions bobbed up and down on it like corks on a pool of water. The sultan would lie down on these cushions and rock himself to sleep as the cushions bounced up and down with his slightest movement."

"That's fascinating," Marilú exclaimed. "What fun it would be to put a large cushion in this pool. To make love on!

Marilú laughed and gave the Vizier a hug, as if to say: "Please do it."

"We'll see," the Vizier responded, and the more he thought about it, the more it seemed to him that it would be fascinating. "I think we'll do it. But I'll have to have a leather mattress made that will be waterproof—quicksilver-proof. You do think of the most extraordinary and delightful things, my love.... But now our *siesta* is over, and I must attend to my affairs. We'll play a game of chess this evening. Goodbye, my sweet."

"Farewell, my love. The hours will seem so long until you return."

The two arose, and parted with a gentle kiss.

CHAPTER 10

Ourda helped Marilú dress for the afternoon, then led her to the music room where Ourda knew Nardjis would be waiting for them.

The music room was one Marilú had not seen before. It adjoined the Salon of the Caliphs and overlooked the terrace and garden. Like the great salon, it was decorated in marble and alabaster, porphyry and mosaics, with elaborate carvings of flowers, Arabic characters, and geometric designs. It was, of course, far smaller than the salon and, despite the luxury of its appointments, gave an impression of simplicity and airiness. Through the large windows and open doors giving on to the terrace, one could see and hear a heavy rain outside, notwithstanding which the room was pleasantly bright with a soft gray light filtering through its translucent ceiling and through the open doors and windows.

Nardjis and Shamsi rose from their cushions to greet Marilú while, from the other end of the room, the girls of the orchestra and their beaming directress left their hassocks and instruments and crowded around her, bowing and smiling, and all speaking at once:

"You were magnificent last night."

"Lady Nardjis allowed us all to go into the salon to listen to you."

"You were wonderful!"

"You probably didn't see us."

"Your voice is lovely, and the song is beautiful."

"I cried and cried when you came to the sad parts."

And the young woman, whose guitar Marilú had borrowed, exclaimed: "I have never heard the bandurria played so beautifully. Please keep it as a present from me. I have another one, and I wouldn't dare play that one after you have played on it. You must teach me that song, and how you get the low notes from the strings. I have only learned to play high notes."

Marilú smiled and beamed, and thanked them all for their compliments, then added that she would love to hear them play, that, except for them, she had never heard a full orchestra, and never musicians of such quality and skill. The girls bowed, smilingly and returned to their hassocks, where they launched into the prelude of a sonata, led by their directress with her waving baton.

Nardjis and Marilú reclined on the cushions at the other end of the room, and engaged in a whispered conversation while partaking of the light refreshments served by Shamsi and Ourda, neither of which occupations interfered with their enjoyment of the music, nor disturbed the musicians who were accustomed to playing as an accompaniment to dining, ballet and other entertainment.

"Tell me," asked Marilú, "what are these affairs that the Grand Vizier attends to every day? Is it hunting, or perhaps some other form of amusement?"

There may even have been a note of jealousy in her voice.

Nardjis smiled as she replied. "No, it is certainly not hunting or amusement that keeps the Grand Vizier busy, but far graver matters, for you may be sure that, if he were free to follow his own desires, he would be with you from morn to night and from night to morn.

"In more peaceful times, he used to do a great deal of hunting, both in the forest on the second terrace, and far beyond the city walls. He and other nobles, including the Prince and the Black Vizier, used to play polo on the drill field, attend cockfights and horse races, and race their horses. They used to hunt deer and hares and wild birds with trained falcons, cheetahs or *saluki*—the oldest known breed of dog, from Egypt and Persia—and the Grand Vizier is a marvellous shot with the bow and arrow.

"But it is months since he has been free to indulge in any amusements. He must be in Córdoba every day to drill his troops and prepare the city's defenses. Today he was busy with the defenses of Medina al-Zahra. For, although the Prince, being of royal blood, is the nominal commander in chief, the actual commanders are the Grand Vizier and under him the Black Vizier. And the Prince, although the bravest of the brave and a mighty soldier, has sadly neglected his own city of Córdoba, and the townspeople are ready to rebel against his regime at any moment. I am told that the same is true of Sevilla and that it is rebellion rather than attacks from without—Christian or Moorish—that most threaten the kingdom of al-Mutamid, may Allah protect him."

"I know of the Christian threat," Marilú interjected, "for King Alfonso *el Bravo* has already reconquered Toledo, and Conchita's father went there to discuss his plans for the defense of Galicia and the expansion of Christian rule to the south of Badajoz. And my own husband has been busy consolidating and extending King Alfonso's control over the Kingdom of Sevilla. But what is the Moorish threat to Sevilla? Moors against Moors?"

"Yes, Moors against Moors," Nardjis replied. "You know how it is, for in Christian Spain, it has been not just Christians against Christians, but brothers against brothers. When your warrior king, Ferdinand, died just twenty-six years ago, after conquering the *taifa* kings of Zaragoza, Badajoz and Toledo, and making them his vassals, his last will and testament divided the kingdom among his sons and daughters."

"That's true," interjected Marilú, "he gave Castilla to King Sancho II, León to Alfonso VI, Galicia to García, Zamora to his daughter Urraca, and Toro to his daughter Elvira. And then King Sancho waged war against his two brothers, and Alfonso fled to Toledo and García to Sevilla. And then Sancho attacked Zamora, and Queen Urraca's partisans killed him. And then Alfonso *el Bravo* became king of both León and Castilla, and afterwards captured García and became king of Galicia. I was less than two years old at the time, but my father has told me of all the events of those bloody times.

"And then, just six years ago, after a rebellion took place against Alfonso's friend, King Qadir of Toledo, Alfonso captured Toledo from the rebels, and made all the party kings—you call them *taifa* kings, don't you?—of eastern and southern Andalucía his vassals. And now he is the Emperor of Spain—Alfonso the Brave!"

"Exactly," chimed in Lady Nardjis, "so you see that in Spain, a war of brother against brother is no new thing. But among the Moors fratricidal wars are even more terrible, and the chief threat to Islamic Spain is not Alfonso the Brave but the brutal, bloodthirsty Yusuf ibn-Tashfin."

Marilú shuddered when she heard that awful name, for she knew that ibn-Tashfin had defeated King Alfonso in a bloody battle at Azagal, near Badajoz, just five years ago, that Alfonso had escaped with only three hundred of his calvary, and that the only thing that had saved Christian Spain from total disaster had been dissension among the Saracens themselves. And she had heard that ibn-Tashfin, to commemorate the battle, had built a minaret fifty cubits high out of the skulls of the Spaniards, and sent back 40,000 more skulls to Africa as a trophy.

Nardjis continued: "And now—you may not know this—Yusuf ibn-Tashfin has his huge army of Berbers, Touaregs and Senegalese at Málaga, under the command of his cousin, and no one knows whether he will first march on Córdoba or on Sevilla. That is why the Black Vizier and the Grand Vizier are both here, to help the Governor of Córdoba and to strengthen the defenses of that city and of Medina al-Zahra. Several months ago the Prince sent his wife and his children and all his treasures to the Castle of Almodóvar del Río, which lies between here and Sevilla.

"If Córdoba falls, Medina al-Zahra will be defenseless, and the enemy will raze it to the ground—this beautiful palace, the Mosque, and all. I weep for the fate of this lovely city, and fear the worst. But God's will be done."

"Oh, that is terrible!" exclaimed Marilú. "Poor Ahmad! And poor you, and everyone! How could Ahmad be so gentle and thoughtful—so kind to me—when he has so much on his mind?"

"You have done much to relieve his mind, my dear. For, since the death of his wife, he has had no solace until you came into his life. And I know that he is better able to face the problems of the day for having you to comfort him each night. But the situation is grave, and God alone knows what will become of us all."

The music ended. The seriousness of their conversation had not deprived Marilú and Nardjis of the enjoyment of the concert, and they hastened to thank the musicians and their directress for their entertainment.

"I don't know which of the three movements of the sonata, I liked best," said Marilú, and she softly hummed a part of the theme of each movement. "It was all so beautiful, and it is the first time—except the concert you gave us in your home—that I have heard a complete orchestra. But this time was even better, because now I am more familiar with the different instruments and could hear each of them as they blended into the lovely harmonies of the whole sonata. You are a wonderful conductor, madame, and all of you are marvellous musicians. Thank you! Thank you ever so much! It makes my poor little song seem so pitiful in comparison."

Nardjis and Marilú took their leave in a flurry of excited goodbyes. "It is still raining outside, so that we shan't be able to go out into the garden," Nardjis remarked. "We had best go to the *hammam* and get you ready for this evening."

They strolled down the long corridor, arm in arm, chatting. Ourda and Shamsi were waiting for them in the vestibule of the *hammam*. Two hours later, the ladies emerged, refreshed, relaxed, and beautifully attired.

In the great Salon of the Caliphs, Marilú noted the large screen at the right and knew that the orchestra would be playing for them behind it during the evening meal. The Grand Vizier rose from his cushions to greet them, the ladies bowing deeply as he approached. He offered his arm to Marilú, and Nardjis withdrew to the rear of the room.

The attendants quickly and quietly brought the basins and serviettes, the tables, jugs, glasses, and platters piled high with food, changing them as the diners finished each course in turn: delicate morsels of fried fish and shrimps; a paella of chicken, mussels, lobster and saffron rice; grilled lamb chops and asparagus; and, for dessert, a bowl of boiled honey, piping hot, into which they dipped slices of pears and bananas and then dipped the dripping fruit into bowls of ice and water which transformed the honey into crisp crust around the tender inside. A clear white wine, sherbets and icy water completed the repast, the diners partaking but frugally of the abundance of viands.

At the conclusion, the Vizier clapped his hands and two girls carried in a small ebony and gilt table, encrusted with ivory and mother of pearl. The chessmen were already set up, ready for play, on a board of white ivory and ebony, set in gold. Other attendants placed two large hassocks at opposite sides of the table.

"Those chess pieces are like those my father has at home," exclaimed Marilú, "except that his set is made of stone, while yours is simply beautiful—it's crystal and red ivory isn't it?"

"Yes. It *is* lovely. It was my father's set, and is much easier to play with than the huge chessmen of the Caliph. But now, my sweet enemy, we must choose sides for the battle—odd or even?"

"Odd!" replied Marilú. The two concealed their fists behind their backs, then quickly brought them forward, Marilú with one finger extended, the Vizier with three.

"You lose," he laughed. "I'll take the white and you the black."

Although skeptical of a woman's prowess at a game like chess, something warned the Grand Vizier that he should not attempt to lure Marilú into an easy defeat with the fool's mate or some similar maneuver. Nevertheless, thinking to confuse her, he decided not to open conventionally, and moved his vizier's soldier to vizier's fourth square. Marilú responded without hesitation, moving her horse to King's elephant three. They played intently, almost evenly up to the nineteenth move, when Marilú, anxious to achieve a quick "check," unwisely sacrificed an elephant in exchange for two soldiers. Eleven moves later, the game was over, Marilú giving up when a checkmate became inevitable.

The Vizier smiled: "You play very well; for a time I was afraid that the best I could do would be to tie you. Do you see where you made your mistake?"

"Yes, my master. I shouldn't have sacrificed my elephant and then, later, after we had both lost our viziers, you took my other elephant in exchange for a rook, and I was lost. But you would have won anyway you are so much better than I am . . . ," she added, looking at her partner admiringly, and reaching for her veil.

The Grand Vizier clapped his hands again, the lights were extinguished and, in a moment, the room was cleared, and the two players were left alone.

They stood up, and the Grand Vizier put his arms around her in a firm embrace, then put his lips to hers and their tongues engaged in a desperate struggle. His robe had become unfastened, and Marilú could feel his strong manroot pressing against her.

He picked her up easily and strode to the alcove with his warm prize in his arms. "I've beaten you fairly and squarely, and you are mine to command. I intend to mount you and ride you and break you as I would an unruly horse."

He loosed the drawstrings of her blouse and pantaloons as he deposited her upon the bed and dropped his robe and turban.

"Cross your legs and squat down tailor-fashion," he ordered. "Now lean way back, with your legs still crossed under your thighs."

Marilú obeyed, her supple back arched, and her head resting on a cushion. She wondered what would come next, although as she saw his naked eager body, she could be in no doubt as to the ultimate outcome.

Brusquely but gently, he bestrode her as he would

a horse, her strong arched back providing a saddle, while, her thighs parted slightly to admit his entry. Slowly at first, at a gentle canter, he rode her, rising and falling but, like a good horseman, never leaving the saddle. His manroot continued to swell and harden with the movement, and Marilú could feel the delicious sensation of his thrusts.

He changed from a canter to a gallop, and Marilú felt wave after wave of emotion pass through her straining body. Rider and horse changed to a full gallop at breakneck speed, groaning and shouting, and then—as a horse would draw up his haunches before a high and wide obstacle and come thundering down on the other side—so, with a convulsive movement, the Vizier came crashing down upon the heaving saddle and let loose a flood into his bucking mount. She trembled in a mighty ecstasy, the bed seeming to melt and flow away from under her. Gently, he dismounted and grasped her around the neck, rider and mount panting and sighing as they lay, utterly exhausted and happy, side by side.

"I think both my legs are broken," sighed Marilú contentedly, stretching them out full length and wiggling her toes. "What a wonderful ride! And what a wonderful rider!"

"My favorite steed," he smiled. "And I think I now have you well trained and eating out of my hand."

"You can ride me whenever you want, my lover—but no more in that fashion tonight. I don't think my legs will ever be straight again."

"Oh, I'm sure they're quite straight . . . and they *are* beautiful."

He stroked her two legs from the thighs to the calves, and pinched her wiggling toes affectionately.

"I think they're still in good working order. Let's see."

And his hands went up her legs again, from feet to

ankles, to knees, along the soft inside of her thighs until he came to what he wanted.

Marilú parted her thighs and her lips and, simultaneously, felt herself entered above and below, with tongue and manroot. She shivered deliciously, then gave herself over ecstatically.

"I'm going to tease you now as you've never been teased before," her lover told her, and at that he plunged full length into her, then withdrew entirely, leaving her quivering and begging for his return. In and out he went, driving full length into her, then withdrawing entirely at each furious stroke. Never had she experienced such tantalizing frustration—nor so delightful a sensation. Full then empty, full then empty, his great manroot never failing in its stiffness, she never ceasing to tremble as she received, then lost the welcome intruder. At last, she could stand it no longer and, as he plunged once more into her writhing body, she clasped her thighs and legs and feet firmly around his waist, and drew him to her so that he could not escape. They groaned and screamed, and in a final ecstasy they lay closely coupled, panting in exhaustion.

After what seemed an eternity, a blissful eternity, he withdrew, and kissed her gently on the eyes. "My sweet, my more than sweet," he uttered, "I do love you so."

"And I you, my darling. How can I ever tell you how wonderful you are."

CHAPTER 11

The hassock-maker at the palace pondered the matter carefully. He was glad of the new assignment, and he did not want to make any mistakes. If his proposed masterpiece, for example, should sink or split down the middle, dumping the Grand Vizier and his blond consort into the pool of mercury, he shuddered to think of the consequences—beheading by the axe, perhaps, or, even worse, boiling in hot oil. No, he must be careful not to make mistakes.

Fortunately, when he was summoned trembling into the presence of the Grand Vizier, and repeated the ritual "to hear is to obey," he had had the foresight to ask that the chief eunuch give him all the cooperation in the way of materials and helpers that he might require. So, almost as soon as he had received his orders yesterday afternoon, he had available an ample supply of assistants and of choice red morocco leather.

He had entered quickly into the spirit of the thing, and had decided almost at once that a heavy leather mattress would not do. It would float, all right—even an iron mattress would float on mercury—but would it transmit to the occupants the buoyancy, the immediate recoil and counter-push, that it would need? No, he had decided that it would not. What he devised, therefore, was a large blanket of soft, supple morocco leather, well pitched on the inside with tar at the seams, and covered with another thin layer of the same material. To prevent any of the mercury seeping in at the edges, which would be disastrous, he decided on a firm, mattress-like leather rim, some eight fingers thick, and twelve fingers high, well-tarred at the seams and covered with another layer of leather.

The completed project, as he had visualized it, would be something like a huge saucer, some twelve feet in diameter, with a somewhat higher than usual rim—a waterlily pad—but octagonal to fit exactly the contours of the pool. It would be moored with silken cords to little silver pilons around the edge of the pool, leaving not more than five fingers margin around the edge. The moorings must be loose enough so that the blanket would not tear under stress and strain.

His assistants had been busy since yesterday afternoon, with needles and thread, tar and glue, and wool stuffing for the rims. It was not yet noon, and his masterpiece—he chose to consider it such— was already complete.

The hassock-maker bowed deeply to the chief eunuch and left the Salon of the Caliphs, his masterpiece floating on the silver pool behind him.

Meanwhile, Marilú had had an uneventful but delightful day. Rising late, she accompanied Lady Nardjis to the *hammam*, lunched on small snails *en casserole*, lamb *en brochette*, pine-nut tarts, and sherbets. Later the two walked together through the garden and sat and talked on the cushions in the gazebo. The garden was a thing of beauty. Refreshed by the rains, new blossoms bloomed everywhere, blending their perfume with the clean smell of damp earth and grass. The rippling brook had become a noisy torrent, and the little waterfall a mad cascade of splashing water. The turtledoves cooed persistently as they flew around the vine-covered pavilion, or chased one another amourously on the garden paths—in short, a paradise of flowers and water and birds, of scents and sounds that in part lulled one's senses, in part quickened them with quiet delight.

The hours passed quickly, and the time soon came for the evening dinner with the Grand Vizier and the night of the silver pool.

Marilú was bursting with excitement as she and Lady Nardjis entered the Salon of the Caliphs. It would be such fun, she was sure, to bounce up and down like corks on the quicksilver bed, to scramble and romp and toss and play as they indulged their passions on a moving mass of mercury. She burned to communicate her excitement and curiosity to the Grand Vizier, to have him share the contagion of her mirth, but she knew that, among the Moslems, it was considered undignified to joke or laugh at mealtime, and that any frivolity was frowned upon.

The Grand Vizier approached and tendered Marilú his arm. He smiled indulgently but, as always, his manner was grave, his conversation serious.

The meal was delicious, beginning with cold fillets of fish in *escabeche*, followed by a thick lentil soup, and, for the *plat de résistence*, a marvellously grilled young kid, browned on the outside, juicy and tender within.

The meal proceeded through the dessert, a caramel custard *flan*, cheese, and fruit. Conversation was sparse, but the animation in Marilú's eyes as she thought of the prospective excitement on the bed of mercury was not lost on the Grand Vizier. And by the end of the meal the twinkle in his eye showed that he looked forward to the delights of the evening just as eagerly as his lovely partner.

The tables, trays and viands cleared away, Marilú reached for her veil, her eyes fairly dancing with excitement. The room was cleared in a trice and the lights extinguished at the clap of the Vizier's hands. The two lovers rose from their cushions, and Marilú could no longer contain herself: "I am so excited," she gushed and she threw her arms around the Vizier, hugging him tightly.

He responded in kind and embraced her passionately, their tongues vying with one another. She could feel his sharp pressure against her, and a feeling of warmth swept over her.

"Come, my sweet," the Vizier whispered, "let's not delay." And they doffed their garments and walked quickly to the pool's edge, arm in arm. He stepped gingerly onto the leather pad which swayed under his weight. "Be careful, dear, give me your hand. You may fall."

Marilú clutched his hand and stepped onto the pad. With her added weight, the two of them, in tight embrace, teetered precariously. She almost fell, he reached for her, lost his balance, and tumbled flat on his back, Marilú on top of him.

She was delirious with joy as she found herself astride her lord and master, his manroot erect and firm at the very gate of paradise.

She had long looked forward to the day when she could ride her paramour, take him by force as he had taken her again and again—and the Vizier had promised he would let her do it "sometime." This was the time. She grasped him and squeezed softly, lovingly. He attempted to right himself, but the tossing bed of mercury gave no purchase for his shoulders and arms, and he could not turn over. He was a prisoner under the urgent weight of his ardent partner. He knew he would be ridden, just as Marilú had said she wanted to ride him, and he was powerless to prevent it. Not that he had the slightest desire to escape such sweet captivity, but he waited eagerly to see what his captor would do next.

He had not long to wait. Marilú, savoring her triumph, was wild with passion. She inserted him into her and rose up and softly, slowly, gaining momentum as she moved. At every downward stroke, the mercury bed pushed her partner upward with increasing force. Fiercely, she rode her charger, and still more fiercely he bucked and cavorted beneath her. Her breasts hung down swaying tantalizingly from side to side. He grasped them, fondled them and squeezed them, then drew her mouth down to his, and they were soon locked in a loving embrace. Meanwhile, she never ceased to ride.

The waves of mercury pushed them from side to side as violently as the impassioned lovers pushed themselves up and down, until at last, in a frenzy of passion, she tumbled down upon him, exhausted and contented.

"Thank you! thank you!" she gasped. "It was sweet of you to let me do it, and I so wanted to. I do hope you're not angry with me, and I do hope it made you as happy as it did me."

"I loved it, my darling. I really did. I never thought I would, and never really thought I'd let you do it. It was wonderful. But you must never breathe a word of this to Nardjis or anyone. It must be our secret alone, and we can do it again."

Still joined together, she extricated herself with difficulty, finding it hard to get any purchase on the swaying raft that would enable her to lift herself from her lover's body. Finally she rose unsteadily, walked or rather fell towards the center of the pad, teetered as though drunk, and collapsed.

The Grand Vizier laughed uproariously, doubled over in mirth. It was the first time Marilú had ever heard him laugh so heartily, and it thrilled her through and through. "All right, my lover, I bet you can't walk on water any better than I can. Just try to come over here, if you can."

The Vizier attempted to rise, tottered from side to

side, and collapsed beside her, the two of them in paroxysms of laughter.

"Oh, my darling," screamed Marilú, "I do love to hear you laugh. Come over here on top of me, if you can. I want you to caress me until I can't stand it any more, and then I want to feel you inside me, pushing me right up to my very womb. I want you to kiss me and love me—oh, my lover, come into me again."

The Grand Vizier grasped Marilú by the waist, attempting, despite the rocking of the leather pad, to mount her. They grappled, their hands and arms and legs striking out in all directions as they struggled to get into position. The exertion aroused their passions to the utmost, and at last the Vizier was where he wanted to be, his hands grasping her, her legs wrapped around him in tight embrace.

"Oh, it feels so good,' sighed Marilú, "come into me, my love."

He thrust into her and bore down upon her with all his force. The mercury reacted with equal force, sending her pelvis up into his groin as hard as he had pressed down into hers. Again and again he thrust, and again and again she responded, adding her own eager desires to the force of the waves of mercury. The quicksilver bed added new strength to his loins, and he felt as mighty as Hercules who had laid and impregnated forty-nine of the fifty virgin daughters of King Thespius in a single night.

His fury aroused her own. Never before had they tossed and twisted, pushed and strained with such violent abandon, until, at last, in an excess of unbridled passion, they collapsed utterly exhausted and utterly content.

CHAPTER 12

"You know," Marilú whispered to Lady Nardjis as they basked alone in the hot pool of the *hammam* together, "I've been practicing those exercises you showed me, day after day, and every time I had a moment to spare. But I don't feel a thing, and I don't think I'll ever learn to be a *kabbázah.*"

"Oh, my darling, you know I told you it might take months before you even *discovered* the muscles you will have to use. Be patient."

Nardjis then called the two little attendants, and Shamsi and Ourda entered the room, ready to complete the ablutions of the *hammam* and prepare their mistresses for a stroll in the garden.

"I told the girls we would have luncheon in the gazebo," said Nardjis, "so let's walk down there together. They will have the food ready for us in a moment."

The two of them walked down the corridor, out onto the terrace, and down the long flight of marble stairs to the middle terrace and the garden gate.

The garden seemed to change with every visit. In part it did, for the gardeners were forever busy pruning, clipping, planting, weeding and performing all the other chores, large and small, that make a garden a thing of beauty and an ever-changing source of delight. But in part it was because each rain brought forth new beauties to admire, and in part because there was just too much for Marilú to have taken in at first glance, so that she was forever discovering some new plant or shrub or blossom, some of them familiar to her but for the most part unknown in her native Galicia.

They walked through aisles of frankincense trees, acacia, feathery tamarisk, and fruit trees—apples, pears, peaches, pomegranates, oranges, lemons—bordered on every side by jasmine, camelia, scented myrtle berries, nenuphars, privet, camomile, violets, eglantine, narcissus and other blooms. The little, vine-covered pavilion stood before them, gay with the cooing of the inevitable turtle-doves and the gurgling of the brook, reduced once more to normal size after the heavy rains of the previous day. Above the entrance arch was an inscription in Arabic characters, incised into the marble.

Nardjis translated: "Here the wicked cease from troubling and the weary are at rest."

"Why that's from the Bible—from the Book of Job, isn't it?" asked Marilú. "How appropriate!"

"Well, in any event, we shall rest here, although we can't be weary, and I don't really think we are wicked, unless love itself be wicked. And here come Ourda and Shamsi with our lunch, which is certainly not troubling us, and I'm sure they're not wicked—just mischievous."

The two girls set down their trays on the little tables in front of one of the marble benches, piled high with cushions, on which Marilú and Nardjis were already comfortably ensconced.

"What are we going to have today?" asked Marilú. "I know it will be delicious. It always is. And I do love these iced drinks. I've had beverages with so many flavors—violet, banana, rose, ginger—what is it today? And what do you call them?"

"They are *sharbah* in Arabic, and that's where you get your word sherbet from, the same as you say syrup for *sharab*, sugar for *sukkar*, and *qandi* for sweets, and many other words you have taken from the Arabic.

The sherbet today is pomegranate. But let's begin with this hot asparagus which is now in season."

Marilú had never tasted asparagus before, and found it delicious with melted butter sauce. Lady Nardjis explained that this was one of the many things that Ziryab had brought to Spain from Baghdad, and that it was still considered a luxury in Andalucía.

The asparagus was followed by a stew of shrimp and fish, and Marilú commented that she had eaten similar stews in Galicia.

"Yes," said Lady Nardjis, "for our cooks are skilled in Christian and Jewish cooking as well as Moorish. But your seafood stews must be much better than ours, for you have so many shellfish and fish from the sea, while our shrimp and fish come mostly from the river. However, we do bring lobster and other things up, alive and swimming, from Málaga or Cádiz. But not in these troubled times."

They discussed the food—the endive salad, the semola cakes dipped in honey, the watermelon. And then, when the lunch was over, and Shamsi and Ourda had left with the trays and tables, Marilú brought the conversation around to the Grand Vizier.

"When we had luncheon beside the silver pool, the quicksilver was paddled by two young eunuchs. Were they ephebes? Does the Grand Vizier make love to them?"

"No, my dear," Nardjis answered, smiling. "The Koran condemns homosexuality and quotes the words of Lot to the people of Sodom: 'What! Come ye with lust unto men, rather than women?' And the Grand Vizier follows the Koran injunction strictly, unlike many of his correligionists who are not good Moslems.

"So you need not fear that rivalry—if that is what has been troubling you. But let's take our nap in the pavilion, so that your mind may be fresh for the chess game tonight, for I know that is what the Grand Vizier is planning. You know, he wants you all alone, with no distractions—no more minstrelsy, and no more dancing girls. You have a monopoly over all his affections and all his senses. And may you well say '*Alhamdolillah!*'—Glory be to God!"

"*Alhamdolillah!*" Marilú breathed fervently, and soon the two were fast asleep on the cushions.

An hour later, they were awakened when Ourda appeared carrying a month old puppy in her arms. "What a darling," laughed Marilú, "would you let me hold him? What kind of dog is it?"

"A *saluki,* my lady—from the Grand Vizier's hunting kennels. Isn't it sweet?" She started to hand the puppy to Marilú when, with a shrill little bark, it jumped out of her arms, and started to chase one of the turtle doves that was strutting after its mate on the garden path.

"Quick. We must catch it," cried Lady Nardjis, and the three women ran after the little dog which scampered along through flowers and ferns and shrubs, up to the edge of a thick woods, barking merrily all the while. Marilú darted for the little creature, and scooped it up in her arms, just as it was about to disappear into the forest.

"Thank goodness you caught it," panted Nardjis. "That is the game preserve and there are all kinds of wild creatures in there—not only deer and rabbits and birds, but wild boars and foxes and other animals that would certainly have killed the poor little puppy."

The three women were panting from their exertion, their garments torn and in wild disarray from the chase through bushes and ferns. The puppy was busy licking Marilú's face, happy to have been the center of attention and to have invented a new game.

"It is a long walk back to the *seraglio,*" Nardjis commented, still breathing heavily, "and it looks like rain."

"Should I carry the puppy for you, my lady," asked Ourda, smiling, her cheeks rosy red from the exercise.

"No, I don't dare let go of it, it is so sweet and cute," Marilú answered happily as the puppy snuggled against her.

They walked quickly back to the palace, Ourda leading the way. The dark clouds gathered overhead and, long before the three of them could reach the garden gate, the rain came down in torrents, drenching them to the skin. Their hair disheveled, their thin garments torn and clinging, the three women were a strange spectacle as they climbed the long flight of stairs leading from the garden terrace to the palace grounds.

"I haven't had as much fun and exercise as this since I left Galicia," Marilú laughed, her cheeks flushed, her long hair hanging down her back in tangled disarray.

Shamsi met them at the entrance to the *seraglio,* aghast to see the two ladiés and her friend Ourda looking like orphans of the storm.

"Goodness, my ladies, we didn't know where you were nor what had happened to you. Thank goodness you're safe. And the *hammam* awaits your pleasure."

A eunuch took the puppy, now sound asleep, from Marilú's arms, and the four women walked, still dripping, down the long corridor to the *tepidarium* room. "There's no use taking off what's left of our garments in the disrobing room," Nardjis remarked, "and it's nice and warm here in the *tepidarium.* My, the bath will feel good after all that running, and I certainly need a good shampoo."

Two hours later, Marilú and Lady Nardjis emerged from the *hammam,* beautifully gowned, and bearing no trace of their merry chase through the brush, save only their still rosy cheeks and sparkling eyes. The Grand Vizier rose to greet them as they entered the Great Hall of the Caliphs.

"We shall meet again, my love, in a battle to the death. Are you prepared?" he asked fondly, proud to have found so worthy a foe in such a beautiful and delightful companion.

The evening repast went quickly, the Grand Vizier and Marilú partaking more scantily than usual of the abundance of viands proffered to them by the attendants, so eager were they and so excited.

Abundance of food there was—a steaming beef broth, a tasty *escabeche* of partridge, morsels of grilled lobster drenched in melted butter and served with crisp but powdery cracknels, roast venison *jardinière*, *blancmange* and hazelnut cookies, fruit, icewater, and milk of almond sherbet.

The meal over, the Grand Vizier clapped, and the great hall was cleared, all lamps extinguished save for a chandelier suspended by a chain over the table that sufficed to illuminate the chessboard and cast a soft glow of light over the players.

The Grand Vizier opened conventionally, moving his soldier to the king's fourth square, unlike the game of the previous evening which he had opened with his vizier's soldier to the fourth square. Marilú responded, moving a soldier to the vizier's elephant's fourth square, and the game went on in silence, the two opponents intent upon the opposing moves of the crystal and red ivory chessmen.

The Grand Vizier manifestly dominated the game, almost from the first move, and then, seemingly distraught, went to pieces at the thirty-sixth move, and after three more moves was forced to give up, a checkmate inevitable.

Marilú was surprised, and not a little dismayed, at the quick change in the tide of battle.

"What happened?" she asked. "Why did you move your horse to king's row five instead of taking my elephant with your vizier? You would have beaten me easily. Were you distracted, or did you let me win on purpose?"

"I would never let you win on purpose, my love. That would be cheating. But I was indeed distracted, and if you will glance down at yourself instead of at the board you will see why."

Marilú looked down and, to her dismay, saw that her sheer blouse had become unfastened, leaving her naked to the waist, her creamy white breasts and red nipples bare. She remembered that her lover had referred to them as twin red roes feeding among the lilies.

She blushed, and reached for her veil as she felt a gently warmth suffuse her whole body. Her companion rose, threw his turban and robe on the floor, and gathered her up in his arms.

"We shall play another chess game in the alcove, my dearest darling," he murmured. "You shall sit facing me, but this time there will be no chessboard between us, and you shall have your will with me as you did at the chess game."

He strode to the bedchamber, Marilú in his arms, pressed to his hairy chest. Seated on the bed, he placed Marilú on his lap facing him, her legs astride his own.

"Ride," he whispered, and he helped her mount, then glued his lips to hers as she rode up and down in blissful ecstasy, feeling him deep within her and giving her the most unutterable pleasure as she writhed and twisted, rose and fell, her arms tight around her partner's waist.

The Vizier alternately fondled her breasts or

pressed them tightly to his chest, his arms clasped round her. Both of them groaned and panted as she increased the pace of her movement, at first rhythmical, then faster and faster, and now convulsive, frantic, and violent, until at last, in a final, pulsating transport of passion, she slumped exhausted on his lap, still linked together, their arms embracing.

They remained in that position, panting with exhaustion. Then, gently, he lifted her from his lap, and lay her down upon the bed beside him, the two stretched out at full length side by side.

"Oh, you wonderful man," she sighed. "I loved that. I like it best when I can face you and kiss you."

"And I too like it best when I can gaze upon you. You are so beautiful, my darling. And rapturously lovely when you are in passion. I love it that way. And you too are wonderful, and in so many ways. I loved your singing, and your playing with that little Galician guitar, and I am so delighted with your intelligence in conversation and in chess—and your laughter, and your sweet tears, and your fun. I love you in all your moods and ways. What I am trying to tell you is that I adore you in all your ways, as a lover, as a companion, in every way. That I would rather know one hundred aspects of a single, lovely woman than one aspect of a hundred women. I have never loved more than one woman and never can.

"Ibn Hazim, may he rest in peace, the greatest scholar of al-Anduluz, who died when I was only thirteen years old—he was an old man of seventy, but I knew him and admired him—wrote that a man cannot love two women, that, if he attempts to do so, it is nothing more than lust which can be called love only in the metaphysical sense and not in the true meaning of the word. He wrote that in *The Dove's Necklace* which you must read some time."

Then they rested quietly in each other's arms, side by side, but by daybreak, when the Grand Vizier rose quietly to be about his affairs, Marilú merely stirred and then turned over to sleep more soundly. He tiptoed out of the room but not without a loving glance behind him.

CHAPTER 13

The dark form tiptoed silently into the bedchamber where Marilú was stretched out on the broad bed, lying on her back, her blond tresses in beguiling disarray, fast asleep.

The visitor whispered softly: "Marilú, it is I. Wake up."

Marilú stirred, her eyes fast closed. She stretched out with feline grace, arched her supple back, twisted her shoulders, extended her long arms and legs, stretched slowly, gracefully, then sank back into the soft comfort of the cushioned bed, her body now bare save for a thin coverlet over one leg.

"Marilú," the visitor repeated softly, bending down over the reclining form.

Marilú stretched out her arms around her morning visitor and drew the dark form toward her and murmured: "Oh, no my darling, not again. Come to me, my love."

"It is I, Nardjis, wake up, my dear." And the bending form let out a peal of laughter that could not be mistaken.

"Oh, Nardjis, I was dreaming," said Marilú, opening her eyes, now fully awake. "It's early, isn't it? I was fast asleep."

"Yes, dear, it is early. The Grand Vizier left instructions that I was to take you to Córdoba this morning to show you the city, the palace, and the great Mosque. We shall then go to the *hammam* in the palace of Dimashk, and you will have lunch with him, and a *siesta,* in the perfumed garden. How does that strike you?"

"It sounds wonderful! A *siesta* with Ahmad in the garden? When do we go?"

"You silly, darling girl," laughed Nardjis. "You didn't hear anything I said—just the *siesta* with Ahmad."

"Oh, but I did hear you. You said Córdoba and the palace and the Mosque, and another palace somewhere, and the perfumed garden. I did hear, and I'm all ready to go."

"We'll have a quick bath in the *hammam,* just a bite to eat, and then we'll be on the way. Córdoba is only a little more than a league from here, and Dimashk less than a league from there. Do you ride horseback, or would you rather go in a coach?"

"I'd love to ride," said Marilú, already out of bed and walking arm in arm with Lady Nardjis. "I've ridden horses with my father since I was a little girl, home in Galicia."

"You use the Spanish saddle, I suppose," Lady Nardjis asked.

"I'd prefer an African saddle, if you have one. I find the high pommel and high cantle of the Spanish saddle uncomfortable, and father always used to say that the Spanish saddle was no good except for tournaments, going full tilt with a lance in your hand. He always had Moorish saddles, made in Córdoba—such smooth, fine leather, and so comfortable to ride."

"Good," said Nardjis, and she gave instructions to Shamsi who was waiting for them in the vestibule of the *hammam.*

"Harkening and obeying, my lady," Shamsi smiled, bowing deeply. Ourda led the two ladies into the disrobing room and from there to the *tepidarium* where she was joined by Shamsi, breathless from her errand. The ablutions in the *tepidarium* and *calidar-*

ium were brief, yet not hurried. The girls gave their mistresses a light breakfast—tea, toasted bread, and fruit—while they reclined in the pool, and then, after a brisk rub with the large Turkish towels, ushered them into the dressing room.

The garments the girls handed to Marilú and Lady Nardjis were much the same as those they had worn on their visit to Medina al-Zahra, except that they were given butter-soft leather boots that reached up to just below the knees. Their heavy woolen pantaloons were tucked into the tops of the boots, and draped down over the outside of the boots in baggy profusion. A white woolen burnous covered their heads and fell in loose folds down to their ankles.

"When we walk around Córdoba," explained Nardjis, "we shall keep our boots on—you will find them comfortable—but we shall let the pantaloons hang down outside the boots to our ankles."

Marilú noted that Shamsi and Ourda remained attired only in their skimpy palace garments, and asked why.

"They will not accompany us today," Lady Nardjis answered. "It will be their day off, and they will be left to their own devices until evening.

Shamsi and Ourda exchanged gleeful glances, but looked downcast when Lady Nardjis added: "Masrur and Ibrahim will ride with us to Córdoba and escort us around the city, and then on to Dimashk."

The two girls brightened perceptibly when Lady Nardjis concluded: "I shall leave you alone with the Grand Vizier in Dimashk, and Masrur and Ibrahim will return here with me shortly after noon. . . . Well, I guess we are ready to leave. Now, behave yourselves, my dears," she added, turning to the two little maids, "you might do some of that sewing you always bring with you, but never seem to have time to attend to. So you may remain up here in the *seraglio* and have your luncheon here."

In the courtyard, Masrur and Ibrahim held the horses for the two ladies to mount. Their own horses were tied to a marble post at the entrance.

"What beautiful animals," exclaimed Marilú as she admired the gracefully arched necks, the finely shaped heads, and small but well-muscled bodies of the four steeds that pawed the ground impatiently before them.

"They are pure-bred Arabian horses," said Lady Nardjis. "You will ride that black stallion whose name is Jet. I will ride the sorrel one."

The two other horses—geldings, appropriately enough—were also sorrel, a smooth, rich reddish brown, but Marilú decided she liked her own jet-black beauty best. She patted its nose affectionately, then stroked its smooth shoulders as she prepared to mount. The stallion attempted to rear as if testing the riding skills of its new mistress, but the firm grip of Marilú's thighs and legs against its sides, and her sure hands on the bridle—for she rode Arab style, with both hands on the reins—showed that he carried an experienced rider, and he stopped his cavorting and settled down, still impatient to be off and away.

"I hope you don't mind that we have given you a stallion," said Lady Nardjis. "We would have given you a mare—a lovely, gentle animal—but you will be returning with the Grand Vizier and he has a stallion, and the mare might be troublesome. But I see you have no difficulty mastering him, and you will see that he has been well trained to trot and gallop and to go directly from a walk to a canter without an annoying jog-trot in between."

They trotted briskly across the broad esplanade to a large iron and bronze gate set in the outer wall surrounding the three terraces of Medina al-Zahra. On each side of the outer gate were vaulted porticos with smaller doors for travelers on foot. Uniformed guards opened the closed the gates for the cavalcade, and bowed deeply, at the same time saluting with a sweeping wave of their shining scimitars.

The road stretched out ahead of them, smooth and beautiful, the center paved with stones like the Roman roads Marilú had seen in Galicia, with broad shoulders of firmly packed earth on which the horses' hooves pounded rhythmically.

"May we canter?" asked Marilú.

"Of course," answered Nardjis, and the four riders broke into a smooth fast canter, the two ladies riding ahead, followed by the two eunuchs, whose scimitar sheaths rattled noisily against their saddle straps.

"You ride well," Nardjis remarked, noting how her companion sat gracefully in the saddle, erect but not stiff, her bottom tucked well under her, and never leaving the saddle by so much as a hair's breadth as she rocked in unison with the gentle canter of her mount.

On they rode, past huge groves of olive trees whose leaves, dark green on top and silver beneath, fluttered in the breeze. The road was edged with flaming red poppies and yellow marguerites, brilliant as buttercups. In some places, the flowers extended out into the fields between the rows of olive trees, making a bright red and yellow carpet as a gorgeous background for the panorama of gnarled and twisting tree-trunks with their green and silver leaves.

The mountains stretched behind them as they passed the rolling landscape, and then the flat plain, on the way to Córdoba. Wheat fields and cotton plants now lined the road and, far in the distance, Marilú could see the high walls of the city of Córdoba, the spires of the Mosque and minaret, the turrets of a huge castle, and, extending out in every direction, the houses and mansions of the largest city she had ever seen.

"It *is* a huge city," Marilú exclaimed in admiration as they neared the city walls.

"It is indeed," Nardjis replied. "There are half a million inhabitants—it used to have eight hundred thousand people in the days of the Caliphate—and it was the greatest city in the world, greater and more luxurious than Baghdad. But now that Sevilla is the capital of the kingdom, it has surpassed Córdoba in size, although not in the magnificance of its buildings. Wait until we enter the walls—you have never seen so many buildings! We can't see it all, because we have to be in Dimashk by the first hour after noon, to meet the Grand Vizier in the garden by the second hour. But we have four hours to spend and we shall see as much as possible.

They passed through a huge bronze gate, saluted by the soldiers who guarded the entrance.

"We are in the Ghetto now," said Nardjis, as they entered a neatly manicured, immaculate *barrio* of the city.

"This is the Jewish quarter. That is the house that was built by Judah ben David. He was the great grammarian, the father of Hebrew grammar. And that mansion is owned by the descendants of the Finance Minister of Ab-ar-Rahman the Great."

"There must be a great many Jews in Córdoba—and rich ones too," Marilú remarked.

"It is said that there are more than three hundred thousand Jews in Spain, mostly in Córdoba, Sevilla and Granada, although they have scattered everywhere since first they came here from the East over eight hundred years ago during the reign of the Emperor Hadrian, and later under the Caliphate of Abd ar-Rahman, of blessed memory. Many of them have become rich as merchant traders, buying and selling everything from jewels, silks, furs, spices and Damascus swords to eunuchs from Greece and slaves from Africa. There are doctors of medicine, bankers, ministers of finance, and other high government officials among them. None of them are really poor, for they work hard, study hard, and save their money. There are no beggars among the Jews. Truly they have prospered greatly under the Caliphate."

"I guess they treat Jews better in Moslem Spain than we do in Christian Spain," remarked Marilú. "Some of them are money lenders in Galicia, but woe betide them if they ever try to collect their debts from a Christian king if he is hard pressed for money. I guess it makes the kings feel almost Christlike when they chase the money changers from their temples, and the poor Jew is lucky if he doesn't lose his head as well as his cash. Certainly, there are no mansions of rich Jews in Galicia, and a ghetto up there really looks like a ghetto. What in the world will happen to them if ever Christian Spain reconquers all of Andalucía?"

"I feel sorry for them," Marilú sighed.

"Well, let's talk about less unpleasant things," Nardjis said, then added, "let's ride on to the palace on the Guadalquivir on the south side of the city. We shall pass many interesting places on the way and I'll point them out to you."

The four riders held their horses to a walk as they rode down the paved streets, and Nardjis pointed out the various *barrios* as they passed by—the shops of the sellers of sweet basil; the bakers' quarter, fragrant with the smell of fresh baked bread; the Garden of Wonders where all kinds of things were sold; the street of the parchment makers, of the cobblers, of the saddlers, and of other artisans too numerous to mention, each trade grouped together in a street or *barrio* of its own.

When they came to the *barrio* of the perfumists, their nostrils were assailed with a variety of fragrances that was nearly overpowering. They paused for a moment, and Lady Nardjis pointed out the shops from whose open doors they could smell the perfumes of rose, orange blossoms, jonquil, jasmine, hyacinth, carnation, and many others—some, familiar flower perfumes, others exotic scents from distant Araby—all, Nardjis, said, used by men and women alike. In other shops, incense was burning on small charcoal braziers to give passers-by a sample of their wares—myrrh and frankincense, sweet aloes, ambergris, benzoin, and other aromatics.

They passed on. At almost every corner there were great basins of gold or silver or copper, or fountains and pools of marble, with clear water running into them. The water, Nardjis said, was mountain water brought by aqueduct to Medina al-Zahra and from there to the palace in Córdoba, the *Alcázar*, from where it was distributed in leaden pipes under the streets to all parts of the city. The avenues and many of the streets were lined with lamp-posts with hanging oil lamps. Marilú marvelled at all she saw, and thought that the city must be a fairyland of beauty by night when all the lamps were lit.

Nardjis pointed out some of the mansions as they rode by—the house of the *Qadi* of Córdoba, the chief justice; that of the *Sahib al-Medina*, the Governor of the City, where Prince al-Mamun stayed in preference to the Caliph's palace, the *Alcázar;* the house of the *Sahib al-Sug*, the Governor of the Market-place; and and many other great mansions. Before one of them, an old woman, meanly dressed, knocked at the front door and was immediately admitted by a eunuch in gawdy costume.

Nardjis explained: "She is undoubtedly one of the bawds of the city. Her specialty is arranging clandestine love affairs for the mistress of the household. She will provide not only a house of assignation, but a lover, and that is the way she earns her living. You see, women in al-Andaluz lead a very unhappy life. The young girls remain completely secluded in the harem under their mothers' care. They go to school, always in the company of other girls, until they are nubile. Then they are even more strictly guarded until they are married, usually at the age of thirteen to sixteen. The marriages are arranged by the parents, and the marriage contract signed, without the prospective bride and groom ever having met except at one or two formal meetings in the presence of their families.

"So it is no wonder that many married women prove to be unhappy with their husbands, and turn elsewhere for the affection they cannot find at home. And, as the husband can have a number of wives, and as many concubines and prostitutes as he wants, according to his station in life and his wealth, it seems only fair that the wife should pay him back in kind. The husband can even patronze one of the prostitutes' guilds, and his wife cannot object."

"Guilds?" asked Marilú in some surprise.

"Yes, I know of three such guilds—there may be more. One is called The Guild of Itinerant Wives and Maidens, another The Sisters of Mary Magdalene, and one is known simply as The Joyous Virgins."

Marilú laughed, but added in a shocked voice, "I think that's terrible. We women ought to revolt unless we are liberated. But I can tell you that it is not only in Andalucía that women are oppressed; it happens in Christian Spain as well. Thank God! I have been fortunate, both in my marriage—my father has always been so kind to me, and would never have forced me to marry a man I did not love—and now as the slave of the Grand Vizier."

"I too have been fortunate, and in nearly thirty years of happy marriage I have never employed a bawd, nor wanted to."

As they passed an imposing and handsome building, Nardjis pointed it out: "That is the library. There are seventy libraries in Córdoba, but that is the main one. It has four hundred thousand books, in all languages and from all parts of the world. But there are more books written in Arabic in the whole world than in any other langugage, so that most of those books are in Arabic. There are all the works of all the great philosophers and mathematicians and poets. Which explains why there is a whole street with no one but parchment makers on it, and another where there are one hundred and seventy calligraphers engaged in nothing but filling those sheets of parchment with beautifully inked Arabic lettering in black and red and gold, and illuminating those pages with the most exquisite pictures in delicate colors and burnished gold. And another street where there are nothing but bookbinders working at their trade. They turn out sixty thousand books a year, each one a work of art. Córdoba, as I told you, is the city of books, the same as Sevilla is the city of music. The people here speak the most elegant Arabic in all Islam, and their speech is full of proverbs and quotations from the books they have read."

They came now to the great market place, vast and thronged with milling crowds of people.

"We shan't go through the market," said Nardjis. "It would take hours, and is not much different from the one you saw in Medina al-Zahra, except that the Córdoba market is even larger, the stocks and variety of merchandise even greater, and prices somewhat lower because of the competition. One's silver *dirhems* and golden *dinars* will go much further here than in Medina al-Zahra—and faster, too, I suppose. There are so many tempting things to buy."

They circled around the iron fence of the marketplace, but Marilú could see through the grillwork the throngs of people in their bright silk or wool garments and white linen burnouses, their caps or turbans, and rope-soled sandals, all busily engaged in shopping at the various stalls or stopping to exchange the gossip of the day with some friend or neighbor. In winter, Lady Nardjis told her, the costumes would be much gayer, for then the men and women would wear a brightly colored Tunisian burnous instead of a plain white one. Or else an even gayer African cloak.

They caught a glimpse too of the stalls and stores piled high with fish and fowl and fruit and flowers, and meats and vegetables of every variety, ceramic ware and fine rag paper from Valencia, glassware from Damascus and cruder glass made in Andalucía. Most fascinating of all were the jewel cases and boxes of every shape and size, carved in ivory or made of ebony and other precious woods inlaid with ivory, mother of pearl, gold or silver, that were a specialty of *Cordobés* artisanship. Marilú had seen and been tempted by these in the shops of Medina al-Zahra, but she had no money, nor any need to buy anything in a palace where everything was given to her in a profusion that reminded her of the fairy stories she had been told as a child.

The four riders hastened on, coming to an imposing structure of white and red marble, with scores of people, young and old, entering or leaving its bronze portals or clustered in groups in animated discussion.

"That is the University," Nardjis said. "It is the first university built in all of Europe, and even today is the greatest, although its prestige has declined since the days of the Caliphs. Because of the University and Library and other centers of learning, Córdoba is still the scientific and medical center of the world, and Christian kings and nobles come here to be cured of serious illnesses, and for operations, because here operations can be performed with anaesthetics unknown in the Christian world.

"Those characters engraved over the center portal read: 'The world is supported by four things only—the learning of the wise; the justice of the great; the prayers of the righteous; and the valor of the brave.'

"But let's hasten on, for it is almost the sixth hour, and I would like you to see the Great Mosque before the crowds arrive for the noonday prayers."

They rode on, coming to a great plaza, on the far side of which loomed a vast Mosque, imposing in its size, but austere in appearance, with its walls of cinnamon-colored stucco and great bronze doors which were closed forbiddingly, as it still lacked a half hour before the *muezzin* would call the faithful to prayer.

The doors, Nardjis explained almost apologetically, had been brought to Córdoba nearly a hundred years ago from Iria Flavia de Compostela when al-Mansur the Victorious had conquered Galicia and destroyed the Church on the Pico Sagro, except for the tomb of St. James. Marilú shuddered when she remembered the tales of the bloody battles waged by Almanzor against her kinfolk, but she knew that a new shrine to the glorious St. James had been built on the Pico Sagro just thirty years after the old church had been razed, and that it would soon be completed. She thought too, with pride, of the cathedral that King Alfonso VI was building on that spot, over the ruins of the IX Century Christian church, which, when completed, would be the greatest church in Christendom.

"Let us dismount here," said Nardjis to Marilú, and then, turning to Masrur, she asked, "Would you and

Ibrahim stable the horses in the caravansarai and then meet us in the *mihrab*. Meanwhile, we shall be seeing the orangerie and the Mosque."

"To hear is to obey, my lady." Masrur bowed respectfully.

"We shall enter the orange garden through the Gate of Forgiveness," said Lady Nardjis and, with Marilú by her side, the two walked through a high arched doorway to the left of the minaret which loomed square and massive on their right.

They entered a broad patio, surrounded on three sides by a high wall, an extension of the walls of the Mosque itself. Directly in front of them stood the main doorway of the Mosque, where two attendants were engaged in swinging open the great bronze doors. To their left and right, on each side of the patio, stood a row of cloisters, while the center of the patio was occupied by three plots of ground on which stood over a hundred orange trees arranged in rows. Scattered among the orange trees, four fountains sent their jets of water high into the air, glistening in the sunlight before falling back into large white marble pools.

"Let us perform the ablution before we go into the Mosque," suggested Lady Nardjis, and the two ladies washed their arms up to the elbows as an attendant hastened to them with towels in deference to their obviously high rank. They then rubbed the moist towels over their feet and ankles.

As they crossed the orangerie, a score of attendants were busy opening smaller doors on either side of the main entrance to the Mosque that Lady Nardjis said was known as the Gate of Palms. Marilú could see a row of columns within the Mosque, behind each doorway, exactly parallelling the rows of orange trees, so that the trees formed an extension of the colonnade within, and vice versa.

They passed through the Gate of Palms just as another group of attendants swung open the other doors of the Mosque, flooding the vast edifice with brilliant sunshine. The effect was dazzling. A veritable forest of delicate columns, of elaborately sculptured marble, jasper and prophyry, no two alike, in serried rows and ranks, formed a bright network of blue and green and scarlet and gold, airy and irridescent. The colors were repeated in the shining tiles and mosaics of the walls and floors. The columns were topped by horseshoe arches of red and yellow stone in dazzling stripes. The ceiling was of cedar and larch, intricately sculptured, enameled and gilded.

An army of attendants was busy unrolling long carpets of esparto grass to protect the floors, prior to the entry of the crowds that would flock to the Great Mosque for midday prayer.

Speechless with wonderment and delight, Marilú stood transfixed as she took in the fairyland beauty of the place. Then, recovering her voice, she exclaimed: "It is a magic forest, Nardjis! But never, not even in my dreams, had I imagined a place as beautiful as this. It's lovely!"

"It is lovely indeed," answered Nardjis, "but let's go to the shrine of St. Vincent where we can both kneel, and you can say a prayer before we meet Masrur and Ibrahim."

"St. Vincent? In a Moslem Mosque?"

"Yes. Three hundred years ago, Abd ar-Rahman I bought the ancient Visigothic church from the Christians, and built the Mosque over it and around it, and *Mozárabes* still come to worship at the altar of St. Vincent over here on our right. The only condition is that they must leave before the Moslem hour of prayer, so as not to disturb us with their bell-ringing and chanting. But this site was originally an ancient Roman temple to Janus."

Several women were kneeling on the floor before the altar, and Marilú and Nardjis joined them. The priest was chanting the *Agnus Dei,* so Marilú knew they were in time for Communion, even though they had missed the early part of the Mass. She remained kneeling for a moment after the *Ite,* and tearfully, gratefully, as she thought how much more tolerant the Moslems were than her fellow Christians, she recited the Lord's prayer in hushed tones, while Lady Nardjis repeated the words of the *fatihah.*

"We must leave now," said Nardjis, as they could see the attendants lighting the myriad lamps and heard the voice of the *muezzin* from the minaret, calling the faithful to the noonday prayer. In addition to the oil lamps, Nardjis said, there were three hundred chandeliers, one of which alone held a thousand candles.

The *Mozárabe* women rose with them and exited through a side door, while Nardjis and Marilú walked straight ahead to a marble platform on which Masrur and Ibrahim awaited them.

Before them was the holy of holies, the *Mihrab,* a small octagonal enclosure with white marble walls, roofed with a single white marble slab carved in the shape of a shell, that reminded Marilú of the shell in the shrine of Iria Flavia, the symbol of St. James. In the center of the *Mihrab* was a pulpit of ivory, ebony, sandalwood, and other precious inlays, on which rested an enormous jewel-studded volume.

"The Koran," Nardjis whispered. "Those gorgeous mosaics over there are Byzantine, the gift of the Emperor Constantine VII to the Caliph."

A silken prayer mat covered the floor in front of the pulpit. There they knelt, while throngs of people started to pour through every door of the Mosque, filing silently down between the columns.

The service over, the two ladies, escorted by the

eunuchs, slipped out through a small door on the right.

"We shall walk over to the palace and the *Alcázar,*" said Nardjis. "Masrur and Ibrahim will leave us inside the gate, and fetch our horses. We must hurry if we are to get to Dimashk in time for your appointment with the Grand Vizier."

They walked down a fine, broad avenue, the banks of the Guadalquivir on their left, and approached the high stone walls of an enormous palace overlooking the river. "That is the old Roman bridge built in the days of Julius Caesar," and Nardjis pointed to a wide stone bridge, arching across the river on their left. "The statue is of the Virgin Mary, dating from Visigothic times. The road beyond goes to Sevilla."

In front of the palace, a fountain spurted a jet of water one hundred feet into the air, but they circled it to the windward side so as to escape its spray.

"This part of the palace contains the administrative offices. It is pretty much run down, and is scarcely used except for the hall of justice where Prince al-Mamun holds audiences twice a week to hear the grievances of the people.... At least, he is supposed to do it," Lady Nardjis added in an undertone to Marilú. "He's not very popular among the townfolk in Córdoba, as I've told you."

A captain showed them through the Hall of Justice, and its adjoining waiting rooms, magnificent, but heavy and somber in appearance in comparison with the beautiful rooms of Medina al-Zahra. The Caliph's throne stood at the far end, of massive bronze and gold. The room was in semi-darkness, with heavy silken draperies covering the windows and doors. The captain offered to have the curtains drawn open, but Nardjis told him that they had little time to spare and would take just a hurried glimpse of *Dar al-rawda.*

She explained to Marilú that *Dar al-rawda* was the House of the Flower Garden, the *seraglio* itself.

"It is vacant now that the Prince has sent his family to Almodóvar del Río and is living in Medina al-Zahra, but we might just glance at a few of the rooms, and I want to show you the harem so that you can see how the Caliph's household lived when the Caliph had hundreds of wives and concubines. King al-Mutamid's father, you know, had eight hundred women in his harem."

The palace, dark and empty, looked dingy beside the beauty of Medina al-Zahra, but Marilú could see that it was indeed magnificent and enormous, with vast halls, long corridors, and great doors of bronze and iron. They went upstairs to a suite of at least a hundred rooms surrounding three sides of a central patio.

"This is the harem. There is the latticed corridor from which the Caliph's wives could see the visitors to the palace without themselves being seen. What do you think of it?"

"I think it's perfectly disgusting," exclaimed Marilú. "I don't see why any man should have all those wives and mistresses, and it must be like slavery to share a husband or lover with so many other women. And the place must be nothing but a lying-in hospital, with a baby born every day, babies and children yowling and crying all over the place, and the women fighting and screaming. I think it's horrible."

Nardjis laughed: "Well, it must have been noisy—except when the Caliph was there, for you remember I told you that the women and children have to be absolutely silent when the master of the house is home. And there wouldn't be a baby every day. Even the most virile Caliph never had more than perhaps fifteen to thirty babies a year. The ways of women are governed by the moon, you know, and there is no way of telling when a woman's moon is most auspicious."

"Well, I still think that a harem is disgusting, and am glad the Grand Vizier doesn't have one. Let's leave."

They followed the captain downstairs.

"Let's just step out onto the balcony, where we can get a fine view of the garden," said Lady Nardjis.

They did so, and Marilú could see a vast garden, much larger than that at Medina al-Zahra, but lacking the rolling hills and distant mountains in the background, and the forest preserve, that gave the latter place its charm. There was a fine view of the Guadalquivir, though, and Marilú could see how the great river wound around the town, bordered by many fine mansions, and disappearing around a bend in the distance. The garden itself, she admitted, would have been the most beautiful she had ever seen, had she not known Medina al-Zahra. She would like to have walked down its shady paths, beside the rippling brook, but was eager to keep the rendezvous with her beloved.

They left the balcony and followed the captain to the courtyard, where Masrur and Ibrahim awaited them, the four steeds pawing the ground impatiently.

Thanking the captain, Lady Nardjis and Marilú doomed their riding cloaks and mounted their stallions, the two eunuchs hastening to mount their own steeds, ready to accompany them on the road to *al-Dimashk.*

"We can make better time, my lady," suggested Masrur, "if we leave Córdoba by the Amir gate and take the road to Dimashk, for we can canter and gallop all the way."

The women spurred their horses, and cantered through the gate, across the plain and up into the neighboring foothills. On a peak to their left, they could see the turrets of a castle in the far distance.

"That is *al-Rusafa*, one of the palaces of the Caliph," said Nardjis. "But *al-Dimashk* is much more beautiful, and its garden is out of this world."

They passed a number of small villas along the road and, further on, several large country houses that Lady Nardjis referred to as *almnnias*, all beautiful with flowers and landscaped trees and shrubbery. Even the fields were gay with blue gentian and lavender growing between the rows of wheat. After a short ride they arrived breathless at the gate of *al-Dimashk.*

CHAPTER 14

The palace of *al-Dimashk* was perched on the top of a steep hill, giving a broad view of the rolling countryside between there and Córdoba, and of the mountains to the north. The mansion itself, snuggled among the green foliage, was a veritable jewel, smaller than the palace at Medina al-Zahra, but just as perfect in its own way. The walls were a pale yellow stucco. Tall and delicate marble columns, topped by alternate horseshoe and clover-leaf Moorish arches, supported the tile roof.

The riders dismounted, and Lady Nardjiš and Marilú entered the palace, greeted at the door by a towering eunuch and two female attendants.

"I'm ravenous," exclaimed Marilú, exhilarated from the ride.

"Well you're also filthy," Nardjis laughed. "It's to the *hammam* for both of us. And then to lunch, and your rendezvous with the Grand Vizier."

As the two attendants led them to the *hammam* along a corridor paved with bright mosaics, Nardjis said that the Grand Vizier would be waiting for Marilú in a pavilion in the center of a boxwood maze.

"I must leave you at the entrance to the maze, and you must find your own way to the pavilion. I am warning you that it is a labyrinth, and you will find it almost impossible to unravel the many confusing paths. The Grand Vizier has forbidden me to give you any hints, except that I am to translate the inscription you will find engraved over the entrance to the maze: 'Follow Your Heart.' That is all it says, and I pray that your heart does not lead you astray."

"Follow my heart," thought Marilú. "What in the world can that mean?"

The *hammam* was by no means as elaborate nor as elegant as that of Medina al-Zahra, but there was an abundance of hot water, and the two attendants, after helping their mistresses to disrobe, scrubbed them vigorously and shampooed their hair until it was silky soft.

"There is no pool here," said Nardjis, "but if you lie down on this bench, on your stomach, you will be given a massage that will relax your muscles, and make you feel like a new woman."

"Doesn't the Grand Vizier approve of the old woman? "Marilú laughed, as she relaxed on the marble bench, while her attendant proceeded to knead and pound the muscles of her back.

She found herself facing a long low window that gave a perfect view of the garden below. She could hardly contain her excitement as she saw, in the middle of the garden, surrounded by a high boxwood maze, the rounded dome of a small marble pavilion. She raised herself on her elbows, and peered eagerly. out of the window, not an easy thing to do, but by this time the *masseuse* had finished kneading Marilú's neck and shoulders and was busy pounding her waist and buttocks.

"Oh, if only I can discover the way to the pavilion," thought Marilú. "Follow your heart? Well, it must mean that I should go as straight as I can toward the pavilion in the center of the labyrinth, because that's certainly where my heart will lead me."

At the entrance to the maze, there were two possible paths, one to the left, one to the right. In her mind's eye, Marilú took the path to the right, then followed the boxwood aisles, twisting and turning.

Wherever she had a choice—to the left, to the right, or straight ahead—she chose the path that seemed to lead closest to the pavilion in the center. "Follow your heart," she repeated to herself. In disgust, she found herself back at the entrance where she had started from.

"I guess I better try the other path—to the left," she thought. "Oh, I know—'Follow your heart' must mean to take the path to the left whenever I can. My heart is on the left side," and by this time it was pounding so hard that there was no mistaking the signals it was giving.

Her eyes eagerly traced the path down the long aisles of boxwood. At many turns, there was no choice; the path turned willy-nilly to the right. But at other junctions, there was a clear choice—left, or right, or sometimes straight ahead. At each such point, her eyes took the leftward turn. Delightedly, suddenly, her eyes emerged at a little clearing just in front of the marble kiosk. It was none too soon, for her *masseuse* had pushed her head and shoulders down onto the marble slab, and was busy giving the final touches to a vigorous massage.

"Follow your heart! Follow your heart! Follow your heart!" Marilú fairly trilled and thrilled to herself. "Darling, darling, Nardjis! She knew I could see the garden from this bench. Oh, she is a dear!" And Marilú's heart pounded "Follow your heart! Follow your heart!" as the maid perfumed her body and brushed her glistening locks.

Her body fairly glowed, and her eyes sparkled with excitement as she threw her arms around Lady Nardjis and gave her a great big hug and a kiss.

"Goodness! What's this for?" laughed Nardjis.

But perhaps she knew, for she looked just as pleased as her companion. Nardjis was attired again in her long riding costume which had been brushed clean while the ladies were being bathed. But Marilú was given only the filmiest of blouses and pantaloons, covered, however, by a long silk robe for the walk through the garden and maze to the pavilion. A pair of golden sandals, and a golden anklet, bracelet, necklace and earrings completed her costume—simple, but undeniably seductive.

They walked arm in arm down to the garden. As they walked, Lady Nardjis commented: "You probably noticed that in the *tepidarium* the windows came all the way down to the floor. Dimashk is the only place I know where that is true. The *hammam*, of course, is in the basement, as usual, but, because the palace is built on a hillside, one of the bath rooms—the *tepidarium*—has a fine vista overlooking the garden, and yet has complete privacy from the outside."

Marilú nodded. Of course, she had noticed the windows. She certainly had! They walked on, down a flight of marble steps, toward the entrance to the garden—a Roman arch, flanked by a high stone wall that hid all but the tallest trees. Above the arch was an inscription in Arabic characters that Lady Nardjis translated: " 'The perfumed garden for the soul's delight.' "

It was indeed a perfumed garden, and one to delight the saddest soul. Marilú's soul was by no means sad, and never before had she seen such a profusion of flowers or such beauty in a garden or in nature—not even in Medina al-Zahra. The fragrance of jasmine, gardenia, narcissus, roses, hyacinths, lilacs, carnations, magnolia, nenuphars, and other sweet-smelling blooms alternated as they walked down the garden path, blending in an aura of scent that was heady but not cloying. A rippling brook followed them, or crossed the path, or hid among the trees and foliage. The silence was broken only by the gurgling stream, the cooing of doves, and the song of a wood-lark.

It was truly a heavenly garden, "Out of this world," Marilú thought—and her rendezvous! She fairly glowed with excitement.

"I must leave you here," said Nardjis. "Follow your heart, and may it bring you to your heart's desire."

She kissed Marilú on the forehead. They had come to the maze. A eunuch, the very one who had met them at the door to the palace, stood at the entrance, his scimitar unsheathed. He smiled and bowed deeply saluting with a wide sweep of his shining sword.

"Enter, my lady. The Grand Vizier awaits. He came here only a moment ago. You may be sure that no one will disturb you. I shall see to that."

Lady Nardjis left, waving to Marilú as she walked back to the palace. Marilú entered the maze, hesitated but a moment, then took the path to the left. The labyrinth was more forbidding than it had seemed from above. The thick boxwood walls were at least six feet high, and grew so closely that not even a rabbit could have penetrated them. The aisles were about two feet in width, bordered on each side with sweet-smelling herbs and flowers.

One could easily be lost in the confusion of such a labyrinth, and it was frightening to think that, if she had not had the benefit of seeing the maze from above, she might well be lost—perhaps forever. Her heart pounded audibly, but she never hesitated. Wherever the aisles offered her a choice of paths, she resolutely took the one to the left, following the pounding of her eager heart. Then, suddenly, she saw before her a small clearing bordered by white camellias and gardenias and, beyond the clearing, a graceful marble gazebo, its delicate columns covered with myrtle and climbing red roses.

The Grand Vizier was standing in the center of the

gazebo on a thick carpet. Behind him, silken cushions were piled in profusion, forming a soft mattress, in front of which a *sefra*—a silken tablecloth—was stretched out on the floor with trays of viands and glass ewers of beverages.

"I have just arrived. You came quickly, my love."

"I followed my heart," Marilú smiled. "And here I am."

"I have little appetite for anything but you, my dear. But you must be starving after your busy morning in Córdoba. So let us eat and drink, so that my appetite for the sweet—so sweet—dessert will be even more sharpened than it is now. Although Lord knows you have never been more lovely, and I have never wanted you more than I do right now. Sit down beside me, my darling."

"Hearkening and obedience, my lord."

And Marilú sat down among the pillows, facing the Grand Vizier, beaming fondly. They ate almost in silence. No words were needed. They hardly noticed what they ate and drank, although it was not because the food and drink lacked anything in delicacy or variety—cold shrimp, cold duck, endives, asparagus, strawberries, icy-cold water, a rose-scented sherbet and, to end the meal a delicious liqueur whose heady fragrance seemed to fill Marilú's head with a gentle intoxicating warmth. Marilú stood up, swaying dizzily in expectation of what she knew was yet to come.

"I think that liqueur has gone to my head; I'm afraid I'm going to fall," she whispered.

The Grand Vizier rose quickly and caught her in his arms. "That silken robe you are wearing must be very warm; perhaps that's it," he smiled.

"And your silk robe must be awfully hot," Marilú replied.

As he loosened the drawstring of her pantaloons.

Marilú felt the Vizier's lance pressing against her navel.

"There's no time to lie down. I can't wait," he groaned, and clasped her to him. Standing upright, he entered her warm, moist garden and tightened his arms around her. Marilú encircled his hips with her arms and pressed him tightly into her. Soon they were locked in hot embrace, their eager lips and tongues exchanging kisses of untold delight, their nether parts kissing in even greater rapture.

How long they remained thus locked in loving struggle, pushing and wrestling, neither had any idea, until at last, Marilú in heavenly access, swayed dizzily as her paramour let loose a flood of rapturous delight that spouted like a fountain to her very womb.

They stood a moment, still locked in each other's arms.

"Oh, my darling, but it was sweet," sighed Marilú "I do love you. It was so sweet, so wonderful and sweet, just as you said."

The Vizier lifted her in his arms, kissed her fondly, and lowered her beside him, nestled among the pillows. "Tell me all you have seen and done today, my love," he said fondly.

She told him of the ride to Córdoba and of their fine gallop to *al-Dimashk*, of everything Nardjis had shown her in Córdoba, all of which had been wonderful and beautiful but most of all, she said, she had been touched by the fact that she had been able to hear a Christian mass in the very midst of that beautiful Great Mosque.

"We're not so very different, are we?" he asked tenderly. "We Moslems and you Christians–we are all people of the Book. We worship the same God, don't we? Do you find Islam very different from Christianity, my love?"

"The chief difference I find," Marilú answered,

stopping a moment to collect her thoughts, "the chief difference betwen Moslems and Christians is in the matter of Jesus. You believe in Jesus as one of the greatest of God's prophets, but you consider he was the Son of God only in the same sense that we are all children of God. I never could understand what was meant by the Trinity and the Holy Ghost, three Gods in One, although the priests have explained it to me again and again. So that, really, I do not know what the differences are between Christianity and Islam. Although I suppose that there must be very great differences, or wise men would not be forever fighting about it."

The Vizier smiled: "Yes, there are differences. And, although we Moslems, like you Christians, worship the God of love, we have been engaged in a Holy War for over three hundred years to compel Christians and other infidels to embrace the faith of Islam.

"The fate of Christianity and of Islam now hangs in the balance here in Spain. With the generals of Yusuf ibn-Tashfin pressing us from the south, and the forces of our liege lord, King Alfonso VI, bearing down on us and on Tashfin from the north, we are like wheat to be ground between the upper and nether millstones. Yet, in the end, I know,—only God is the Conquerer."

"But why," asked Marilú, "can't you make peace with Tashfin and together submit to Alfonso as the Emperor of all Spain? Or, if you can't make peace with Tashfin, why can't you, my love, flee to Toledo and join your army with that of King Alfonso? I do so hate to think of you facing the hazards of war."

"The Vizier pondered, then replied: "Ibn Hazim, my precious, has written the answer:

A man must do
What he must do;

Some men are false,
Some men are true,
And some men flee
While others fight;
Each man must do
What he deems right.

"Tashfin is the enemy, and I must fight."

Marilú sighed: "But let us, you and I, not be enemies, my love. Let us embrace one another, even if I do not embrace your religion, nor you mine. And she put her arms around the Vizier's waist and kissed him warmly, deeply.

Aroused, he drew her close to him. His hands stroked her hair, her face and shoulders, then slipped down to fondle her creamy white breasts.

They sank down into the pillows again at last, fully satisfied and blissfully content.

"Let us take a short *siesta*, my darling," the Vizier murmured, "here in this garden, safe from prying eyes with only the brook and the doves and songbirds to disturb us. Close your eyes."

He kissed her lids softly, and they were soon sound asleep in each other's arms.

They awakened to the loud cooing of a couple of amorous turtle doves who had ventured into the gazebo, and were rapt in lovemaking right before Marilú's and the Grand Vizier's startled eyes.

"Let us go and do likewise," laughed Marilú. "They're trying to show us how."

"I'm too tired and too lazy, and I don't want any more," replied the Vizier, lying on his back, his manroot belying his words.

Whereupon Marilú leaped upon her lover, pinning him to the ground and inserting his pin where it would do the most good. Thus made secure in her seat upon him, she rode her steed at a canter far more thrilling than any she had enjoyed that morning.

Laughing and gasping, rider and steed pursued the sport, Marilú rising and thrusting her pelvis into his, and twisting her seat tantalizingly in the fast-moving saddle, while the Grand Vizier lay flat on his back and enjoyed himself beyond measure. Up and down, from side to side, they rode, and rolled, the canter quickening to a gallop, and then to a full cavalry charge, until the fair rider, faint from emotion and exertion, slumped down into her still jerking saddle, and enjoyed rapture beyond any in her experience.

The vizier pulled her to him and kissed her until he too was overcome in ecstasy, and a torrent of love spurted upward into Marilú's eager womb. They lay there, exhausted but happy.

"It was such fun, my darling," whispered Marilú. "Thank you, thank you. You are so good to me. And so good *for* me, too," she added. "And, you know, I think this perfumed garden is the most beautiful, most wonderful place I've ever seen. I love it!"

"And I think *your* perfumed garden the most beautiful, the most wonderful I've ever seen," the Vizier responded with a smile. "And I love it!"

"My perfumed garden?" Marilú queried, puzzled.

"Don't you remember the song of songs which is Solomon's, my dear? Where the bridegroom tells the bride: 'A garden enclosed is my spouse, a spring shut up, a fountain sealed. Thy plants are an orchard of pomegranates with pleasant fruits, with camphor and spikenard and saffron, calamus and cinnamon, with frankinsense, myrrh and aloes—a fountain of gardens, a well of living waters, and streams from Lebanon.'"

"Yes, I remember the words, but I never realized what was meant by the garden of the bride. But now

I recall that the bride replies: 'Awake, O north wind, and come blow upon my garden that the spices thereof may flow out. Let my beloved come into his garden and eat his pleasant fruits.' "

"Then you must also remember that the bridegroom answers: 'I am come into garden, my beloved. I have gathered my myrrh with my spice. I have eaten my honeycomb with my honey.' So you see, my love," the Vizier continued, "the garden is one where the only hill is the Mount of Venus, and where the deep valley is a spot of incomparable beauty and delight, a 'well of living waters.' So let me come once again into your perfumed garden, my beloved."

"Ever hearkening and obeying, and with joy and gladness, my master, my love," smiled Marilú drawing the Vizier close to her breast as she lay upon the pillows.

And there followed an interval of unutterable bliss, not plunging and passionate, but laden with sweetness and contentment as the Vizier came once more into the perfumed garden, and both sated themselves to the full with the rapture of their intertwining bodies.

They rested briefly in each other's arms, wholly content, wholly satisfied. Until at last the Vizier whispered in Marilú's ear: "You're marvelous, my love. And now you know why the builder of this palace called this place 'The perfumed garden for the soul's delight.' He knew the song of Solomon and he knew the double meaning of the words. But we must get up now. I have work to do at Medina al-Zahra. . . . I'll race you back to the Dimashk palace."

"No, you won't, you big bully you," Marilú screamed, grabbing him by the arm. "You know I can't possibly run as fast as you. All you want to do is leave me in this labyrinth, so I'll never find my way out. We'll put on our robes, and you will escort me back to the palace like a gentleman. . . . Oh, I do love you so, my—my stallion! I'll tell you what we can do, my love—I'll race you back to Medina al-Zahra on horseback."

"A good idea," responded the Vizier, as they walked back together down the narrow aisles of the maze, arm in arm. "You may very well beat me at that. Your stallion is as fast as mine, and will be carrying less weight. We'll see. I really do have a lot to do at Medina al-Zahra. The news is not good. I'll tell you more about it tonight. A courier will be racing back from Tashfin's headquarters and I'll have the latest word."

The Vizier seemed rapt in thought, and they walked on in silence, taking comfort from each other's closeness. The eunuch greeted them at the entrance to the maze, bowing majestically, and saluting them with a sweep of his scinitar: "I trust you have enjoyed your *siesta*, my master and my mistress."

"We have, Yahia, we have indeed," the Grand Vizier responded abstractedly, and they walked on through the garden to the palace, where they parted with many a backward glance.

Marilú's maid hastened to dress her in the riding habit and burnous she had worn when she arrived, but by the time Marilú reached the vestibule of the palace, there was the Grand Vizier ready to leave, while the two stallions, held by a groom, were pawing the ground impatiently.

"We'll trot to the gate, side by side, and then we'll race straight down the road, and the Devil take the hindmost," shouted the Grand Vizier as fiercely as he could to his laughing partner.

They took off at the same moment, leaving the guards at the gate agape with astonishment, as the two stallions burst forward into a fast gallop. The hood of Marilú's burnous fell backward, and her long hair streamed wildly behind her in the wind. She was leading now, but by no more than a horse's length as the Vizier's pure white stallion strove to overtake Marilú's black one. On they galloped at full speed, scattering chickens, ducks, sheep and pigs, and startled peasants, as they sped down the road, neither gaining an advantage but Marilú's charger still maintaining its one-length lead.

The outer gate of Medina al-Zahra, with its welcoming statue of the smiling Lady Zahra on top, loomed in the distance. The Grand Vizier, in male pride, spurred his mount on with all his strength. His stallion, seeming to gather new vigor from his master's efforts, spurted forward, drew even with Marilú's and then rushed on to lead its rival by two full lengths as they came to a halt at the gate.

"You ride well, my dear," panted the Grand Vizier, both of them breathless and exhilarated from the ride. "In fact, I've never known a woman who was your equal. You amaze me, and delight me, more and more every day. But, easy now, through the gate. You must keep your mount down to a trot across the esplanade and through the inner gate.

The Vizier wondered, as he spoke, whether his companion was horsewoman enough to control her steed and bring it to a trot after the excitement of the extended gallop. He looked at her proudly, affectionately, as she showed her mastery, and they trotted briskly across the esplanade, side by side.

How lovely she looked, despite the bulk of her riding habit! The long burnous hung down gracefully over her legs and around the cantle of her saddle. Her hair, in glorious blond disarray, streamed behind her like a golden pennon. The Vizier's heart was hopelessly enmeshed in those tangled tresses, and he decided that tonight, of all nights, he must unburden himself to his love.

Two grooms were standing within the inner gate to take their mounts, while Nardjis, Shamsi and Ourda waited eagerly to greet their returning master and mistress. The Grand Vizier hastily but fondly took his leave and disappeared down the palace corridor to the administrative quarters.

Lady Nardjis embraced Marilú affectionately: "Well, I see you found your way through the maze, my dear. I'm so happy for you. And for Ahmad too. I've loved him since he was a child, and I've never seen him so utterly happy. And I know.... But you must be tired, my dear. And you must get a nap as soon as we can get these dusty clothes off you, so that you will be fresh and ready for this evening's entertainment.

CHAPTER 15

The many events of the long day in Córdoba and al-Dimashk had proved to be exhausting, for it was not until evening that Marilú awoke from her nap, rested but dishevelled. Ourda was there to await her pleasure. She handed her mistress a long cotton robe, and led her to the *hammam* where they found Lady Nardjis and Shamsi chatting in the disrobing room.

The *hammam* proved relaxing and refreshing as always, and the garments Marilú was given after her bath were snowy white, the long robe worn over her blouse and pantaloons being of a heavy iridescent white taffeta, sparsely but richly embroidered with gold. Lady Nardjis too was garbed entirely in white, and so were Shamsi and Ourda as the four prepared to leave the *hammam* for the Salon of the Caliphs.

The simple white was most becoming, and a happy change from the brilliant colors they had worn on all previous occasions. Nardjis reminded her that this was the doing of Ziryab the Persian, whose influence on customs and costumes in al-Andaluz seemed all-pervasive.

"Ziryab laid down the rule," Nardjis said, "that, each year, after the twenty-first day of the second month of *Rabi'a*, anybody who is anybody must be dressed in white. To wear colored garments, except in the wintertime, just isn't done."

She smiled: "You see, we women are not only the slaves of our masters, but of a man whom we never knew, and who died over two hundred years ago. . . . Well, I must admit I like the change, and you look lovely in that long white robe, set off only by the golden embroidery that matches your earrings, bracelets, anklet, and necklace. And that sapphire ring you always wear, that matches the deep blue of your eyes—a lovely ensemble. I really think that white does more for you blonds than for us brunettes."

"Thank you. You are always so good for my morale," said Marilú.

She reflected that the ring, a heavy gold band, carved in the form of an angel holding in her hands a brilliant sapphire, had been given to her by her husband Gonzalo. Had she been faithful to him? Not merely faithful in body—she felt that, as a slave, she was forced to submit to her master and was absolved of carnal sin—but had she been faithful in mind and soul? Had she been an angel, as Gonzalo had whispered to her when he gave her the ring?

She had not, and it weighed heavily on her conscience. An unfaithful wife, a fallen angel—not that she had ever for one moment ceased to love Gonzalo, her husband and the father of her children, but that she could not help loving Ahmad as well, and with all her heart and body and soul. A mortal sin, she knew!

It was the hour of vespers. She excused herself from her companions, saying she wanted to be alone for a few minutes. Returning to the disrobing room, she knelt beside one of the marble benches. As always, at that hour, she recited beneath her breath the Lord's prayer and what she remembered of the vesper service. As she came to the *Confiteor*—"I confess to almighty God, to blessed Mary ever virgin . . ."—she struck her breast three times and repeated: "*Mea culpa, mea culpa, mea maxima culpa,*" beseeching the Virgin Mary, and Michael, John, Peter, Paul, and all the saints, to pray to the Lord God for her. She wiped a tear from her eye, comforted by prayer, and rejoined her companions in the vestibule of the *hammam.*

As they walked down the corridor, Marilú, to erase from her mind the problems that were troubling her, asked Nardjis brightly: "Are we the only ones who ever use the *hammam*? Doesn't the Grand Vizier ever use it?"

"Oh, yes indeed! It is one of his pleasures, and the only thing that relaxes him after a long day's work. He uses it every morning while you are still asleep, and every evening, as soon as you and I have finished, and while we are still in the dressing room. He almost invariably has a steam bath and massage, but he does not loll for an hour in the pool, nor does he take another hour to have his hair brushed and set and get himself attired for the evening. So he is always ready to receive you in the Salon of the Caliphs." Nardjis smiled as they entered the great doors "And there he is."

Attired all in white, a heavy white silk robe embroidered with gold, a white silk sash, a white turban bearing an enormous diamond, white and gold sandals, the Grand Vizier had never looked more majestic nor handsomer, Marilú thought as she bowed gracefully, then placed her arm in his as he led her back to the cushions at the far end of the great hall.

The orchestra was already seated, the women smiling at Marilú as she and her escort took their places. They were not hidden from view this time but, instead, two large screens had been placed together at one side of the room, their purpose not revealed to Marilú until the evening meal was over.

The meal was served as usual, silently and quickly, by smiling attendants, as slim and graceful in their scanty costumes as the dancing girls Marilú remembered from her first evening with the Grand Vizier—to quicken his desires, she thought, not that the Grand

Vizier's desires ever had to be aroused by extraneous entertainment.

The meal was delicious, and superabundant—cold *hors d'oeuvres*, a tasty stew of calves' trotters and tripe, a splendid roast capon served with asparagus and a chestnut stuffing, a compote of ginger and cumquats with crisp ladies' fingers, and the inevitable ice-water, sherbet, nuts and fruit. The ride had added zest to Marilú's always healthy appetite, and she ate rather more than usual.

"I am afraid we serve rather a skimpy meal here," the Vizier remarked. "My companions would be dismayed to know how I am starving you. They always have at least ten courses, and wine and liqueurs as well. But I find that, when I am working hard and have no time for hunting or sports, I simply cannot eat more than a light meal. I trust you don't mind."

"My no means," Marilú replied. "I've never eaten so well in all my life. Everything is delicious, and there is always more than I could possibly eat. Besides, I don't want to stuff myself, and be too languid to enjoy the evening's entertainment.

She gave her partner a smile that was all warmth and affection, and that turned into a soft laugh as she saw the Vizier's heavy robe rise perceptibly below his sash.

He clapped his hands. The tables and trays were cleared away immediately, leaving only the baskets of fruit and the crystal decanters and goblets for the Grand Vizier and his companion to refresh themselves during the evening's entertainment. The music, which had played softly all during the meal, changed to a slow march, practically a dirge, and from behind the screens to the left trooped a score of dancing girls who paraded solemnly across the room in front of the quicksilver pool.

To Marilú's amazement and amusement, they were

covered from head to toe in long and bulky white burnouses, their pretty faces peeking out from the folds of their hoods, looking as ridiculous as Shamsi and Ourda had looked when they were wrapped in their long robes for the trip to the market-place in Medina-Zahra.

"Cocoons, all of them," thought Marilú. "Crazy cocoons! They look like a parade of mourners at a funeral. How silly! And especially for dancing girls."

The row of dancers, still all facing to the right, came to a halt. From behind the screen came another figure, similarly attired, and Marilú recognized the sparkling eyes of the lovely dancer who had so entranced her the first night in the great hall. Like the chorus of dancers, she too walked solemnly across the room and came to a halt, still facing to the right, in the center of the room.

Suddenly the music changed, its tempo shifting from *largo solenne* to *allegro*. The dancers about-faced, and pranced across the room from right to left. Marilú shrieked with astonishment, then burst out laughing. They were naked! Or almost so, only a thin black ribbon of a girdle around their waists helping to hold up the costumes on the other side. The costumes were nothing but half-shells, covering the dancers completely when they faced to the right, and uncovering them just as completely when they turned around to the left.

"Like oysters on the half-shell," thought Marilú. "So luscious on one side, and just big heavy shells on the other. How beautiful they all are, so young and slim, and all looking so mischievous and delighted at the trick they've played on us."

The dancers, including the petite *prima ballerina*, pranced gaily back toward the screen in time with the music. They turned again and pirouetted across the room, looking even more ridiculous and amusing as, at every turn, they displayed first their heavy cloaks and hoods, and then their shining naked bodies.

Back toward the screen they danced, and then, one by one, as they came to the screen, they discarded their burnouses which remained stiffly upright on the floor, while they whirled and turned into the center of the room, now altogether naked save for the tiny black ribbon that encircled their waists and loins.

The burnouses then suddenly came to life, and headless and topless, chased after the dancing girls who dodged them in graceful whirls and turns. As the headless burnouses chased their owner around the floor, Marilú could see that they were each supported by a child in a short white dress and slippered feet.

"They certainly could not be more than eight or nine years old," thought Marilú, "and they must have slipped out from behind the screen when the dancers left their burnouses on the floor."

The merry chase continued, the topless burnouses racing after the whirling dancers in a sort of game, while Marilú and the Grand Vizier laughed until the tears fell down their cheeks. The rest of the audience were similarly convulsed, although those who were watching from behind had missed the shock of witnessing the hooded mourners transformed suddenly into naked dancers.

The children and the burnouses disappeared. The music became slower and more sensuous and the row of almost naked dancers, the *prima ballerina* in the center, undulated suggestively, their thighs and lower legs, their hips, arms and graceful hands, their firm, young breasts waving from side to side in time with the music. One by one they whirled around the tiny woman in their center, embraced her longingly, then danced off the stage and disappeared behind the screen.

Finally, only the *prima ballerina* was left alone in front of Marilú and the Grand Vizier. She approached sinuously, tantalizingly, coming to a stop immediately in front of the watching pair, and so close that they could smell the heady fragrance of her perfume. Her smooth olive skin, scarlet lips and pearly teeth, firm breasts, rounded thighs, and broad hips beneath the slimmest of waists, her long neck, shining dark eyes and jet-black hair, made her what Marilú knew to be the ideal of Arabian womanhood—even to the rounded depth of her navel and the prominence of her *mons veneris*, covered but by no means concealed by the black silk ribbon around her loins.

The dancer, feet together, swayed voluptuously before them, her arms and hands waving with snake-like sinuosity as she extended them at full length, upwards or sidewards, then clutched suggestively at her breasts or buttocks or drew them down her sides and loins in passion-filled caresses. As the tempo of the music quickened, so did her movements, until at last her pelvis was jerking up and down in fervid abandon.

Marilú could contain herself no longer. She reached for her veil, heaved a deep sigh and cast upon her companion a look of such utter longing that her meaning was unmistakable. The Grand Vizier, equally moved, clapped twice and dancer and audience disappeared. The lights were snuffed, the great doors closed, and Marilú and the Vizier were left alone in semi-darkness. They rose, panting heavily, and the Vizier seized his fair companion in his arms.

"Not here. Not here, my love," Marilú gasped.

The Vizier lifted her in his arms as though she were a child and strode to the alcove, their lips pressed firmly together. In their haste they each grabbed and pulled the drawstrings of their partner's pantaloons, and the Vizier hurled Marilú down upon the bed and was immediately on top of her and into her, plunging and pushing.

Overflowing with the intensity of their mutual passion, Marilú suddenly felt herself shaken by a tremor such as she had never before experienced. The bed—the very earth seemed to be shaking and floating away from under her. Her whole body, and that of her paramour, dissolved and vanished. Nothing was left—nothing but manroot and woman-sheath, white-hot and flaming, one irresistibly piercing, the other closely enveloping.

The truth burst upon her with the force of supernatural revelation, a glorious all-encompassing revelation—for the first time she found herself gripping, squeezing, pressing the great manroot within her, with every muscle from the very lips to the deepest depths, constricting, holding, embracing, passionately kissing the precious treasure she held within her.

She gloried in the revelation of her new-found art, and now consciously bent all her efforts to the sweet, sweet task, squeezing the beloved manroot with the full length of her enveloping sheath while with her lips she held him prisoner in such tight captivity that not a drop of his vital force could escape her grip. Gradually, her body and that of her lover began again to materialize. Arms, hands, thighs, calves, buttocks, breasts, necks, heads and, above all, their straining lips, mouths and tongues, came back to life, tossing and writhing in passionate embrace, and with an incandescent heat that she had never before dreamed possible.

Her lover too was overcome by this strange new passion. "My God! he screamed. "I have never loved, nor been loved, like this before. You are killing me!"

Marilú could stand no more. Her aching sheath released its grip and was at once inundated to overflowing with a torrent of love, hot and burning, and oh, so satisfying. Lover and beloved sank down into each other's arms, still joined together, utterly exhausted, completely satisfied, and divinely content.

"Oh my very dearest," the Vizier panted, "you have never loved me like this before. It has been Paradise on earth. My sweetest sweet, my adored, my beloved, I do love you so!"

"And I you. You have filled me so full of ecstasy. You have made me lie down in green pastures, you have led me beside the still waters, you have restored my soul, your rod and your staff they comfort me, my cup runneth over."

The words of her favorite psalm had come to her mind naturally, taking on new meaning as she expressed her inmost thoughts to her lover, with no intention, no idea of sacrilege or parody. Nor did the Vizier, religious and devout as he was, see any impropriety in this use of words, familiar to them both since childhood. In its new context, the beautiful language of the Holy Book expressed exactly what he knew his companion felt deep within her heart, and which he wholly reciprocated.

After what seemed an eternity of tender bliss in each other's arms, the lovers drew apart. The Grand Vizier then seated himself upon the bed. "Come here, my love. Sit down here. Upon my lap. Like that. So that I can hold you close, and talk to you in whispers—for what I have to tell you is so sweet, so intimate, that I wish to whisper it only into your pearly ears, so that not even the air around us can know what I am saying."

Marilú snuggled close to her lover, hanging on his every word.

"You must know, you cannot fail to know," he whispered, "that I love you. With all my heart, with all my soul, with all my being, I do adore you, and you only. I want you for my wife, my only wife, heart of my heart, soul of my soul, flesh of my flesh. I cannot ask you now to marry me, and for two reasons. So you must not say now whether you will or won't. Some day—and soon, I trust—if Allah so wills, we shall be joined together as man and wife.

"But there are two reasons, yes, three reasons, why I cannot ask you now. Many Moslems, you know, have married Christians. Abd al-Aziz, the son of Musa, the conqueror of Spain, took as his wife the fair Queen Egilón, widow of his vanquished enemy, King Rodrigo. The Sultana Aurora, who became the wife of al-Rumaikiya, had entered his harem as a Christian slave and was his favorite concubine—your case will be the same as hers, if Allah so disposes. And another Aurora, as rosy and fair as her name, was a Christian, a Basque, who became the wife of the Caliph al-Hakim II, and, so we are told, the lover of the conqueror al-Mansur.

"But all these women, and there were many more, before they could become the wives of Moslems, had to embrace the faith of Islam—not renounce their belief in Jesus Christ nor in the Virgin Mary, but only to believe that there is only one God and that Mohammed, upon whom be the benediction of Allah, is his Prophet.

"That is one reason why I cannot ask you now to marry me, but I believe that it would truly be no obstacle, so let me get on to the other two reasons that may bar our path.

"In the first place, the Marqués de Clavijo is still alive. My outposts and my couriers have kept me informed of his whereabouts, and he is now at Alarcos, not more than thirty or forty leagues to the north of here, in command of the southern marches of the Kingdom of León and Castilla.

"He is charged with seeing that the northern provinces of King al-Mutamid, who, as you know, pays tribute to the King of Spain, remain loyal to the leige lord, Alfonso VI. This is in preparation for the ultimate struggle between the invader, Yussuf ibn-Tashfin, and the Emperor of Christian Spain, for King Alfonso was defeated once by Tashfin and narrowly escaped being slaughtered with all his army. He is determined not to let that happen again, and he is aware of Tashfin's presence, with his advancing armies, in al-Andaluz. Yet I doubt very much that his spies have kept him as fully informed as we are with our couriers and outposts throughout the south of Andalucía.

"Now, I realize, my love, that so long as your husband lives, you cannot marry me. Neither your faith nor mine would allow it and I cannot take as a wife one who would be so false as to break her marriage vows. So long as you are my slave, you cannot be held to blame for what you do, but you cannot be my wife while the Marqués de Clavijo lives. But in these troubled times, no man can be sure today what fate the morrow may have in store for him. And, if God so wills that your husband shall die, then do I intend to ask you to be my wife. You may be sure, my love, that I shall not knowingly be the instrument of his death, for our marriage—if we marry—must not be polluted by his blood on my hands."

Marilú felt grateful to the Grand Vizier for raising and resolving the problem that had been uppermost in her mind. She burned to have the Grand Vizier for her own, yet she had never ceased to love her husband, and her Christian faith was too deeply embedded in her conscience for her ever to contemplate a bigamous marriage.

"And the third reason, my love," the vizier continued, "is that a sword of Damocles is suspended above my head. The next few days—at most a week or two—will tell when it will fall, whether I shall die in battle and be transported to join my ancestors in Paradise, or whether I shall enjoy Paradise on earth with you. God only knows, and I cannot ask you to be my bride until I know the answer."

"Oh, my beloved," begged Marilú, "none of us knows where we shall be tomorrow, but do not, I beseech you, speak of death. What will be will be, but I cannot, do not want to think of you as dead."

"No, my love. No more do I—not while I have you to look forward to, if God so wills. But I can tell you this: I would rather die as a lion than live as a donkey, and if Tashfin conquers al-Andaluz, we shall be no more than beasts of burden for our conquerors.

"Now I must tell you," the Vizier continued, "our couriers have brought us news this afternoon of the movements of Tashfin's troops. They are under the command of his greatest general, Sirr ben-Abu Bakr, no relation, by the way, to the Black Vizier who is descended from ben-Bakr, the first Caliph of Islam. The Emir Sirr is probably descended from slaves of the *banu* Bakr, the Bakr tribe, and has taken their surname. But a great general he is, perhaps the greatest in the world today.

"His forces are encamped at Ecija, just nine leagues to the south of us. It is gentle, rolling country—the *campiña*. You and I, my love could ride the distance in a day, but great armies move slowly, and General Sirr has with him the most enormous catapults, the heaviest battering rams, the greatest engines of war that have ever been built in the history of mankind. These will slow him down. And there is the Río Genil, as well as several minor streams, for him to cross before he can get to the banks of the Guadalquivir. And at each stream, even though they are no more than *arroyos*, our troops can harry him by night, and further delay his passage. We should be able to delay him for at least a day or two at the Genil River—we don't dare deploy our troops in force that far away from our base—and it could be a week, perhaps two weeks, before he can reach the walls of Córdoba. And he won't dare come to Medina al-Zahra until Córdoba is razed to the ground.

"But it is neither the weakness of the fortifications of Córdoba, nor the strength of his armies, nor the power of his engines of war, that are the greatest dangers. Our cavalry is the equal of Tashfin's in skill and courage, if not in numbers. Our walls and gates are the stoutest in all al-Andaluz, and our bowmen the best in Spain. Protected by the castellations and turrets of our walls, they can shoot down Tashfin's men as fast as they can be brought to man the catapults. And we can pour down molten lead by the cauldronful upon their engines of war. So that, even though they use the stoutest oaks from the forest of the Guadalquivir in the battering rams which they bring up from Ecija, the walls of Córdoba-and the walls of the *Alcázar* and the *al-Kazaba* within the city walls—can withstand the assault as they have withstood other assaults for centuries.

"No, our walls and gates will hold. It is the enemy within the gates that I fear most. The populace of Córdoba is so rebellious under the governorship of Prince al-Mamun—in fact the people of Sevilla and of all the other towns in the Kingdom of al-Mutamid are so discontent under the rule of the *banu*-Abbad tribe—that we cannot be sure that our gates will not be flung open by some traitor from within. Our soldiers are unsafe in the very streets of Córdoba, and our water supply and food supplies may well be cut off by the very people we are protecting from the enemy. We shall be fighting, to tell the truth, in hostile territory.

"But that is to paint too black a picture. Only God

knows what the fate of battle may be, and all I can say is that Prince al-Mumun and the Black Vizier and I shall fight to the death, if need be.

"But today we do not know whether the Emir Sirr intends to attack us here in Córdoba, or whether he will march on to Sevilla. Ecija is about midway between the two cities, and the road is equally good in either direction—West to Sevilla or North to Córdoba. Our walls are stouter; on the other hand, King al-Mutamid's army in Sevilla is greater than ours in Córdoba. So, until the die of battle is cast, we shall not know what fate has in store for us. And, I, my darling, cannot ask you to become my bride so long as your husband lives, and so long as the outcome of the war against the *Almorávides* remains undecided."

"I tremble, my love, to think of you waiting so bravely for the call to arms," Marilú sighed. "Come to my arms, my darling, and comfort me. I need you so."

Marilú flung off her robe and clasped her arms around the Vizier's neck. The Vizier gently lifted her from his lap, threw off his cloak, and drew her to him on the bed. He pulled Marilú's right leg over his left, shoulder, and placed her other leg between his thighs. In that position, as close to one another as two human beings can be, he pierced her pulsing flower with his manroot and plunged it home. She grasped him, and he her, both struggling to make the close contact ever closer. Marilú pressed her lips to his, and strove to make her tongue penetrate as deeply into his mouth as he had penetrated her below.

She felt his strong manroot reach her womb and then, imprisoned within her as far as it would go, she constricted her vulva to prevent her precious captive from escaping. Her inner muscles rippled back and forth, squeezing him in the most rapturous of kisses.

"My God!" the Vizier groaned. "You are a *kabbázah* such as I have never dreamed of. I can't stand it any longer. No, don't stop, my darling. I love it. Kiss me below as I shall kiss you above."

And he plunged his tongue ever deeper into her ravished mouth, at the same time lunging and plunging, grinding and churning his pelvis into hers, his manroot seeking the new pleasures it had discovered in the raptures her newly-found arts gave him.

"Oh, my darling," cried Marilú, her ecstasy blending with his. "It is more than I can bear. Oh, my God!"

The last was uttered as she felt her lover pierce some secret place inside her. Her thigh between his thighs pressed its soft inside against his firm scrotum and caressed it as he plunged and churned. Her other leg, over his shoulder, seemed to open up new places within her for his great rod to probe.

"His battering ram," she thought, "has battered down my gates, and I have opened them up to him from within. But I have him captive, and he can't escape me. And I shall squeeze him to death with love."

She increased the pressure of her sheath upon his manroot, glorying in the new-found strength that Nardjis, dear Nardjis, had taught her.

"Oh, my God! my God! I can't hold out any longer!" she screamed aloud.

With relief, she let loose her hold, and shook convulsively in a violent frenzy as a volcando of hot flowing lust exploded from his loins and invaded her inmost depths.

"Oh, my love, you are wonderful. Hold me to you. Don't let me go," she sighed, panting and gasping.

She lifted her leg from his shoulder and placed it along and over his left leg, her other leg still between his thighs, and the two of them still linked in sweet embrace.

"I'd like to stay like this," the Vizier said, "from now till morning."

"With you inside me? I couldn't stand it. We'd

never get to sleep," Marilú protested. "Look, I feel it already growing inside me. Oh, my God, how can you? It's moving around like some wild thing. It's getting bigger and bigger. No, I won't let you do it again. You can't. I won't. Oh, dear God! Please do."

The Vizier rolled her over on her back, still inside her, and thrusting furiously, up and down, around and around, his sword became more and more piercing and plunged to its hilt within her sheath. Marilú churned and rolled, gasping and groaning, until, in ecstasy, she bit his shoulder, sinking her teeth into its sinews until he screamed.

"You vixen you!" he exclaimed.

The sharp prick of her teeth acted as a spur that caused him to redouble his bucking and plunging, and he groaned and gasped as Marilú moaned and sobbed beneath him. They heaved in violent ecstasy until Marilú, clutching him desperately, shoved against his loins in a paroxysm of passion that left her too exhausted to maintain the constriction of her sheath. A torrent flowed into her vitals in a mighty thrust from her still plunging lover. The thrust brought on a wave of wild convulsions that stirred her very being, wave after wave.

"I'm drowning," she cried. And with that, she collapsed, limp and exhausted beneath the full weight of her lover who lay panting and moaning above her.

It was some time before either had the strength to disengage. Then, lovingly, he removed his weight from his partner's gleaming body, kissed her fondly on her tight-closed eyelids, and murmured: "If I should die tomorrow, my own dear heart, I shall die content. I shall have known such love as I have never known before, complete and consummate. Let us sleep now, my precious, for we do not know what the morrow holds for us."

"Don't speak of dying, my love, for we have only

begun to live. Let's sleep, my dear, and may you sleep with the angels," Marilú whispered, using an expression meaning "Happy dreams," but that carried with it unsuspected premonitions of what the next days might bring.

CHAPTER 16

It was not yet daybreak. The small alcove was lit with the yellowish light of six oil lamps in sconces on the walls. Marilú opened her eyes sleepily, started to stretch, then sat up suddenly, sensing that some new and grave turn in events must have taken place since the forebodings voiced by the Grand Vizier on the previous night.

The Grand Vizier, in chain armor and helmet, a scimitar and scabbord buckled to his sash, was talking to Lady Nardjis.

"Just leave the hot tea for Marilú beside the bed, Nardjis, and please wait for me outside. I may have some last-minute instructions to give before I bid you farewell." Turning to Marilú, he added: "Drink that hot tea, my love. I have news for you—whether it is good or bad, Allah alone knows—but I have come to say goodby."

Marilú slipped on her robe and sat upright on the edge of the bed, sipping the tea which seemed to quicken her senses. She listened eagerly: "Please speak, my lord, and tell me all."

The Grand Vizier paced slowly back and forth and quickly outlined the course of events. "The army of General Sirr has been reinforced with new contingents from Africa. The people of the *campiña* are in rebellion and many new recruits have joined the foe. His forces now far outnumber the combined troops of the King in Sevilla and ours in Córdoba and Medina al-Zahra. He has deployed a strong body of troops from Ecija in the direction of Sevilla to cut off any possible aid from that direction. His main force has crossed the Genil with most of his engines of war, and is proceeding toward Córdoba with a speed that we had not thought possible. It will still be two or three days before he can arrive at the city gates. We shall deter him by every possible means, and shall make a desperate stand to prevent him from crossing the Guadalquivir and reaching the road to Medina al-Zahra. I must leave for Córdoba. Prince al-Mamun and the Black Vizier are already there. The soldiers will be assembling in the courtyard by daybreak."

Marilú's lips trembled but, recovering quickly, she said bravely: "I shall go with you, my lord, and await the outcome of battle in Córdoba, so that I can be near you."

"Impossible!" The Grand Vizier shook his head.

"Entreat me not to leave thee, or to return from following after thee," Marilú pleaded, "for whither thou goest, I will go . . . thy people shall be my people, and thy God my God."

"No, my dear, that will not be possible. I shall not remain in Córdoba, but shall engage the enemy in battle as far south of Córdoba as I dare. And I shall feel more at ease knowing that you are here in Medina al-Zahra, or that you are following my instructions for flight. Listen closely now to what I have to say."

He spoke quickly, decisively. "Lady Nardjis will remain with you and your two friends, come what may. If General Sirr crosses the Guadalquivir and heads toward Medina al-Zahra, she will take you at once, accompanied by a squad of eunuch guards, to Ghafik and then to Mérida, by a back road through the mountains that will avoid Córdoba and all contact with the *Almorávides*. From Mérida, you can safely proceed to Christian territory and on to Toledo. A captain and forty men will remain behind to defend Medina al-Zahra as long as possible, to prevent the enemy from following you. They can hold out for two days, maybe more, but it will be enough to permit you and your friends to escape with Lady Nardjis. This is essential, for no more cruel foe has ever lived than the *Almorávides*, and I shudder to think what would become of you if you were captured. Not to speak of this magnificent city of Medina al-Zahra which will be razed to the ground, and all its inhabitants murdered.

"The women of the palace have already been evacuated to Sevilla—yes, including your little Ourda and her friend, and the orchestra of musicians. Sixty women in all. Your husband has a sizeable army—perhaps a thousand men—in Alarcos, some thirty-five leagues away, more than a day's ride for even our fastest couriers, for it is a mountainous route and hazardous. I shall despatch two of my most trusted men to ride there and warn your husband of your presence here, and of your imminent danger. I have had Lady Nardjis write a message for him which I know he will heed, but, to convince him that it is not a trap, I must send him that ring you have been wearing. He knows it, doesn't he?"

"Yes," Marilú replied. "He gave it to me."

She slipped the ring off her finger and handed it to the Grand Vizier, her face pale and her hands trembling as she did so. The Vizier went to the arras that shut off the alcove from the Salon of the Caliphs.

"Lady Nardjis."

Nardjis answered immediately: "Yes, my lord."

"Here is the ring. You know what to do. Pray God that my couriers arrive quickly. And please return here, dear friend, after you have given them the letter."

"With love and obedience, my lord." And Lady Nardjis hastened off.

The Grand Vizier let the curtain fall closed, and

then continued: "My couriers will ride all day and part of the night. They will bivouac overnight close to the Christian camp, so that their horses will be fresh and rested by morning. And then, if Allah wills, it should be no more than a two days' ride for your husband and his army to reach here—his cavalry, at least. His wagons and supplies will take longer. I pray in my heart that he may rescue you before the *Almorávides* arrive, but God's will will be done.

"Now, listen carefully. If the Marqués de Clavijo should reach here in time to rescue you and your friends, you must insist on taking Lady Nardjis with you. On my instructions, my company of soldiers here, and my two couriers will flee immediately to Sevilla as soon as they know that the Christians are arriving. Lady Nardjis would be alone if you desert her—alone to be murdered by the *Almorávides*—and she has been my closest friend ever since I can remember. Will you give me your word that you will help her—as she will help you if the *Almorávides* should reach here first—will you promise?"

"I promise, my lord. She too is my dearest friend." Marilú's lips trembled again, and her eyes were wet with tears.

"Then, one more thing. If the Christians do rescue you, you must ask your husband to tear down the inside walls of the dungeon in which you were first confined when you were brought to the palace. Lady Nardjis will show you where the dungeon is.

"They are false walls—no one knows this but I, not even Nardjis; I learned it from my father who, in turn, learned it from his beloved Walládah, daughter of the Caliph al-Mustakfi—within that wall lies *the hidden treasure of Abd ar-Rahman!*

"I have never seen it—no man has ever seen it for over a hundred years—but it is the greatest treasure of jewels and gold and precious objects that has ever been assembled by any monarch in the history of mankind, greater than the treasures of Solomon or of Haroun al-Rashid. I feel that I am right in turning this secret over to you. There is no way, no possible way, for this treasure to be transported to King al-Mutamid in Sevilla. Furthermore, it is not his treasure, not the treasure of the *banu* Abbad, but that of the Umayyads. If the *Almorávides* take Medina al-Zahra, they will destroy the palace and the treasure with it. On the other hand, this kingdom and all within it are subject, under solemn treaty, to our liege lord, King Alfonso. There are no members of the *Umayyad* dynasty living on this earth. If that treasure belongs to anyone, it belongs to the Emperor of Spain, and your husband will take it to him.

"Among the treasures, I am told, there is a small iron casket, conspicuous because it is so inconspicuous—a plain casket of solid iron among all the treasures and caskets of gold and silver. In that casket, there is said to be the *al thu'ban,* the famous dragon necklace that the Caliph Haroun al-Rashid gave to his wife Zubayda and that was said to have cost him ten thousand golden dinars. It was stolen from the palace at Baghdad, brought to al-Andaluz by a merchant, and given by Abd ar-Rahman II to his favorite, al-Shifa. You must ask that that casket be given to you as part of your husband's share of the booty which he will give to King Alfonso. Accept it then, as a gift from me—in memory of me—for I have a premonition that I shall not see you again, that I shall die in battle against the forces of Yussuf ibn-Tashfin."

"You are so kind, so thoughtful, my love," said Marilú, "but pray do not speak of death. Only God knows where and when we are doomed to die, and we must not try to guess his plans. I, at least, cannot think of you as dead. When you leave me, I shall say

'God be with you,' and have no thought save that you will return."

"If God is not with me, my love, then I shall be with God. But tell me—I have given you my instructions, and you will follow them—is there anything more you would like to ask me, any request you wish to make? If so, my love, I am yours to command."

Marilú remained silent for a moment, deep in thought. Then she said: "You have told me, my dear one, of the things that may or may not come to pass, and, against my will, you have forced me to contemplate the possibility that you may never return. So I do have one last request to make of you—a strange request, perhaps. As soon as you have departed, would you have Lady Nardjis give me a glass of wine, drugged with *bhang*, the same as she gave me when first I arrived at the palace. And have my friends Zoraya and Conchita also drugged."

The Grand Vizier listened, puzzled, but remained silent.

Marilú continued: "Then, when we are all sleeping under the influence of the *bhang*, have us bathed to remove every trace of perfume from our hair and bodies. Then have us dressed in the same dirty clothes in which we were attired when we were brought here, and left in the dungeon, handcuffed together, exactly as we were seven days ago, with only Lady Nardjis to attend to us.

"And thank you, my lord and master, for this, and for all you have done for me—for your kindness, your thoughtfulness, your fine companionship, and all your love. Thank you, thank you; I can never be sufficiently grateful to you. And that will be my last request to you—unless and until you return."

The Grand Vizier looked at Marilú with admiration and astonishment. "Oh, wisest of women. Your are remarkable. No wonder you vanquished me in chess—you have looked two moves ahead, while I have thought only of the next move. My mother, the Princess Walládah must have been a woman cast in the same mold as you, beautiful and intelligent beyond compare, passionate and compassionate. Yet you are more than these for, with all your wisdom and all your passion, you can romp as merrily as a child. Through you I have learned what I had never before suspected—that love can be a source of laughter and merriment as well as of rapture and ecstasy.

"Oh, I do love you, my darling, as I have never loved before. You are wonderful, and Allah has been good to me to have given me these seven days of Paradise on earth before he gathers me up to Paradise in Heaven—if that be His will.

"My dear, it shall be as you request. Lady Nardjis will attend to everything. And now, farewell—my *wife*—if that be the will of Allah."

"Goodbye—my *husband*—if God so wills."

They embraced tenderly, both choking with emotion. The Grand Vizier left the room, not daring to look back. He gave his final instructions to Nardjis, waiting outside the alcove, then kissed her forehead affectionately, and departed.

Marilú sank down on the bed and sobbed as she had never sobbed before. It was all over, she knew in her heart of hearts.

From the courtyard below came the clang of men in armor, of horses neighing and pawing the ground, striking the cobblestones with their hooves, of coats of mail and shields, helmets and vizors clashing in the early dawn as the soldiers assembled their gear, eager to depart on what might be their last campaign. They buckled on their scimitars, slung their bows and quivers of arrows over their shoulders, or grasped their spears or lances proudly. A sharp word of command, the clatter of men in armor mounting their steeds, the staccato of horses' hooves, and the column was off and away, down the road—to victory or death.

PART II

THE RESCUE

CHAPTER 17

The two couriers had galloped over thirty leagues in twelve hours, putting up for the night in an olive grove just five leagues south of their destination—Alarcos. They had tied their horses to trees, allowing the animals enough rope so that they could find ample forage and water by the banks of a stream that coursed alongside the grove. The couriers had only their long burnouses to shelter them from the night air, and their *haiks* rolled up under their heads as pillows.

They had slept soundly after their hard ride and, at the first peep of the early morning sun from behind the hills, they were wide awake and ready for the next short leg of their journey. They refreshed themselves in the brook, said their morning prayers, and brushed and curried their waiting horses, then munched on two large loaves of bread they had brought with them in their saddle bags. With a shout, they were up in the saddle again and galloping along the last fifteen miles of road that separated them from the Christian encampment.

The Spanish camp was alive with the bustle of early morning preparations, the stable sergeants supervising the brushing, currying, watering and feeding of the horses, the teamsters washing their supply wagons and readying their harness and gear, the cooks with their great brass pots and cauldrons preparing breakfast for a thousand hungry soldiers, and the soldiers themselves scurrying across the camp ground in one direction or another. Beside the road, the tents of perhaps a hundred camp followers were also stirring with life, the women shaking out the blankets that had been put to such hard use the night before, and busy with their own pots and pans and household utensils.

As the couriers drew nigh, one with a white pennon affixed to his lance as a sign that they were messengers of peace, they were surrounded by four sentries, also on horseback, who approached them with a menacing air.

"A message for the Marqués de Clavijo. Urgent!" shouted the courier with the white flag.

"This way." And two of the sentries, their swords drawn, escorted the couriers to a large red and white striped tent in front of which three officers, seated at a small table, were having their morning meal.

The couriers dismounted and bowed low. "The Marqués de Clavijo?" asked the messenger who had carried the pennon.

"Speaking. What brings you here?" The speaker, a tall, powerfully built man with broad shoulders and a weatherbeaten face, remained seated as he addressed the messenger.

"Your lordship, we come from the palace of Medina al-Zahra with a message from the Lady Nardjis, chatelaine of the palace. Your lady, the Marquesa de Clavijo, and her two companions, the Condesa de Andrade and Condesa de Ayala, are held prisoners in the palace. They await only the arrival of your lordship to be released. It is urgent, your lordship. For, at any time, the troops of General Sirr may arrive before the walls of Medina al-Zahra, and the lives of the *marquesa* and her friends will be in the gravest peril. In proof of what I say, I bring you the ring of the Marquesa de Clavijo."

The courier reached in his pocket and drew out the ring which he handed to the *marqués* with a bow.

Clavijo jumped to his feet at the sight of the ring, which he knew so well, and steadied himself by grasping the table. His two companions were equally moved.

"The letter." The *marqués* spoke brusquely.

The messenger handed the letter to Clavijo, who proceeded to read it aloud for the benefit of his companions. It was clear and precise—an urgent appeal to come immediately to rescue the three ladies, and to bring a sufficient bodyguard, and at least twenty supply wagons to cart off the rich booty contained in the palace.

"How do I know that it is not a trap—that my wife and her companions have not already been slain?" Clavijo demanded.

"You have our lives at stake for that," replied the messenger. "The palace is deserted except for the three ladies, guarded by Lady Nardjis who alone has the keys to the dungeon, and, I believe, a servant or two. I have not seen the ladies, as they are locked in a dungeon in the palace. The Grand Vizier, the Black Vizier, and Prince al-Mamun are in Córdoba. There is a squad of eunuch guards at the gates of the palace, and a company of forty soldiers in the town of Medina al-Zahra to defend the walls of the town.

"If the army of ibn-Tashfin arrives at Medina al-Zahra before your lordship, those soldiers will defend Medina al-Zahra to the death, hoping to give your wife and her friends time to escape by a back road through the mountains, accompanied only by Lady Nardjis and a squad of eunuch guards. If your lordship arrives before the *Almorávides*, the eunuchs and the forty soldiers will flee to Sevilla, leaving no one but the women in the palace, and, down below in the city, those townsfolk who have not already fled.

"The soldiers and guards await only my signal to let them know you are coming. When we arrive at

Monte de la Novia, overlooking the town of Medina al-Zahra, I shall give the signal, and you will yourself see our soldiers and guards flee the palace long before you can get there. They will have a headstart of nearly three leagues. As I say, your lordship, you will have our lives at stake against treachery, and I pray that, when you have rescued your ladies, you release us and let us follow our comrades, for we should be in Sevilla to defend our King al-Mutamid."

"Very well." The Marqués de Clavijo spoke decisively. "Jorge and Roberto, you will get the troops and at least twenty wagons ready to leave as soon as possible. We shall take eight hundred men in all, leaving two hundred here at Alarcos. It will take us more than a day to reach Medina al-Zahra, but we shall camp as far south of here as we can reach on the first day's journey, perhaps at Monte de la Novia or just north of there. The wagons must travel day and night, with changes of horses and teamsters, so as to be in Medina al-Zahra as soon as we are. Every rider must have a lead horse as well as his own, so that we should be able to make thirty leagues before sundown. I shall ride on ahead with fifty men—yes, I know it is risky, but you two will not be far behind, and I wish to arrive at the palace as soon as possible.

"Jorge, you will see that my fifty men are ready, with provisions in our saddle bags. I shall want to leave in ten minutes at the most. And, Roberto, you will see to the wagons and our cavalry. Sergeant, give these two couriers some hot tea and breakfast, and some provender for their saddle bags, including oats for their horses."

Clavijo retired to the tent, and came out five minutes later ready for the ride. His two horses and those of the Saracen couriers were saddled and ready. The soldiers were busy readying their own mounts. In another five minutes, the company was mounted, and away, at a full gallop down the road to Medina al-Zahra.

At the palace, early the next morning, Lady Nardjis had just finished her morning task, attending to the needs of her three charges, when the walls of the dungeon reverberated with the clarion call of a war trumpet in the distance.

"Oh, thank God! Thank God!" Nardjis cried, and sank to her knees overcome with emotion, the tears streaming down her cheeks.

"What is it, Nardjis dear?"

"What's happened?"

"Why are you weeping, my dear?"

The three prisoners, immediately solicitous, realized that the trumpet blast must portend something of grave import, but it was hard to reconcile heartfelt thanks to God and her equally heartfelt sobbing.

"Oh, it's glorious news," Nardjis told them through her tears. "I'm just crying for happiness after all these days of anxiety. The war trumpet has just sounded the calls of boots and saddles, and retreat, meaning that they have received the signal that the Spaniards are arriving to rescue us. They must now be on the mountain top where the couriers were to give the signal. So that it will be more than half an hour—nearly an hour before they can reach us. But they are here, my darlings, they are here! May Allah be praised!" And Lady Nardjis again burst into tears.

Marilú, Conchita and Zoraya, equally overcome with emotion, made the sign of the cross, and sank to their knees in prayers and tears.

When Nardjis had recovered somewhat from her first joyful but tearful reaction, she explained that in a few minutes the palace guards and soldiers would be galloping off on the road to Sevilla, leaving them and the cook alone in the palace. "If the *Almorávides* had been approaching," she went on, "our outposts overlooking the road to Córdoba would have given another signal, and the trumpet would have sounded assembly, and the call to arms. And we four would have had to prepare for our escape through the mountains, a difficult and a dangerous trip. Oh, my darlings, it won't be long now. Dry your tears, and I shall wait for your husband and his men at the inner gate to lead them to the dungeon."

She locked the door as she left, for she had not yet heard the clatter of hooves that would reassure her that the soldiers and guards had actually left them alone in the palace, and she still had to protect her charges against any possible intruder from the populace in Medina al-Zahra. Left alone to their thoughts, Zoraya and Conchita could not keep their minds off their beloved Roberto and Jorge—pray God they were alive and on their way! A gentle glow of affection suffused their entire bodies, and they closed their eyes as they envisaged the joy of a reunion with their lovers.

For her part, Marilú pondered again Zoraya's words of the previous evening, and vowed that when she was reunited with her beloved Gonzalo she would let him know the full force of her affection. She would never again play the modest but dutiful wife submitting to the embraces of her lawful husband—she would be a woman in every sense of the word and deed, ardent and passionate.

She realized that the supreme ecstasy that she had experienced in the arms of the Grand Vizier came, not so much from his talents as a lover—for he was in no wise superior in that respect to her dear Gonzalo—but from the fact that she herself was overcome by the excitements of the abduction, the *hammam* and its voluptuous perfumes, the sensuous music and dancing, and above all the knowledge that she was a slave, a slave whose sole function was to satisfy the passions of her lord and master. And, intoxicated by these emotions, she, Marilú, had given herself without restraint, eagerly, ardently and passionately, to the raptures of love. It was that which made the difference. It was because she had given herself, as a woman and not as a lady, that she was able to feel the dark winds of passion throughout her innermost being, and could impart those same feelings to her lover.

Well, from now on, she would give herself just as fully—even more fully and with no restraining feelings of guilt—to her own, her lawful husband. And she would tell him how much she had missed him, how much she wanted him, so that he would understand this strange new access of passion in a woman who had heretofore always been so modest—loving but in a discreet and ladylike fashion. And now she was a *kabbázah!* What ecstasies lay in store for them! What delights and what happiness!

The reveries of the three women were interrupted by the clatter of armed men running down the corridor. A smiling Nardjis opened the dungeon door, and in burst the Marqués de Clavijo, his sword drawn, followed by half a dozen of his men.

"Oh, Gonzalo! Gonzalo! How I have missed you!" cried Marilú, the tears streaming down her face. "It has been so long, so terribly long, my love!" She attempted to rise, but couldn't, manacled as she was to her two companions.

"And I've missed you, my love, my own sweet precious!" Gonzalo murmured, choking with emotion. He threw down his sword, and embraced his wife as best he could in her uncomfortable position. "Do you have the keys to these handcuffs, Lady Nardjis?" he asked.

"No, my lord, the chief eunuch had the keys, and he has been gone for many days. But I've brought these tools." And Lady Nardjis handed Gonzalo the hammer and chisel.

"You break open these manacles, sergeant," Gonzalo ordered. "My hand is too shaky."

With one blow, using the stone floor as an anvil, the sergeant shattered the handcuff on Marilú's right wrist, then repeated the operation on the other handcuff. Gonzalo lifted her gently to her feet, as she swayed dizzily in her new-found freedom.

"Oh, it is so good to be able to put my arms around you, my lover," moaned Marilú through her tears, as she felt her breasts crushed against the chain mail of her husband, whose strong arms encircled her and drew her to him.

Meanwhile the sergeant had chiseled loose the dangling handcuffs from Zoraya's and Conchita's aching wrists, and they too rose shakily to their feet, embracing with affection and tears both Nardjis and the cook who had entered the dungeon to see what, if any, orders might be given her.

As soon as they had recovered somewhat from their emotions, Conchita asked eagerly: "Cousin Gonzalo, is Jorge Rodríguez with you?"

"And Roberto Ayala?" asked Zoraya. "Are they alive, my lord?"

"They are both alive and well," Gonzala smiled, for he was not unaware of the tender passions his two colonels entertained for the two women—for the lovely widow, Zoraya, and for the child who stood beside her. For Conchita, disheveled as she was, looked like a child of scarcely fourteen years—what a sweet girl she was, this little cousin of Marilú's. "And you two girls had better get yourselves cleaned up and dressed, for you look a sight. And Roberto and Jorge will be here any minute—in an hour or so at the latest, I should say. And you too, my love, what a mess, what a sight you are! But what a sight for sore eyes, all three of you—what a lovely sight, and how sore our eyes are from weeping for you!"

"I'll take them away and refresh them," said Nardjis. "We'll all dress in riding clothes so that we can accompany you, for we must leave as quickly as we can before Tashfin's army arrives. I am told they are battling outside the walls of Córdoba now, at the bridgehead south of the Guadalquivir. Meanwhile, the cook can show you the other dungeon, my lord, the *oubliette* where I have hidden all the treasures of the palace, for fear that the *Almorávides* might get here before your men arrived. How many men do you have, and how many wagons?" she asked.

"There will be eight hundred of us as soon as the rest of my troops arrive. Why do you ask? And some twenty-five or thirty wagons."

"Good," said Lady Nardjis. "I was thinking that maybe you would like to send a squad of your men down to the barracks in Medina al-Zahra. The two couriers who brought you here can show them the way, and then I suppose you will release them. And the cooks in the barracks can let you have eight hundred loaves of bread, and I'm sure they can roast half that many chickens for your lunch. It will take at least an hour to load your wagons, and, if they don't get here for another hour, there will be plenty of time to cook the chickens. Our cook can roast a half a dozen or a dozen capons for your officers."

"Good idea," said Gonzalo. "Sergeant, take a squad down to the town, and release the two Saracen couriers after they have shown you the way to the barracks. Tell the cooks and the townsfolk that there will be no sacking or looting of Medina al-Zahra, and they will be glad to provide you with provender. Oh, yes, and oats for the horses. I'll have one or two of the wagons sent down as soon as they arrive."

"Just a moment, Gonzalo, my love, before Lady

Nardjis takes us away," said Marilú. "There is something I have to tell you—something I have kept to myself because I did not know whether you would arrive in time to rescue us before the *Almorávides* got here.

"While I was in captivity," she went on, "I heard a voice—it was not a dream, Gonzalo, believe me—I heard a voice, a deep, solemn voice, such a voice as I imagine Saint James the Apostle spoke with when he came down to earth to lead our troops to victory at the Battle of Clavijo. And that voice commanded me that, if I were rescued from here by Christian men, I must not step outside of this dungeon until I had seen its walls demolished—demolished from within, I was told. And I was told that this would lead me to great treasure, but that all I should ask for myself—there would be caskets of gold and of silver, studded with precious stones, but all I must ask for myself would be a small casket of simple iron. Gonzalo, I cannot leave this dungeon until you obey that voice, so help me God!"

"These dungeon walls must be thirty feet thick," said Nardjis.

"Nevertheless, we must obey that voice," answered Gonzalo. "It may indeed be the voice of the Apostle himself. Captain, there was a battering ram in the courtyard. I saw it on the left as we came through the gate. Have your men bring it here."

Nardjis remained dubious of the possibility of razing the dungeon walls, but was impressed by Marilú's gravity as she spoke. In a few minutes, the captain reappeared with twenty of his men, lugging the massive wheeled scaffolding from which the battering ram—a huge log of iron-bound oak—was suspended by two heavy chains.

"You had better all stand on that side of the dungeon," he said, "while we try this ram against the walls on the other side."

The men placed big chocks of wood behind the four wheels of the machine, letting the ram itself come to rest some three feet away from the dungeon wall. They gripped the iron spikes on each side of the log, and pushed it back as far as the chains would let it go. Then, with all their strength, abetted by the great weight of the log itself, they heaved it against the wall of the dungeon.

"My God! It's a miracle," exclaimed Lady Nardjis. "That must be the hidden treasure of the Caliph Abd ar-Rahman. Praise be to Allah!"

The others in the room crossed themselves in amazement. A whole section of wall had crumbled with the force of the blow, revealing that the inner wall of the dungeon was nothing but a false wall, of a single row of bricks covered with stucco. Behind it was a vault some ten feet deep reaching from the floor to the ceiling. And within the vault lay pile after pile of golden bricks, in front of which were half a dozen leather trunks of various sizes.

Gonzalo opened one of the larger trunks, whose leaden seal had been broken with the force of the blow. "There's your iron casket, my dear. A pretty rusty one. And no key. But, in any event, we mustn't open it until we get to Toledo, for the King has a right to share in all our loot, and these trunks and treasures must be opened by his appraisers. Captain, try the ram on the other walls of the dungeon."

The soldiers moved the heavy machine to another spot on the same wall, with the same result—another large vault, divided from the first opening by a solid masonry arch and wall. And within the vault, the same treasures—bars of gold, and leather trunks, bound with heavy straps and sealed with great leaden seals. The people in the room moved around to make way for the battering ram as the soldiers placed it in turn against the two other walls of the dungeon.

The inner wall, with the door to the dungeon, was solid stone a foot and a half thick, so that there could be no concealed vaults within that section, but the other three walls contained three vaults each, which now lay open to view, piled high with bars of gold and leather trunks.

"Captain," exclaimed Gonzalo, "there will be loot enough in here to make us all rich for the rest of our lives, even after the King has taken his share of the booty. Tell your men of their good fortune. There is no use sacking the rest of the palace until we see whether we can carry any more of this hidden treasure. Gold is a pretty heavy load, you know, and these trunks are hardly light," he added, hefting one of the smaller trunks which he judged must weigh at least a hundred pounds.

"Have this battering ram removed, so that we can load the booty as soon as the wagons arrive, and then leave us alone in here. I want to talk with my wife and her companions, and with Lady Nardjis."

As soon as the ram had been removed, and the soldiers gone, the Marqués de Clavijo turned to his wife. "You have discovered a fortune here for us, my love. Let's see what's in this small trunk," he added, turning to one of the smaller coffers whose seal had also been broken by the battering ram.

He led Marilú by the arm to the vault, unstrapped the trunk, and opened its lid so that the two of them could peek within. "My God! my love," he whispered to Marilú, "it's full of diamonds. With layers of silk between. The large trunk, my dear, was full of jewelry and caskets, all wrapped in silk, but if these smaller trunks contain nothing but precious stones, the value of this treasure is incalculable.

"We cannot expect just to give the King his legal share of a fifth of all our booty. We'd never live to tell the tale. This treasure does not belong to us, but to all Spain, and the King will be most generous if he lets us have a tenth of it—for us, our officers, and our soldiers. Keep the secret of this trunk to yourself, my love. I shall want to discuss with Jorge and Roberto what we must do, and meanwhile we must not let the soldiers have even an inkling of the value of this treasure, or they will be mutinous if they do not get their usual legal share. And it would mean their death if they attempted to demand it. They will have a rough idea of the value of the gold, from its weight, but they can have no conception of the contents of these trunks, nor of their value.

"Lady Nardjis," he continued, no longer whispering, "what is the meaning of this inscription on the bars of gold? And I see the same sign on all the leaden seals on the trunks."

Nardjis tried to lift one of the golden bricks, but it was too heavy. She examined the seal with awe. "It is the seal of the Caliph Abd ar-Rahman, my lord. It is indeed a miracle. This treasure has been hidden for at least one hundred and thirty years. There have been rumors of its existence, but neither King al-Mutamid, nor his father Mutadid, nor any of the kings of Córdoba before him, have ever been able to discover it. I doubt whether Almanzor himself knew where it was, or it wouldn't be here now.

"And to think that my own dear Marilú discovered it. Surely, it must have been the voice of Saint James that she heard. It is almost enough to make me a Christian, my lord."

"I'm glad you said that, Lady Nardjis, and brought me back to my senses," said Gonzalo, "I was so amazed at this discovery that I had forgotten I was a Christian. Let us all get down on our knees—and you too, my dear Lady Nardjis, for your God is our God—and let us give thanks that God, in his mercy, has revealed this treasure to us. And even more, that he has been gracious enough to let us rescue my beloved wife, and her dear companions, and you too, Lady Nardjis, for you women are worth more than any treasure on earth."

He got down on his knees, and the four women did likewise, the four Christians making the sign of the cross, and Nardjis too, remembering that Marilú had not been ashamed of following Moslem customs in Córdoba and in Medina al-Zahra. The tears streamed down their faces, including the weather-beaten face of the Marqués de Clavijo, as they thanked the Lord for his grace and mercy.

"And now, Lady Nardjis," Gonzalo said, rising from the floor, "let me have the key to the dungeon, and then you might take these three lovely women and refresh them for our trip to Toledo. Roberto and Jorge will truly be here any minute now. And you wouldn't want Jorge to see you like that, would you, Conchita?" And he gave his young cousin a loving hug and a kiss, beaming with affection. "And I hope that makes you jealous, Marilú, my darling, because I think that Conchita is the sweetest young thing I know, even if she does look like an unholy mess with her hair in tangles and her dress in rags."

"It does make me jealous, my love," Marilú laughed. "And you better not let Jorge catch you."

The four women left the room happily arm in arm. Gonzalo buckled the leather straps on the two trunks that had been opened and, taking the hammer that Nardjis had left, he carefully hammered the leaden seals in place, taking care not to efface the Caliph's seal. It was impossible to tell that they had been broken open, and Gonzalo leaned back and admired his handiwork. He decided to go back to the courtyard to see how his captain and men were getting along, and he closed the dungeon door as he left, locking it behind him.

The soldiers were in the outer courtyard, outside the palace gates, busily brushing, currying, and watering their horses. They cheered when their general appeared at the gate, and the captain saluted and said that they were all overjoyed at the news of the hidden treasure. Gonzalo lined up the men, and told them in detail of Marilú's miraculous discovery, then warned them of the dangers of loose talk. If ibn-Tashfin's army learned in any way of this treasure, they would be pursued all the way to Toledo, and surely murdered, every one of them.

He made them swear the most solemn oath, by Saint James the Moor-killer, not to tell anyone of the great treasure they had found—to tell no man or woman, in Medina al-Zahra or anywhere, until they had delivered their booty to the King in Toledo. And he said that he would exact the same oath from their campanions who should be here shortly, and that the treasure would be shared equally with the two hundred men left behind in Alarcos because, whether their share was divided among eight hundred men or one thousand men would make little difference to any of them, but it would be most unfair to deprive their comrades of their just share because they had the bad luck to be left behind.

Then the sergeant who had taken his squad to Medina al-Zahra saluted and addressed the *marqués*: "We shall have the eight hundred loaves and eight hundred chickens, my lord, not just four hundred. And there are plenty of oats for our horses. We must send a wagon down—two wagons, I suppose—as soon as they arrive. We can then pack the oats and chickens and bread in our saddle bags, and let our lead horses carry them, so that we shall have those two wagons for the loot.

"The townsfolk were so delighted that we shan't be looting down there, that all the women in the town, it seems, are helping the cooks kill and prepare the chickens. And there are very few people left in Medina al-Zahra, my lord. It seems that most of them have fled. And the rest of them will be leaving soon."

"Thank you, sergeant. You have done very well. And captain," Gonzalo added, "let me know just as soon as our sentries see the rest of our forces. You should be able to spot them at Monte de la Novia where the Saracen couriers gave the signal this morning to the soldiers in Medina al-Zahra.

"Monte de la Novia," he repeated to himself, "what an appropriate name—Sweetheart's Mountain—and what sweet hearts it has led us to!"

"My general, there they are!" exclaimed the captain, pointing to a cloud of dust upon the mountain top. Evidently the wagon train, driving the whole night through, had reached Monte de la Novia ahead of the cavalry who had perforce slept at least part of the night. The dustcloud was quite obviously that of at least a score of supply wagons, and not that of mounted men.

"I'll wager that the horsemen overtake the wagons, and get here first," said Gonzalo with satisfaction. "But it will be at least three quarters of an hour before they reach us. Line them up for me when they come, and let me know. I want to tell them of the treasure, and have them sworn to secrecy. The two colonels will want to rush off to see our ladies, and I can tell them about the treasure later. And now I must go and see how the women are getting along."

The Marqués de Clavijo turned back to the palace and walked down the corridor, admiring everything he saw. It was magnificent—undoubtedly the most beautiful palace he had ever seen. He could hear the gay sound of women's voices at the far end of the corridor.

"Marilú, Lady Nardjis, are you in there," he called through the closed door.

"Yes, we're almost through, and putting on our riding habits," answered Nardjis. "You can come in in just a moment."

"Well, hurry up, because our friends will be here soon. We spotted them on top of Monte de la Novia, and I'm sure that at least two of them are galloping here as fast as they can, to see their own sweet *novias*."

"Come in, come in, Gonzalo," screamed Conchita and Marilú.

Gonzalo entered the vestibule and then the dressing room of the *hammam*, admiring the elegance of its architecture and equipment, far beyond anything he had ever seen or imagined. The women were attired in their riding habits, minus their boots and burnouses which lay on the marble bench in front of them. They were busy brushing each other's hair, the two blondes and the two brunettes apparently vying with one another to see which shade could acquire the higher gloss.

"Go into the other two rooms," squealed Conchita, "and see what a wonderful place this is."

Gonzalo passed through the *tepidarium* into the *calidarium*, impressed by everything he saw. He returned to the dressing room. "I wish I had time to see the whole palace, Lady Nardjis," he remarked. "It is truly magnificent. But our friends will be arriving any minute now. Let's meet them at the gate, and then you women might take Colonel Rodríguez and Colonel Ayala down to the dungeon to show them the treasure."

"You may not know it, cousin Gonzalo," said Conchita, "but we've decided that we're going to get married before we leave here."

"No, not before we leave here, you silly," corrected

Marilú, "but this evening when we arrive at El Viso. We shall have time to get to El Viso this evening, shan't we, dear? I just can't take the responsibility of having these two women traveling with us, four or five nights to Toledo, and not married—and the men they love traveling with us. And I am responsible for Conchita, you know. Well, I'll tell you all about it later, my love. There's so much to tell you."

"Yes, we should arrive at El Viso tonight with time to spare," Gonzalo said, "and if we can put up at your lovely house, Zoraya, it would be very helpful. Especially if you and Conchita are going to be married tonight. But you haven't asked your suitors yet. How do you know they want to marry you?"

"Oh, we know they want to marry us, all right," Conchita answered. "They've been pestering us long enough. And, anyway, we don't ask them. They ask us. And they will. So that's settled, cousin Gonzalo, and you have to help us."

"All right, Conchita darling, but I'm going to take another kiss, now that you're beautiful again—and before Jorge gets here."

"Am I really beautiful, cousin Gonzalo?" asked Conchita as she snuggled delightedly in his arms. "Do you think Jorgito will think I'm beautiful?"

"So it's 'Jorgito' now, is it? And next, I suppose, it will be 'Jorgito, darling.' Yes, I'm sure he'll think you're beautiful, although I don't know why. And come over here, Marilú, my love, and give me a great big hug and a kiss; you look so beautiful to me, and I think I do know why."

He embraced Marilú lovingly, and they walked down toward the gate arm in arm, followed by Lady Nardjis with Conchita and Zoraya by her side.

As they reached the inner gate, the two colonels, followed by their cavalry, galloped full speed across the *place d'armes*, pursued by the wagon train careening across the yard. The colonels leaped off their horses at a bound, barely nodded at their general and his lady, and sprang toward Zoraya and Conchita, who greeted them with open arms.

"Oh, Jorge, Jorgito, I've missed you so," sobbed Conchita. "I love you so much, and have so longed for you and prayed for you to come." And a flood of tears flowed from her eyes without restraint as they clasped one another lovingly in their arms.

"But you never gave me any indication before that you loved me. You *know* I have always loved you. But I thought you were in love with Santiago. Poor fellow! He died in a foray near Alarcos. He was a brave man, and I miss him."

"I shall miss him too," said Conchita. "I did like him very much, and I even thought I loved him. But I was only a little girl then. I've aged terribly these past ten days, and now I know that I never did love anyone but you, Jorgito. And, oh, I do love you so. Thank you for rescuing me. And now please come and see the dungeon where I was imprisoned until cousin Gonzalo came."

Meanwhile, Zoraya, sobbing in Roberto's arms, was saying: "I knew you'd come, Roberto. And I've missed you so. I've longed for you day after day, and it's been so long. And I've been thinking things over all the time we were imprisoned here, and I know that I do love you."

"Will you marry me, then, my darling? You know I've loved you ever since I've known you, and I've been so lonesome without you, and so worried about your safety."

"Of course, my love, I'll marry you—and just as soon as we get back to El Viso this evening, the sooner the better. But let me show you the dungeon where we were imprisoned until the Marqués de Clavijo rescued us. It was vile down there. We were handcuffed together and, if it hadn't been for Lady Nardjis who took care of us—she is the lady standing at the gate with Marilú and Gonzalo—we'd have starved."

Gonzalo threw the dungeon key to Roberto, and the two couples, Roberto and Zoraya, Jorge and Conchita, walked down the corridor arm in arm.

"My it's grim in here," exclaimed Jorge as they entered the dungeon.

"Yes, it was horrible," said Conchita excitedly. "And there are our handcuffs on the floor. The sergeant broke them open for us with a hammer and chisel. Lady Nardjis took care of us. She's lovely. You'll love her. Let's go in that vault over there. It's dark in there and I want to show you the treasure Marilú discovered. Come along."

She chose the darkest of the nine vaults, to show her sweetheart the treasures of Abd ar-Rahman.

"When the Marqués de Clavijo rescued us," Zoraya was telling her sweetheart, "we were simply distraught and in rags. But let me tell you about the treasure of Abd ar-Rahman, and let me show it to you," and she led her *fiancé* to the next darkest of all the vaults.

From the sighs and giggles and impassioned words of love that issued from the gloom, it was clear that the two colonels were less interested in the treasures of the dead Caliph than they were in the two very live treasures they held in their arms. Long before they emerged from the darkness of the vault to the semi-darkness of the dungeon, don Jorge had proposed to doña Conchita and she had accepted lovingly.

"We're going to be married, Zoraya," Conchita squealed with glee.

"And so are we, my dear. But we better get out of this dungeon now before the soldiers come to load the treasure onto the wagons. And I expect that our loves will want to have a word with their general before he dismisses them for dereliction of duty." The two women walked affectionately down the corridor arm in arm, as the colonels rushed off to report to the Marqués de Clavijo.

Gonzalo had just finished his allocution to the men, swearing them all to the darkest secrecy. "And now, sergeant, if you will take two of the wagons down to the town, you can get our provisions for us. Meanwhile, Captain Escobar, will you see to the loading of the treasure under the supervision of Colonels Rodríguez and Ayala. I'll have a word with them before they join you.

"And, you teamsters, remember, you are not to overload the wagons. I don't want any broken axles, and you know what the roads are like. We shall be traveling as fast as your horses can pull you, with two shifts of teamsters and two shifts of horses for each wagon. We shall only go as far as El Viso today, so you can make it in a day. But, remember, gold is heavy. Heft one of the bars, and you can tell how many you can safely pack on one wagon. And put the trunks on top of the gold bars, with everything securely tied down and covered with canvas.

"You will each be held responsible for broken axles or any trouble with your loads, so look to it. I'd rather leave some of the booty behind—although with twenty-five wagons I don't think we'll have to—rather than have a broken axle, perhaps with the *Almorávides* hot on our trail. All right, men, you are now the richest soldiers in all Spain—that is, if you're careful, and fast in the loading."

The men cheered again, enthusiastically. Gonzalo then explained the matter of the treasure to his two aides, including the revelation of the voice to Marilú, which they agreed must have been the voice of Saint James the Apostle himself. And the three of them went off to supervise the unloading of the treasure from the vaults, and its careful loading onto the supply wagons. Gonzalo counted the trunks and gold bars as they were loaded. At least two million dinars, some ten tons of gold, he calculated roughly, probably more. And the value of the jewelry and gems in the trunks—incalculable, but at least five or six times the value of the gold, he surmised. There was no way of knowing until the King's appraisers examined the precious stones and jewels.

Meanwhile, Lady Nardjis was showing Marilú, Zoraya and Conchita around the palace. They exclaimed with amazement as each new architectural wonder was revealed to them. The tapestries and carpets alone, they knew, represented wealth far beyond anything they had ever imagined possible.

"Let's see if they have finished loading the wagons, now," said Nardjis. "There may still be space for some of the treasures I have hidden in the *oubliette*."

They found the Marqués de Clavijo in the courtyard, and were joined almost immediately by the two colonels who had finished supervising the clearance of the vaults. "There are still three empty wagons," said Gonzalo. "I suggest we keep two wagons empty for emergency—broken axles or something—and that we load the third wagon with the most precious things in the *oubliette*. No glassware or ceramics, Lady Nardjis. Too breakable. But anything else that you suggest as especially precious. Jorge and Roberto, would you wait outside with the wagons. I'll go with the four ladies to the *oubliette*—their taste will be better than mine—and please send me a squad of men to carry the things back to the wagons. We should be ready to leave in twenty minutes."

In the *oubliette* by the light oil lamps Marilú saw the Caliph's chess set in one corner of the room. "I think the King would be pleased to have that, and the table too. They are the most beautiful things I have ever seen in all my life. Too big and heavy to play chess with, but the King will love it. And that little chess set and table. Gonzalo, could we take that back to Galicia with us?"

"I think the King will let you have it, so long as we give him that jeweled one. It is gorgeous, isn't it? And, say, among those jewels over there, couldn't you two love-birds find a couple of rings that will do for wedding rings. And two for Roberto and Jorge. Believe it or not, we soldiers don't carry rings around with us."

Zoraya and Conchita selected two lovely rings for themselves, and two massive gold bands for the prospective grooms. Conchita, undecided, selected two extra rings so that Jorge could determine which pair he liked best. It was agreed that they should take back with them, for the King to dispose of, all the jeweled caskets, laden with gems, the gold and silver goblets, dishes, and plates, and many other precious objects that Nardjis showed them.

In a storeroom down the corridor, there were yards of silken fabric and a number of leather trunks, into which they loaded all the smaller, more fragile objects, packed down tightly with the silk. Lady Nardjis suggested that they fill all the wagons to the top with tapestries, rugs and curtains from the great Hall and other rooms of the palace, which the soldiers did. Each wagon was then covered with heavy canvas, well secured with hempen ropes.

In ten more minutes, the cavalcade was off amidst the rattle of armor, the clangor of wagon wheels, and the sharp staccato of hooves on the cobblestones. A vanguard of five squads, with its troop guidon and five pennons, rode on ahead, under a captain and five sergeants. On each flank were two squads with their sergeants and pennons, to keep a sharp outlook along the hills on either side of the road. Then came the main body of men with the wagon train in their midst, and the two colonels on either flank, their standards and the general's banner flying gaily in the wind, along with the guidons and pennons.

Zoraya, Conchita and Lady Nardjis rode side by side, ahead of the wagon train, to avoid its dust, while, directly ahead of them, Marilú rode side by side with the Marqués de Clavijo. She had important things to discuss with him. The rear guard, also a troop of five squads with its captain and sergeants, brought up the rear. And along they went, at full gallop, eating up the miles, on the long first leg of their journey—some fourteen leagues between Medina al-Zahra and El Viso. But it was only a little after ten o'clock—the men had been up early and had worked quickly. Barring accident, they should easily reach their destination before sundown, even at the slower pace necessitated by the wagon train.

The gates of Medina al-Zahra were soon left behind, and Lady Nardjis burst into tears as she thought of all that beauty left for the destructive vandalism of the *Almorávides*. The world would never again see the loveliness of the Caliph's gift to his mistress.

Farewell to Medina al-Zahra and the palace of the Caliphs! And hail to Toledo and the castles of Christian Spain!

CHAPTER 18

As the cavalcade left the gates of Medina al-Zahra in the distance, Lady Nardjis pointed out the great aqueduct of Valdepuentes, a many-arched structure, built by the Caliphs but in Roman fashion, that stretched ten miles across hill and vale, in some places over thirty feet high, bringing the clear pure water from the high sierra to al-Zahra's palace and town.

They passed green fields of sugarcane, the grass-like leaves rippling in the breeze; great olive orchards with dark green and silvery leaves; here and there an ancient cork tree, some stripped of their bark and others that had been stripped a decade ago and now growing a new five-inch covering of cork to be stripped again a decade hence. There were broad fields of low-growing grapevines, the grapes still small and green; and everywhere, along the road and extending between the rows of cultivated crops or trees, flaming red poppies and bright golden daisies, as well as other wildflowers.

"I wonder why the vines here grow on the ground," Marilú remarked, "so that you'd have to stoop to pick the grapes. It must be backbreaking. Not like home in Galicia, where the vines grow on trellises and you have to stretch to pick them."

"I guess it's because the people of Andalucía have been under the Moorish yoke, and before that the Roman yoke, for so many centuries that they are used to stooping, while in Galicia we are always reaching up to heaven," Gonzalo answered. "But, really, I don't know why. Custom, I suppose, and the fact that farmers never change their ways from one generation to the next."

Four miles from Medina al-Zahra, they passed the ravine of the Pedroches river, no more than a trickling *arroyo* but with a gorgeous panorama, over valleys and hills, of Córdoba and the broad fields of Andalućia beyond. Further on, along the Ollenas highway, next to a great nine-arch bridge over the Guadiato river, Lady Nardjis told them that the beautiful Morrish castle and mosque at the old Spanish town of Santa María de Trasierra had been built during the administration of Almanzor, of revered or hated memory, depending on which side one stood in the wars between Christians and Moslems.

Just beyond was the imposing Obejo castle, overlooking the Valley of the Guadiato, and all along the way they passed Moorish castles high on the mountain tops, and *Mozarabe* Christian monasteries built like fortresses, with high stone walls to protect them from Saracen raids during these years of intermittent war and peace. Seven leagues from Medina al-Zahra, they came to the City of Villaviciosa, passing the charming X Century buildings and gardens known as the *Huerta de los Arcos,* from the beautiful Moorish wall and arches that surrounded the fields. And so on, through the town of Villaharta, never stopping for more than a few minutes, and then only to change horses every three or four leagues along the route.

As they rode, Marilú explained to Gonzalo her plans for the marriages of Conchita and Zoraya. "All three of us were so frightened, so upset by the abduction, and the long imprisonment, never knowing when we were going to be raped by our captors, and so lonesome for the men we had left behind us, that we could think of nothing but love and lovers. And, after twelve days, Zoraya, who has been widowed nearly a year and has been in love with her cousin, Roberto, for all that time, is just burning for love.

"You know that St. Paul says it is better to marry than to burn, and while that doesn't sound like a very strong recommendation for marriage, I can tell you that it is terrible to burn for twelve days and not be married. Please don't be shocked, my love, but I am burning for your embraces more than I can tell you. I have missed you so much, and from now on, my dearest husband, I am going to be the most ardent, passionate wife in all of Spain. I do love you so."

"I shan't be shocked, my darling," laughed Gonzalo. "And you won't find me lacking in passion or ardor either."

"You never are, my sweet. But I don't know how Zoraya stands it—nearly twelve months! She simply has to get married immediately.

"And poor Conchita," Marilú went on? "she's in a worse fix than either of us, so young and innocent, and yet so eager to become a woman."

And Marilú went on to describe Conchita's experience with the Abbot of Santa Eufemia—how the old priest had nearly seduced her in her innocence by using a religious ruse.

"That bastard! That son of a she-dog!" exclaimed Gonzalo. "I'll rip out his damned heart! I'll kill him! That poor child! And you excuse my language this time, my love. Poor, poor little Conchita. And that God damned abbot! Why can't he be satisfied with his mistresses, like the rest of them? I shall indeed kill him—and we shall be passing by his damned monastery tomorrow."

"My love, that's what I wanted to talk to you about. You agree, don't you, that Conchita and Zoraya must get married to Jorge and Roberto as soon as possible—before we put up for the night at El Viso.

But had you thought of the banns—three Sundays before the wedding?"

"No, I confess that hadn't occurred to me. How do we get around that?"

"That's what I've been planning—plotting, if you like. If I can get to see that horrible Abbot of Santa Eufemia—I wouldn't dare trust you to speak to him alone, you'd murder him—and if I tell him what I know about him and Conchita, I know he'll find some way to get around the banns. He'll have to, because I'll want you to be waiting in the next room when I talk with him, and he'll know that if I tell you what happened, you'll—you will cut out his heart," and Marilú smiled.

"I damned well will!" he exclaimed. "But do you think he can find any way to dispense with the banns?"

"He will," answered Marilú, to save his own skin. And there must be some way to do it. After all, this is wartime. But leave that to me. I promise I shall find a way. And you can tell him of the threat of the *Almorávides*, and scare heaven out of him. I bet he'll want you to escort him to safety to one of the older, fortified monasteries. Just don't lose your temper.

"So what I want to do—and I hope you'll agree, my darling—is for us two to ride on ahead. We can go much faster than these wagons. And we can get to Santa Eufemia, make that horrible priest ride back with us to El Viso, and get there before Conchita and Zoraya arrive with the wagon train. And then we'll make that son of a she-dog, as you call him, marry the two of them. And that's that. Will you do it, Gonzalo? Please, my love."

"Of course, I'll do it. And I think you're right. It will work. It has to. And I guess there's no use my murdering that damned priest unless I'm ready to kill half the priests in Spain. Thank God they have their mistresses, or no honest women would be safe from their lust. But we shall have to have two squads of men accompany us. We can't travel alone in this part of the world. And the soldiers will help put the fear of God into the shriveled soul of that damned abbot.

"But we're arriving at Espiel now. You can see that ancient Visigoth church at Cerro del Germo, way over there at the left—in the distance, on that mountain top. This is a mining region here—more mining than farming. We shall be taking the road to the right to Puerto Calatraveña. We must stop here for lunch, and I'll tell Roberto and Jorge that we shall be riding on to Santa Eufemia to fetch a priest for the marriages tonight.... But remember, not a word about that old son of a she-dog to anyone. Jorge must never know what Conchita's been through. Well, here we are."

The cavalcade drew to a halt at the crossroads. They all dismounted, and the soldiers proceeded to take off the saddles and substitute long ropes, tied to halters, instead of the bridles. The teamsters' horses were unhitched from the wagons, and all of the animals were led down to the stream that ran through the gulley below. Not before the soldiers had brought up buckets of fresh clear water, however, for themselves and their officers.

The old cook got down from her wagon, somewhat stiff from the ride, and laid out five beautifully roasted and browned capons on a blanket on the grass for the general, the two colonels, and their four ladies. The capons had been well-wrapped, and were still warm and steaming. Loaves of bread, endives, pastries, and baskets of fruit completed the luncheon, which they ate picnic-fashion in the shade of a huge cork oak.

"My, I've never had an army lunch as delicious as this before, my general," Roberto remarked as he chewed away at a juicy capon leg. "You ought to change your commissary, General, or I'll join up with the Saracens."

They were all in high spirits from the exciting and happy events of the morning, and Lady Nardjis reflected on how gay and informal this luncheon was, in contrast to the seriousness and grave demeanor of the Saracens, with hardly a word spoken during the whole course of a meal.

Gonzalo outlined his plans for him and Marilú to ride on ahead, beyond El Viso to Santa Eufemia, to get a priest for the weddings—an old friend of Conchita's father, he said, from Galicia. He called to one of the captains and gave instructions for the two squads and a captain to accompany them. "And better have your men get ready for the next leg of our trip. We should leave in ten minutes."

The soldiers had meanwhile been eating their loaves and chickens—a more abundant feast than they were accustomed to on their long rides. Some were brushing and currying their mounts, which had been fed a small amount of the oats and allowed to pasture on a long tether under a grove of olive trees. Others were already saddling their mounts or harnessing the wagon horses.

In a few minutes more they were all on the way, Marilú and Gonzalo galloping on ahead with their escort, followed by the lumbering wagons and main force of soldiers, with their vanguard and rearguard and riders on the flanks spread out as before.

Just beyond Espiel, Marilú and Gonzalo came to Puerto Calatraveña, and beyond that the plateau of the Pedroches, a flat and rocky plain covered with boulders of every size and shape, and not pasture enough to feed a goat—nothing but spiny holly oak and evergreen holm oaks growing wherever there was a crevice between the rocks to feed their roots.

A dreary place, thought Marilú, but she was happy to be riding alongside her husband, and exhilarated by the fast gallop along the fine, smooth dirt road. Five leagues farther on, Gonzalo pointed out the lead mines at Alcaracejos; and then they passed through Villaralto and arrived at El Viso.

"We shall just stop here a moment. I must give instructions to Zoraya's majordomo that we shall all be here this evening. He will want to prepare a banquet for us, and rooms for us and the honeymooners. My sergeant will arrange for stables and quarters for the men right outside the gates. And then we will be on our way."

El Viso was a beautiful town. The great Madroñiz castle dominated the town, but there were many other fine mansions, Zoraya's one of the most beautiful.

"I'm a bit homesick for this place," Marilú said. "We were so happy here with Zoraya before the kidnapping. And, oh, my darling, we're going to be so happy tonight, you and I. And Zoraya and Roberto, and our darling Conchita and her Jorgito. I shall always have an affection for El Viso, my love."

"And I too," Gonzalo replied, "but not until we had rescued you. Until then, I thought it the most damned place in all the world. And your poor father and mother back in Galicia, and Conchita's father, not knowing of your rescue, and no way to let them know. Even the children must be wondering why you have been away so long. We must send a courier on ahead from Toledo as soon as we arrive, with the news of your rescue and of Conchita's marriage. I know the old count will be delighted. He has always liked Jorge, and was so afraid that Conchita would be giddy enough to marry a poet. Poor Santiago! He died a hero. . . . But we must get on to Santa Eufemia."

They rode on in silence, rapt in thought and with mixed emotions respecting their visit to the Abbot of Santa Eufemia. The countryside was beautiful here, far different from the Pedroches plain. Olive groves, corn and other cereals on every side, flocks of sheep pasturing in the meadows—large Merino sheep that the Arabs had brought to Spain many years ago. In every field were rows of bee hives of plaited straw, with hundreds of honeybees buzzing around with tireless energy.

But the travelers had no time to engage in bucolic contemplation. Three leagues beyond El Viso they came to the town of Santa Eufemia. The monastery stood on a hill to the right, its walls of white limestone from a nearby quarry not yet completed.

"You speak to the old abbot first, Gonzalo," said Marilú. "Throw a scare into him about the *Almorávides*, and let him know that we are Conchita's cousins, and that you have just rescued us from the Saracens—also that your army will be in El Viso tonight and on its way to Toledo tomorrow. Then tell him that I want to speak to him alone—the old she-dog."

"All right, my dear. You're learning to speak my language."

They drew up before the gate of the monastery, the soldiers milling around, as Gonzalo, in a stentorian voice, announced that he had urgent business with the abbot, Dom Gregorio.

"Just a minute, my lord," answered the monk who opened the gate. "The abbot is at prayers."

"No, not just a minute. Immediately!" stormed Gonzalo, and he rode through the gate, followed by Marilú and his men. "And you run as fast as you can and tell him we are coming."

The monk gathered up his skirts and ran off to the monastery as fast as his fat legs would carry him. Gonzalo let him get to the door, and then he and

Marilú and the captain and sixteen soldiers dismounted, the latter hitching the thirty-eight horses to the rail outside the monastery. Gonzalo burst through the front door without knocking, followed by Marilú and his men, whose swords clanked menacingly as they entered the vestibule.

The abbot, Dom Gregorio, was just coming down the corridor, trailed by the monk who was still panting hard. "What is the meaning of this intrusion?" he demanded.

"Intrusion nothing," replied Gonzalo. "We're here on business. And our business is urgent and of the utmost gravity. I am the Marqués de Clavijo, and this is my wife, María Luisa Andrade de Araujo."

And Gonzalo proceeded to outline his business, just as he had agreed with Marilú beforehand. The Marqués de Clavijo was famous, and his terrible temper equally so, and Dom Gregorio spoke with the greatest deference.

"I shall be glad to speak with your gracious lady in private, my lord Marqués de Clavijo. Come this way into my office, my dear."

Marilú wondered whether it was the same office that Conchita had told her of, not that she was in any fear as to her own chastity. The old abbot was too frightened and shaken for that, she knew. She barely sketched what Conchita had told her—enough so that the old abbot would know that she knew the whole story. Then Marilú added: "I would hate to go into all this with my husband—for Conchita's sake as well as for yours, my lord abbot."

She then quickly told the abbot what she wanted, saying she was sure he would find a way to dispense with the banns. Dom Gregorio reflected for a moment, his head in his hands.

"What did you say were the names of these four people, my dear. Write them down for me on this piece of paper, would you—the two women and the two men."

Marilú did.

"A miracle! A miracle, my dear!" exclaimed the abbot. "It is amazing! To think that, just four Sundays ago, as I was at my prayers, I heard a voice, the voice of San Geminiano. And it commanded me to post the banns for just those two couples. They are all recorded in the daily record of the monastery which I shall show you—but let's not waste time with that now. We have urgent business to attend to, as the Marqués de Clavijo has said.

"Will you excuse me while I dress for the ride down to El Viso, and I shall wish to have two of my priests accompany me. They have fine bass and baritone voices, and will assist me at the mass. There is a chapel in the mansion there, isn't there? Well, let me get ready, and I'll be with you and your husband in a few minutes."

The abbot left Marilú who rejoined Gonzalo to break the good news—everything was settled, as she was sure it would be. "The old son of a she-dog," growled Gonzalo. "You should have been a diplomat, my love. You'd make a fine, conniving cardinal, you would. But I'm glad you're not. The more I know you, my dear, the more amazed I am at you."

Meanwhile the abbot hastened down the hall. "Fra Antonio," he bellowed. "And Father Higinio and Father Francisco. Come here at once, I need you."

The three monks came running to Dom Gregorio's office. Addressing himself first to the priests, he told them that they would accompany him to El Viso to assist at the nuptial mass, stay there overnight, and return with him the next day. As a reward, he promised to take them with him to the Hermitage of St. Peter, under the escort of the army, where they would be safe from the *Almorávides*.

"Now, get packed, and get my things ready, including my Missal and vestments, becuase we must leave as soon as possible." The two priests left, and the abbot turned to Fra Antonio. "You are a month behind in entering our minutes in the monastery's journal, are you not?"

"Yes, my lord abbot, but it has not been my fault," the monk excused himself. "You know we still have no gold leaf and no red pigment to illuminate our books with, and it is only last week that we were able to get a supply of Chinese ink from Toledo. But I am working as fast as I can, and shall have our journal brought up to date—not illuminated in red and gold, but up to date—just as fast as I possibly can."

"That's all right, Fra Antonio. No excuse is necessary. Now I tell you what I want you to do," and the abbot lowered his voice to a conspiratorial pitch. "You will enter these names among the banns for four Sundays back. I had meant to give them to you before, but omitted to do so. I can assure you that the names have been posted on the chapel door, and you are not to enquire into that. The marriages are to take place tonight, this twelfth day of June in the year of our Lord 1091, and will be celebrated by me and by Fathers Francisco and Higinio in El Viso. You understand? And all entries are to be brought absolutely up to date and without fail—and be ready by eleven o'clock tomorrow morning. In Chinese ink only—the gold and red illumination can wait. And I don't care if you have to work all night and all morning—but it must be done.

"And your reward will not only be that you will accompany us to the Hermitage of St. Peter tomorrow—with the completed journal under your arm, you understand?—but that you will be installed at St. Peter's as their chief calligrapher. And there you will find all the gold leaf and red pigment, and other pigments too, that you will need, not only for this journal, but for the parchment sheets of music that you love so well to illuminate. And no one—absolutely no one—must know that you made all the journal entries today. Is that clear?"

"Perfectly, my lord abbot. And it will be done. I shall put all other tasks aside and get to work on this immediately."

Dom Gregorio put on his riding boots and a long burnous over his robe, and carefully rolled up the vestments he would need for the nuptial mass that evening. He joined Gonzalo and Marilú in the vestibule where they had been waiting impatiently, in the company of the two priests who were already attired for the trip, with their vestments rolled up to be placed in their saddle bags.

The horses were ready and rested, and the riders were soon off in a cloud of dust for their nine mile trip back to El Viso. Gonzalo and Marilú galloped back at the head of the column, followed closely by the three clerics, with the rear brought up by the two squads of cavalry.

"You ride well, my darling," said Gonzalo "at this rate, we should be back in El Viso an hour before vespers—well before the others arrive with the wagon train. And your plot worked wonderfully. I'm already beginning to entertain less violent feelings toward the old abbot.

"And I truly can't blame these priests for lack of chastity. Lord knows that, after twelve days of celibacy, I'm as rutty as any stallion, and am ready to mount my sweet mare as soon as I can get the men and wagons stowed safely away and attend to my duties as the King's general."

"I'm anxious too, my love, and there's nothing I'd like better than to bed you just as soon as we arrive at Zoraya's," Marilú responded. "But, remember that, for Roberto and Jorge, this will be their wedding night. They have been riding hard all day and a good part of last night—and you too, my darling. Don't you think that, for Conchita's and Zoraya's sakes, at least, you should all take a two hour *siesta*. And we shall all need a good hot bath.

"Why not plan the wedding for the eighth hour after noon, and the banquet for an hour later, at complins? And let them sleep until noon the next day. You remember how we were on our wedding night. And, believe me, Gonzalo, I want you more tonight than I have ever wanted you in all my life, and we shall have many things to occupy us during the night."

"You think of everything, my love. And I *am* exhausted, and suppose Jorge and Roberto are too, not just from the hard ride, but from the strain of not knowing whether you three were alive or dead, and then all the confusion and strain of all the things that have happened in the past twelve hours. And you three girls must be just as exhausted after the strain and anxieties, not just of twelve hours, but of twelve days.

"So, it is agreed, and I shall give the orders just as soon as the others reach El Viso. But we shall be up at eleven tomorrow morning. No good soldier can sleep until noon. And I shall send a captain on ahead to make a place for us at the old Moorish castle at Almadén, just six leagues beyond El Viso, a short ride for the second night of the honeymoon."

They soon arrived at Zoraya's mansion, where the majordomo was waiting to receive them. "Everything has been ordered for tonight, my lord, and I and all the servants look forward to seeing our beloved *condesa* again—and the other two gracious ladies, too, my lord."

Gonzalo gave the necessary instructions. "Captain, I

shan't want any of the men to leave the palace grounds this evening. Too much danger of loose gossip if they go down to the city, for ibn-Tashfin has spies everywhere, and especially in the brothels. And no drinking—absolutely none. So you might ride into town with a couple of your men, and bring back a wagon-load of women for this evening's entertainment—two wagon-loads. And none of the women must be allowed to leave the camp until we are on our way at noon tomorrow. I noticed two large wagons in the stables as we passed by."

"Very well, my general, it will be done. By your leave," and the captain went off to give the necessary orders to his men.

"And, Dom Gregorio," Gonzalo continued, "the wedding will be at the eighth hour after noon, so you gentlemen have nearly three hours to get ready. But don't fail to be back here in time. The nuptial mass must be at the eighth hour sharp."

"Very well, my lord *Marqués*. I think that Fathers Francisco and Higinio will accompany me to the town to visit some of our parishioners, for we don't often get down to El Viso and must attend to our flock. But we shall be back in time, I can assure you, my lord."

And the abbot departed with his two campanions. "Let's get our vestments and things ready for the nuptial mass in milady's chapel, and then I think we should pay a visit to the house of the Sisters of Saint Mary Magdalene. I don't think my wandering thoughts will allow me to officiate at two weddings, with two such luscious brides, unless I have first appeased my own far from cold desires. What do you say?"

"Agreed and agreed," answered Father Higinio, and Father Francisco added in his *basso profundo*: "It is our duty to know when our wayward sisters indulge in sin so that we may grant them indulgence thereafter."

Scarcely had the Marqués de Clavijo finished his arrangements with the majordomo for the quartering of the troops, the stabling of the horses, the storing of the wagons in the iron-grated courtyard, and the tents for the camp followers, than the wagon train and its escort clattered through the outer gate of the palace grounds.

Marilú embraced Conchita, Zoraya and Nardjis affectionately, and whispered that everything had been arranged, and Gonzalo told them, and Jorge and Roberto, of the plans for the wedding and banquet.

"Now, if you gentlemen will excuse me," said Zoraya, "I should like to make our household arrangements. Marilú and Conchita and Lady Nardjis can take their *siesta* with me, and the majordomo will conduct you gentlemen to the large guest room for your *siesta* whenever you are ready. And I shall have three bridal suites ready for this evening—that is, unless you military men have other more important things to attend to tonight."

"That will be fine, Zoraya," and Gonzalo smiled. "You are certainly a most gracious and thoughtful hostess."

Turning to his companions, he added: "The wagons can all be stored in the courtyard here. The gate will be locked, and the wagons are practically pilfer-proof with all those carpets and tapestries under the canvas and on top of the treasure. We shall have a squad and a captain mount guard outside the courtyard gate all night long on a four hour shift. And now I want to give instructions for the night's bivouac, and warn the men again of the dangers of gossiping."

He lined up the men, told them of the arrangements that the captain was making for the evening's entertainment, and gave strict orders that no one was to be allowed to leave the palace grounds and that drinking—even of wine—was to be absolutely prohibited until after they had left Alarcos, far enough north to be relatively safe from pursuit. The wagons were safely stored side by side in the courtyard, and the great iron gate securely locked.

"Well, gentlemen," Gonzalo said, turning to Roberto and Jorge, "I think everything is under control, and we had best retire for a *siesta* before this evening's activities. We must all be pretty well exhausted."

"I know I am," said Jorge, "but when I see Conchita—isn't she a darling?—I feel I simply can't wait for the wedding."

"And I'm just as anxious to be wed to the loveliest woman I have ever known," said Roberto, "but we shall all be better men after a couple of hours' sleep. So let's go—and happy dreams."

The three officers went off together, tired but happy, while the captains attended to their many duties.

CHAPTER 19

Two hours later, the three priests and the two happy couples, with Gonzalo, Marilú and Lady Nardjis—no less blissful, to be sure—were assembled in the little chapel, devoutly expectant.

The priests, dignified and solemn, vested as for mass but without their maniples, stood before the altar, which was brightly lit with twinkling candles. Four minstrels in their gay, many-colored costumes stood ready to add their voices, and the sweet sound of a harp, a lute, and two *vihuelas*—the last being diminutive guitars played with a tiny bow—to the chanting of the priests.

All was in readiness for the marriage ceremony. Gonzalo and Marilú were to act *in loco parentis* for Conchita and Zoraya. Nardjis stood by with the four golden rings, ready to hand them to the brides and to the bridegrooms, each of whom was to act as best man for the other.

Marilú and Nardjis were in tears as Conchita and Zoraya in turn repeated the vows: ". . . to have and to hold, from this day forward, for better, for worse, for richer, for poorer, in sickness and in health, until death do us part."

Dom Gregorio boomed forth: "*Ego conjungo vos in matrimonium, in nomine Patris, et Filii, et Spiritus Sancti.*"

The priest used the Roman rite, new to this reconquered region, and introduced into Spain only twenty years earlier by the crusading clergy of Cluny. Most of the Mozarabic Christian churches in the region had stubbornly clung to the old Gothic liturgy despite the pressure of the conquering armies and clergy of Alfonso VI, who was himself a lay brother of Cluny Abbey, and who addressed the Benedictine monks of Cluny as *fratres carissimi.*

The aspersion of the brides and grooms, the blessing of the rings, the *dominus vobiscum* and the response, *Et cum spiritu tuo,* followed by the marriage prayer, were concluded, and the two tearful, happy couples were united in holy matrimony.

The priests then donned their maniples, and began the ordinary of the mass. The two fine baritones and the deep bass of the three clerics joined in the *Kyrie, eleison* and the *Gloria in excelsis Deo,* to the accompaniment of the minstrel chorus, and the mass continued—chanted, sung and spoken—down through the concluding prayers and benediction. The service was over, the priests were thanked and dismissed, and the others—so closely united in marriage and companionship—embraced one another in tears and laughter.

Lady Nardjis invited her friends to accompany her to the dining hall, taking Gonzalo's proffered arm, with Marilú clinging to his other arm. The brides and grooms followed and were soon all seated at a beautifully appointed table, with Lady Nardjis, as hostess for the evening, at the head. The banquet was served Morrish style, with one course following the other, and although every course was delicious, and the wine superb, it is improbable that any of the guests knew, much less cared cared, what they were eating or drinking.

The final toasts over, they all embraced one another, their eyes glistening with tears of happiness, and then quickly left for their respective suites.

"Just a moment, my love," Zoraya whispered to her husband. "I do want to speak with Conchita for just a minute. She seems so frightened. I shan't be more than a minute, my dear." And she beamed so entrancingly at her husband that he couldn't refuse her.

Zoraya, alone with Conchita in the dressing room gave her an affectionate kiss, and whispered, "I know you're going to be very happy, my sweet."

"I already am," Conchita smiled. "Happier than I have ever been in all my life. Isn't Jorgito grand? And I'm not scared at all—just a little frightened."

Zoraya hurried back to her own bridal suite where Roberto was pacing back and forth. "I thought you'd never return," he whispered in her ear. "You've been gone so long."

"Only one minute, my love," laughed Zoraya, "but it seemed so long to me too."

"Oh, my love, I have so longed for this moment," sighed Marilú, alone at last with Gonzalo in their bedchamber. "And don't be shocked, because you are going to find me the most wanton woman in all Spain tonight, my darling."

"Oh, I do love you, my own, my sweetest one," he whispered, "more than I ever have in all our happy married days—and nights."

Her eager fingers hastily undid the buttons of his jacket and shirt while he just as hastily removed the lovely, filmy garments that Nardjis had brought for Marilú from the palace of Medina al-Zahra.

"Come to me, my husband, I can't wait," Marilú whispered, as she saw her husband's great manroot hard and tumescent, pointed to the ceiling.

She had slipped a pillow beneath her as her husband laid her down with gentle roughness on the bed, and she rejoiced to feel him penetrate her to her very womb. Love had never been as wonderful as this, she thought, as she grasped him and drew him into her ever deeper.

And then she felt her muscles contracting in the ecstasy of *kabbázah* as she held her husband tight within her from end to end.

"Oh, my darling, my darling," he groaned. "Hold me! hold me! it's wonderful."

And he plunged and pressed, in and out, and round and round, his powerful back and thighs straining to the utmost as he thrust into her again and again. Marilú, her thighs and legs wrapped tightly around his waist, churned and writhed in passionate embrace, the two of them groaning and panting in pain and rapture. Never before had she experienced such unadulterated rapture! Never before had he known the delights of love so keenly, so overwhelmingly!

They kept it up, it seemed, for hours, until, at last, she could hold out no longer, and she released her *kabbázah* grip with a sigh of relief. Instantly, in a paroxysm of mutual passion, she felt herself inundated with a torrent of delight as her husband sank down into her arms, rapturously content.

They remained coupled in each other's arms, panting and exhausted.

"I am so full and happy, my husband," Marilú sighed. "I could feel you so hard and strong within me. I have never loved as I loved tonight. And it will be like this for ever and ever, my husband. I do love you so."

"You love me *so?*" he asked, as he pressed deeper inside her.

"Yes, my love—*sō*," and she again compressed her muscles. "Oh, my God! my God! not again," she screamed, as she felt him grow hard and stiff inside her.

But it was too late to stop the onward flow of passion, and again the two writhed in amorous embrace. Again and again they were drowned in wave after wave of rapturous delight as Gonzalo plunged full into her very vitals, and Marilú grasped him with the full force of her strong muscles from her vulva to her womb. Around and around and up and down they churned and writhed, as he explored her secret parts. He was supported on his elbows now, and squeezed and fondled her breasts and nipples, swollen in passion.

The waves of ecstasy flowed over them and through them again and again without ceasing, until at last, in a full flood tide of rapturous passion, they once again relapsed into each other's arms, utterly exhausted and sublimely satisfied.

"Oh, my darling wife, my dearest Marilú," he sighed. "How I have missed you. And how glorious it is to be reunited again. I love you, *Marquesa*."

"And I love you too, *Marqués*," she whispered. "I'm so happy! I just hope our little Conchita is just as happy. And Zoraya too. But they couldn't be. No one, no one in all this world, could be as happy as I am. I do love you so. And now you must behave, you wicked man. And get some sleep. Remember, you are an old married man—a married man with two lovely children.

"How I miss them, the darlings," she continued. "We must get back to them as soon as we can. Maybe we have made a little boy tonight to keep them company. I hope so. And I want him to be as strong and brave as you are, my husband."

"I miss our children too, my love," Gonzalo whispered. "But when I'm with you like this I can think of no one else. Let's get to sleep, my precious. But don't be surprised if I come over to your side of the bed again tonight. I want to make up for those long nights without you."

The sun did not penetrate through the drawn curtains until late the following morning. Marilú awoke, stretched lazily and sinuously with catlike grace as she was wont to do. Gonzalo, flat on his back, watched her with affectionate amusement, his manroot rising again as he saw the contours of her graceful body. She watched excitedly as his great rod became stiff and tumescent before her eyes.

"You lazy loafer, you," she laughed. "I'm going to take you now as you've taken me all evening. It's going to be love, love, love, and here I come."

She jumped astride her husband's prostrate body, and quickly inserted him. She rode him and rode him, posting up and down in a frenzied trot on her rampant stallion, and then sitting down closely in her saddle at a full and ever-faster gallop.

"I told you that you ride well, my darling," he laughed as he grasped her swaying breasts and fondled and squeezed them affectionately.

But they were soon engaged in too desperate a course for further talk, as the fair rider and her plunging steed galloped and galloped in wild abandon. It was difficult for her to control her *kabbázah* muscles in this position, but she did so, and kept a firm seat in the saddle, clutching with all her strength the stiff rod that held her in her place.

"Oh, my God!" she screamed as she could hold out no longer, and a fountain of hot spray rose into her from her prostrate mount. She sank down into his embracing arms, rapturously exhausted.

"I don't think I'll ever be able to take you again," she sighed. "You're so strong and I feel so weak, so tired—and, oh, so full and contented. Let me just rest beside you until I get my breath."

"Well, my darling, you've taken me thoroughly enough for one night—for many nights—and I enjoyed every minute of it. It's morning, and I have to be about my affairs. We'll leave right after lunch. You can get together with the ladies while Roberto, Jorge and I are busy. . . . I wonder how things have gone with them. I know they've been very happy. I'm sure of it."

After her bath, Marilú wandered down the hall where she saw Zoraya standing contentedly in one of the small living rooms. "Oh, Zoraya, you've been such a wonderful hostess. I'm so happy I could purr! Last night was more wonderful than any I've ever known or dreamed of. And it's because I truly gave myself without restraint—like a woman. Thanks to you. . . . And you, my dear?"

"Ecstatic! I can't tell you how happy I am."

Conchita burst into the room, bubbling with excitement. "It was heavenly—absolute bliss. I've never known there could be such ecstasy as this, even in my dreams. Oh, it's utter rapture to be married. I'm so happy, and I can never thank you enough, Marilú, nor you either, Zoraya darling."

"And we've been very happy too, my dear," Zoraya smiled. "Marilú's been telling me. She didn't have to tell me though; I could see it in her eyes. And Roberto and I have had a heavenly time. Oh, my precious Conchita, I hope you were as happy as I."

"I was," Conchita replied smugly.

"Me too," smiled Marilú. "But now we'd better be going. Here comes Nardjis." And the three of them hugged and kissed Lady Nardjis until all four were breathless.

"My, oh my, you're smothering me. And I'm so glad to find you three so happy. But hadn't we better join the gentlemen? It's time for lunch."

The three priests joined them at the table, all animosity gone by this time. They chatted gaily during the meal, all of them very contented with the way things had gone.

"I am very grateful for your agreeing to take us on to the Hermitage of San Pedro," said Dom Gregorio. "And I would like to pick up Fra Antonio at the

Monastery. It will only take a minute. He is in charge of the monastery journal, and I want to show you that the banns for your weddings have been posted for the past four Sundays—a miracle—the voice of San Geminiano.

"And with your permission, my lord *Marqués*, I'd like to take Fra Antonio with us, and the monastery journal too. I plan to have him appointed chief calligrapher of the Hermitage, and I want him to finish illuminating the text of the journal. We can all fit in one of your empty wagons with our things. Our old bones can't stand the long trip from here to Orgaz on horseback."

"Very well," said Gonzalo. "I'd like to see that journal. And it is a miracle, although I confess, Father, that at first I didn't believe you. But after these marriages, so happy that I know they must have been ordained in Heaven, I'd believe anything. Let's be on our way. It's only a short trip this time—a little over six leagues to Almadén. But the soldiers are ready to leave, and I want them to have plenty of time to grease the axles, and repair the harness, and have all our fighting gear in readiness for the long trip to Alarcos tomorrow. Let's go."

In another few minutes the cortege was again on its way, the ladies of El Viso waving goodbye to the soldiers whose needs they had attended to so assiduously the night before. As they rode through the gates, Marilú, Conchita and Zoraya looked back affectionately at the mansion where they had spent so many happy hours. The three ladies, and their friend Nardjis, rode together, chatting happily, as the general and his two colonels rejoined their troops.

And, by early afternoon, the cavalcade had arrived at the ancient Moorish castle of al-Madén. Lady Nardjis told them that the name was Arabic for 'mines,' and pointed out the great cinnabar deposits at the side of the road, the deep vermillion pigment standing out like a bloody scar against the brown earth.

"They use that pigment to make paint," Nardjis explained, "but the chief use for cinnabar is to make mercury. They roast the cinnabar and the quicksilver comes trickling out from the bottom of the furnace. It's fantastic!

"And over there, just beyond the hedge of blue gentian and lavender, those thistles, taller than a man, are the giant teasels they grow for carding wool. They use the dried flower; it's all prickly, and it pulls the wool until it's soft and flannely all over."

"You know so many things, Nardjis," said Conchita admiringly.

"Well, all this region used to be part of Islamic Spain, not so many years ago, and I've traveled all over here, and to Toledo too, when my husband was alive. So, you remember the things you did together. And you don't forget." She was silent.

The castle of al-Madén was enormous, and well furnished, although in more Spartan fashion than Zoraya's mansion, and certainly not to be compared with the magnificence of Medina al-Zahra. It was a fortress, rather than a palace, but accommodations were adequate for the three couples and Lady Nardjis. An inner courtyard gave ample room for the wagons, safely stored behind a pair of heavy iron gates. The soldiers and horses camped in the outer courtyard, within the castle walls, and the same arrangements were made for a visit from the ladies of the town—an essential for a happy army.

Chatting gaily, the four ladies entered the castle, and were shown to their rooms by a smiling majordomo. They were soon joined by the three husbands who had been busy attending to the storing and guarding of the supply wagons, and giving orders for the rest of the day and night.

After a light supper in the great dining hall, Conchita remarked shyly: "I'm tired, and I'd like to go to bed early."

"Well, I'm *not* tired, and I'd like to go to bed early," laughed Zoraya, as she linked her arm with that of her husband, who beamed at her with almost fatuous devotion.

"And I'm not tired either," said Marilú, "but I do think we should all get a good night's rest."

"Well, so long as you three women have made up your minds," Gonzalo grunted, "I guess there's nothing for us men to do but to turn in too. Will you excuse us, Lady Nardjis?"

And in a few minutes, the three couples had left for the second night of their happy, happy honeymoon.

"Do you think I'm adorable, Jorgito?" asked Conchita, as they closed the door of their apartment behind them.

"Of course, you're adorable, my darling," he laughed, "utterly and devastatingly adorable. And I adore every bit of you, from head to toe. I adore these adorable lips," and he grasped her in his arms and pressed her to him as he planted his lips on hers.

"And I adore these adorable, sweet breasts," he whispered, fondling them affectionately, cupping them in his hands and caressing them tenderly.

He kissed them ardently, caressing them with his tongue, until Conchita cried: "I can't stand it any more. I can't stand it, Jorgito darling. No, don't stop, Jorgito. I love it."

"And I adore those adorable legs and most adorable thighs," he whispered, as he lifted Conchita up in his arms and laid her on the bed, stripping off her clothes as he did so. His hands caressed her feet, her ankles, and her calves, lingeringly, lovingly—then passed up higher to the tender inside of her thighs, which he covered with passionate kisses.

"Oh, don't, don't, Jorgito darling," sighed Conchita.

"And I adore that adorable you," Jorge whispered, as he transferred his kisses still higher, his beard mingling with the soft blond hair between her thighs, and his tongue caressing the red lips he found beneath. "I adore this adorable little flower of yours, my sweetest sweet. I adore all of you, utterly and completely, my own adorable little wife and lover."

"Oh, Jorge, take me," Conchita panted. "I want you so much. I need you so much. Take me, quickly, Jorgito, please."

"No, my adorable one," he teased, "I'm going to let you take me."

And he stretched out on the bed, on his back, his feet against the footboard, and his knees raised at an angle. "Now, you mount me, my adorable wife. Mount me as you would a horse, and I shall be your stallion. My knees will be the cantal of your saddle, and you will bestride me, and ride me. Now, don't come squashing down on me, but post up and down gently, as you would at a trot."

"Oh, I love this," exclaimed Conchita, as she posted up and down on her bucking mount. "I love it. It gives me squiggles all up and down my spine. It's wonderful, Jorgito. Keep on bucking. I love it."

And she increased the pace of her trot as she felt him penetrate further and further, sending thrills and chills into every part of her body. Jorge grabbed her pendant breasts as she bent over her prancing steed. He squeezed and fondled them as they had never been fondled before and kept grinding his pelvis up and down and from side to side until at last Conchita screamed: "I can't stand it any more."

And she sat down firmly in the saddle, writhing and squirming, but never leaving her seat by more than a hair's breadth, as she started off at a canter and finally broke into a full gallop at hair-raising speed. Her charger followed her every movement, plunging and falling up and down, from side to side. And then, in a final frenzy of passion, he lunged into her, and squirted a fountain of heavenly elixir into her heavenly body.

"Oh, my God! my God!" she moaned. "It's wonderful! It's wonderful, Jorgito, and I love you so." She sank down into his arms, the two still linked together, panting and sighing. "You're so wonderful, Jorgito, so strong and wonderful," she sighed. "And I'm so full, so full and contented."

"And you're so adorable, my darling sweet," he murmured as they lay down side by side in one another's arms. "Does that answer your question, my adorable precious? Do you believe now that I adore you?"

"Oh, I do. I do indeed. It's been wonderful. And I've never enjoyed a ride as much as I enjoyed that one. And I love to have your great big root inside my little flower. Let's talk rude, Jorgito darling. It makes me feel so wicked and passionate, Jorgito, and I am wickedly passionate—for you alone, my lover."

She bent down and gave him a kiss, full of ardor and passion, and he rolled her over on her back, planting a warm kiss deep within the recess of her neck and shoulder.

"Oh, Jorge, lover, take me again, take me again and again. I want you to take me," she moaned, wrapping her thighs around his waist as she felt him penetrate her yet again and the two of them writhed and churned and groaned in mutual passion.

CHAPTER 20

They left the castle of al-Madén early the following morning, the cavalcade spread out as usual, with two squads at right and left to guard the flanks of the column, and vanguard and rear guard stretched out a thousand yards away from the wagon train and main body of troops. As the column turned east at Saceruela, three leagues north of Alamadén, the captain of the right guard spotted two horsemen on the horizon, galloping northward at full speed. His own squads were invisible, hidden by a clump of trees.

Sending one of the sergeants back at a gallop to the main column, in order to have a squad from the vanguard head off the two riders from the front, he deployed his own men through the shelter of a ravine until they were on the far side of the approaching riders. At a given signal, his troopers galloped with drawn swords toward the two riders from the side and rear. With a squad in front, and two squads of men charging them from the right and rear, the two strangers had only one way open, and they galloped westward, only to be met and captured by the main body of Gonzalo's forces.

They were brought, unresisting, alongside the wagon train to be questioned by Gonzalo. But they refused to answer any questions other than to say that they were couriers of the Princess Zayda, wife of Prince al-Mamun. As such, they demanded to be released, saying they were on their way to Alarcos to report to Princess Zayda.

Lady Nardjis and her three friends were on the far

side of the wagon train where they could see and hear, without being seen by the two couriers. Nardjis whispered to Marilú: "I know one of those men—the sergeant. I am sure that I can make them talk if your husband will do as I say. Do you think you can call him over here without their suspecting anything?"

Marilú beckoned to one of the captains and gave him brief instructions. The captain rode through the ranks of wagons and whispered a few words to Gonzalo. Gonzalo turned to Roberto: "Would you take over the questioning, and don't let these men go until I return." Turning to Jorge, he added: "Let us dismount here, rest a few minutes, and change horses. I shan't be long."

Jorge shouted the order to dismount, and the troopers got off their horses and wagons. The prisoners were made to dismount and turn their horses over to a trooper. Gonzalo himself dismounted, handing his bridle to one of the soldiers, then walked through the ranks of wagons to where the four ladies stood.

"My lord," whispered Lady Nardjis, "I know one of those men—the sergeant, and I feel sure I can make him talk if you will do as I suggest. I don't like the look of things, and I mistrust the Princess Zayda and all her men."

"I don't like the look of things either," said Gonzalo. "What do you suggest?"

"Well, my lord, put me in one of the empty wagons as a prisoner and have my hands tied behind me. Then, have those men thrown into the wagon. Have the sergeant who puts them in say something horrible to me, as rude and vulgar as he can be—as though he hated all Saracens, and me especially. If you will do that, then I am sure I can establish a friendly enough relationship with the two prisoners to get them to loosen their tongues and tell me what's going on.

"From the fact that they were riding from the

south, and that the Princess is north and east of here, I'm very much afraid that they may have been plotting, perhaps even with the *Almorávides*, and that we and all our wagons may be in grave danger."

"I'm afraid you may be right about the danger, Lady Nardjis," said Gonzalo. "I hate to put you to this trial, but it may save our lives."

He called to one of his sergeants, a brutal looking giant of a man, but obviously no man's fool.

After a few words of instruction, the sergeant led Lady Nardjis off and helped her up into one of the two empty wagons. He tied her wrists firmly behind her and fastened them to one of the uprights inside the wagon.

"I hate to do this to you, my lady, and I am going to be so violent to you when I put the prisoners in here that I am afraid you'll hate me for it—but I understand what you are trying to do. God be with you, my lady."

He left her there and, a few minutes later, he and his men returned with the two prisoners, their hands tied behind their backs. "Get in there, you swine, you," he ordered roughly, as he tied their wrists to the wagon. "No, not you, you bitch," he snarled at Lady Nardjis. "It's not time for you just yet. I'll let you have it soon enough, you Saracen she-dog."

He jumped off the wagon, the tailgate was closed and locked, and the three prisoners were left there almost suffocating under the tent-like canvas roof.

"That dog of a Christian," cried Nardjis, "he'll die before he rapes me, the dog. I have a dagger in my bosom, and when he unties my hands and takes me to the bushes, I'll plunge it straight into his heart. And then I'll come back here and cut your bonds, and we'll escape together." And she sobbed bitterly.

"Why, Lady Nardjis! It's you. What are you doing here? What happened? Don't you know me?"

"Yes," exclaimed Nardjis, looking up. "You're sergeant Abdullah, the bodyguard of the Princess Zayda. How glad I am to see you. We'll help one another escape, and maybe you can steal some horses when we come to a stop."

"You ask what I'm doing here," she went on. "Those dogs of Christians found me in the palace of Medina al-Zahra. They had heard tales of the hidden treasure of the Caliph Abd ar-Rahman, and they tried to force me to tell them where it was. As though I'd know, the stupid fools. When every king of Córdoba and Sevilla has tried in vain to find it for over a hundred years. If it really exists at all—if it's not just a myth.

"And when I wouldn't tell them where it was—I couldn't—they were going to torture me, but decided they better get away before General Sirr arrived, so they've taken me prisoner to torture me in Toledo. And they have enough treasure in all those wagons of theirs to satisfy even the avarice of their Christian king—practically all the rugs and tapestries and precious things they could find in the palace."

"Oh, my poor Lady Nardjis," said the sergeant. "I feel so sorry for you, and wish I could help you. But I can't. And if that dog of a sergeant tries to rape you, may Allah help you to kill him as he deserves. But don't try to come back here to rescue us. It will be safer for you to escape alone. And we shall be rescued anyway, I can promise you that. We have just come from Córdoba on a mission from Princess Zayda. The troops of Prince al-Mamun and the Black Vizier have been utterly routed, annihilated, and Córdoba and Medina al-Zahra have fallen.

"And General Sirr, at our request, is sending a task force of twelve hundred men to attack the wagon train and recapture the booty, which he will divide with Princess Zayda in return for all her provinces in this part of the country. King al-Mutamid has made her Queen of all this region between Córdoba and Toledo, and she has many loyal followers because of her beauty.

"Anyway, we are sure to be rescued before dusk today—our spies tell us the Marqués de Clavijo only has six hundred men, and the *Almorávides* will outnumber him two to one, not to mention the matter of surprise. And I advise you to wait and be rescued with us, unless that dog of a sergeant, may Allah shrivel his black soul, attempts to take your honor. And may Allah bless and protect you, Lady Nardjis."

"Thank you, Sergeant Abdullah," Nardjis replied. "But why didn't you ride past us at night while we were alseep at Almadén? Then you could have gotten to Alarcos without the Spaniards having seen you."

"That's what we wanted to do," the sergeant replied. "Our two comrades, who left Córdoba three hours before us, must have passed you in the night, and are now well on their way to Alarcos and the Princess. But we were delayed, which is why we were caught, and why we are here."

The wagon had been rattling along at a steady pace all during this conversation and, in due course, came to a halt again, as it came time for the next change of horses. The tailgate opened, and the Christian sergeant jumped inside.

"Come along, you Saracen bitch," he growled as he untied her hands, keeping tight hold on the rope still fastened to her left wrist. "I have a little business to do with you. And you two over there, you better shut your God damned mouths, or I'll break your damned jaws for you," he added, as the two Saracens started to protest.

He pulled Lady Nardjis out of the wagon, and slammed the tailgate shut. "Oh, my lady, please forgive me, but I wanted to convince those two spies that you were truly a prisoner. I do hope you were able to discover what you wanted."

"I did indeed," said Lady Nardjis, still somewhat shaken. "And I do thank you—although it was horrible. I'd dread to really be your prisoner, sergeant. Would you really be as vicious as that?"

"Not really, my lady, certainly not with you. But the general is waiting for us."

Gonzalo, Roberto and Jorge were waiting as Nardjis and the sergeant approached. Lady Nardjis was too upset to smile, but she said at once: "I got what I was seeking, my lord, and thanks to this sergeant who truly frightened the heart out of me with his roughness."

She outlined what she had learned from the prisoners.

"Twelve hundred men," Gonzalo repeated gravely. "And we may expect the attack today. Well, forewarned is forearmed. We shall do what we can. Let us be on our way. I'd rather be on the other side of the Guadiana and Bullaque rivers when the attack comes.

"Reinforce the guard on the right flank, Jorge. We shall be continuing east, and the *Almorávides* will be coming from the south. But give strict instructions that our men are not to fight a holding action unless it becomes imperative. We shall need all the soldiers we have right here at the wagon train. The essential thing is that we be advised immediately—*immediately*, you understand—as soon as the enemy is spotted.

"Our outposts should be strung out so as to get the widest possible view of the landscape, and as soon as the enemy is sighted they should send their fastest couriers to me at once, and then all rejoin our main column. The rear guard, vanguard, and left flank too. Is that clear?"

"Yes, my lord," Jorge replied, and Roberto nodded

his assent: "I shall give instructions to the left flank and rear guard, and bring the vanguard closer to us. I gather there is no further danger from the north or east."

"Right," said Gonzalo. "We shall keep Zayda's men prisoners at least until after the attack."

The column moved ahead at an accelerated pace, the men alerted and ready. Seven leagues further on, after only the briefest of stops for a change of horses, they came to the town of Luciana on the banks of the Guadiana at the mouth of the Bullaque River. They forded the stream at a point that Gonzalo knew well from his previous crossings.

"Well, thank goodness, we have left that behind us," grunted Gonzalo with satisfaction. "The terrain is better for our purpose on this side of the river. And further on, we shall again have the Guadiana on our flank. Now let them come—the sooner the better."

The column moved on steadily. Just before the town of Piedrabuena, a courier came galloping up at full speed. The enemy had been spotted crossing the Guadiana at the same point that Gonzalo's forces had crossed a half hour earlier. No, they themselves had not been seen, the courier was sure of it.

"Roberto, order the rear guard and right flank squads to join us immediately, without being seen, if possible. I can see that the left flank squads are already coming, as they were ordered to do. And you, Jorge, bring back the vanguard to join our main column." The two officers were off at once.

Gonzalo reflected: "The *Almorávides* must have left the main road from Córdoba to Alarcos, moved west to Almodóvar del Campo, and are trailing us here."

He examined the terrain around him. Straight ahead, the road ascended a steep hill toward Piedrabuena to the east. There was a deep ravine to their right between them and the river. No attack could come from that side. To the north, on their left, was a long steep hill, topped by a thick grove of trees and underbrush. So the enemy would be coming from the west, from behind their column.

The two colonels had completed their mission. Gonzalo gave the battle instructions. "Jorge, you take the wagon train up that hill on the road ahead of us. You will have two hundred cavalry with you. Send the womenfolk beyond that point, to the hill on the north, where they will be hidden by the forest. And let the end of your wagon train be visible from below, with a rear guard just behind it, so that the enemy will think it is the main body of our troops. When the eneny approaches from the bottom of the hill, you will have your men fire three volleys of arrows, no more, and then come charging down the hill straight at them with your lances.

"Roberto and I shall be hidden in the forest with six hundred men at the top of that hill to the north. As the enemy charges up the hill to strike your forces, Jorge, and when they are half way up the hill, Roberto's and my men will let fly three volleys of arrows. We shall be on foot, and hidden in the forest, so that our shots should have maximum effect, and the enemy will not know where the arrows are coming from. They will assume that they come from the main column up ahead. As soon as we fire the third volley, we shall leap on our horses, and come charging down that hill with our lances, striking the enemy on their left flank. And then, may God favor the side of Saint James and of Castilla and León! Is that clear"

"Yes, my general," answered the two colonels, and Jorge galloped away to carry out his orders. Roberto and Gonzalo gathered the main body of troops—six hundred men—and disappeared in the forest and underbrush along the top of the hill paralleling the road.

Marilú, Conchita, Zoraya, and Lady Nardjis waited

at the crest of the hill to the north and east of the scene of the prospective battle. From there, they could see without being seen, and they were tense as they watched the landscape. A single squad of soldiers waited with them, with their horses tethered to the trees, in the event the course of battle should require them to flee. Meanwhile, the four ladies tried to withhold their tears, as they prayed for victory and, above all, that their three beloved husbands should survive the onslaught of the dreaded *Almorávides.*

Jorge's forces, including the wagon train, were grouped somewhat below the crest of the hill so that, when the enemy came into sight, they would still be heading eastward along the road.

They had not long to wait. The Saracen army came galloping down the road. Their vanguard allowed their main column to join them, and then they charged up the hill at top speed, scimitars flashing in the sunlight. Jorge's forces made what seemed to be a desperate attempt to bring the last of the wagons over the top of the hill. A hundred of his men, as a rear guard, shot three volleys of arrows from horseback, discarded their bows, and came charging down the hill, lances poised, straight for the Saracen army. A second group of one hundred men, still on foot, shot three more volleys of arrows, taking careful aim, then left their bows, leaped on their horses, and charged down the hill after their comrades, lances in hand. The arrows had taken their toll of the enemy, but the *Almorávides* charged up the hill, scimitars waving, ignoring their fallen comrades, and shouting their fierce war cry.

Three well-aimed volleys of arrows from the six hundred soldiers on their left flank took a terrible toll of the charging Saracen troops, and then, with a wild cry of "Saint James, León and Castilla" and "Cierra Espana"—"Close ranks, Spain"—Gonzalo's and Roberto's troops came flying down the hill straight for the enemy's flank. Caught by surprise, at least four hundred of the *Almorávides* were impaled on the lances of their enemy. Six hundred more had been shot from their horses by the volleys of arrows from the front and flank. A scant two hundred were left to defend themselves with their scimitars against the flashing swords of nearly eight hundred Spaniards.

The outcome of the battle was not long in doubt. Outnumbered, the Saracens fought valiantly, and thirty-five Spaniards fell before their scimitar blows. But, at last, the din of battle was over. The *Almorávides* neither asked nor were given quarter, and every last man was slain by Spanish swords—all but two, two men who galloped down the road at full tilt away from the scene of battle.

"Follow me," yelled a Spanish captain, and two sergeants wheeled around to pursue the fleeing Saracens.

"Let them go, captain," Gonzalo commanded, and the captain and sergeants turned, crestfallen, back to their commander.

"But, General, we could have caught them, and made it a total victory," protested the captain.

"If any horsemen in Spain could have outridden those Saracens, you three could do it," Gonzalo smiled. "And I believe you could have caught them. I know you are disappointed, captain, but there are two reasons I wanted them to escape. One is that I wish to be on our way as soon as possible to make up for lost time, and the other is that I want them to carry the news back to General Sirr of the annihilation of his task force."

"But they will say that they were attacked by five thousand men, my general. They will never admit that they were vanquished by a mere eight hundred.

"So much the better, captain. All the less likely that General Sirr will come marching up here with his army. He is more likely to conquer Sevilla first to protect his rear. And I doubt whether he will attempt to attack Toledo until next Spring, probably not even Alarcos. So you have done magnificently, and I appreciate your valor and loyalty."

He shook their hands warmly.

"Roberto, would you send out some varlets with glaives of mercy to help any wounded Saracens on their way to Paradise and to capture stray horses and any other booty. And have some of the varlets count approximately the number of enemy dead. I would like to leave here in half an hour if we can."

The four ladies came riding down to the field, accompanied by their escort. "You were wonderful, Jorge," cried Conchita as she sprang off her horse and fell sobbing into his arms. "You were so brave, my love, and I was so afraid you would be killed."

Zoraya likewise took refuge in Roberto's arms, the tears streaming down her face.

Marilú beamed at Gonzalo through her tears. "My hero! You were wonderful! And how I love you, and how frightened I was when I saw those terrible *Almorávides* charging straight up the hill after Jorge and his men. How could you do it? There were so many more of them, and you killed them all."

"Choice of terrain, my love," Gonzalo replied simply. "Terrain and expert archers. That, and our lances, and the fury of our charge. After that, it was four to one, and simple. And Saint James and God were with us!

"But, Lady Nardjis," Gonzalo added, "we owe it all to you. If it hadn't been for your warning, we would have been taken unaware, and God knows what would have happened to us. My wife has been dinning your praises into my ears ever since we left Medina al-Zahra, and I know that she and Conchita and Zoraya love you as their dearest friend. I have known you simply as a charming, a lovely and intelligent person, but never until now have I appreciated your true worth. You are a remarkable and a wonderful woman. You have saved all our lives, believe me. Please let me embrace you as I long to do, and from now on please let me call you Nardjis, and you call me Gonzalo. You are very dear to me, and I want you to consider us as all one family."

He put his arms around Nardjis and kissed her tenderly on the forehead. With his arm still around her waist, he asked: "Now tell me, Nardjis dear, what should we do with your two prisoners? Should we kill them? Dead men tell no tales, you know."

"Perhaps, Gonzalo, it would be just as well to have them tell some tales. Let them see what has happened to their allies, and let them repeat the story to Zayda. We may learn something interesting. But keep me out of sight, until you put them back in their prison wagon. Let them assume that I have escaped, because I don't want Zayda to know I am with you—not yet, anyway. She knows me well, and we may learn more if I am kept in hiding."

Gonzalo kissed Nardjis again on the forehead, and said: "I am going to put you in the wagon with the priests, if you don't mind—just for a few minutes while I let these prisoners look around. And then it is back in the prison wagon for them, and on to Alarcos."

One of the captains came riding back. "We have lost thirty-five dead, my general, thirty-five of our good companions. We've brought their bodies here, sir. And we have counted over eleven hundred of the enemy dead; there may be more."

"Thank you, captain," said Gonzalo gravely. "You may let the men know that the widows of these brave thirty-five, or their next of kin, will receive their share of the booty. I know that is what all our men would want. And, in just a few minutes, you can put their bodies in the wagon the priests are riding in so that we can take them to Alarcos for a Christian burial. The priests can travel on horseback—it is only six leagues more.

"And, sergeant," he continued, turning to the giant soldier who had put the prisoners in the wagon, "let your prisoners out of the wagon. Keep them tied up and put them back in the wagon quickly, but I want them to see that we have annihilated the twelve hundred men sent out to murder us—and lost only thirty-five of our men. Let them see all that. And, oh, sergeant, that Saracen bitch"—the sergeant blushed under his tanned face—"that Saracen bitch you tried to rape stabbed you and got away, escaped. Let them know that too. And curse her all you want. It may be helpful. And thank you for being such an accomplished actor."

Gonzalo's instructions were carried out to the letter. The Saracen couriers were dumbfounded when they saw the scene on the hillside, and noted a scant thirty or so Spanish bodies to be loaded into the wagon.

And within less than half an hour, the cortege was again on its way, passing the silver, lead, iron and manganese mines of Calatrava on the banks of the Guadiana, near the site of the ancient Roman city of Cretum, from which they could see the old Roman bridge, still in use at the river crossing. From there, they galloped past Valverde, with its great copper mines and magnificent pine forest, until they crossed the river again and came within sight of the ramparts and towers of Alarcos perched on a plateau overlooking the river and plains below. Vineyards the olive groves covered the fields around them.

"We shall be staying at the castle of Alarcos," Gonzalo told Marilú. "Even before I knew that the Princess Zayda was going to be there, I had sent word on ahead, and my men—the two hundred I left behind in Alarcos—have moved from their encampment and are occupying the grounds within the castle walls. They have prepared the castle for our return, and you may be sure that, if the Princess Zayda attempts to stay there, they will escort her to the palace just outside the walls where King Alfonso generally stays—really, a more comfortable place, but no courtyard for the protection of our wagons. So we shall soon be there, dear. And I'm tired."

"You must be, my dear, after that battle. And I don't look forward to meeting Princess Zayda this evening, as I suppose we shall."

CHAPTER 21

The cavalcade passed through the gates of the city to the sound of wild cheers from hundreds of the soldiers of the Marqués de Clavijo who had remained in Alarcos over the past week, but who had heard the news of the vast store of booty that their comrades were bringing them. Less than an hour earlier, advance couriers from Gonzalo's fighting troops had brought, not only that great news, but also word of the magnificent victory over the army of the *Almorávides*. The wagon train and its escort were therefore hailed as conquering heroes, and followed with shouts and cheers and waving arms as they wound their way through the city streets, from the great walls of Alarcos to the equally massive fortifications of the castle itself.

The most vociferous cheers were reserved for the Marqués de Clavijo and for his gracious wife, Marilú, to whom the voice of Saint James the Apostle had revealed the whereabouts of the treasure of Abd ar-Rahman. The story of the revelation of Saint James had gone from mouth to mouth, acquiring new facets of circumstantial evidence as it circulated until, finally, the accepted version was that the Apostle himself had appeared before Marilú in her cell, halo and all, and surrounded by a great aureole of blinding light, but invisible to her cellmates. And that, in a great booming voice, the Apostle had commanded her to destroy the walls of the dungeon. Upon the arrival of her rescuers, the manacles of the three women had dropped like magic from their wrists, and, at a touch from Marilú's outstretched hand, the twenty-foot thick walls of the dungeon had crumbled into dust.

There were conflicting versions, of course, but the less elaborate stories brought by the soldiers who had actually entered the dungeon were cast aside as sacrilege, and it became the better part of valor for them to keep their doubts to themselves. So the more heavily embroidered tale became established gospel, and there were even those who swore they saw a halo of light around the golden hair of the conqueror's wife as she rode through the city, bowing right and left in grateful acknowledgement of the cheers of her admirers. In any event, the radiance of her beaming smile and yellow hair were as bright as any halo, and soldiers and townsfolk easily lost their hearts to this lovely redeeming angel.

Nor were the others in the cortege lacking in admirers. Jorge and Conchita, Roberto and Zoraya, the Lady Nardjis whose great wisdom had made possible the escape from Medina al-Zahra, the captains and sergeants down to the humblest soldier, were all conquering heroes, and the outbursts of joy and jubilation were so spontaneous as to remove any possible doubts as to their sincerity.

But there were more important things to attend to. The supply wagons had to be safely stowed away in the great courtyard of the castle, behind the iron gates. And other arrangements had to be completed for the night's encampment, both within and without the castle.

Gonzalo approached the four holy men who had dismounted from their steeds, somewhat stiff in their joints from the jolting of the wagon and their subsequent six-league ride on horseback. He addressed Dom Gregorio: "*Padre*, would you be good enough to make arrangements at the Church for a Christian burial service for these thirty-five good men who died in defense of their king and country. Tomorrow morning for the eighth hour after midnight, *padre*. I don't care if the gravediggers have to work all night. It must be done, and they will be compensated for their pains. We shall make a suitable donation to the Church, of course."

"Very well, my lord *Marqués*. It shall be as you say," and the old abbot bowed and went quickly on his way.

Turning to the prisoners, still tied in the wagon, Gonzalo said: "Gentlemen, my captain and two squads of my men will accompany you to the palace where the Princess Zayda is staying. If it prove that you are in fact her couriers, then my apologies to you for the inconvenience we have put you to, and my profoundest apologies to the Princess, which will be conveyed on my behalf by the captain and will later be repeated by me in person.

"But, if it appear that you have played us false, then we shall leave your punishment to the discretion of the Princess Zayda herself. You will understand our predicament, I trust, gentlemen, because at our last stop you must have had some idea of the dangers we ran in journeying from Medina al-Zahra to Alarcos, and we could not afford to take the slightest chance with our lives or with our booty.

"And, captain," he added, "you will do me the favor to invite her highness, the Princess Zayda, to accept our humble hospitality, and to dine with us and with our ladies at the eighth hour this evening. And, if she would do us the honor, we should be most appreciative if she would come to the castle at the seventh hour to sip a wine of honor with my wife and her companions, and to converse with them until the hour for dinner. The Princess, captain, is a most distinguished personage, and must be treated accordingly."

The captain left with the prisoners in tow, their bonds removed, and their scimitars and horses returned to them. Two squads with two sergeants accompanied them to the palace of the Princess, within the city walls and just outside the walls of the castle itself.

"And now, Roberto and Jorge, and you four lovely ladies, including my own adored Santa Marilú—I understand from the plaudits of the crowd that you have been beatified, my dear—would you all come with me to my apartment. I have a few words for you in private."

"In the first place," he continued, as they closed the door of the apartment behind them, "remember that no one knows a thing of the Princess Zayda's duplicity except the seven of us in this room. And, of course, the Princess herself and her immediate confidants. It is true that those two prisoners know that they have revealed certain facts to Nardjis whom they believe to have escaped—Nardjis will remain concealed for the immediate present—but they will never divulge this to the Princess. For, by now, they will know that it was a grave indiscretion, for which they would pay with their lives. So no one but ourselves—no one, I repeat—knows of the duplicity of the Princess or of the fact that, through Nardjis's shrewdness, we were able to defeat the *Almorávides.*

"Let us keep it that way. I shall divulge these facts only to the King himself, for his protection from the wiles of the Princess, for you and I all know her to be a very subtle and wicked woman. I understand, too, that she is reputed to be one of the most beautiful and seductive women in the world, and the King, you know, is not immune to women's wiles. So, as I say, I shall tell him the facts.

"In the second place, remember that the Princess is a very powerful and very wily woman. We cannot afford to have her for an enemy. If the King submits to her charms, and I am sure he will, she will be the most powerful woman in Toledo, and we especially cannot afford to have such a woman as our enemy while she is in Toledo and we are far away. So, remember, that none of you, no matter what your personal opinion of the woman may be, is to give the slightest hint to her or to anyone of your true feelings. We must always treat the Princess with the highest deference—in fact, with the deepest admiration and affection, and let her know it in our words and in our manner. What do you say to that advice, Nardjis? You know the Princess well, whereas I know her only by reputation."

"Gonzalo, you are an amazing man," Nardjis replied. "You are so completely right in everything you say, so wise not to make an issue of this woman's treachery despite what we now know of her actions, that I am lost in admiration. And she is indeed one of the most beautiful and intelligent women in all al-Andaluz. I have never known a man who did not succumb completely to her charms when the Princess had any reason to want to inveigle something out of him.

"You will excuse me, Marilú and Conchita and Zoraya for saying it, but I truly believe that, if the Princess so desired it, your three devoted husbands would be in bed with her this very minute, or at any time that she wanted. If there is any woman who is truly irresistible, it is she."

The three men laughed out loud, while their wives listened in shocked disbelief, and even a shade of annoyance, from which, however, they soon recovered.

Gonzalo continued: "And, in the third place—about this treasure—Roberto and I have been talking things over together, and what I am about to say is wholly his idea although I agree with him entirely, and I hope you will too.

"Do you know what Roberto's nickname is among his fellow-officers, Zoraya? No? Well, it's *'el sesudo'*—the brain! Your husband doesn't talk much, but when he does, I've always found his ideas worth listening to.

"Well, you all know that, under the laws of Christian Spain, and under both Spanish and Moorish custom since time immemorial, all chattels, all objects of value, and all prisoners, constitute the booty of war, and belong to the warriors who captured them—the Saracens call it *'ghanimah.'* And, under Spanish law, the King is only entitled to a fifth of that booty. On the other hand, all conquered territory, and all money captured from the enemy, constitute what the Saracens call *'fay'*, and belongs to the sovereign.

"Now this booty we have taken is no ordinary loot, as you know. I should judge that we have at least ten tons of gold, worth between two and three million dinars. And from what I have seen in the large and small leather trunks, I should guess that the precious stones and jewelry—and this does not include the rugs and tapestries—are worth at least five or six times that much. This is only a wild guess, of course, but what I want to impress upon you is that we have taken perhaps ten or twenty million dinars of loot, and if we attempted to give the King only his legal fifth share of that vast wealth, our heads would soon lose all physical contact with the rest of our bodies.

"I am serious about this. And that does not go into the question of whether this is booty looted from an enemy, or whether it belonged to the King by right as the only legal successor of Abd ar-Rahman. Nor whether the gold bars are chattels or money. These bricks of gold are minted with the seal of the Caliph. Does that make them money? These are points that I would not advise any of us to argue. Also bear in mind that no one but the seven of us in this room has any concept of the value of this treasure—and we ourselves have only the vaguest idea of its real worth. So none of our officers or soldiers will demand that the booty is for them, minus only the King's fifth share. They don't know, and they never will know, the actual value of all this loot.

"And, as for us, what I am saying is that, if we insist on our legal rights, we shall get nothing. In my experience, I have found that all governments and all sovereigns are without shame when it suits their purpose to ignore the law. As Saint Augustine says: '*Quid sunt regna nisi magna latrocinia quia et latrocinia quid sunt nisi parva regna?*'—'What is a king but a mighty robber, since what is a robber but a little king?'

"In the final analysis, what part we get of this booty depends not on the law but on the generosity of our sovereign. And what could we possibly do with ten or twenty million dinars? We shall all be rich beyond human desire if we get the tenth part of that—for us, for our officers, and for our men. And, of course, you know that there are established rules for the division of the booty among us all according to rank.

"So, what I propose, gentlemen—and you ladies should listen because it concerns you too—is that I send a message to King Alfonso telling him of this loot, and saying that, under the circumstances, the booty does not belong to us who have taken it, but that it is a treasure that belongs to all of Spain. Hence, that we shall place it *all* at his disposal, as Emperor of all Christian Spain, and that if he, out of his bounty, should graciously favor us and our officers and men with any portion of this great wealth, we shall be forever grateful to him. It is my thought that he will be so delighted, amazed and overwhelmed by our loyalty, and by the magnitude of this enormous wealth, that he will be most generous.

"What do you say, Jorge? Roberto and I cannot offer to sacrifice your share, unless you consent. Legally, assuming the loot is worth twenty million dinars, your share—and Roberto's too—would be about one and a quarter million dinars each. If King Alfonso should give us a tenth part of what we are entitled to, you, Jorge, and Roberto, would each have one hundred and twenty-five thousand dinars. What Nardjis's share would be—for she played a soldier's part in preserving the loot—and what Marilú's share should be—for she discovered it—I do not know. What do you say?"

"What in the world would I do with a million dinars?" exclaimed Jorge. "A hundred thousand dinars and I shall be richer than I ever dreamed—richer, I believe, than any man in northern Spain, other than the King himself. So, for my part, I agree. Furthermore, I have all the treasure I want right here in my arms," and he gave Conchita an affectionate hug.

"As for me," Nardjis added, "I don't feel that I am entitled to any share of the booty. I am so grateful that you have rescued me from the *Almorávides*, and I ask for nothing more."

"And my share—if any—belongs to you," concluded Marilú affectionately, her arm around Gonzalo.

"Very well," said Gonzalo. "Just one more thing. Lady Nardjis is going to keep out of sight when the Princess Zayda comes to talk with you ladies. She may learn something of value, and the Princess may talk a little more freely if Nardjis isn't there. But Nardjis will join us at dinner—the Princess is bound to learn sooner or later that she has come up from Medina al-Zahra with us, and we can't afford to have Princess Zayda believe that we have put something over on her. Do any of you have any suggestions, or anything to add to what I have said?

"No? Well, then, let us all get a little sleep. Jorge may not believe it. He is still a young man. But there is nothing that takes it out of a man like a battle, physically and mentally. I am sure we are all exhausted, and you ladies too, for we have all been under terrific strain. But, gentlemen, let us three take our siesta together in this apartment, while you four ladies go to Nardjis's apartment. I don't know how you other two gentlemen are, but, as for me, I could never get to sleep with my Saint Marilú roaming around the apartment—I'm afraid she would lose her sanctity on the spot, and neither of us would get any rest."

"I agree," exclaimed Jorge, "and I can assure you that my little Conchita is more devil than saint. And, in spite of my youth, I do feel battle fatigue and need some sleep."

"Again I say that you are a wonderful man, Gonzalo," said Nardjis. "You are so wise in all your plans. And, knowing the Princess, I am sure that she will accept your invitation. Her couriers will have told her that her friends, the *Almorávides*, have been annihilated. And when the rumors of this booty reach her—and they will—she will be more than eager to come over here and make new alliances. Better watch your husband, Marilú," she added wickedly.

The four ladies departed, with all seven of them feeling more closely united in conspiracy and affection than they had ever been before. The three men quickly stripped themselves of their heavy boots and clothes, down to their undergarments, and were sound asleep. The soldiers, too, were enjoying a well-earned *siesta*, save only for the guards at the city and castle gates, and at the locked gate to the courtyard, and those watches were manned by the troops that had remained at Alarcos and had not undergone the strain of battle.

Promptly at the seventh hour after noon—within the ten minutes of grace allowed to royalty—the Princess Zayda appeared at Alarcos castle, accompanied by two of her handmaidens. She was received most graciously at the doorway of the castle by Marilú, Conchita, and Zoraya.

The four women embraced affectionately, and Marilú led the way to a small salon, rather overfurnished, with a combination of Moorish luxury and rustic Spanish chairs and tables. The Princess and Marilú sat beside one another on a small, well-cushioned divan while Zoraya and Conchita seated themselves on cushions placed on the floor beside the couch. They had decided that an atmosphere of easy informality would be most appropriate for the occasion.

Marilú spoke to the two maids who hovered around them: "If you will just leave the wine and cakes on the table there, we can serve ourselves. Thank you." Turning to the Princess, she added, "There is so much we have to talk about, and I am sure that you prefer to be alone. My husband and his colonels are sleeping now after their hard day, but they will join us for dinner."

The maids left silently, together with the two ladies in waiting of the Princess.

"Well, before anything else," Zayda remarked, "I want to tell you how sorry I am about your captivity in Medina al-Zahra. We women are the slaves of men, whether we are married to them or not," she sighed.

"In our case," Marilú replied, "we were handcuffed together in the dungeon and I understand that the two viziers and the Prince, your husband, were in Córdoba every one of the twelve days that we were at Medina al-Zahra. So we were indeed captives, but hardly slaves. It was a hardship, a terrible hardship, and we were truly frightened, not knowing what was to become of us—but all's well that ends well, and I'd rather not think of that horrible experience any more. Instead, let us drink to the future, to your happiness and to that of the Prince, whom I hope to meet some day."

As she spoke, Marilú filled four crystal goblets with sherry and passed them to her three companions.

"My husband, alas, is dead, and so are the two viziers, but let us drink to ourselves and to the future." The princess raised the glass to her lips, and the others did likewise. "They were slain before the walls of Córdoba on the twenty-fifth day of the second month of Raba's—let me see, that would be June 12th by your calendar, just three days ago today. I am a widow.

"The very morning of his death, my husband received a letter from his father, King al-Mutamid, that the King showed me. I know it by heart: 'Never be discouraged, my son, for death is easier to bear than disgrace. A prince should never abandon his palace until he is carried to the tomb.' It was prophetic, but Allah's will be done. And those savages, the *Almorávides*, carried his head around the walls of Córdoba on a lance—perhaps the heads of the two viziers as well. They were all killed in the same action. And then, General Sirr's army razed the town and palace of Medina al-Zahra to the ground—the most beautiful spot in all al-Andaluz, lost to the world forever. God's will be done."

"I am most distressed to hear that, my lady," Marilú sighed. "Our hearts go out to you in your sorrow. So we shall never see those three brave men who were, I know, loyal subjects of the Emperor Alfonso, as well as of King al-Mutamid. How in the world did you escape from the clutches of their enemies?" Marilú filled the Princess's glass again.

"I appreciate your sympathy, my dear. I was safe, because my husband had sent me and our children, together with all the treasures of our household, to the castle of Almodóvar del Río. But the news of General Sirr's advancing armies was so frightening that I fled to Sevilla with the children, and took refuge in the palace of my father-in-law, King al-Mutamid. The King was gracious enough . . . thank you," the Princess remarked as Marilú again filled her glass to the brim, "this wine is delicious; it must be from Jerez de la Frontera."

"It is, your highness. And my heart is torn to hear of your plight. My husband will be most distressed, I know. You were saying . . ."

"Where was I?" asked the Princess. "Oh, yes, I was saying that King al-Mutamid was most gracious. Before I left his palace—I spent three nights there—he deeded over to me all the regions of the former Kingdom of Toledo between the Tajo River and the Guadiana, that had been annexed by the Kingdom of Sevilla. My realm includes the castles of Cuenca, Veles, Ocaña, Consuegra, and many others. And he made me Queen of all that region—my title is 'Queen of Toledo'—and he authorized me to seek the protection of the Emperor Alfonso the Brave, for my kingdom and for his."

"Then you are a queen, your majesty," said Marilú in awed tones, filling her own and Zayda's glass to the brim. "Allow me to drink with you—let us all drink, ladies—'long live the Queen!' And you must tell us, your majesty, all about your coronation."

"There was no coronation, my dear—just a simple ceremonial transfer of the deeds and titles, attested to by the Royal *Escribano*. I have the deeds with me to take to King Alfonso. You see, King Mutamid is a most generous man—and what a man!" Zayda's eyes sparkled as she spoke.

"The very first day I came to the palace, and after I had put the children to bed and we had had dinner, he took me to his apartment for a private talk. He wanted to hear all about his son and the defense of Córdoba, and he expressed his fears that the *Almorávides* would take the town, and that al-Mamun would be slain. That may have been why he wrote the letter.

"Anyway, he played the lute for me—he is a marvelous musician, you know—and he played so sweetly that tears came to my eyes. And then he was so sorry for me that he put his arms around me to comfort me—this is just between us women, you understand—and, as he drew me to him, I could feel his great manroot swelling under his robes. I had always been attracted to him. He had a terrific reputation—hundreds of wives and concubines. And then too he is a poet and so am I. So then he tried to comfort me because of all my troubles, and he remarked that it was awfully warm in the palace—it was—he took off his robe and I let him take off mine. And then I couldn't help noticing.

"And being a weak woman, as you know—I've never told anyone about this—I was so curious. I took him in my hands and told him that I knew he must have comforted hundreds of women. And then, before you know it, I was flat on my back on his bed, and he was inside me. I've never experienced anything like it. And I'm naturally of a very affectionate nature, and so let him have his way with me again and again.

"And the next day, after lunch, when he took his *siesta*, I offered to massage his back for him, and he massaged me until I couldn't stand it any longer. Longer—it couldn't have been any longer. It was this long, really." And Zayda put her hands some two feet apart.

"And so it went on for three days, all afternoon and

all night long, and we talked and talked to one another, and finally he made me a queen—said that, after all, I shouldn't be sleeping with him if I was only a princess, or something like that. And for the first time, I think, I was glad I was married to Prince al-Mamun, and had such a wonderful father-in-law.

"But that's not what I wanted to talk to you about. I think this wine must have gone to my head. I wanted to ask you about the *Almorávides* attacking your supply train—you wiped them out, didn't you?—and about the booty you are bringing back—they tell me you discovered the hidden treasure of Abd ar-Rahman. Is that true? And is it really worth millions of dinars?"

"Yes, your majesty," Marilú replied. "We wiped them out. There were twelve hundred of them and only eight hundred of us, but we killed every last man of the *Almorávides* and lost only thirty-five of our men. But then, we had my husband, and Zoraya's and Conchita's husbands to lead our soldiers, and God must have wanted Alfonso's side to win, because God had made Alfonso Emperor of all Spain. As to the treasure, it is true. I heard a voice commanding me to destroy the dungeon in which we were imprisoned and, when my husband came to rescue us and remove our handcuffs, I told him of that voice. And he had his men knock down the wall of the dungeon, an inner wall, a false wall—and there it was. I haven't the faintest idea how much it may be worth, but I know that Abd ar-Rahman's wealth was supposed to be fabulous. Anyway, we are taking it to King Alfonso. It is his by right, not ours."

"That's a fascinating story," said Zayda, "and perhaps you can do me a favor."

"With pleasure, your majesty, if it lies within my power," said Marilú, realizing that she was drawing out of the Princess—or Queen, if that's what she wanted to call herself—information that could be helpful to Gonzalo. She was glad that Lady Nardjis was hidden behind the screen in front of the back door to the salon, because Nardjis, with her superior knowledge of Islamic Spain, would draw conclusions that might not occur to Marilú. "What is it that I can do for you, your Majesty?"

"Well," answered Zayda, "I suppose your husband knows King Alfonso very well. And I suppose that, as he is bringing back this huge treasure, he will have the king's favor more than any other man. Do you suppose that your husband would be willing to introduce me to the king? I am going on an official mission, as I told you.

"But even more than that. I am going to confess to you that I have always been in love, desperately in love with King Alfonso the Brave from hearing about him even though I've never seen him—'*de oidas, que no de vista,*' as you would say. I understand he is a terrific man, as well as a great king, and I have made up my mind that I am going to marry him. I am going to offer him my Kingdom of Toledo, and my most precious treasure—myself. And men tell me that I am no mean prize."

"But the king is married," exclaimed Marilú, a bit bewildered. "He's married to Constance of Aquitaine."

"Yes," said Zayda, "but, of course, Constance is his second wife, because his first wife was Ynés, the daughter of the King of Sevilla, my husband's aunt. And kings can arrange these things in ways that ordinary mortals can't. And tell me, how does this Queen Constance compare with me?" And Zayda rose from the couch, turned around, and beamed a smile on Marilú and then on Zoraya and Conchita—a smile that would have melted any male heart.

She was indeed lovely, perhaps the most beautiful woman, Marilú thought, that she had ever seen. No, not as lovely as Zoraya, because Zoraya's inner charm, the loveliness of her character, shone through her eyes and made her own loveliness a thing of transcendent beauty. But the Princess was indeed perfect—small, with a waist tinier than Marilú's own, her head carried proudly on a slim and graceful neck, her complexion faultless, her hair jet black, her arms—and from what one could see through a revealing, close-fitting dress, her legs—were faultless. And her bosom, straining to be seen beneath her low-cut blouse, was perfection itself. There was no doubt that she was beautiful, even to Marilú who was revolted by what Zayda had told of the affair with her father-in-law, and by what Nardjis had reported of the Princess's conniving with General Sirr. And her avarice and ambition!

But, in spite of her disgust for the woman, Marilú had to admit to herself that she was indeed an extraordinary beauty. And Nardjis was right. She must be careful not to let this woman alone with her husband.

"Your Majesty," said Marilú, answering Zayda's question, "you are the most beautiful woman I have ever seen. Queen Constance is not known for her beauty, and her constancy is undoubtedly far greater than that of her husband, who is reputed to be most inconstant."

"Then do you think you could persuade your husband to introduce me to the king," Zayda insisted. "And I should like to have a few words with your husband alone—before dinner, for at dinner we can talk nothing but generalities, and I am leaving for Toledo the first thing tomorrow morning. Do you think your husband would see me now in private—just for half an hour?"

"Oh, my God, this is it; I can't leave that woman alone with Gonzalo," thought Marilú. But she smiled sweetly and replied: "My husband has been sleeping, but I shall see if he is awake, and if he can see you. Will you excuse me? I shall go to his apartment at once."

She slipped out the back door, behind the screen, and Lady Nardjis tiptoed out of the room with her, hidden by the screen. When they were safely down the corridor, Marilú grasped her friend's arm, and gasped, "What an awful woman—with her own father-in-law. And now she wants to supplant poor Queen Constance. She is unspeakable, Nardjis. Do you think I can trust her with my husband?"

"Frankly, no, my love," Nardjis laughed. "But you can trust Gonzalo, my dear, and after you tell him what we have just heard, you need have no worry. But I certainly wouldn't want to leave her alone with Gonzalo for half an hour."

"You tell him what the Princess told us, Nardjis," pleaded Marilú. "I'd rather you tell him. I'm too angry and jealous, and he might think I was exaggerating."

"All right. I think that might be better. And I want to tell Gonzalo how wonderfully you handled the conversation. You are a born diplomat. And how many glasses of wine did you give that monster? I could hear the bottle gurgling, but didn't dare peek."

"Four," Marilú replied, and she smiled wickedly. "*In vino veritas*, you know."

They knocked at Gonzalo's door. "Come in," he boomed and, as Nardjis and Marilú entered the room, he asked, "Well, what did you learn?"

"Nardjis was hidden behind the screen, and she'll tell you everything. I was too busy talking with the Princess to be sure I got it all."

Lady Nardjis related the whole story from beginning to end, not omitting a single shade of meaning, right down to Zayda's suddenly avowed infatuation for King Alfonso as soon as she had reassured herself as to the existence of the treasure trove. Gonzalo gasped or grunted from time to time as the story unwound.

"What a bitch!" he exclaimed. "What a complete and unadulterated bitch! And what a dangerous woman! I'm glad you didn't antagonize her, and I'll be careful that I don't. And you say she is very beautiful—surpassingly lovely to look at?"

Marilú looked pained. But, whether Gonzalo noted this or not, he went on: "I tell you what you do, Marilú. Tell the Princess I'll be delighted to see her. And send her up here. But, if I don't come out of here in ten minutes, have Roberto come into my room without knocking—on some military pretext, you know—and the three of us will go down to the dining hall together. Ten minutes—no more, my love," then, seeing her face brighten up, he added teasingly, "I can be faithful to you for ten minutes—couldn't get my pants off in that time."

"You brute, you horrid man you," exclaimed Marilú, not at all displeased, as she could see that Gonzalo was as much revolted by Zayda's character as she herself.

"Wait a minute, my love," said Gonzalo. "It just occurred to me. You say that the Princess will be leaving here early tomorrow morning. Give me just five minutes then. There is something I must attend to right away. Tell the Princess that I can see her in five minutes. And give me a kiss, precious, before you go."

He kissed her tenderly, and whispered in her ear: "Don't worry, my dearest. I shall never be unfaithful to you. I love you, *Señora Marquesa.*"

"And I love you too, *Señor Marqués.*" And Marilú left the room, holding tight to Nardjis's arm. Nardjis excused herself, saying that she would join Marilú again by dinner time. And meanwhile she would go and get Roberto.

Gonzalo, left alone, stepped to the casement window, and called down to the guard below. "Sergeant, would you find Captain Escobar and tell him I would like to see him urgently."

"Very well, my general. I know exactly where he is. He will be here in a moment, sir."

A minute later, the captain knocked at the door. "Come in, captain, I'm glad you could come. I have a mission for you and your two sergeants that is most urgent, and will be a great service to me and to the King. Could you three be ready to leave by daybreak tomorrow, to ride post haste to Toledo and deliver a message to the King in person. It is the most urgent, most secret message you have ever carried—it has to do with the treasure, of course, and other matters, and is for the King's eyes only—no ministers, no chancelors. I shall write that on the envelope, and you must insist on it.

"I shall prepare the message tonight. Please come to my apartment tomorrow at daybreak. Don't hesitate to wake me if I am still asleep. If you knock hard enough I shall hear you. And, meanwhile, captain, you and the sergeants must get a good night's sleep. Lord knows, you three have had a hard day. I myself saw you strike down one Saracen with your lance and kill two more with your sword. And now, goodnight, and God be with you."

"Goodnight, my general. We shall be delighted to be of service, and you can count on us, sir."

Hardly had the captain left the apartment than Princess Zayda came to the door, escorted by Marilú. "Allow me to present my husband to you, your majesty. Her Royal Highness, the Princess Zayda, Queen of Toledo. My husband, don Gonzalo, Marqués de Clavijo."

"I am honored, your majesty. Pray come in and sit down, and if I can be of service to you, do not hesitate to command me."

"I'll leave you two here," said Marilú. "We shall all be waiting in the little salon, until you are ready to dine."

Marilú ran back to the salon as fast as she could. "Come on, Zoraya and Conchita, let's find Jorge and Roberto and Nardjis right away. Nardjis is probably with Roberto right now, Zoraya—alone in your apartment. What do you think of that? After all, Zayda is alone with my husband. I think I'm going to latch on to Jorge, Conchita."

The three women ran down the corridor to Zoraya's apartment where, sure enough, Nardjis and Roberto were engaged in lively conversation. "See, I told you, Zoraya," Marilú laughed. "Here they are, and right in the bedroom. Get Jorge for me, Conchita dear. I can't wait to tell the men all we have heard from the Princess Zayda. Nardjis has probably already told Roberto."

"She has," answered Roberto, "and I'm not going to wait until the ten minutes are up. I'm going to wait outside Gonzalo's apartment right now, and if I heard any strange noises—or if I don't hear any conversation at all—I'm going in. Anyway, we'll meet you down in the salon in ten minutes."

Conchita entered the room, bubbling with excitement, with Jorge on her arm. "Let Nardjis tell Jorge, Conchita," suggested Marilú. "You're too excited. And I'm too angry."

So Nardjis outlined what she had just related to Roberto and, a few minutes earlier, to Gonzalo. "The bitch!" exclaimed Jorge. "The dirty bitch!"

"Why that's almost exactly what Gonzalo said," Marilú laughed.

"And Roberto too," said Nardjis. Anyway, we better

be getting down to the salon. I do hope that Gonzalo is not succumbing to the wiles of that dirty, complete and unadulterated bitch—let's see, have I forgotten anything—oh, yes, bastard. That's what Roberto said. I'm just quoting you gentlemen. We ladies would never think of using such language."

Her persiflage was interrupted by a kiss from Marilú, right on the mouth, and the four of them hastened back to the salon. "Some more glasses, please," Marilú said to the maid who had come to clear the table, "eight glasses and another bottle of sherry."

They were sipping sherry and chatting gaily, when Gonzalo entered the room, the Princess on his arm, followed by Roberto. "Roberto interrupted us with a question about the night watch," said Gonzalo, "but I told him that I had already given orders to the captain of the guard. So here we are. Lady Nardjis, I believe you are acquainted with her Majesty."

The Princess looked surprised. "It is so good to see you, Nardjis. I didn't know you were here. No one had told me, and I assumed that you had gone to Sevilla with all the other women from the palace. Anyway, you will be glad to know that they all arrived safely.

"Lady Nardjis came up from Medina al-Zahra with us, your Majesty," Gonzalo explained. "She had taken care of my wife and her companions all the time they were in the dungeon, and we wouldn't think of leaving her down there at the mercy of the *Almorávides*. It's lucky we didn't, after what you have told us—the palace and town razed to the ground, and not a person left alive.

"And, your Majesty, allow me to present Colonel Jorge Rodríguez de Saa, the husband of my cousin Conchita. Jorge, the Princess Zayda, Queen of Toledo."

"I am honored, your Majesty," said Jorge, with a grave bow.

Conchita choked on her sherry. "Went down ... the wrong way," she gasped.

A butler came to the door: "Dinner is served, my lady."

"Allow me, your Majesty," said Gonzalo, proffering his arm to the Princess. "Jorge, would you be good enough to escort my wife, so that you will have charge of the two Andrade cousins. And, Roberto, would you escort Lady Nardjis and Zoraya."

The dinner was Spartan by the standards of Islamic Spain, sumptuous by Christian standards, but the Princess, accustomed as she was to the more luxurious banquets of Sevilla and Córdoba, took matters in her stride. She flirted outrageously with Gonzalo on her left, and Marilú was forced to admit to herself that Zayda really was a beautiful and a charming woman, vivacious, captivating, and highly intelligent.

But, as the Princess had said, at banquets one speaks only of generalities, and, when the dinner was over, very little had been said by anyone, although they all conversed incessantly and in the most animated fashion. At long last, or so it seemed to the three wives, liqueurs had been served, and the evening came to an end.

"You must allow us, your Majesty, to escort you back to your palace. Jorge, Roberto and I shall be honored to accompany you."

The Princess might have preferred to be alone with Gonzalo, but there was nothing she could say and, to Marilú's relief, the three men escorted Zayda and her two maids of honor back to the palace.

"I shall see you, I trust, in Toledo, your Majesty," said Gonzalo as he bade her adieu. "And it will be my pleasure to present you to the King and Queen."

The three men returned to the castle, exclaiming almost in unison: "What a bitch!"

"But isn't she beautiful?" added Jorge.

"Gorgeous," Roberto said.

"And that's what makes her dangerous," concluded Gonzalo.

They parted, each for his own apartment, where their wives were waiting for them with open arms.

"Tell me, Gonzalo," asked Marilú as she helped her husband off with his coat and other garments, "when you were alone with the Princess—for ten whole minutes—were you aroused?"

"Yes, my love. But I've been saving myself for you—and I'm going to take you right now!" And he grasped her around the waist, flung her down on the bed and proceeded to suit the action to the word.

"Oh, that was wonderful," gasped Marilú, as they lay there panting side by side. "But do you know, I do believe you were thinking of that Princess Zayda all the time you had me. You're just a nasty old man, you . . . you brute."

"Well, do you believe I'm thinking of Zayda this time?" he laughed, as he pinned her down to the bed again, and loved her until she could stand it no longer.

"No, I really don't, my love. I know you can't be thinking of anyone but me, because I can't think of anyone but you. And I want to tell you how wonderful I think you are. Youi were magnificent, and oh, so brave, on the field of battle. And so wise and strong in every way. Nardjis is right. You are just the most wonderful man in all the world, and I do love you."

"And I love you too, my darling, But I must go into the next room now, and write a letter to the king, because Captain Escobar is coming at daybreak tomorrow to carry it to Toledo. I'll show you my rough draft in the morning. The letter itself will be gone by the time you wake. So go to sleep, my love, and I'll try not to awaken you when I come to bed. Goodnight, my sweet, and happy dreams."

And Marilú did drop off to sleep—to sleep and happy dreams. But before sleep closed her eyes, and after Gonzalo had left the room, she had time to reflect once more on all that had happened to her since her abduction from El Viso. She knew now that she loved Gonzalo, had always loved Gonzalo. Her affair with the Grand Vizier had been an infatuation—yes, and desire, but never the deep, burning, all-possessing love she felt for her husband. She was grateful to the Grand Vizier for his having released her from her ladylike inhibitions, so that she could be truly a woman, able to love her husband as he deserved. But she realized that it was more a matter of the sensuous environment into which she was thrown—the voluptuous and exotic baths, perfume, music, dancing, food—than of the Grand Vizier's person or personality. He was, beyond doubt, an extraordinary person, but Gonzalo was his superior in every way. And she knew she must erase Medina al-Zahra from her memory for ever. For Gonzalo—to whom she was bound in holy Christian wedlock—was her own and only love. And with these thoughts, she drifted off into contented slumber.

Conchita, in the sheerest of gowns, was waiting impatiently for Jorge's return. He entered the apartment, closed the door behind him, and proceeded to take off his boots and garments.

"You're not even looking at me, you horrid man," pouted Conchita. "I bet you think the Princess is more beautiful than I, and you don't want me any more. I hate you."

Jorge proceeded to enumerate each of Conchita's charms, as he had done the night before. Not neglecting to fondle and caress and kiss each charm in turn, he went on to explain, to Conchita's entire satisfaction, how superior her charms were to those of the Princess Zayda, visible or conjectured. And he went on to put to use simultaneously all of Conchita's various charms that he had so lovingly and meticulously described.

"Well, are you satisfied now, my dear, that you are far superior to the Princess Zayda in every way?"

"Oh, I am satisfied, my love," murmured Conchita, still panting, "so wonderfully satisfied. And I think you are the bravest, strongest man I ever saw."

And she grasped him and they lay there panting, side by side, in each other's arms, and hopelessly in love.

Roberto opened the door to his apartment and closed it softly behind him. Zoraya was waiting for him in bed. "Come to me, my husband," she sighed. "I do want you so."

Roberto flung off his boots and garments, and in a moment the two were linked in passionate embrace, leg to leg, thigh to thigh, breast to breast, and mouth to mouth. They gasped and moaned and twisted and writhed until it would seem that the very walls of the castle would come tumbling down around them. And still Roberto lunged and plunged ever deeper into his love. Until, at last, Zoraya could no longer contain herself. Her muscles relaxed in a final orgasm, and she relapsed on the bed, panting and gasping. A flood of heavenly delight inundated every nook and cranny of her body and she sighed with pleasure as Roberto groaned in ecstasy—then slumped down into Zoraya's arms, the two of them overflowing with contentment.

"Oh, my darling," Zoraya gasped, "I have never known such happiness as you have given me, this night and every night. You are so wonderful and I do love you so."

"And I, my dearest one," Roberto panted, "have never known how wonderful it could be. You hold me so tight down there. I didn't know it was possible for a woman to do that. And, oh, my dear, it gives me such pleasure... But you say you have never known such happiness. Weren't you happy with Raúl?"

"Sublimely happy, my love—and for many years. They were the happiest hours I had ever known—until I met you. But you are so much stronger, so much more ardent that what I say is true: 'I had never known such happiness as you have given me.'

"But I must tell you also that I loved your cousin with all my heart and all my soul. It would be unfair to the dead if I tried to deny it. Raúl was a perfect husband, kind, considerate—a wonderful man in every way. And he was very fond of you, Roberto, as you know. You were his favorite cousin—and mine too. And I am so happy, so deliriously happy, Roberto, that now you are my husband, for I love you more than life itself.

"And perhaps I should tell you that I never realized until today how much I really loved you. When I saw that Saracen strike at you from behind—his awful scimitar flashing through the air—I died, Roberto, I died. My heart stopped beating. And then that brave sergeant of yours pierced the Saracen through and through with his sword, and saved your life. He saved my life too, Robert. I could not have stood being widowed twice. It was then that I knew how much I loved you.

"But it is not because of your bravery that I love you, Roberto. It is because you are so kind, so thoughtful, so loving—it is because we were made for one another, darling. I cannot count the ways in which I love you—but in every way, my husband."

"You've never talked with me like this before, my love," Roberto murmured. "And you've made me very happy—very happy, my dear. And I love you when you are gay, and I love you when you are serious. I love you when you are crying, as you were this afternoon after the battle, and I love you when you are laughing. I love you in all your ways, and all your moods—when your spirit is fanned by the gentle breeze of laughter or by the dark wind of passion.

"Yes, you are right. We were made for one another."

And again Roberto clutched her in his arms, and again they writhed and twisted frantically in every direction, heaving and panting and groaning until once again they sank down in a wondrous ecstasy of pure delight. And so it went throughout the night and well into the early morning—two souls with but a single passion.

CHAPTER 22

At daybreak, the Marqués de Clavijo was awakened from his sound sleep by a knock at the door, at first hesitant and then authoritative.

"Thank you, captain," said Gonzalo drowsily. "Here is the letter to the King, and God be with you!"

He handed the captain a large envelope, sealed with red wax and bearing the imprint of the Clavijo seal. "For the King's eyes only" it read in bold script on the face of the envelope. The captain took it with a bow, and Gonzalo wearily returned to bed without disturbing his wife.

An hour later, the bright sunlight filtered through the curtains, arousing them both. "I'm too tired, my love," murmured Gonzalo, as he watched his wife stretching sensuously on the bed. "I was up late last night writing the letter to the King, and Escobar got me up at daybreak. We must be at the funeral service in an hour, you know, and then we have a seven hour ride ahead of us. I would like you to read my first draft of the letter while I shave. It is rather crude in style, I know, but I did not dare confide this matter to a scrivener."

He left for the washroom, while Marilú, wide awake, sat up in bed and perused the letter.

"To his most serene and most Christian Majesty don Alfonso, by grace of God King of Castilla and León, and Emperor of all Spain,

In the first place, your humble servant, Gonzalo Araujo y Pérez, Marqués de Clavijo, presents his apologies for the crudity of style of the present missive which is attributable, not to disrespect, but to the fact that the matters treated in this letter are of too delicate and secret a nature to be entrusted to an escribiente, *and are hence indited by its author in crude Galician rather than in Latin or in pure Castilian.*

In the second place, your servant wishes to inform your Majesty that, thanks to the miraculous intercession of Saint James the Apostle, whose voice instructed my wife, María Luisa Andrade de Araujo, to destroy the dungeon in which she lay in durance vile, I bring to your Majesty the renowned hidden treasures of the Caliph Abd ar-Rahman III, which were concealed in the walls of that dungeon, as well as other booty from the palace of Medina al-Zahra. Among those treasures are over ten tons of golden bars, and many leathern trunks and coffers sealed with the leaden seal of the great Caliph, whose contents, judging from that of two trunks, accidentally opened in the demolition of the dungeon, consist of precious gems and jewels, so that the total value of this treasure must certainly exceed some ten million dinars, perhaps several times that sum.

In the third place, the colonels under my command, don Roberto Ayala y Fernández and don Jorge Rodríguez y Saa, together with your humble servant, have agreed that this vast booty does not rightfully belong to us and to our army, with only the conventional one-fifth share going to your Majesty's treasury, but that it is the heri-

tage of all Spain, and hence belongs to your Majesty as Emperor, and that it would constitute an outrage against the laws of nature and of nature's God, and against the rights of the people and sovereign of our beloved country, were any contrary disposition to be made. We are therefore bringing this great treasure to you and to you alone, and if your Majesty should, in the exercise of that royal generosity for which he is so rightly acclaimed, deign to distribute any part thereof to us and to our army in recogniton of our services, we shall be profoundly grateful. Our officers and soldiers can have but little knowledge of the true value of this treasure, and your humble servant will at the proper time make bold to suggest a plan to your Majesty whereby they will be most grateful for a distribution based upon your Majesty's generosity rather than upon the ordinary disposition of the booty of war.

In the fourth place, it is my duty to inform your Majesty that our wagon train bearing this booty was attacked near the town of Piedrabuena by a force of Almorávides from the invading army of General Sirr ben Abu Bakr, numbering twelve hundred men, our own forces consisting of only eight hundred officers and soldiers. But that, owing to the wisdom, foresight and shrewdness of one, Lady Nardjis, a Saracen noblewoman who is accompanying us on our journey, and of whom I shall tell your Majesty further in due course, and owing to the intervention of Saint James the Moor-slayer, upon whom we called for aid, God enabled us to annihilate that attacking force, slaying every last man with the exception of two who escaped to tell the tale to

General Sirr, while we lost only thirty-five men of your Majesty's army.

In the fifth place, your Majesty is advised that, within twenty-four hours after your Majesty receives this letter, the Princess Zayda, widow of Prince al-Mamun, will arrive at Toledo with a message from King al-Mutamid and a burning desire on her part to see your Majesty. But it is my duty to advise your Majesty that we have proof that the said Princess Zayda did treacherously plot with General Sirr to seize this treasure which we are bringing to your Majesty, and that it is by reason of this connivance that we were attacked by the Almorávides and came perilously close to losing both the treasure and our lives. And that we have proof, too, of other iniquities of the said Princess Zayda that it will be my duty to communicate in due course to your Majesty. That, nevertheless, the Princess Zayda is a woman of such surpassing charm and beauty, and so infatuated with your Majesty 'de oidas que no de vista', *and at the same time a person so influential with your subject, King al-Mutamid, for reasons that it would be indelicate for me to relate in this letter, that your humble servant makes bold to suggest that your Majesty will not wish to punish, nor even offend that lady, and that it will be to your great personal pleasure and profit, at some later date, to grant her an audience.*

In the sixth place, it occurs to your humble servant that, if the Princess Zayda should learn of the true value of the treasure we are bringing to your Majesty, she might well be tempted to communicate with her coplotter, General Sirr, whose invading armies, far outnumbering your Majesty's forces, might postpone their present seige of Se-

villa—they have already taken Córdoba—and march directly upon Toledo, thereby endangering not only the treasure, but your Kingdom and the safety of your Majesty himself. That, for this and other reasons, which will be explained to your Majesty at an appropriate time, it would seem highly desirable that no rumor of this treasure be allowed to circulate within your Court, or within the City of Toledo, and that your Majesty be absent from the City of Toledo when the Princess Zayda arrives, and until your humble servant can deliver to your Majesty in person the treasure which he is bearing.

In the seventh place, to attain this end, your servant humbly suggests that your Majesty may wish to appoint a secret rendezvous, somewhere between the City of Toledo and the town of Orgaz, at which meeting place your humble servant can turn over this treasure to your Majesty. And that your Majesty bring with him to this rendezvous as many trustworthy appraisers and experts in gems and jewels and rugs and tapestries and other precious objects, with their scales and other instruments, as can be found in the City of Toledo, and that your Majesty and these appraisers depart from Toledo in the strictest secrecy, and that no one appraiser be allowed ever to know the total value of the treasure, but only that part thereof which he himself appraises. And, for the guidance of your Majesty, your humble servant with his troops and the wagon train of treasure will be passing this night at the Hermitage of Saint Peter in Orgaz, and can be at the rendezvous appointed by your Majesty, the following morning as early as your Majesty may wish—the earlier the better, for the magnitude of this treasure, filling twenty-three large wagons, is enormous, and its appraisal will take a score of appraisers the better part of a day to evaluate. That, if your Majesty will send word to your humble servant at the Hermitage of Saint Peter, tonight or by dawn tomorrow, of the time and place of the appointed rendezvous, your servant will, please God, be there without fail, to place at your Majesty's disposition this treasure which your servant and your loyal and grateful soldiers so proudly bring.

Your most humble and obedient servant,
CLAVIJO

Marilú read the letter, her appreciation of her husband's tact and wisdom growing apace as she perused its seven important articles. The avarice of King Alfonso the Brave would, she knew, induce him to obtain the treasure at the earliest possible minute, and the idea of a clandestine extramural rendezvous would appeal to his instinct for secrecy. Whether or not he would respond to her husband's loyal and generous gesture with suitable generosity of his own was an unknown factor, but she realized there was no alternative.

"That's a wonderful letter, Gonzalo," she called through the bathroom door, "and, while it might not be as flowery as a Castilian *escribiente* would make it, it strikes me as extremely courteous, clear, and convincing. And I'll be dressed in a minute, just as soon as you can let me in there."

"Come right in, my love, I'll be through in a minute." And when he, in his undergarments, embraced her tenderly in her thin shift, and felt himself rising to the occasion, he murmured, "I just wish we had a few minutes time, my dearest—but we don't.

"Captain Escobar took the letter this morning. He and the two sergeants will be in Toledo by early afternoon. There are posts every three leagues, where they will change horses, never stopping except for a moment or two. The sergeant will carry a lance with three scarlet pennons, so that they can be seen from a distance by the sentry at the post, and three horses will be ready and saddled at the gate. Scarlet, as you know, is the color of Clavijo, so the sentries will know that the remounts are for my couriers."

They finished dressing, and met the others in the dining hall. "We have fifteen minutes—just time enough for a cup of hot tea and a bite to eat," said Gonzalo. "I can hear the soldiers assembling down below for the funeral procession. It is a sad occasion for all of us. I knew every one of those brave men personally—the flower of Spain."

With muffled drums, the funeral cortege wound its way slowly through the city streets, on horseback and on foot, the thirty-five coffins draped in purple carried on five large drays, each pulled by four black horses. Dom Gregorio and his three fellow clergymen walked alongside the drays, preceded and followed by an honor guard of mounted soldiers, their swords drawn.

The funeral services were conducted by the local priest garbed in the black vestments of mourning. As he pronounced the dread words of excommunication against witches and warlocks, wizards and diviners, and all those who lay violent hands upon priest or cleric, Gonzalo started as he realized how close he had come to committing this deadly sin. He stared in silence at the flickering candles around the coffins as the three priests from the Monastery of Santa Eufemia, also garbed in black, joined in the *Kyrie eleison,* the *Gloria in excelsis Deo,* and the solemn *Dies irae*. As they came to the *Pie Jesu Domine, Dona eis requiem*—"Jesus, kind! Their souls release, Lead them thence to realms of peace"—the faces of Marilú, Nardjis, Zoraya and Conchita were bathed in tears, and they could hear around them the sobs of their husbands and of the soldiers, trying hard to stifle their emotions.

The slow procession from the church to the cemetery was preceded and followed by black-hooded hired mourners in trailing black robes, as well as by the clergy and companions in arms of the dead and others who grieved for the fallen heroes. The thirty-five catafalques were borne by an equal number of squads of soldiers, acting as pall-bearers. The priests conducted the simple burial service, and the coffins were lowered into the graves to the sobs of the four women and of the others who had accompanied the corpses from Piedrabuena. Further back, the townsfolk gathered in respectful tribute to the brave men who had given their lives for their King and country.

When the last prayer had been said, the last spadeful of earth spread upon the graves, Gonzalo gave the orders for the long journey to Orgaz.

Shortly after leaving the walls of the city behind them, they came to the village of Peralbillo Alto where they forded the River Guadiana, the wagons going over a small bridge, one by one, with all the horses at a walk so as not to shake the stone piers beneath them. As they turned north, they passed a wide swamp to the west of the highway at Fernancaballero, then on past Malaón and Fuente el Fresno. Six miles beyond, they followed the twisting road over the Calderina ridge, nearly four thousand feet high and rich with coal and graphite deposits, that separated the Tajo basin from that of the Guadiana. After fording the Algodor river, wagons and horses, they came to a dreary wasteland, flanked by a broad pasture—the Dehesa de Guadalerza, with its imposing castle in the distance.

After many stops, to change horses and for a light lunch, they came to Los Yebenes and then to Orgaz.

There Dom Gregorio asked if he and his fellow clergymen might descend from their jolting wagon, and go the last five miles of the journey on horseback, so as to arrive at the Hermitage in the dignity befitting a visiting abbot. The request was granted, and the three priests and the monk brushed out their rumpled garments, and mounted stiffly on the four horses placed at their disposal.

Down a winding road to the left, past the little village of Arisgatas, the cavalcade proceeded. As they rounded a bend, the great walls and towers of the Ermitá de San Pedro de la Mata de Casalgordo loomed before them, an ancient Visigoth chapel and monastery, dating from the VII Century. It was a bit out of the way, to the southwest of the direct route to Toledo, but it was the only spot for miles around where adequate accomodations could be found for the travelers.

The abbot had sent word ahead, by one of the soldier couriers, so the monks and priests of the Hermitage were ready for their arrival. They were welcomed at the gate by the Abbot of St. Peter's. who was outranked in the hierarchy by his colleague from Santa Eufemia, and hence doubly deferential, although the rank of the Marqués de Clavijo would in itself have ensured them a respectful welcome.

Four small apartments, each with two rooms, one large, one small, had been set aside for the distinguished visitors, the delegation from Santa Eufemia being lodged in another wing of the cloisters, while the soldiers set up their encampment outside the monastery but within the monastery walls. There was an iron-gated courtyard for the wagons which were guarded by two captains and four squads of soldiers in two-hour shifts.

The Abbot of St. Peter's led the visitors to their rooms, and announced that dinner would be served at seven, after vespers, if that suited their convenience. Gonzalo thanked him and, when they were alone, he suggested that they go to Lady Nardjis's apartment if she would be good enough to let them use one of her rooms as a living room for their group, where they could converse in privacy.

"I am absolutely exhausted," he said. "I was up until late last night composing this letter to his Majesty, and I shall leave this draft for you to read while I take a nap—alone," he added, smiling affectionately at Marilú. "I suggest that you, Roberto and Jorge, may want to do the same, which is why I asked for two rooms for each of us. Meanwhile, Marilú, my dear, would you write letters to your mother and father to let them know we are safe, and that we hope to be back in Galicia within two weeks. They can tell the children we'll be home soon. And you can tell your parents all about the treasure, the attack, Conchita's marriage, and anything else you want.

"Conchita, you might write to your father, and please send him our fondest love, and perhaps, Roberto, you may wish to write to your family in León to tell them of your marriage, and to say that you two will see them soon. I hope that we can all leave Toledo together in three or four days at the most, and we can separate at Sanabria, where you two can leave for León, while the rest of us go on to Galicia. We can send the letters on by courier tomorrow morning—there are courier posts all the way, as you know, from here to Toledo, and on to Iria Flavia and León, so the letters will arrive by post long before we get there.

"And now, if you will all excuse me, I am going to sleep. I find that writing a letter—at least, a letter to the King—is more exhausting than fighting a battle."

Marilú left with Gonzalo, her arms around his waist. "I know how tired you must be, my love, and I shan't disturb you. I'll write to your family too, and I'll let you read my letters tomorrow morning. After supper tonight, we shall be too busy for you to read them, because I shall want to tell you how much I love you."

The others remained in Nardjis's apartment, while Roberto read Gonzalo's letter aloud.

"I do hope the King is generous," remarked Conchita. "I hate to give up all that treasure, which really should belong to us and to the soldiers. And maybe I'm treasure enough for Jorge, as he says, but he can't spend me and I can't spend him, and I'd like a little spending money—a lot of money—to start housekeeping."

"What do you mean, he can't spend you," Zoraya laughed. "I bet you are both pretty spent, night after night—and how many times is it each night?"

"I shan't tell you, you wicked woman," laughed Conchita, "but it's too many times to count. I run out of fingers."

And with that, the four newlyweds left for their separate quarters, to sleep, to write, or for such other diversions as might suit their fancies. Nardjis was left alone, heavy of heart, as she alone of all that happy group had no loving spouse to share her joys and sorrows.

At the seventh hour after noon, they were all assembled together again, this time in the long dining hall of the Hermitage where they were served a simple but abundant meal, accompanied by gallons of red wine, and followed by a delicious liqueur which the Abbot of Saint Peter's said had come from another Benedictine monastery. The Abbot and some of his priests were with them at table, together with Dom Gregorio and his colleagues, and the conversation was merry and animated.

By this time, the hazards of the journey, and the

services rendered by the priests of Santa Eufemia, abetted perhaps by the warmth of the liqueur, had mellowed the feelings of the four women and of Gonzalo toward Dom Gregorio.

"After all," Gonzalo reflected, "even Saint Augustine had prayed: 'O Lord, make me chaste—*but not yet.*' And surely little Conchita was luscious enough to tempt even a saint."

Jorge and Roberto, of course, were not privy to the secret of Dom Gregorio's attempted seduction of Conchita, so the three of them shook hands warmly with the four clerics after Dom Gregorio had explained that he and his friends were so stiff and tired from the journey that they would not be up to bid them farewell the following morning. Conchita and Marilú even allowed the old abbot to plant a fatherly kiss upon their brows as they said good-bye, knowing that he was not in a position to plant horns upon their husbands' foreheads.

Just as the abbot was bidding the company farewell, Captain Escobar made his appearance at the door, triumphant.

"Come in, captain," beamed Gonzalo. "And bring your two sergeants with you. Wait a minute, Dom Gregorio, I want you to see three true soldiers, the finest horsemen in the King's army. Nearly sixty leagues in a day! It would take us four days' hard riding to do as much."

"We'd have been here three hours earlier, my general," smiled the captain, "but we couldn't get in to see the . . . the person to whom we had to deliver your message."

Gonzalo rose, and embraced the three couriers, and as he gave Captain Escobar an *abrazo,* he whispered; "Any message?"

"No letter, mv general, and the King seemed vexed at being disturbed," Escobar whispered in his ear.

"But as soon as he was half way through your letter—well I have never seen his Majesty in such good humor. And he told me he would not take time to write you a letter, but would meet you tomorrow morning at the ninth hour after midnight at the castle in Almonacid de Toledo. And he asked me to convey to you his warmest regards and his deepest appreciation. Yes, general, those were his very words."

Gonzalo gave the captain another *abrazo,* and whispered: "Magnificent, captain. You and your sergeants have done a fine job, as I knew you would. Would you give word that we must all leave here at the seventh hour. But don't divulge our destination—to anyone. I shall give the orders in the morning. And get some rest yourselves after you have eaten." Turning to the Abbot of St. Peter's, he added: "My Lord Abbot, it is too late for these gentlemen to mess with the troops. Would you be kind enough to give them supper here? And of the best—the same fine food you have been good enough to give to us. They won't want much wine—they will be riding again tomorrow, but I would like them to taste that fine liqueur you served to us."

That arranged, the three couples—the general, the two colonels, and their wives—pleaded extreme weariness as they excused themselves from the table, and, together with Lady Nardjis, the seven were soon on their way to their separate quarters. And, although the morning found the three wives and husbands still busy at their lovemaking, the time came when all were perforce compelled to leave their warm beds and prepare for the events of the day.

CHAPTER 23

Shortly before the seventh hour, the troops were ready to be on their way—destination top secret. As the Marqués de Clavijo and his comrades in arms, with the four ladies, came down the steps from their apartments, Roberto said: "My general, Jorge and I have been talking, and we are struck with admiration for the *esprit de corps* you have fostered among your men—your real interest in them as individuals. Truly, sir, it is unique in the King's army. You have a reputation for being the sternest taskmaster in the whole army—and with the most terrible temper—yet your men would follow you to the gates of Hell. Every day, Jorge and I get a lesson in the principles of leadership. Last night, for example . . ."

Gonzalo interrupted: "Thanks, Roberto. I appreciate it. But the only secret is that I do in fact love my men, and would willingly go *through* the gates of Hell with them. But let's be going. We have ample time—two hours for seven leagues—but we must not be late."

The Abbot of St. Peter's was at the gate to bid them *pax vobiscum.* The three officers thanked and embraced him, the ladies kissed his ring, and, in a clattering of boots and saddles, wagon wheels, and clanking swords and the sound of hoofbeats on the pavement, the cavalcade was off and away.

Down the narrow road they went, back to the junction with the main highway. They continued north past the town of Mora.

"Those empty fields you see there," Gonzalo told

Marilú who was riding beside him, "are not idle. I have passed by here in the autumn and seen those fields covered with purple crocus. Yes, in the autumn—it is a special variety. They make saffron from the stigmata—the saffron that you have with rice and chicken and many other dishes. Each crocus has three stigmata, that must be picked by hand, and it takes four thousand blossoms to produce an ounce of saffron powder, so you can see that there must be huge fields of flowers to supply the market. Way over there to our right you can see the towers of the castle—one of the most ancient in this region."

On they rode in silence, green fields on either side of them, the mountains in the distance. As they turned a bend in the road, Gonzalo pointed to the walls and turrets of a great castle, high on a mountain top. "That is the castle of Almonacid de Toledo—our destination. It's a new fortress, built to defend the approaches to Toledo—the hill is nearly three thousand feet high, and with a view over the surrounding countryside that would be hard to equal between here and Córdoba. It will take us nearly half an hour to get to the top of that hill, but we shall arrive on time."

The cortege was admitted through the gates, and rumbled on, past the fortifications, across a broad *place d'armes* to the gate of the castle itself. They dismounted, and Gonzalo strode to the gate, followed by his entourage of the two colonels and the four ladies. To their amazement, the King himself was there to greet them, a handsome figure of a man, not yet fifty and as vigorous as a youth of twenty. They bowed deeply, but the King strode forward and gave Gonzalo a warm *abrazo*. His Majesty was greeted by shouts of "*Viva el Rey*" from the troops, and he waved his arms in response, smiling broadly in manifest satisfaction.

"Have your men unhitch the wagons here. They

will camp and stable their horses in the *place d'armes,* and our men—there are two hundred men from the palace guard with us—will take the wagons and arrange them in the inner courtyard. They know exactly how we want them placed." The King used the royal plural as he spoke.

Gonzalo gave instructions to one of his captains, and the King continued. "Now you three gentlemen—and you ladies—come with us. It will take a little while to get the wagons ready, and we wish to talk with you, and hear all about your great adventure."

The King, preceded by two of his captains, led the way through the gate, across the inner courtyard, to the door of the castle which was opened by two servants in livery. They went up the wide stone stairs, the King and Gonzalo side by side, followed by the others. An arched gallery, one flight up, encompassed three sides of the courtyard; the fourth side, through which they had entered, was taken up by the massive iron enclosure and gates. Some of the wagons were already being pushed and wheeled into place by the King's guard.

"They will be lined up, side by side on two sides of the courtyard," explained the King, "their tailgates toward the center, so that the heavier goods—carpets and so forth—can be unloaded in the center of the courtyard to facilitate inspection and appraisal. The canvas covers will be removed from the wagons, so that everything will be in plain sight from above, and our guards will be watching from all around the gallery, so that there can be no pilfering by the appraisers or anyone else. We have twenty-four appraisers, and they will be divided up into twelve teams—each team expert in some particular field, jewelry, rugs, pearls, gems, *objets d'art,* and so forth. Our men will have to unload the wagons, and then regroup the booty so that each class of goods will be by itself. The gold bars will be stacked against that far wall. As you can see, we have one hundred guards lined up on this gallery, keeping a sharp eye on what's going on, and a hundred more below attending to the wagons.

"Now, come on in here with us—it will be half an hour before the stuff is ready for the appraisers, and before there is anything worth looking at. As you may imagine, we are full of curiosity, and we will go out on the gallery again to see what there is. Incidentally, there is no one in Toledo—*no one*—who knows where we are. I have my Chancellor, Treasurer, Minister of War, and Royal *Escribano* with us, and a score of their aides. We left Toledo at noon yesterday—the troops by the south gate, as though they were going on manoeuvres, and we and our ministers by the north gate, as though we were going on a hunt—bows and arrows, dogs, falcons and everything. The lady—Princess Zayda—had not yet arrived at Toledo. But come this way."

The King led them into a small salon, dismissed his two captains and the butlers who had laid out a table with sherry and refreshments—shelled nuts, cakes and other delicacies. The King's cupbearer sipped a glass of the sherry while the Royal Physician sampled the viands as a precaution against poison, and then left the room, bowing deeply.

"And now make yourselves at home here," said the King, graciously. "We shall not be disturbed. And, Marilú, would you serve the sherry. We're parched. And you must be Conchita, aren't you? We remember that your father presented you to us a month or so ago. But you were only a child."

"I *was* a child, your Majesty," Conchita curtsied. "But I am a woman now—over fifteen, and married to Jorgito, to Colonel Jorge Rodríguez, I mean," she added, blushing shyly.

"Well, congratulations, Rodríguez," smiled the King. "You certainly have good taste in women. She is darling—looks exactly like you, Marilú. Your cousin, isn't she? And Rodríguez, you better keep your little wife away from us."

"I shall, your Majesty," said Jorge. "I mean—excuse me, your Majesty," he stammered, "I mean, I shall obey your orders."

The King laughed, and gave Jorge and Roberto an *abrazo*. "And now, Clavijo, you must present these other ladies. I have not had the pleasure." And his eyes took in Zoraya's beauty with the appreciation of a connoisseur.

The introductions over, they seated themselves around the room, and Gonzalo related the crowded events of the past six days, while Marilú served the sherry and Conchita passed the nuts and fruits.

The King raised his glass: "To our most loyal and devoted generals. And to their lovely wives, and to Lady Nardjis, without whose help none of you would be here today."

"To your Majesty," they responded.

And Roberto added respectfully: "Rodríguez and I are colonels, your Majesty, not generals."

"Not from this moment, you're not," retorted the King. "Clavijo, you are now Commander-in-Chief of my Army—old Arteaga is dead, you know—and you two, Ayala and Rodríguez, are generals. We have already informed the Minister of War of our decision, and your engrossed commissions will be ready by evening. And now, let us go out on the gallery and see what there is to see. You ladies can then leave us. We know you will wish to prepare for lunch, and there are many things we shall wish to discuss with your husbands."

Down below, the wagons were lined up in a hollow square. The canvas covers were off, and the contents, as well as the larger items of booty, could be clearly seen from the gallery, while the high sides of the wagons concealed the goods from anyone not directly facing the tailgates, so that no one person standing below could have any concept of the magnitude, variety, and value of the booty in its entirety.

The appraisers were already hard at work, each team discussing values, agreeing, and then marking the items, either individually in the case of the larger items, or by groups, as in the case of a trunkload of pearls which were being sorted out in boxes by size and color. The King beamed, and the others gasped with amazement, as they saw the incredible variety of the items, probably the greatest collection of wealth that had ever been displayed to view at any one place and time in all the history of the world.

"It takes your breath away," said the King. "And now let us go back to the salon for a moment. There is one thing we had forgotten to mention to you—something that concerns all of you personally."

"Oh, the iron casket," exclaimed Marilú excitedly. "There it is, down there. Tell the King about it, Gonzalo."

Gonzalo related to his Majesty Marilú's account of the voice she had heard in Medina al-Zahra.

"It is all I want, your Majesty," said Marilú. "I was commanded by that voice to ask for it—if your Majesty would be so gracious as to give it to me."

"What, that rusty old box down there?" asked the King, and he called out to one of his captains below. "Captain, would you bring that iron box up here, and something to smash it open with if there is no key attached to it."

He led the group into the salon again. "Another sherry for us all, Marilú. We shall need it." The King smiled. "I want to tell you all of your share of this booty."

At that moment, the captain entered the room, carrying the rusty casket, followed by a sergeant with a hammer and chisel. "Open it," the King instructed. The sergeant placed the casket on the stone floor and, while he steadied it with his hands, the captain dealt it a sharp blow on its hinges with the hammer and chisel. The casket, rusty with age, flew open. Inside was what appeared to be a copper necklace, so covered with rust and decay that only a few jewels of apparently negligible worth were visible.

"But that bauble is nothing, my dear," said the King. "Of course, you may have it. We shan't even take the trouble to have it appraised. It is yours."

"Thank you, your Majesty. That is all I want. That is all that the voice commanded me to ask for." Marilú realized that the necklace must be more beautiful, more valuable than appeared, but she confessed to herself a sinking feeling of dismay as she saw what the King had called a "bauble"— it certainly looked it.

"You may go now, captain," said the King. "And thank you." Then, turning to Marilú, he added: "And, my dear, you will have that trinket, as Saint James has apparently commanded you to have it. But that will by no means be your share of the booty. Now, listen to what we have to say.

"In the first place, Clavijo, we were struck by your letter. And we agree with you that this treasure is the heritage of all Spain. But we have decided that, inasmuch as, in the case of the usual booty of war, the booty goes to those who capture it, with one-fifth share for the sovereign, so, in this case, where the booty goes to us, we should give one-fifth share to those who have discovered it and brought it to us.

"Usually, as you know, the booty is divided into three parts, after deducting the King's fifth—one-third for the generals, one-third for the other officers and non-commissioned officers, and one-third for the men.

The share in each category is, of course, divided by rank. Of the generals' share, Clavijo, you would take half, and the other half would be divided between your two generals. All that is as it should be, and those proportions will be followed in the case of this booty.

"So, we have decided that one-twentieth of the value of this treasure shall be for the soldiers, one-twentieth for the officers and sergeants, and one-twentieth for your generals. That leaves one-twentieth more to make up the one-fifth share that we said would be deducted from our portion. And that twentieth, my dear Marilú, goes to you, because without your intervention and that of Saint James the Moor-slayer, there would be no treasure to divide.

"And as for you, Lady Nardjis, your share shall be that of captain of the army, for your services have been at least equal to that of any of our captains. And from what we can see, a captain's share should suffice to make you a very wealthy widow."

The three generals knelt down to kiss the King's ring, thanking him profusely for his generosity. The four women, also kneeling and grasping his hand to kiss his ring, were too overcome with emotion to more than mumble their thanks.

"Oh, and we may add," said the King, "that all the appraisers are sworn to absolute secrecy, under pain of death, as to their particular appraisals. And none of them will have any idea of the value of the entire treasure. Each of the teams will hand us their separate valuations, signed by both appraisers. And no one, but those of us here in this room—not even our Chancellor and Treasurer—will know the value of the booty as a whole. We alone will know it, and we shall have to know it in order to arrive at the value of each twentieth part.

"And, Clavijo, when you announce to your officers

and men what their share is to be, you are not to mention it as one-twentieth, but state the value in golden dinars. And we suggest that they receive their shares in coined gold which our Treasurer will provide, less only the usual seigniorage for the cost of mintage. The vast amount to be distributed will avoid any possible dissatisfaction as to whether or not we may have received more than our usual fifth share. You understand, Clavijo? Any questions?"

"Yes, Sire, it is quite clear," replied Gonzalo. "Your plan to announce the distribution in dinars is precisely what I was going to suggest, but your Majesty has anticipated me. And again we must all thank you for your generosity. Might I ask your Majesty, however, in view of the fact that my wife will be so magnificently endowed, that my share be one-quarter of our twentieth, the same as that of my fellow-generals, and that the difference be divided up among my troops—there are approximately eight hundred and fifty men, and one hundred and fifty sergeants and officers. I plan to give their proper share to the widows of the thirty-five captains, sergeants and privates who have died in battle."

"And half of my share," interjected Marilú, "I would like, if Gonzalo is willing, to give to the Cathedral at Iria Flavia de Compostela that your Majesty is so generosly constructing, in honor of Saint James the Apostle." The Marqués de Calvijo smilingly indicated his complete agreement.

The King smiled with pleasure. "Of course, Clavijo, your quarter share will be divided as you say. It is generous of you, and we shall make the calculations this afternoon, when all the appraisals are in. And, as for your generosity, my dear Marilú, it touches us to the heart, because, of all the works we are undertaking in Spain, and the one for which we most desire to be remembered in history, it is the cathedral in Iria

Flavia that is closest to our heart. Some day, when it is completed, your city will be known as Santiago, in honor of the Saint, and pilgrims will come from all over the world to worship at his shrine.

"As you know, we are already building a highway to that Shrine, and it will in time be the finest highway in all Spain. So to match your generosity, we shall have our Treasurer donate an equal amount for the completion of the cathedral. And now, ladies, don't let us detain you any longer. We shall see you at luncheon. We have business with your husbands. We shall all stay here over night, and return in triumph to Toledo tomorrow—to a banquet tomorrow night at the palace."

"Thank you again, your Majesty," murmured Marilú, as the tears welled in her eyes again. "You are so generous, and Iria Flavia de Compostela and its cathedral mean so much to me."

"Oh, your Majesty," Conchita burst in, "these rings—Zoraya and I, and Jorge and Roberto each have one—we took them from the treasures in the palace, not the hidden treasure of the Caliph, but the palace itself. We wanted them so that we could get married, but I guess now that they belong to you, we stole them. But please don't take them away from us, your Majesty. I love my ring so much."

The King smiled. "No man must remove a wedding band from another man, my dear, nor from his wife, so our only recourse would be to chop off your fingers. And we don't have our chopper with us. Oh, we have an idea—the rings will be our wedding present to you. Part of our weddding present—we know exactly what we shall give to you two brides, we saw the very thing in the courtyard. You shall have those gifts at lunchtime. But as we have already given you a first wedding present, we are entitled to kiss the brides."

And the King seized Conchita in his arms and exacted his kiss, then put his arms around Zoraya, and did likewise. Zoraya could feel—there was no doubt about it—the King's renowned member pressing against her most uncomfortably. But what could she do about it—what could she do if ever the King caught her alone in the palace? After all, Alfonso is the sovereign, and she his subject. She tried to take her mind off the question, but it was impossible. At last, the King removed his lips, but Zoraya had the uneasy feeling that he was just biding his time for a more direct attack upon her honor. *Pobre de* Roberto!

The four ladies bowed out, leaving the King alone with his generals. "And now, gentlemen," said the King. "There are a few matters we should like to clear up. First tell us what you know of the movements of General Sirr. Is he likely to move on to Toledo?"

"Your Majesty," answered Gonzalo. "It is my belief that he will have been so taken aback by the defeat at Piedrabuena, and by the exaggerated reports of the strength of our little army that the two who escaped will undoubtedly have brought him, that he will decide he had better protect his rear before moving north. So he will concentrate on Sevilla, and on mopping up the territory between Sevilla and Alarcos, before he moves north. Sevilla can hold out at least until September, possibly later, which means that the *Almorávides* will not be ready to march on Toledo until next spring. And Alarcos, with some changes that I would like to suggest to your War Minister, can hold out against a siege for a considerable period—three months, maybe six months.

"But, in my opinion, we should not attempt any serious defense—ambushes and obstacles, yes, but no last-stand defense—south of Alarcos. And when Alarcos does fall, and it almost certainly will in time, we must at once withdraw our remaining forces under cover of night, and retreat to Toledo. The castle here at Almonacid de Toledo is well constructed, and will hold out for considerable time, inflicting tremendous damage on any attacking force. Toledo itself is impregnable.

"But, your Majesty, if you attempt to make a stand anywhere between Córdoba and Alarcos, or anywhere between Alarcos and here, you will risk annihilation. It could be a repetition of that terrible battle at Azagal five years ago—only worse. Do you agree with me, Roberto and Jorge? You know the terrain as well as I."

"Yes, your Majesty," said Roberto. "Gonzalo—I mean the Marqués de Clavijo—is right. It would be suicidal to attempt a defense at any but the best fortified places, and at places where our flanks are protected by a river, so that we can retreat to the rear."

Jorge nodded his head in agreement.

"That seems to make sense, Clavijo," agreed the King. "You will see the Minister of War at lunch, Clavijo, and we shall tell him that we are impressed with your views. And then you can go over them at length with him tomorrow in Toledo."

"And your Majesty," continued Gonzalo, "that brings me to another thing I wished to discuss with you, if I may. King al-Mutamid has made the Princess Zayda queen of all the region between the Tajo and the Guadiana. I can sketch it out for you on the map later. It is now known as the '*Tierra de la Mora Zayda*'. And she is bringing her deeds of sovereignty with her, and intends to offer all that territory to you in exchange for her hand in marriage.

"Yes, your Majesty," Gonzalo went on, noting the expression of amazement in the King's countenance. "She intends to be your wife. That is your affair, not mine. But, as your general, I wanted to warn your

Majesty that her deeds to that region are not worth the parchment they are written on. Ibn-Tashfin's army will sweep through all that territory without resistance."

And Gonzalo went on to inform the King of the manner in which the Princess Zayda had inveigled King al-Mutamid into making her 'Queen of Toledo' as she styled it. And of her conniving with General Sirr in the attack on the wagon train at Piedrabuena. And of her sudden infatuation with the King as soon as she had heard that the treasure belonged to his Majesty, not to the army. "Not that she doesn't have good reason to be infatuated with your Majesty, treasure or no treasure," Gonzalo added.

"What a bitch that woman is," exclaimed the King. "What a complete and unadulterated bitch."

Gonzalo laughed. "Excuse me, your Majesty, but those are the very same words I used when Marilú and Lady Nardjis repeated what the Princess Zayda had revealed to them. With all respect, your Majesty, I can see that the Galician tongue is not so very different from the Castilian, after all.

"Yes, your Majesty, she is a bitch. But she is one of the most beautiful women I have ever seen—simply luscious. Her breasts, her waist, her legs—what I could see of them—are divine. And she is charming, vivacious, intelligent and amusing—a talented poetess, and what a woman! She seems to have the faculty of arousing a man—when she wants to—beyond anything I have ever seen before.

"If you will excuse me, your Majesty, for saying it, but, after ten minutes alone with her, I was aroused. And all she was trying to do was to seduce me into arranging an audience with you. If I hadn't arranged in advance for Roberto to interrupt our little *tête à tête*—well, it probably would have turned into a teat *à* teat, your Majesty."

The King exploded with laughter. "Well, we see that we shall have to meet that lovely bitch. Have her at the banquet tomorrow night. And if she is as luscious as you say, Clavijo, we shall be busy with affairs of state for the next week or more. We shall bid you goodbye after the banquet, and that will be the last you will see of us for a fortnight."

"Very well, your Majesty. I shall send a courier on ahead today to advise the Princess Zayda that you will expect her at the banquet tomorrow. But, your Majesty, my wife and I have not seen our parents or children for so long, and they and the Conde de Andrade, Conchita's father, must be frantic about the women being captured by the Saracens, and imagining all kinds of terrible things. I did send a message ahead by post yesterday, reporting that Marilú and Conchita are safe, but we had hoped to set out for Galicia three days from now, if your Majesty will permit—with Jorge, of course. And Roberto is equally anxious to see his family in León, and introduce his lovely bride to them. So we would be most grateful, your Majesty, if we might be permitted to leave on the morning of June 20th, after two days in Toledo. We would return immediately, Sire, if Tashfin's army does march north before spring."

"Why, of course, my son, and Rodríguez and Ayala, too," said the King. "You would be unnatural if you didn't want to get home after all you've been through. And, as we say, we shall be busy with affairs of state. The more we think of it, the more we like the idea of seeing that Princess Zayda, and the fact that she is such a bitch makes it all the more exciting. We always have liked bitches. So, after the banquet tomorrow night, we shall bid you and your fair ladies farewell—and that charming widow Nardjis—and we shall see you in the spring.

"And now you had better join your ladies, and prepare for lunch."

"Very well, your Majesty," said Gonzalo, as he and his companions bowed, and backed out of the room.

"You laid it on pretty thick, Gonzalo," commented Roberto, "about that 'luscious' Princess, and your erection, and all that."

"Of course, I did, Roberto, and for a very good reason," Gonzalo answered. "The erection is true. She is terrifically seductive—but not half as beautiful as your lovely Zoraya, nor, if the King's tastes run to blondes, not nearly as lovely as Conchita or my own darling Marilú. But I didn't like the way that royal lecher kissed Conchita and especially Zoraya, and that is why I had him practically drooling over Zayda, which is what I wanted.

"And, another thing—I wanted us to get away from Toledo as soon as possible, not only for the honor of our wives, but before the King changes his mind about the division of the treasure. And the day after tomorrow, I'd like to go down to Toledo with you two, and arrange with a banker I know to take charge of sending the treasure on to Galicia and León, where it will be safer.

"Now, at luncheon today, I imagine the King will be so interested in the appraisal of the treasure that he won't have his mind on women, but, for tonight, it's strictly a case of 'Romans, guard your wives; here comes that bald-headed adulterer,' as they used to say when Julius Caesar came to town.

"So I'm going to arrange for Marilú to plead that they are all overcome with weariness, and ask to be excused from coming down to dinner. And then, if the King is willing, I'm going to suggest that he invite the captains in to dine with him, and they'll all get drunk together. Let me play it by ear, and when I see a good opening, I'll plant the bug in his ear."

"Gonzalo, you are remarkable," said Jorge. "You may not have noticed, but he gave Marilú a pat on the bottom as she left the room."

"I noticed," commented Gonzalo drily. "But let's join the ladies."

They found the women in Marilú's apartment. Gonzalo drew Marilú and Nardjis aside and explained what they should do. "But not until evening; all four of you must be present when the King gives instructions for us to choose our part of the loot. Meanwhile you two must do whatever you can to make sure the King is never left alone with Conchita or Zoraya."

"Especially Zoraya," Nardjis assented. "The poor girl was distraught when we came back to the room. She is so in love with Roberto and yet she knows that the King has a . . . has a terrible reputation."

"Well," said Gonzalo, as they joined the others, "if you five intruders will please get out of our apartment, we can get ready for lunch, and I advise you all to do the same."

CHAPTER 24

The King was jubilant. He entered the room wearing a smile that was all-embracing, and bearing under his arms two golden caskets identical in size and workmanship, but varying in design. They were of massive gold, encased on top and on the sides by an elaborate golden filigree of leaves and underbrush. On one of the caskets, a fawn, rampant, disported with a fleeing nymph, while on the other, a similarly rampant Cupid pursued a nearly naked Psyche. He handed the latter casket to Conchita, and the other to Zoraya, and then exacted his kiss from the brides. This time Conchita as well as Zoraya felt the pressure of the royal member against her middle, and realized that it was not only the King's smile that was all-embracing.

She uttered a sharp squeal of shock and fright, and then, to disguise her uneasiness, she asked, "How do you open this thing, your Majesty? There's no key or keyhole."

"We shall be delighted to show you how to open your little box, my dear, and yours too, Zoraya," and it was clear that the King's play on words was not unintentional. "Let us show you. The appraiser showed us how."

The King took Conchita's casket, moved the Cupid and the Psyche together and the top of the casket flew open. He did the same with Zoraya's casket, pushing the fawn and nymph together. The two girls giggled with delight.

"Oh, thank you, thank you, your Majesty," said

Conchita, while Zoraya added, "It's a lovely wedding present, your Majesty."

"And if either of you needs any further help in opening your little boxes, we shall always be ready to assist," said the King with a smile that carried just the suspicion of a leer.

"And, gentlemen, I've brought you your commissions," and he laid down on the table three handsomely engrossed and sealed parchments that he handed to Gonzalo, Jorge and Roberto. They knelt and kissed the King's ring as they thanked him for his royal grace.

"We have further news on the appraisal," the King added. "The gold bars weigh eleven tons, worth two million, seven hundred and fifty thousand dinars—not far from your estimate, Clavijo. The gold is twenty-four karat, attested by the Caliph's seal." The King drew a sheaf of papers from his pocket.

"But you are way off on your guess as to the value of the entire treasure, Clavijo." Their hearts sank. "It is appraised at seventy-four million, four hundred thousand dinars—seventy-seven million, one hundred and fifty thousand dinars in all."

They all gasped in disbelief.

"That means that each of you generals is entitled to nine hundred and sixty-four thousand, three hundred and seventy-five dinars. You, Marilú, are entitled to three million, eight hundred and fifty-seven thousand, five hundred dinars. And you, Lady Nardjis, to over eighty-three thousand dinars, the same as the twenty-three captains and the two captains' widows. Here are the exact figures, Clavijo, so that you can make the announcements to your men after lunch."

"This is overwhelming. I do not know how to thank you sufficiently, Sire," said Gonzalo. "You are most generous, most gracious, and I know I speak for all of us when I say that we thank you from the bottom of our hearts. We are all rich beyond any possible dream." And he knelt again and kissed his sovereign's ring.

"There are not enough gold bars to pay the entire shares of your officers and men in gold, Clavijo," the King continued, "but never mind. Our Treasurer will pay their full shares in minted golden dinars in Toledo tomorrow. Now remember, you are not to speak of twentieths or shares—just announce the exact amounts in dinars. Only we eight have any concept of the total value of the treasure.

"Now we have already selected from the treasures in the courtyard those things which we especially desire—some of the larger gems, some of the caskets, jewels, the golden goblets and plates, carpets and tapestries, and so forth, which we particularly liked. We have not taken our full share. We shall do that later. After each of you have selected your shares, we shall simply remove the remainder."

"Your Majesty," Marilú broke in, "there is the Caliph's chess set and table that I told Gonzalo must be given to the King. It is the most beautiful thing that I have ever seen, and only a King's palace is worthy of it. I do hope your Majesty saw it, and liked it."

"We did indeed, my dear, and we agree that it is exquisite. It will truly be the most beautiful thing among all my treasures—the most beautiful inanimate thing, at least." The King went on: "After lunch, we should like you to go through the courtyard and select all the things you want, taking your complete shares, and loading everything you take into the wagons which should be locked and covered for the trip to Toledo tomorrow. The Treasurer's aides will follow you and tally each item as you take it, until your full quota is reached. And then, we shall have all the remaining things packed into other wagons for us, including the gold bars.

"Incidentally, we have asked the appraisers who have sorted out the pearls to make up half a dozen matched strings for necklaces that we may wish to give away from time to time. One necklace will be made up for us to give to the Princess Zayda tomorrow night. We suggest that you may wish to have them sort out some matched strings for yourselves, as otherwise you may end up with a number of assorted pearls, and not enough of any size or color to make a necklace. . . . Now let us all go in to lunch."

The King's physician and cupbearer sampled the food and wines, as usual, before the meal was served. During the course of the luncheon Gonzalo addressed himself to the King: "Sire, if you are willing, I would appreciate your accompanying me when I make the announcement to the troops. I would like your Majesty to witness their enthusiasm when I tell them of your bounty, and I want them to see their sovereign in person so that when they fight and die for King and country, they will know that it is a sacrifice that any Spaniard should be proud to make. With your permission, Sire, I shall send a messenger down now, so that they will be assembled in the *place d'armes*."

"Very well, Clavijo. We shall be proud to see your troops."

The luncheon over, they went below, standing on the terrace overlooking the drill field. The troops were assembled before them, standing stiffly at attention. Gonzalo bellowed: "At ease! I present your sovereign, his most serene and most Christian majesty, don Alfonso, by grace of God King of Castilla and León and Emperor of all Spain."

Three lusty cheers rent the air.

"And now, gentlemen, I wish to tell you of the spoils of war that his Majesty has most generously allotted to you as his most loyal subjects. You know the rules for its division among you, so I shall just give you the total amounts. And, gentlemen, these sums will be paid to each of you tomorrow in golden dinars by the Royal Treasury. I have already told you that the widows or next of kin of those who died at Piedrabuena will receive their proper shares. The appraisals of the booty have been completed, and to you officers and non-commissioned officers will go the sum of four million, three hundred and thirty-nine thousand, six hundred and eighty-eight dinars. To the troops will go a like amount."

The hurrahs were deafening. Cheer after cheer split the air. Some of the men embraced on the field, others sobbed unashamedly, while still others were stricken dumb at the magnitude of the great wealth they were to receive. The captains could quickly calculate that, for each of them, it meant nearly eighty-four thousand dinars, a princely fortune, while even the humblest private would get over five thousand dinars, more than any of them could earn in a hundred years.

"Your Majesty," said Gonzalo, "I believe you will excuse the lack of any acceptance speech. This demonstration speaks for itself."

The King, obviously pleased, and overcome with emotion, raised his arms high above his head. "Our most loyal subjects," he said, "that distribution of what God has given us is our pleasure. You well deserve it. Now let us give thanks to God and to Saint James the Moor-slayer for what they have, in their great bounty, bestowed upon us."

They knelt and prayed, the soldiers on the drill

field, and the monarch with his attendant generals and ladies upon the terrace.

"We are pleased, Clavijo, that you suggested our presence during the announcement," said the King, still manifestly thrilled. "Now, you ladies and gentlemen, go about your business in the courtyard, while we retire to our private chapel for an hour of prayer. Let us meet again in the salon right after vespers for a sherry before dinner."

They walked in silence back to the castle, Gonzalo at the King's left, the others following. The King left them at the castle door, while the others remained in the courtyard, in the hollow square between the rows of wagons. The appraisers stood before their respective wagons, and a group of five young men, with tally sheets in hand, waited to jot down the value of each item that might be selected by each of the five recipients—Gonzalo, Roberto and Jorge, Marilú, and Nardjis.

The selection of the treasures took far less time than they had expected, chiefly because there were relatively few things they wished to acquire as permanent possessions. But the display of treasures was breathtaking, and the seven happy new plutocrats wandered among the wagons in admiration as their carpets and other things were being stacked away in three separate wagons, two destined for Galicia, one for León. The five leather trunks with the gems were placed in a fourth wagon, for they would be unloaded in Toledo. The strings of pearls were left with the jeweler-appraisers to be strung into necklaces for tomorrow's banquet.

There was ample time for them to get ready for their six o'clock appointment with the King, and the seven met in Lady Nardjis' apartment to go over the events of the past seven hours.

"I am devoted to the King," said Zoraya. "He is kind and generous and intelligent, and every inch a King. I would truly lay down my life for him—but I am so afraid of his intentions, and am terribly worried."

"And I'm devoted to him too," said Roberto. "I am ready to lay down my life but not my wife for him. And I'm worried too."

"Me too," said Jorge, and Conchita added: "I'm just plain scared to death. Just never leave my side for a moment, Jorgito darling."

Lady Nardjis outlined briefly what she and Marilú proposed to do, and asked the others to play their parts. "And we can just pray for the best, my dears," she concluded. "So far, fate has treated us well. May the blessed Virgin Mary protect you!"

"Thank you, Nardjis," said Marilú, "but I hadn't expected to hear that prayer from a Moslem."

"Well, as you know, we Moslems believe in the virginity of Mary, the Mother of Jesus, and I confess that I find myself becoming more of a Christian and less of a Moslem each day. I have come to love you three so much, and your husbands too," Nardjis added, smiling at the three generals, "that it is hard not to accept the beliefs that have made you what you are.... But it's time for us to dress."

A few minutes later, the three men made their way to the salon where they were joined by the King. "Where are the ladies?" the monarch asked, plainly put out by their lateness.

At that moment, the four women appeared at the door. Nardjis had powdered the faces of the three wives until, in the dim light of the salon, they looked like ghosts. Marilú faltered to her knees: "Excuse us, your Majesty. We are not well—the events of the past two weeks—everything. And we feel terrible. Would your Majesty excuse us if we don't join you for sherry?"

She burst into tears. And her two companions looked as if they were ready to do so at any minute.

"Why, of course, my dear," said the King, instantly sympathetic, and still grateful to Marilú for discovering the great fortune that had come so him to unexpectedly. "You excuse yourselves, and we hope that you will feel better soon."

Lady Nardjis knelt. "May I stay a moment, your Majesty. I'd like to drink your health on my behalf and on behalf of my dear companions. They are so anxious to thank you for all your bounty, to thank you personally, and they are weeping as much because they cannot do that tonight, as because they are unwell. They simply will not be well enough to join us for dinner—a cup of hot bouillon in their rooms is all they will be able to ingest.

"They are merely overwrought, your Majesty, as you can understand. The abduction, the imprisonment in the dungeon, the constant fear of rape, the excitement of the rescue, the attack by the *Almorávides*—and now they are overwhelmed by your Majesty's most gracious generosity. It has just been too much for them. You are so kind, your Majesty, and they are so devoted to you. But you will understand. . . . And Gonzalo, Roberto and Jorge, if his Majesty will permit, I think you really ought to join them now and have a light supper at their bedside. They cannot bear to be separated from you after those twelve days in Medina al-Zahra."

"May we, your Majesty?" asked Gonzalo. "Our place is by our King, but it is also by our wives. Would you spare us this evening? We would like to pledge your health in wine, and again give our thanks and our devotion, but if you will be so gracious as to excuse us, we would indeed like to join our wives."

Then, as if in an afterthought, he added: "Your Majesty, may I ask that you invite my twenty-three captains to dinner in our place. They are devoted to you, would lay down their lives for you—as we would too. But it would be just such a gesture as this—your inviting these simple captains to dine with their sovereign—that wins battles for your Majesty against the Saracens. They would never forget it. And you, Sire, would enjoy it, I am sure—to be with your brave comrades at arms. Some day, you will be fighting side by side with them again on the field of battle, and you will know that you can count upon them to the last man, to the last breath of life."

It was not for nothing that the King was known as Alfonso *el Bravo*. The evocation of past battles and future glories struck a resonant note in his warrior's heart, and he responded: "You go along, gentlemen. Your place is by your wives' bedsteads tonight, and we pray that they will be recovered by morning. We shall all meet tomorrow at nine o'clock for the return to Toledo—better make it eleven. We may do some heavy drinking tonight. The trumpets will be sounded at ten tomorrow. Goodnight and God bless you and your wives. And you too, Lady Nardjis. We know that you will take care of them."

The four discreetly withheld their rejoicing until they were safely back in Lady Nardjis' apartment, where they had all agreed to meet if the King gave his consent. They all embraced affectionately, and Gonzalo twitted his wife: "What an actress! What a performance you put on!"

"I wasn't acting, my dear," Marilú replied. "I really am overcome, and Conchita and Zoraya too. And I think we three should go to bed, and have nothing but a good hot consomme for supper. You three men can sit by our bedsides and have a light buffet. I am not up to anything else tonight. It has all been so confusing, so upsetting. And Zoraya and Conchita tell me they feel the same way."

So again they went their separate ways, a quiet night indeed for six amorous honeymooners.

CHAPTER 25

The sun filtered through the drawn curtains. A beam of light struck Conchita's eyes as she lay in bed, on her back, smiling happily, her head framed in an aureole of golden hair. She stirred uneasily, tried to avoid the light then opened her eyes, fully awake. It was seven o'clock. She had slept ten hours, and had awakened refreshed, fully recovered from the indisposition of the evening before.

"Wake up, Jorgito. It's morning, and we have all morning to play," she burbled, pushing her husband with her elbow, then gazing at him affectionately as he opened his eyes drowsily.

Conchita threw back the sheet. "Wake up, you lazy-bones," she laughed, her happiness and eagerness mounting rapidly as she saw him begin to stiffen, then rise perceptibly.

"Oh, I can't wait for you, you loafy lazer," she cried. "Here I come!"

And with that, she hurled herself upon her husband and started riding him as madly as though she were in a desperate race. This time, no easy trot, no gentle canter as a preliminary, but a full, mad gallop in a wild and glorious cavalry charge. Boldly she rode and well, into ecstasy, into Heaven.

Jorge drew up his knees, pushing his fair rider down upon him until her breasts dangled against his chest, then grasped the waving orbs and tried to bring them to his lips. The effort to bring these luscious fruits within reach was tantalizing, and increased the ardor of rider and steed alike. They heaved and plunged in a rhapsody of ardent passion, groaning and panting as Conchita's rhythmic rise and fall sent delightful tickles and tremors along the full length of his root, the full depth of her flower.

She cried out in a paroxysm of rapture as he seized her waist and pulled her down into his churning pelvis, then let loose a fountain of rapturous lust that penetrated her very vitals and left her collapsed and exhausted upon his chest.

"Oh, Jorge, Jorge," Conchita moaned. "You fill me so, I'm so full and happy."

They lay almost motionless, savoring to the full the joy of passion.

Meanwhile, similar scenes of love were being enacted in two neighboring apartments.

The trumpet call, loud and peremptory, interrupted their reveries, and sent them, and others in the palace, scurrying to get ready for the last leg of their journey to Toledo. A light snack for breakfast, served in their apartments, and the three couples, and Lady Nardjis, were downstairs on the terrace well before the eleventh hour, ready for the short ride to Toledo.

The wagon train was already out on the drill field, the horses harnessed and hitched, the canvas covers battened down, and the four special wagons, labelled by destination, in the van of the procession. The troops, those from Alarcos as well as the two hundred men of the royal palace guard, stood by their horses, awaiting the order to mount. The King's ministers and their aides stood on the terrace, ready and waiting, conversing with Gonzalo, while their steeds milled nervously around, their bridles held by the castle grooms.

The castle doors opened again, and the King, flanked by his attendants, came out smiling and nodding to those below.

"We are glad to see so many shining faces this morning—certainly a big improvement over last night," the King said, addressing his words to the group of ladies who curtsied at his approach. "We hope you are all completely recovered, my lovelies."

"We feel fine this morning, your Majesty," replied Marilú, speaking for all of them. "We were just so completely exhausted last night—and we just went to pieces when we finally reached here, and could feel safe and secure at last, after so many weeks of horror and tension. And now we are all so happy—and terribly, terribly grateful to you, your Majesty."

"Well, this June eighteenth is indeed a glorious day," the King commented, addressing his words to the whole company on the terrace. "It will be a triumphal procession to Toledo. This day will go down in history, and, mark my words, people living in the Twentieth Century will still cherish the memory of the eighteenth day of June."

The procession wheeled around the drill field, the King in the van, mounted on a magnificent black charger, Gonzalo riding proudly at his left.

Leaving the walls of Almonacid de Toledo behind them, the cavalcade took the highway to the north, proceeding at an easy gallop, troopers and wagon train alike. Past the granite foothills of the mountains of Toledo, they crossed the Tajo River over the ancient Roman bridge, which would be replaced two centuries later by the Bridge of San Martín.

The great City of Toledo, high upon the steep hillside, above the walls, loomed before them. At a strategic point stood the great fortress of the Alcázar, built by Alfonso just four years earlier, on the site of a III Century Roman camp. Its walls and gates were, as Gonzalo had said, impregnable—and looked it. This was their destination. The long procession assembled in the inner courtyard of the Alcázar, the riders dismounted, and the wagons were unhitched and stored at the far end of the field, protected by a double guard of Gonzalo's troopers and of the palace guard.

The King engaged in conversation with Gonzalo, the others in his entourage standing at a respectful distance. "We are sorry, Clavijo, that we cannot offer you and your party our hospitality within the Alcázar, but it is still only a fortress, as you know, and we have scanty accommodations outside of our own apartments. We shall be busy from now until evening, unloading the wagons—except for yours—and placing their contents in our own vaults, until we can transfer it to our palaces in Burgos and elsewhere.

"The Treasurer will be ready to distribute the booty to your troops at the fourth hour after noon. He has the complete payroll, with the amounts beside each name. And the widows or heirs should be there to receive their shares. . . . And we have many other things to attend to. But we shall expect you all at the banquet at eight o'clock. You will be in the salon half an hour earlier for a sherry and to be presented to Queen Constance. And be sure you have the Princess Zayda with you."

"Yes, your Majesty. We shall be quartered at my house, immediately outside the Alcazar gates, and I shall conduct the Princess Zayda here in person. Until then, Sire," and Gonzalo bowed and rejoined his friends.

Roberto gave the necessary instructions to Captain Escobar, now Colonel Escobar, and chief in command of the troops. And the three generals and four ladies mounted their horses and set off at a brisk trot to the mansion of the Clavijos. It was only a short distance, but the hill was steep, and it was easier to ride than walk.

"It is so good to be alone again—and home, and safe," sighed Gonzalo, as they were welcomed by their servants at the gate.

"And now, let's just have a simple lunch, and relax—no troops, no Dom Gregorio, no Zayda, and no King—just ourselves, a happy little family."

"You know what I'd like to do after lunch," said Marilú. "I'd like to take a good long walk. I haven't had a walk since I don't know when. And I need to stretch my legs."

"Good idea," said Gonzalo. "And I'd like to get away from the palace. We can ride to the top of the Peña del Moro, have a lovely walk through the gardens of the Hermitage of the *Virgen del Valle* and in the *cigarrales*—and take a siesta among the trees, if you wish."

"*Cigarrales*?" asked Nardjis. "Surely, cigars don't grow in the fields here in Toledo. But anyway, I think I'll stay here and rest while you all go for a walk."

"Well here in Toledo," Jorge laughed, "the *cigarrales* are olive orchards on the other side of the river—a simply delightful spot and perfect for a walk and for a lazy *siesta*. And I think a walk is a wonderful idea. What do you say, darling?"

"Wonderful," said Conchita, "but let's eat. I'm starved."

"Right away, my dear," smiled Marilú. "I suppose we're all hungry. Come along, it's ready right now," she added, as she noticed the butler at the door ready to announce luncheon.

Luncheon was suckling pig, beautifully browned outside, and tender and juicy within. "I thought we'd all appreciate this for a change after our stay in Islamic Spain," said Marilú, "and I sent word ahead by yesterday's courier to have it ready. But we have some lovely lamb chops for you, Nardjis, if you'd prefer."

"No, darling. That's thoughtful of you, but we Moslems—except the very strict ones—are absolved from dietary laws when eating in other people's houses.

The Koran tells us that when we are forced to transgress those laws, 'then verily God is forgiving and gracious'. And, as I told you yesterday, I'm beginning to feel more Christian than Moslem."

After they were all served and Nardjis had tasted the succulent meat, she exclaimed, "I can assure you, Marilú, that it's no sacrifice to eat this dish. It's the most delicious thing I have ever eaten."

Luncheon over, the others left Nardjis in the house, and, accompanied by three mounted soldiers, were soon on their way, crossing the Tajo by the same bridge over which they had come on entering the city. Turning left off the main road, up a steep mountain path, they came to the Hermitage of the *Virgen de la Cabeza,* from which vantage point they had a magnificent view of Toledo to the north, and, looking south and east, of the mountains and of the winding Tajo River.

Turning left again, on what was nothing more than a trail, along which they had to ride in single file, they came to another hermitage, *Ermità del Virgen del Valle.*

"This used to be the Monastery of San Pedro and San Félix, centuries ago, before the Moorish conquest," explained Gonzalo, for the benefit of Zoraya and Conchita who had never been there before. "And now, after the *Reconquista* by King Alfonso, it is once more dedicated to religious purposes. But let's keep going on horseback, up to the Peña del Moro. The soldiers can then come back here with the horses, while we take our walk and *siesta.*"

The trail followed the outline of the deep ravines that split the solid granite rock on either side of them. It wound along, going up and up, the granite boulders alternating with patches of olive orchards and moors carpeted with wild thyme.

"We shall have to dismount here, and continue

climbing on foot to the summit—that is, if you are all willing. It's quite a climb."

They all agreed, and the soldiers took the horses, to meet them later, down below. It was a difficult climb indeed, crawling around and over huge granite boulders carved by nature into the strangest shapes.

They came out on a plateau of solid granite on which stood great granite boulders of strange shapes and sizes, perched so precariously, it would seem, that at any moment they might be expected to fall clattering down into the valley below. The panorama was stupendous, and the day so clear they could see for miles in every direction.

The climb down the other side was just as difficult, and here the three husbands preceded their wives, catching them in their arms as they jumped down from boulder to boulder.

"The olive groves—the *cigarrales*—begin here," said Gonzalo, "and although it didn't look it when we rode up here, we can follow the moors and olive groves as we go down, almost without a break, winding our way alongside the ravines. But be careful because, if you fall into one of those crevices, a broken leg would be the least of your worries."

They came to the end of one of the *cigarrales*, to a broad moor fragrant with thyme. "We go through the woods there at the far side," said Gonzalo, "and on to another olive orchard."

They crossed the moor, and Conchita exclaimed, "I'm tired. I'd like to take my *siesta* right now—but in the woods, in the shade, not out here in the sun. Look—there are three paths there, all going in the same direction. Why don't we explore, each of us taking a separate path and, after our *siesta*, we can all meet at the far side, in the olive grove."

"Well, there are six of us, and only three paths, so I guess I'll have to go with you," Jorge grumbled.

The three couples split up, each taking their separate way, completely secluded by the trees and heavy underbrush.

"Wow, I'm dead," said Conchita as she and Jorge came to a grassy knoll enclosed by trees and bushes, and circled with a fringe of thyme. "Let's take our *siesta* here, Jorgito," she said.

They sat down upon the soft grass side by side, their knees drawn up, and Conchita clasped her arms around Jorge's neck.

Then, the sound of passionate sighs coming through the woods from two directions further aroused Jorge's ardor, and he and Conchita were soon linked in amorous embrace. Again and again, they essayed their passion and their moans and groans mingled with those on either side.

And then, all was quiet, as three happy couples took their *siesta* in the thyme-scented wood.

Marilú stirred, awakened by a sharp cry she could hear on her right. Startled, she was about to jump to her feet when she recognized it not as the roar of some wild beast but as the voices of Zoraya and Roberto, panting and moaning in ecstasy.

"Gonzalo darling, come to me again," she whispered.

Soon two more voices joined the first two, and then a fifth and sixth, and the woods resounded with scurrying rabbits and songbirds and the sighings of love.

Some time later the three couples emerged from the woods and met in the open spaces of the olive grove.

"Goodness, I've never seen so many rabbits in all my life," laughed Conchita.

"Nonsense, my crazy little cousin," Marilú said. "There are millions of rabbits in Andalucía. That's why the Carthaginians called the country '*Ispania*,' when they came here fourteen centuries ago, from their word *'sphan,'* meaning rabbit. And, you know, a country that has so many rabbits must be a rich country, because, in a poor country, the people would eat the rabbits—and the doves too."

"Yes," put in Zoraya, "when I lived in Cádiz, I was told that Andalucía was the richest land in all the world, and that it was because, in Andalucía, Moslems, Jews, and Christians could all live together in peace, people of each religion—and race—contributing to the greatness of the country. And I suppose that, if ever the people of any one of these races and religions become so powerful and so intolerant as to wipe out the other religions and races, then Spain will lose its greatness and become poor. And people will eat the rabbits, and this land will no longer be the *Hispania* we know today."

"You're getting philosophical, Zoraya," commented Marilú. "Anyway, I've had a marvelous *siesta.*"

"And I must say, I do like a walk in the country," added Gonzalo. "So invigorating!"

The others agreed that the walk had been a wonderful idea. And then Zoraya shrieked: "Look at the back of your dresses, you two—all green and full of leaves and grass. And your hair is all tousled—you look like something the cat dragged in."

"I can't imagine how that could have happened," Conchita laughed. But look at yourself, Zoraya. Speaking of grass and green leaves. And even a witch couldn't have hair as mussed as yours. Goodness!"

"I guess you men better help brush us off," said Marilú. "It's all your fault."

"Mine? I was asleep," said Roberto. But they did help one another to get brushed into some semblance of decency, and the three soldiers were discreet enough to hold their tongues when they met them at the bottom of the hill. But grass stains are grass stains, and the three ladies bore their green stigmata until they were safely back at the Clavijo mansion.

"You must all have had a marvelous walk," exclaimed Nardjis, as she saw them enter the room. "As for me, I've had a wonderful *siesta* and am ready for the banquet—I have only to put on my evening gown. And that nice jeweler has sent around our necklaces. They are gorgeous.

"Why don't you all have a cup of hot tea with me before you take your baths. You can sit down, and keep your backs to the wall when the maid comes. You men don't seem to have any grass stains on you—oh, my but look at your knees! Goodness! Better get down and pray—here comes the maid now."

The maid left the tea things, and Jorge exclaimed impetuously: "Oh, Nardjis, I love you—and I've probably told you that before. I love everybody in this room. Even Conchita."

"You better, you brute!" Conchita smiled.

When it was time to leave for the Alcázar, Gonzalo said, "I've ordered a coach for you six, and I'm taking another coach to fetch the Princess. You four ladies look lovely with your necklaces—perfectly adorable."

"Well, you better take a good hard look, Gonzalo," replied Marilú. "I don't like your being alone with that Zayda in a coach, and I don't want you to forget that you have a lovely, adorable wife waiting for you."

"Zayda won't have anything to do with a mere general, Marilú," commented Roberto. "She has bigger game in mind for tonight. You can trust him."

"Thanks," said Gonzalo. ". . . for nothing. You underestimate me. And I don't know that I trust myself in matters of this kind. And now I have to be going. See you later . . . maybe."

The Princess was lodged in another mansion a half

mile further on. She was ready to leave when Gonzalo came to the door. "Please come in," she smiled.

"Your highness, we must be off at once, you know." He hesitated.

"You extraordinary man," the Princess laughed. "I know you're not impervious to my charms. I know you're attracted to me. We women have ways of telling. But I've never known a man so shy. Well, at least you may kiss my hand, and help me on with my wraps. Don't you like me?"

"Oh, my lady, please don't ask me that." And Gonzalo blushed as he answered her. "No man could fail to be susceptible to your charms—and I am a man. But I am a man sublimely happy in my marriage, and I don't dare allow my wandering thoughts and hot desires to swerve my mind for one minute away from my own dear wife. If I did, I would be hopelessly lost, for you know, my dear Princess Zayda, that you are a most fascinating, a most seductive woman.

"But I am taking you to meet Alfonso *el Bravo* whom you will find to be truly an extraordinary man. And I would rather that you remember me always as the person who introduced you to the King. I can forewarn you that he is already inflamed by what I have told him of your charms."

Zayda snuggled close against him in the coach, evidently intent on teasing him to the limit—not more than teasing, for she was a woman who would keep her eye resolutely on the main chance and allow nothing to stand in her way. To Gonzalo, more and more uncomfortable, the coach ride seemed interminable, although it was not more than three or four minutes to the inner doorway of the Alcázar.

He offered the Princess his arm as they entered the fortress, and they went straight to the small salon, where the others were already gathered. Zayda greeted the ladies and the generals affectionately, and Gonzalo then introduced her to the others in the room—the Chancellor, Ministers of State, and other important officials, and their wives, all of whom Gonzalo knew from previous royal affairs.

The doors opened and, with no fanfare of trumpets, but with a hush as dramatic as any fanfare, the King entered, with Queen Constance on his arm. They seated themselves side by side on two of three chairs at the far end of the room. There was no doubt for whom the third chair had been ordered. From the moment he entered the room, the King had eyes for no one but the Princess Zayda, who was undoubtedly one of the most beautiful women ever to grace the royal presence.

Gonzalo stepped forward, the Princess on his right arm. He bowed low to the King and Queen. "Your Majesties, the Princess Zayda, daughter-in-law of King al-Mutamid, widow of the late Prince al-Mamun, Queen of all the Regions between the Tajo and the Guadiana. Princess, their Majesties, don Alfonso and doña Constance." He bowed again and took a step backward.

The King and Queen extended their hands to be kissed, and Queen Constance remarked, "You are truly lovely, my dear, won't you sit down," and she indicated the armchair on her husband's left.

Gonzalo now came forward with Marilú on his arm—as the guests of honor in view of their glorious achievements. They were followed by the other guests in order of rank. The King and Queen were particularly attentive to Conchita and Zoraya and their smiling husbands and when Lady Nardjis came forward on the arm of the Lord High Chancellor, a bachelor, the King personally introduced her to Queen Constance as "that remarkable Moslem lady of whom we have told you."

Following the ritual of tasting the wine by the royal *copero,* butlers circulated among the guests, passing around silver trays with crystal goblets of pale dry sherry.

"To their Majesties, don Alfonso and doña Constance," boomed the Lord High Chancellor, and Princess Zayda rose from her seat, glass in hand, to join in the toast.

The King now took a glass and handed one to his Queen. Then in a gesture, extraordinary for royalty, he raised his glass, and toasted: "And to our three brave generals, heroes of the Battle of Piedrabuena, and to their charming wives, rescued from Saracen captivity; to Lady Nardjis without whose help none of these, nor any of their soldiers, would be alive today; and to the Princess Zayda whose radiant beauty graces our humble board tonight."

They all drank, and with that eight-barrelled toast, it was possible for even the honored guests to join in the round. A butler announced the dinner, and this time, to Marilú's relief, it was the Lord High Chancellor who escorted Princess Zayda to the table, while Gonzalo came in with his wife and Lady Nardjis on his arms.

The company was seated, with the King at the center of a long table on a dais, the Queen at his right, the Princess at his left, while behind him stood the ever-vigilant cupbearer and physician. On each side were the seven guests of honor, with the Chancellor again beside Lady Nardjis with whom he was by this time conversing in animated fashion. The other guests were seated at an even larger table facing the dais.

The King could not take his eyes off the fascinating lady at his left—or his hands either, until Princess Zayda, embarrassed, whispered to him: "Your Majesty, please, this is a tablecloth, not a bed-sheet."

Her smile took any possible sting out of the words,

and the King smiled back, and whispered: "That will come later, my dear. Meanwhile, there is a little gift I should like you to accept—from the treasure stores of the Caliph Abd ar-Rahman."

And he fastened around Zayda's neck a pearl necklace which was truly one of remarkable beauty.

The Queen paled visibly, and whispered to her consort: "My dear, I am afraid you will have to excuse me. I am feeling faint, and am afraid I must retire. It must have been the sherry."

"I am sorry, my love. I do hope you will recover." And the sincerity of the King's affection for his Queen, and his genuine concern over her state of health, had no relevance to the fact that his left hand was now located well above Zayda's knee and engaged in exploring as far beyond that spot as he could reach without overturning the table.

"Please, your Majesty," Zayda protested, after the Queen had kissed her goodbye and left the room, accompanied by one of her ladies in waiting. "Please, your Majesty, there will be time enough for that later. I am fascinated by your Majesty, totally overcome by your charm, Sire. I have longed to meet you for years, and what I now see so far surpasses everything I have heard that I am eager to get to know you better—much better, your Majesty—but, please, not yet. Let's just eat for now, and let me be delighted with the wit and charm of your conversation, and by that fine, resonant voice of yours that sends thrills up and down my spine. Please . . . you nearly made me spill my wine."

The King desisted for the moment, and the two engaged in lively conversation, oblivious to anyone else in the room.

"I think we'll all be safe this evening," Marilú whispered to Gonzalo, "Your plot has succeeded marvelously. But the poor Queen. I don't see how she stands it."

"If it were not Zayda, it would be someone else," whispered Gonzalo. "And, believe it or not, the King is devoted to Queen Constance. They are both devout Catholics, so there is no question of Zayda supplanting Queen Constance in his affections—merely in his bed. And that has always been his happy hunting ground. But we must stop this whispering—not that anyone is noticing. They are all watching Zayda and the King."

And it was true. Every eye was turned toward the center of the head table, and course after course was served, with hardly anyone aware of what he or she was eating or drinking. But all things must come to an end, and, as the final liqueur was poured, the King summoned Gonzalo: "Come around to the front of the table where we can talk to you, Clavijo. We shan't be able to see you tomorrow, or for a week at least—affairs of state, you know."

"Very well, Sire," Gonzalo replied, "And we are all going off to Galicia, or to León—you know you gave us your permission yesterday, your Majesty."

"Let us say goodbye to all of you," and the King nodded to the others to join Gonzalo in front of the table, where he could see them. "Goodbye my friends, goodbye, and thank you for everything. *Bon voyage* to all of you, and God be with you."

CHAPTER 26

At breakfast the next morning in the sunny dining room of the Clavijo mansion, Marilú broached the matter that she and her four women companions had been discussing.

"Gonzalo, if you and Roberto and Jorge don't mind, we four would like to go to the market today, and spend all day there, buying all the things that we can get here in Andalucía and that we can't possibly buy in Galicia or León—soaps and perfumes and spices, and chinaware and silks, and especially the tiles and lead pipes and things we need to build a Moorish bath in our houses back home—just like we have here in this house in Toledo, but even better. You remember you saw the *hammam* in the palace of Medina al-Zahra, heated with hot water running under the floor. And, although we don't need anything as luxuriously decorated as that, a hot bathroom would be wonderful on those cold days in Iria Flavia. May I, Gonzalo? You're so rich now, we can be extravagant for the first time in our lives. And Nardjis knows the market in Toledo, and prices and quality and everything."

"Of course, my love," Gonzalo answered. "I think it's a fine idea. Buy everything you need or want, and get some presents for the children, and your parents. What do you say, Jorge? And Roberto?"

The other husbands agreed enthusiastically, and each of the three gave his wife a list of some of the things that he would particularly like to have her buy.

"I tell you what, ladies," said Gonzalo. "You four come with us, right after breakfast, to the house of Samuel Leví, the banker I was telling you of. It will ease your minds to meet him and know the arrangements we can make with him for converting all those precious stones into gold or money. And, Nardjis, you can decide whether or not you want to make the same arrangements we do."

There was, of course, no question then or at any time in the minds of any of them that Gonzalo, in the exercise of his power of *patria potestas* under the laws of Gaius and Justinian that had prevailed in Spain since the Roman conquest, as well as under the pre-existing common law, had full power of disposal over Marilú's share of the treasure, as well as over his own. What was hers was his; what was his was his own.

"We shall all go down in the royal coach together," said Gonzalo, "and I shall have three supply wagons come with us. You may need that many to carry all you are going to buy, and it can all be repacked this evening for our journey home tomorrow. We three shall have to leave you after we finish our business with Leví, because we shall be discussing military matters with the Minister of War, but you four can stay in town as late as you want. So far as I am concerned, Marilú my sweet, you have *carte blanche* to buy everything you wish."

Breakfast over, they all gathered in the vestibule, ready to take off on their banking and shopping expedition, the women bubbling over with excitement at the thought of being able to buy everything they wanted and, for the first time in their lives, with no need to economize.

Outside, the three supply wagons and a squad of soldiers waited, plus the teamsters, coachmen and footmen, and the royal coach itself—the most magnificent vehicle in all of Christian Spain. Drawn by four black horses, a postilion mounted on the left lead horse, two coachmen in front, two footmen in the rear, all in the royal livery, the coach was a spacious closed carriage suspended on steel springs between two huge wheels in back, two smaller ones in front. The outside was red and gold with decidedly more gold than red, elaborately carved and ornamented, and bearing the castle and lion that were the emblem of Castilla and León. The inside was upholstered in green and gold brocade covering tufted cushions of softest down and forming two couches facing one another, with ample room for the four ladies on the rear seat and for the three men on the front. Two crystal vases in golden brackets held bouquets of red and white roses.

Two of the supply wagons, at Gonzalo's order, left the cortege to go to the Plaza del Zocodóver, Toledo's main plaza, where they would wait for the ladies at the market-place. The third wagon, with the five leather trunks containing the jewels, followed the coach across town, past the Cathedral, down the same narrow streets they had traversed the previous day to the Plaza de la Judería, the center of the Jewish quarter. On the right stood a handsome mansion, one of the finest in Toledo.

"Well, here we are," said Gonzalo, as the carriage came to a halt in front of the great doorway.

The soldiers unloaded the five trunks and carried them upstairs to a large salon where the visitors were met by a venerable Jew and a younger man, both of them wearing yellow skull-caps. Gonzalo instructed the soldiers to accompany the wagon to the Zocodóver and wait for them there, and to have the troduced the members of the party to Samuel Leví carriage wait outside the Leví mansion. He then in-who, in turn, introduced the younger man as his son, David.

"Before we get down to business," suggested don Samuel, graciously, and in a voice that Marilú thought was one of the most musical and resonant she had ever heard, "I would be honored if you would join us in a glass of sherry."

They seated themselves around a great, carved oak table at one end of the room, which was luxuriously furnished in Mozarabic style with carpets and tapestries fully as fine as those of the palace of Medina al-Zahra. A full-bodied *oloroso* sherry was served from a crystal decanter standing on a silver tray, and poured into delicate crystal goblets that don Samuel passed to each of his guests.

As they sipped, don Samuel told them, "Knowing the purpose of your visit, my lord *Marqués,* I took the liberty of asking Ahmad ibn al-Jassas to join us. He is the great-great grandson of the al-Jassas of Baghdad who in his time was the greatest jewel merchant in the world—so wealthy that, after the Caliph al-Mugtadir had confisicated sixteen million dinars of his wealth, he was still the richest man in Baghdad other than the Caliph himself.

"His descendant, Ahmad, is one of the leading gem merchants in Toledo, and should be here in half an hour. But before he comes, I would like to discuss with you ladies and gentlemen in private some general ideas that I think may suit your purpose. And let me do the bargaining with ibn al-Jassas. For, although he is a completely scrupulous man, he is also a shrewd merchant, and his initial proposals are likely to be quite unacceptable. First, let me just glance at the gems and at the appraisal sheets to have some idea of the basis of valuation."

David opened the trunks for inspection. In each, the various kinds of jewels were separated by class, by size and by quality and color, each lot wrapped in silk, and with a separate appraisal tally.

"I should like to have seen the pearls," commented don Samuel. "From what I hear, they must be magnificent, but I agree with the appraisers that, for your purposes, the other gems are more marketable, and more durable in the event that we are dissatisfied with the offers we are able to get here in Toledo, and must ship the stones to India or elsewhere. Personally, I would never buy pearls of that antiquity, except as jewelry, not as an investment.

"The two merchants who appraised the stones yesterday have privately committed themselves to me to taking all or any part of the treasure at the appraisal price less twenty percent, payable in monthly installments over a period of five years, so we have at least a basis for our discussions with ibn al-Jassis.

"At present usury rates, payment over a five-year period means a discount of over twenty-five percent, but, in any event, I believe we would be well advised to insist on immediate payment, or, at the most, payment over a one-year period. Conditions in Spain are too risky for you to sell on credit. And I would, in any event, retain possession of the gems for your account, releasing them *pari passu* as each installment is paid. . . . David, what do you think of the gems, and of the appraisals?"

David had meanwhile been laying out on the table, on black velvet-lined trays, the sapphires, rubies, diamonds and emeralds from the lightest of the five trunks—that of Lady Nardjis—with the tally sheets alongside each lot.

"They are truly magnificent, father. I have never seen so large or so fine a collection in my life, and we know that this trunkful is only a small fraction of the total. As to the appraisals, I would say they represent a fair balance between what a willing and knowledgeable buyer and a willing and knowledgeable seller might agree on. Obviously, when one attempts to dispose of such an enormous quantity of gems as this, one must expect to sell at a considerable discount, so I consider the offer you were able to get from the two appraisers not unfair. They will have to market the stones all over the world—India, Damascus, Baghdad, and in every city of Europe—no one market could absorb all of them."

"I agree," said don Samuel. "The valuation is just; the appraisers had no idea what disposition the King intended to make of these gems, and no reason either to exaggerate or to underestimate their value. But I am going to try to do better—and particularly with respect to the time of payment. Gentlemen—and ladies—what do you think? Shall I bargain on the basis of the appraisals? The best I can really hope for is a price of perhaps ten to twenty percent below the appraisal, payable over a one-year period. What do you say?"

Gonzalo answered: "I speak for all of us. We are anxious to sell. We leave the bargaining entirely in your hands."

"Good! I might say that I have two other possibilities—one the sale of the gems in India, but it is risky and will take time; the other, to try to sell them to King Philippe in Paris. My oldest son, Solomon, is in Paris as our representative with a banking house there. And King Philippe has committed so many robberies of the Church and of the nobility—he is probably the richest and most hated man in France—that he is a likely buyer for at least part of this collection. His parents, the good King Henry and Anne of Russia, would turn over in their graves if he spends his money in that way, but that need not concern us.

"But there is another aspect of the business I'd like to take up with you before ibn al-Jassas gets here. You will probably want gold bars or minted gold dinars in Iria Flavia and in León. And you may wish to leave some dinars here with me in Toledo—we can discuss how much at your convenience. I would pay you usury on that amount at the usual rates. For the payments outside Toledo, we would not ship the actual gold to those cities. There is an abundance of gold in León, and my nephew, Moses, would undertake to pay you the dinars, don Roberto, immediately, or as soon as he receives word of payment to me here—say, within ten days from each payment here, at the most. The *agio* for payments in León is five percent, in other words, you would pay five percent for the transfer from here to León.

"Now, in Galicia, there is a shortage of gold, and today's *agio* on Iria Flavia is ten percent. Furthermore, it will be impossible to guaranty full payment there in less than a year. But I happen to know that there are considerable quantities of gold going from Cádiz and Oporto to Iria Flavia—a flight of gold in fear of the depredations of the invading army of ibn Tashfin. And large amounts of gold are also being poured into Iria Flavia by King Alfonso for the construction of the Cathedral. So I feel sure we can complete the payments in much less time than a year, and I would be willing to charge the same *agio* as for León—five percent."

"Would Abraham be willing to do business at that rate, father?" asked David.

"Yes, he will, if I agree to it," replied don Samuel. "Gentlemen, you may be amazed at our mention of these other bankers. Abraham is my first cousin. We have relatives or friends in all the banking centers of Europe and the Levant, and we send our younger sons to serve as apprentices with the great bankers in France and Germany and elsewhere. They are of marriageable age, and many of them do marry into those banking families, so that there is in fact a great family of bankers all over the world—fathers, sons, uncles, nephews, and cousins—and we all do business with one another on the basis of the most absolute faith and confidence.

"In times of danger, as in Andalucía today, we send our money and our treasures to some safer city. We have long since removed practically all our wealth from Sevilla, Córdoba and the other cities of Andalucía, and we have very little left in France for fear of their predatory King Philippe.

"And we send monthly statements of account to all the other banking houses, so that we know how we stand, and how many dinars we have deposited in each place, and where we have overdrafts that must be repaid. If ever you wish to remit from one city to another, you can do so through us or through our correspondents, paying whatever the *agio* may be at any place and time. I shall give you letters to Moses in León, and to Abraham in Iria Flavia, before you leave.

"And one more thing, if you wish to make any purchases in Toledo, my son David can accompany you, and make any payments you need and charge them to your account. I advise you to buy whatever you need because prices here are always much less than in León or Galicia, and today there are many bargains to be had because of the fear of Tashfin. If you were in Sevilla, you could pick up even greater bargains. . . . Now, are there any questions before our prospective buyer arrives?"

"No, I think not," Gonzalo replied. "You have made everything quite clear. And our ladies will be spending all day—and a good deal of money—in the market, so we would indeed appreciate it if your son David were to accompany them. We three shall remain here to complete the arrangements and sign any papers that must be signed. Nardjis, will you want to leave any money in Toledo, or will you have it all remitted to Iria Flavia?"

"No," said Lady Nardjis, "I shan't be returning to Toledo, and I would indeed appreciate it all being remitted to Iria Flavia, except for the amounts that Señor David Leví spends for us here. And, Gonzalo, you can sign any papers that need to be signed for me."

"That won't be necessary, my lady," said don Samuel. "So long as you wish to have everything sent on to Iria Flavia, I'll have the papers drawn up immediately, with only the amounts left in blank. And we shall insist on handling your sale on a cash basis. It is not too large a sum for ibn al-Jassis to pay. . . . And I think I hear him at the door now. David, would you ask the *escribano* to draw up the papers for Lady Nardjis."

A moment later, a dark handsome man, with a neatly trimmed black beard, entered the room accompanied by a younger man, the latter wearing a yellow caftan. Don Samuel introduced everyone—Ahmad al-Jassis, and that gentleman's "personal Jew," Isaac Toledano. The sherry was passed again, and then don Samuel opened the conversation.

"We have been looking at this trunkful of gems," he said. "They belong to Lady Nardjis. We have not yet opened the other trunks, but we understand that their contents are much the same as this, excepting that they comprise a much larger amount, particularly that trunk there"—he pointed to the one bearing Marilú's name—"which contains more than twice as much as all the other trunks put together. Would you like to examine one of the other trunks, don Ahmad? We'll leave you and don Isaac alone, so that you can talk in private, and I can be showing the others some of my Persian manuscripts over there by the window."

"Let me just look over the stuff you have on the

table right now, and check it with the appraisal sheets," al-Jassis replied. "And then, I'd like to put this stuff back, and open up"—he chose at random—"that trunk over there."

He and Toledano examined the gems on the table minutely, comparing them with the tally sheets, and taking them tray by tray to the window to inspect them by daylight. Don Samuel, meanwhile, at the other end of the room, showed his visitors a number of parchment-bound volumes containing the most exquisitely illuminated Persian miniatures on every other page, interspersed with an equally beautiful text in cursive Arabic writing, rich with burnished gold leaf and vivid coloring, the blues predominating. They laid the small volumes down on a table when al-Jassis spoke to them.

"We've finished our inspection of these gems, at least for the time being. Let's put them back in the trunk, and spread out the other stones. You have more trays, I assume."

David wrapped and put away Nardjis's gems and then he and Isaac lifted the other trunk, which proved to be Jorge's, and put it at one end of the table. David then placed the velvet-lined trays along the length of the table and, package by package, unwrapped the jewels, laying them out, lot by lot, in each of the trays, with the tally sheet beside each tray. It made a gorgeous display—emeralds, rubies, sapphires, diamonds, of every color—brilliant against the black velvet background. But al-Jassis and Toledano seemed quite unimpressed, and said nothing, although don Samuel, smiling, said that it was the most beautiful collection of gems he had seen in all his seventy years. It was.

One by one, Toledano took the trays over to the window where he and al-Jassis commented beneath their breath on them and on the appraisals.

"Not a bad collection," said al-Jassis aloud after the last tray had been examined. "And I am interested. But the appraisals, of course, are grossly exaggerated. Not that I am impugning the expertise or the integrity of the appraisers. You and I know them well, don Samuel. But they have obviously put down the retail value of the stones—the price at which you or I would sell them to some wealthy person who was very anxious to buy. And I am willing to take the entire lot—at a fair price—although I can see that it is going to take me many years to dispose of them in Baghdad and elsewhere. Most of the gems were probably stolen from Baghdad in the first place, but that's neither here nor there.

"I tell you what—without even looking at the other trunks, I am willing to accept the appraisals according to the tally sheets, and will pay you fifty percent of the appraised value, less a ten percent commission, payable over a period of five years. What do you say, Samuel?"

"What I would like to say, don Ahmad," the old Jew answered, "I could hardly say in the presence of these ladies. But let's get down to business—and I'll omit the usual formality of telling you that I am willing to do business with you only because of my affection for your father and for young Toledano's charming wife. If you are really interested, we can come to an agreement. If not, I have reason to believe that I can dispose of a good part of these stones in India, and of the remainder in Paris, through my son, Solomon, who has exceptionally close connections with the not unsusceptible finance minister of *lè Roi* Philippe.

"In the first place, before we discuss price, let us get the terms of payment straight. I want cash for my clients, payable now on delivery."

"That's impossible, don Samuel," replied al-Jassis.

"Even at the price I offered, which I must emphasize is reasonable under the circumstances, I could not possibly assemble the necessary number of dinars in less than a year."

"Well, let's make it a year then, payable in equal monthly installments, the gems to be released to you *pari passu* as payments are made. That is for those four trunks there. The little trunk would be paid for in cash, which would not strain your exchequer."

"Agreed—provided the price is right," answered al-Jassis. No, no more sherry, I thank you. After the deal is over, I shall be delighted to drink your health and that of these charming ladies and gentlemen."

And so the bargaining continued for the better part of an hour with much scribbling of calculations and references to King Philippe and India and Baghdad, until, at last, a price was reached—the appraised values less a discount of ten percent.

"I could do better, I am sure, my friends," concluded don Samuel to his clients, "but it might take time, and I advise you to accept this offer from my good friend, Ahmad ibn al-Jassis."

"His 'good friend'," laughed al-Jassis. "I'd hate to think how he would bargain with an enemy. But a bargain is a bargain, and I will admit now, that it *is* a marvellous collection. Marvellous! I trust that I can dispose of it without loss. That is the risk. And let me propose a toast to the health and happiness of all of you, and especially a toast to doña Marilú, Marquesa de Clavijo, without whose miraculous revelation, this treasure would have been destroyed by the vandalism of those savage *Almorávides*."

They drank each other's health in utmost convivial-ity after the hard bargaining of the past hour. David summoned the *escribano* again and the papers were prepared for Lady Nardjis's signature.

"And now, gentlemen, I trust you will all do me the

honor of having luncheon with me while these charming ladies and my son David spend part of their new wealth, and the rest of the day, in Toledo. It will take a couple of hours before all the papers can be ready for our signatures and you, my good friend, don Ahmad, will wish to divide the gems up into lots for the first installment. My friend Toledano can audit the tally sheets and make an inventory of the gems with my clerk, separating them into lots for the twelve monthly deliveries and payments. And the *escribano* will then draft the necessary *escrituras*."

It was so agreed and, amidst many *abrazos* among the men, and much hand-kissing in taking leave of the women, the four ladies, accompanied by David Leví, went off in the royal carriage to the Plaza del Zocodóver. There they found the supply wagons and soldiers waiting for them beside the ancient Moorish gateway that, since the *Reconquista*, was known as the "Arch of the Blood of Christ."

"Let's go first to buy the tiles and artefacts for our baths," suggested Lady Nardjis. "One of the wagons can follow us, because the tiles are heavy. And, if I remember, the tilemakers are right down that side street there."

"It hasn't changed, my lady," David smiled. "They have been there ever since the time of the Caliph."

At that moment, a tall man, in handsome but somewhat ragged clothes, crossed their path, bearing on his back a heavy load of silks.

"Abdullah!" exclaimed Lady Nardjis. "What are you doing here, and how is it that you are working as a porter?"

"Lady Nardjis! How happy I am to see you!" the tall man exclaimed, laying down his burden. "And what a surprise! As you know, my wife and I left the palace two months ago to see my mother who was dying, may her soul rest in peace. And then the news

about Tashfin was so disturbing that we didn't d
go back to Medina al-Zahra. And I have been unabl
to get a job here as a cook or carpenter, or anything else, and am working as a porter around the marketplace. Rosa is earning some money as a laundress just a few blocks from here.

"May I bring her—she would be so delighted to see you, Lady Nardjis. Lord knows we have had little enough happiness since we left the palace, and there could be no greater pleasure than to see you again, safe and sound, Allah be praised."

"We shall be at the tile shops, looking around," said Nardjis, "and perhaps you would be good enough to help us purchase some supplies. You know these things so much better than I. And I'll introduce you and your wife to my friends when you return."

"I'll be back instantly, my lady," said Abdullah, his emotions welling up in his throat as he spoke. And the tall man disappeared in the crowd with his burden.

"Abdullah came to the palace as a cook," Lady Nardjis explained, "but he proved to be so expert at so many things—carpentry, plumbing, painting, masonry, stucco work—that he became the chief assistant to the *kahraman,* sort of an assistant majordomo and handyman. A jack of all trades, and master of all of them. And his wife Rosa is the best dressmaker and seamstress in all Córdoba. Her name was Ourda, but we called her Rosa because at first she worked as an assistant to a dressmaker whose name was also Ourda. But we found that the older Ourda was making money on the side—perhaps that is not the way to describe her position—by accepting the favors of numerous gentlemen callers. So we fired her."

"I see," quipped Zoraya. "She hemmed and whored."

"Pay no attention," laughed Marilú. "Go on."

"Well, I've just been thinking," Nardjis resumed.

"Marilú, you would find that Abdullah and Rosa would be ever so helpful to you in Iria Flavia. He is a marvelous cook. And there simply isn't anything he can't do. He could certainly supervise the installation of the baths better than anyone I know.

"And, Rosa, as I say, is an excellent dressmaker—the best and fastest I've ever known. She could make all the children's clothes, and yours and Gonzalo's too—and sew the curtains, and everything. And they are both lovely people. If you think you could use their services, I know they'd be overjoyed to come with us to Iria Flavia. And they can help us right now around the marketplace. They will know qualities and prices, and shops, much better than I."

"It's a wonderful idea, Nardjis," exclaimed Marilu. "I hope you don't mind our taking your time with this, don David, but I am sure Abdullah can make our shopping easier and faster."

"Of course not," answered David, "A knowledgeable fellow like that can be a big help. I know nothing of merchandise—merely how to pay for it."

By that time, they had arrived at a small alley with tilemakers' shops on every side. Scarcely had they started to look at the various wares than they saw Abdullah and his wife running toward them, smiling from ear to ear. They bowed low to Lady Nardjis and kissed her hands, shedding tears of happiness to see their former mistress. Nardjis quickly introduced them and Marilú asked if they would like to go back with her to Galicia. They accepted with alacrity, tears running down their faces as they embraced one another in sheer joy.

"Well," said Marilú, "would you, Abdullah, start by helping us with our shopping."

She explained quickly what they wanted for the three mansions in Galicia—including the castle of Conchita's father—and the one in León. "And kitchen utensils, household goods," she added, "everything that you think we should have.

"And you run back to your house, Rosa, and pack all your belongings in the wagon, and then come back and help us buy silks and other things, and presents for the children. And, oh, yes, I'll be glad to advance you both two months' wages so that, if there is anything you need for yourselves, vou can get it in the market here. There is very little to buy in Iria Flavia."

Abdullah and Rosa thanked Marilú profusely, Rosa exclaiming: "Our belongings, my lady. We have nothing. A small bundle which I'll fetch instantly—and then meet you at the silk shops. And I have enough dirhans in my pocket to pay our rent—not on our house, my lady, but for a single room which we share with two other couples."

She was gone. The others, with Abdullah's expert advice, bought everything that was needed to install a bath in each of the four mansions. Abdullah's knowledge of the merchandise, and his keen bargaining, saved the ladies at least a third of the prices originally asked.

From the tilemakers' shops, they went on to other shops carrying every class of cooking utensil, pots and pans, and so forth, mostly of heavy brass. Again Abdullah helped them choose what was necessary.

From there, they walked back to the marketplace proper—a typical Moorish *suk* surrounded by high walls with heavy iron gates. They walked immediately to the silk market where the tiny stalls and shops were laden with silks of every description, the best coming from Granada and Damascus.

By that time Rosa was there to help them, as Abdullah had helped with the household goods, and they bought in profusion, for themselves, their parents and children. Bolt after bolt of rich gold and other brocades, heavy grenadines, satins, taffetas and voiles, in white and black, and every shade of gold, yellow, blue, green and red, met their eager eyes, and were added to their pile of purchases. One lot in particular caught their fancy—a number of bolts of brilliantly striped silk, and not even Nardjis had seen woven striped silk before.

"They are just beginning to wear this striped material in Damascus, my lady," said Rosa. "And this is the first shipment that has come to Toledo. Everyone is talking about stripes but only the ladies of the *avant-garde* of fashion have dared to buy it. But it is predicted that stripes will soon be the rage all over Spain. Do buy some. I'd love to make it up for you, and I have some ideas on cutting it."

The four ladies could hardly resist this appeal to be in the forefront of fashion and each bought several bolts in various colors.

They were not interested in jewels or trinkets, nor in the leather from Granada, nor in the gold and ivory filigree and marquetry work, nor in the Tabaristan and Armenian carpets that filled the shops on every side—they had all they wanted of such things from the booty of Medina al-Zahra. But they bought abundantly of the soaps, perfumes, and myriad other articles they saw on every side, including tea and saffron and other spices, chinaware, crystal goblets well-packed in straw, presents for the children, and many other objects, including ream after ream of fine white paper, made from pure linen rags. Marilú said it was almost impossible to buy anything for writing in Galicia, except parchment, and Nardjis commented that this was strange, inasmuch as they had been making paper in Valencia for two hundred years, and in Baghdad for three hundred years. It was a Chinese invention, she said, like the black ink of which they also bought a supply in the form of little bars that could be ground up and mixed with water, as needed.

Marilú's eyes lit upon a display of swords with both blades and hilts intricately inlaid with damascened gold. "Oh, I would love to get one of those for Gonzalo," she said. "Would you help me choose one, Abdullah?"

"Not one of these, my lady," said Abdullah. "Not if you value your husband's life. Unless it is only a dress sword you want. If you want the finest Toledo blades, there are two swordmakers who are preeminent—Badr and Tarif, both grandsons of the swordmakers for the court of the Caliph al-Hakim II, over a hundred years ago. And their sons too are working in the same shops their great-grandfathers worked in, and making swords that in temper and strength, and fine cutting edge, rival the best that are produced in Damascus. You can choose without a qualm any weapon that either of those makers recommends as his best. And there will be no bargaining there. There can be no bargaining when the life of the Marqués de Clavijo may be at stake."

"Abdullah is right," commented David. "Badr and Tarif are famous and, while we Jews have no use for swords, we are not unaware of their value. But the hour is late, and I suggest that you let me take you to lunch, and you can buy the swords afterwards. I know a small restaurant whose food conforms to the Hebrew and Moslem dietary laws, and it is the best place in Toledo. I especially recommend the squab, and with squab you may eat butter, and then some of the most delicious pastries you have ever tasted."

They ordered Abdullah and Rosa to go back to the Clavijo mansion with the soldiers and wagons so that the wagons could be packed for the trip next day. Marilú asked the coachman to be ready to return with the carriage in about an hour and a half.

David then led them upstairs to a tiny restaurant

over what seemed to be a private house next to a synagogue—a place that they certainly would never have discovered by themselves. The squab, served with asparagus, was indeed superb, grilled to a turn on a spit over a flame of small faggots, and delicately spiced—a mere touch of basil that did not detract from the fine flavor of the fowl. The pastries melted in their mouths— "So good I'm tempted to turn Hebrew," said Conchita as she ate her third little tart. A faintly perfumed Chinese tea completed the meal.

After lunch, with David as an escort, the four ladies walked from the restaurant to the swordmakers' shops where they saw the men hard at work, sparks flying, hammers pounding the hot steel on anvils, jewelers chasing the fine gold and silver work on the blades and hilts and guards, hammering fine wires of precious metal into the engraved steel, until steel and gold and silver were one solid piece. The silver would then be oxidized, giving the beautiful gold and black ornamentation in the intricate designs that are a specialty of Toledo.

"I'd like a sword for Jorge, too," said Conchita.

"And you don't think I'd let you buy swords for Gonzalo and Jorge," Zoraya laughed, "without my getting one for Roberto so he can defend himself."

They entered one of the shops and were greeted by the proprietor, the famous swordmaker Tarif. Introductions were quickly completed and Tarif, a courtly Arab of more than middle age, was manifestly delighted to have as prospective customers so renowned a general as the Marqués de Clavijo and his two closest companions in arms whose fame, as well as that of the Marquesa de Clavijo and of Lady Nardjis, was the talk of the town.

"I have just what you want for your husband, Marquesa," said the swordmaker with a smile, "and for General Ayala as well," he added, turning to Zoraya.

"But for General Rodríguez, milady," he concluded, smiling at Conchita, "I shall have to take you across the street to my friend and rival, Badr, who has made the only sword in all Spain worthy of the strength of arm of your husband."

Conchita beamed as the master swordmaker escorted the ladies and David into his shop and unlocked a cabinet in which were hung two truly splendid and terrifying swords.

"I made these blades a year ago—as fine as any I have ever made—intending to show them to King Alfonso and let him take his pick. As you can see, one blade is longer than the other, and I thought the King might like to handle them both to see which one best suited him. But the King is often in Toledo and I can make another for him at any time, while I understand that your husbands, miladies, will be leaving shortly.

"Your husband, *Marquesa*, is above average height and the longer blade will be ideal for him. You may not know it, but he is reputed to be the finest swordsman in all Spain with the possible exception of the Cid Campeador. While your husband, Señora de Ayala, is said to be fast at the thrust. This sword, slightly shorter and not quite so broad, will be perfect for his style.

"Both swords seem to be very broad," enquired Marilú, "and what is the purpose of that channel that runs down the blades on both sides?"

"They have to be broad to cleave through a man's helmet or coat of mail, and the channel serves two purposes—it make the blade lighter without detracting from its strength, and it lets the swordsman withdraw his sword easily when he thrusts through his opponent's body, because the blood can run out and the air rush in through the channels."

The four ladies shuddered at the thought and

turned to admire the exquisite black and gold tracery on the hilt and guard—the latter a simple cross.

"You can see that there is a blank space in pure gold on the hilts. I intended to have a lion and castle engraved on that spot whenever the King chose which weapon he preferred. But your husbands can have their crests engraved there whenever they have a day or two to spare in Toledo.

"And these are the scabbords," he concluded, showing Marilú and Zoraya two simple, reinforced leather sheaths with steel points, and steel bands at the top and eight inches below for the insertion of the leather straps that would fasten the scabbord to the saddle or to the sword belt. The accoutrements were strong and simple, as becomes a weapon for a soldier rather than a courtier, but they were handsomely inlaid with gold and silver to match the design of the hilts.

Marilú and Zoraya were delighted with their purchases, knowing how pleased Gonzalo and Roberto would be with these magnificent weapons. And David arranged with Tarif that he would send the money by messenger as soon as he returned to his office.

"Now, let's go across the street, miladies," Tarif suggested. "My rival, Badr, has a sword that he made some years ago for the Cid. But the Cid is now in exile, and just a year ago he captured the fabulous sword, Colada, from Count Berenguer of Barcelona, and will not be in the market for another weapon."

"I've heard of the sword Colada," interjected Conchita. "Is Badr's sword as good as that? Because I wouldn't want anything but the best for my husband, you know."

"I think I can reassure you on that point, milady," responded Tarif. "The swords we master swordmakers forge today in Toledo are equal to the best that have come from Damascus. Or, rather, from Isfahan in Persia, for that is where the so-called Damascus blades are made. But, of course, a famous sword such as Colada is valued for its antiquity as well as for its quality, and it is said that Berenguer paid ten thousand golden marks for it. And if anyone could find King Arthur's Excalibur or Roland's Durandel, they would be worth even more because of their greater antiquity and renown. But the two swords I have sold you, and Badr's sword, are every bit as fine.

"Look at the little mark on these two blades, just below the hilt—a letter "O" placed over the letter "T". That is the mark of the Toledo swordmakers' guild, and means that the blade has been tested by experts and found to be of Toledo's finest quality. Not one sword in ten thousand bears that mark. And the Badr sword I speak of also has this mark. Well, let's go and see it."

And he led the ladies and David to a workshop almost directly opposite.

"I've brought you a customer, Badr," he called out. "The wife of General Jorge Rodríguez."

"For the blade I made for the Cid, of course. Come in," Badr replied.

Introductions were completed, and Badr laid on a table in front of his visitors a huge sword.

"My, it is heavy," gasped Conchita. "I can scarcely lift it even with two hands. . . . It's that big iron ball at the end of the handle. Why do you have to have a big weight like that at the wrong end?"

"That's the quillon, the pommel," laughed Badr. "It prevents the sword from slipping out of a man's hand when the hilt is wet with sweat or blood. And if it weren't for that weight, you couldn't lift the sword at all. . . . Vásquez," he called out to one of his apprentices. "Bring me that sword you are balancing. And the pommel."

A young man approached carrying an unpolished

blade in one hand, and in the other a flattened iron ball with a hole in one end. The master swordsmaker kept the quillon in his hand and laid the sword on the table.

"Now try to lift it, milady," he said, turning to Conchita.

Conchita tried with all her strength. "I can't lift it at all. It's too heavy," she panted.

Badr fitted the pommel to the end of the hilt.

"Now try it," he said.

Conchita lifted the blade easily with two hands, hardly believing the testimony of her own eyes. "It's lighter than the sword I'm going to buy for my husband. And thank you for taking the trouble to show me."

The deal was soon concluded. Badr provided a scabbord simliar to those made by Tarif, but with the gold and black design matching that on the sword itself. With many bows and expressions of mutual appreciation David and his four charges left the swordmakers, well satisfied with the afternoon's business.

"When you give a person a blade of any kind," David advised, "you should give him a coin to ward off ill luck. So let me give you each a silver dirhem to give to your husbands. And now, if you would be good enough, I would appreciate your letting me off at my house so that I can present to my father the accounts for what you have spent. I am sure that you have shopped wisely. Abdullah and Rosa were a big help. And, as for me, it has been a privilege and a pleasure to accompany you. I do trust we shall meet again."

He kissed their hands as he left the coach, and the four ladies waved goodbye.

"It's early yet," said Conchita, as the carriage sped across town, "and I'd like to go to the Cathedral. We will be just in time for vespers, and we haven't been in a Christian church since we were kidnaped—just that blessed chapel of Zoraya's where we were married."

"Might I accompany you," asked Lady Nardjis. "I feel the need of prayer."

"Of course," Marilú responded. "It never occurred to me that you would not join us. It will be a comfort to me if you would kneel beside us as we pray. And we can have the swords blessed in the church."

Marilú gave instructions to the coachman who left them at a side door to the Cathedral where, he said, they would find a sacristan to take them to the priest before the vespers service. But the sacristan, whom they found almost as soon as they entered the door, insisted on taking them to see the Archbishop himself.

"Dom Benaldo," the sacristan murmured, bowing deeply to his superior. "This *señora* is the wife of the Marqués de Clavijo, and these are the wives of Generals Rodríguez and Ayala. They wish to attend vespers and would like you to bless these Toledo swords they have just bought for their husbands. And this *señora,* your Grace, is Lady Nardjis, that brave Saracen woman who saved them and their husbands and all their troops from an ambush by the *Almorávides.*"

Turning to his charges, the sacristan continued: "My ladies, Dom Benaldo de Sedirac, Archbishop of Toledo."

"Delighted to meet you," smiled the Archbishop, "and particularly glad that I can welcome you to this ancient church. It was built by Saint Eugenio, the first Bishop of Toledo, nearly six hundred years ago during the reign of the Gothic King Recared, brother of Saint Hermenegildo. A hundred years later, after the conquest of Toledo by Tarik, it was made into a Moorish mosque. But I have had the honor of consecrating it again under the Roman rites by order of Queen Constance. I came here only a few months after King Alfonso, may God exalt him, captured Toledo six years ago. It is fortunate that you came to the Cathedral, for the parish churches in Toledo still cling stubbornly to their Mozarabic Gothic ritual in spite of the missionary work that we priests from Cluny Abbey have done over the past years.

"Come with me to the altar and I shall bless these swords to your husbands' use, and then you may kneel down there below for the vespers service."

The good Archbishop took each of the three swords in turn, unsheathed them, and recited the ritual blessing.

"And now let me bless you lovely ladies before I bid you goodbye. You will find a priest in each of those confessionals, and there is still time to confess before vespers. And, Lady Nardjis, I am pleased to have you worship here."

The four women knelt and kissed the Archbishop's ring as he said benediction over them. Marilú, Zoraya and Conchita then left to enter the confessionals, Nardjis going straight to the first row of benches where her friends would join her after confession.

The service over, they repaired to the carriage and, in a matter of minutes, were once again in the Clavijo mansion where, after the presentation of the swords, for which the women were lovingly embraced by their grateful husbands, they all enjoyed a magnificent dinner, at which Marilú dazzled everyone, and inflamed Gonzalo, by wearing the necklace she had found in the iron casket, now polished and resplendent, and which Nardjis recognized as the fabled and fabulous dragon necklace given by Caliph Haroun al-Rashid to his beautiful wife Zubayda.

And afterwards, in order to rest for their long

journey next day, they had all retired early, the three couples to a night of brief, yet tender and sublime, lovemaking, their final night of starry rapture in the golden city of Toledo.

PART III

THE REUNION

CHAPTER 27

"You're up early, my love," whispered Gongalo, as he opened his eyes and saw Marilú at the other end of the room, busily trying to adjust a ball-shaped package on her breast, suspended by a ribbon around her neck.

"It's the dragon necklace, my dear," Marilú replied, "and I've been trying to find some way to take it with me on the trip. I can't just wear it around my neck, or it will bounce up and down, so I thought I'd tuck it in my bosom. Does it look all right? Is it too conspicuous?"

"Yes, my love," laughed Gonzalo.

"I guess it is," sighed Marilú. "Maybe I could wear it like a chastity belt." And she unwrapped the silk covering and suspended the golden dragon in front of her like a fig-leaf.

"Well, I admit I've never seen your little garden look prettier, my sweet," Gonzalo smiled, "but do you think it is proper to have a dragon with light brown hair? And, as a chastity belt, I really don't think that dragon will give you much protection. Come over here, and we'll try it out."

Marilú moved over beside the bed, still clutching the dragon, with its brilliant diamond eyes and bejewelled body, in front of her as a circlet of chastity. She made no resistance as Gonzalo removed the shining beast, and laid it carefully on the night table, nor was her resistance much more than a teasing gesture as he grasped her around the hips and dragged her down upon the bed beside him.

Marilú shrieked with pain and pleasure as he thrust into her. "Oh, Gonzalo! Gonzalo! You've struck my womb. You're hurting me so. Please don't stop. *Ay! ay! ay!* Gonzalo!"

They came almost simultaneously, but Gonzalo still kept his member pressed close within her. "Lie still, my love," he whispered. "Don't move. Let us savor this moment. Don't move. Be still."

But although they kept their bodies motionless, Marilú found it impossible to quiet the palpitating muscles deep within her as she felt his manroot grow stiffer, bigger, pulsating with life. Suddenly, neither could stand it any longer, and the fierce struggle began again, stronger and more turbulent than before. Wave after wave of rapture flowed over her, and again and again she came, gasping and groaning. But still he kept lunging and plunging, insatiable in his passion.

"Oh, Gonzalo, Gonzalo, I can't stand it. You're killing me. It won't stop. It keeps on coming. Gonzalo! Oh God! Oh God!"

At last the battle ended, and Gonzalo lay, utterly spent, upon her breast, still deep within her, but quiet and wholly satisfied.

"You fill me so full, my husband. I'm so full, so happy. I do love you so, Señor Marqués de Clavijo."

"And I love you, Señora Marquesa de Clavijo," he whispered as he withdrew and lay beside her, his arm under her head, her head resting gently on his breast. "And your dragon was no protector of your chastity, my sweet. He didn't even bite me."

"I guess he's scared of you. You are so fierce, you know, he must think you're Saint George–Saint Gonzalito, anyway. But I've decided to put the necklace in my bosom, only not wrapped into a round ball–just wrapped in that piece of silk between my breasts, so that I'll just have one big buffet across my front like an old lady."

"Good idea. And I'll still love my little old lady—my dragon woman," Gonzalo whispered affectionately. "But now, let's get bathed and dressed—and no monkey business in the bath. There's no time for it." And he gave her a fond pat on the bottom.

Lady Nardjis was already at the breakfast table as they entered the dining room. The others joined them a few minutes later, smiling so happily that it may safely be assumed that they had also partaken of the joys of early morning love.

A few minutes later, they were all at the front gate of the mansion. A squad of soldiers was waiting, ready to mount, and holding their steeds by the bridles and their lead horses by the halters. In addition, they held fourteen other horses for the seven at the gate.

"The wagons!" exclaimed Zoraya. "Where are the wagons?"

"Don't worry, dear," laughed Roberto. "They left at daybreak with another squad of soldiers, and will be traveling twelve hours a day, with two shifts of teamsters and horses, while we shall be riding only seven hours each day, from eight to four, allowing an hour for lunch and changing mounts. So we shall all be together with the wagons, and with Abdullah and Rosa, for each night's bivouac.

"You and I shall leave the others on the eighth day, at Sanabria, and we should reach León late that night. They will have two more days' riding than we, to get to Iria Flavia. It will be an easy ride most of the way—about seventeen leagues a day. We could go faster, but we have to think of a suitable place to stay each night."

"It won't be such an easy ride over the Sierra de los Gredos," Conchita interjected, "and Jorge told me that's the way we're going. *Papá* and I came over the Guadarrama range, a little further north, and it was hard riding over the mountain pass. But beautiful!"

Gonzalo, Roberto and Jorge were carrying the three shining swords their wives had bought for them in Toledo. They inserted them in the sheaths that hung straight down on the near side of their saddles, so that they could be drawn with one sweeping movement of the right arm. They mounted and Jorge, in the pride of possession, drew his blade and exclaimed: "These are wonderful weapons you've given us—so perfectly balanced."

Roberto and Gonzalo followed suit, and Gonzalo used his weapon to give the signal to the troops to gallop forward before he reinserted it in the scabbord. Their wives beamed to see the manifest pleasure their husbands took in their new weapons, and it thrilled them to watch the warlike sweep of their swords flashing through the air. The scabbords were so firmly fastened to the saddles that the blades could be drawn with a single hand, although it was necessary for the men to use their left hands, holding the bridle, to steady the sheath as they reinserted the blade.

They rode down the steep incline to the Plaza del Zocodóver, and then down an even steeper and longer hill past a Moslem mosque on their right.

"That's the Mosque of Bib El Mardom," said Nardjis, recognizing it as the place where she used to worship on previous visits to the city. "It once was an old Visigoth Christian temple, but it was converted to a mosque three hundred years ago. I suppose that some day it will become a Christian church again."

As they rode down the long, steep hill past the mosque, they got a splendid view of the rolling countryside to the north of Toledo until, at last, they came to the great Arab walls that surrounded the city, and the old Bisagra gate, which the guards swung open to let them through.

"I can see why they call it the Bisagra gate," said Conchita, "because '*bisagra*' means 'hinge,' and those hinges are the biggest I have ever seen."

Nardjis laughed, "Only in this case, '*bisagra*' comes from the Arabic '*bib shara*' which means 'gateway to the fields'."

"I thought it was called '*bisagra*' from '*via sacra*'," said Gonzalo, "but I'm sure you must be right. Anyway, this is the gate King Alfonso rode through when he entered the city six years ago. And over there, beside that tower on the banks of the River Tajo, are the Cava baths where King Rodrigo first saw Florinda, the daughter of Count Julian, bathing naked in the river. He fell in love with her and seduced her on the spot."

"I guess these kings are all alike," Marilú commented.

"All men are," Zoraya put in.

"In some ways," Gonzalo admitted, "but a king is able to do what we other men only wish we could do. . . . That other gate over there is the Bib al-Makara that was built by King Wamba three centuries ago, just before the Moslem occupation. It has been restored recently, so the stones are mostly new. And just beyond you can see that temple. It is really beautiful inside, but we can't stop. Originally, in the IV Century, it was a hermitage erected to Santa Leocadia after her martyrdom. Then, three centuries later, when Santa Leocadia appeared before San Ildefonso and the King and all the people, the hermitage was converted into the great temple you see now.

"And now you must say goodbye to Toledo. Our next stop, for lunch, will be at Torrijos. Let's gallop."

"I hate to leave Toledo," sighed Marilú. "Of course, I want to get home to Galicia, but so many wonderful things happened to us in Toledo—the division of the treasure, the shopping at the Zocodóver market, this lovely jewel I'm carrying in my bosom, and being so close together with you, Gonzalo, and all of us. And you men look so brave and beautiful with those shining new swords by your side.

"And I loved El Viso too, with such wonderful memories. And your rescuing us at Medina al-Zahra. Oh, we've had such marvelous adventures, Gonzalo, and I've never been so happy as I am today."

They rode on and on at a steady gallop, crossing the Guadarrama River, past olive groves, sheep pastures, and fields green with growing crops, and brilliant with the wild flowers that bloomed along the edges of the field and invaded the meadows and orchards on either side.

Shortly after passing through the picturesque little town of Torrijos, Gonzalo announced: "We are going into that woods for a shady place to have lunch, beside the old Roman hot springs where we can relax."

The baths were in ruins, but the hot spring was bubbling away, and its water was hot enough to make a refreshing drink of linden tea from the package of leaves that Roberto had brought in his saddle bags.

"Now you must just leave us alone for lunch," said Conchita. "You've been after us day and night for days, and we women never have a chance to talk together by ourselves. So you three go over there and have lunch with the soldiers if you want, but leave us alone."

The three husbands went off laughing. As soon as they were out of hearing and the four women were seated together on the stones of the old Roman bath, eating the meat and bread they had brought in their saddle-bags, they began to talk of their plans for the future, of their plans to visit each other, and of their plans for the children they hoped to have.

But they were soon on their way again, reaching Maqueda shortly before four, a picturesque little town with buildings dating from the successive occupations of the Romans, Visigoths, and Moslems. They put up in a rather dilapidated Moorish mansion, large enough for their needs, but primitive in its facilities compared to the Clavijo mansion in Toledo.

The food that the servants of the house prepared for them that evening was likewise farm style, but delicious and abundant—a rabbit stew, full of farm vegetables, and, for dessert, cheese and fruit. The wagons drew up as they were eating, and the soldiers set up their tents in the courtyard and were served the same substantial mess that their generals had eaten in the dining room. Leaving one squad of men to guard the baggage, and taking turns, the soldiers likewise found the same sort of entertainment in the village that their superiors were enjoying even more ardently within the mansion.

And so they set out again the next morning, traveling almost straight west, descending into the valley of the Alberche, crossing that stream near its junction with the Tajo, and riding along the right bank of the Tajo, to Talavera de la Reina, the old Roman town of Talabriga. To their left, they could see the fine Roman bridge across the Tajo, with its thirty-five stone arches, and a smaller bridge further along the stream. The old Roman walls and turrets, and a number of square Moorish towers, linked the two bridges. But the fortifications were in ruins and had not yet been repaired. They put up for the night at the hermitage of the Virgen del Prado, Spartan in the simplicity of its architecture, but Lucullan in the magnificence of the food and wines that they were served by the abbot and monks who were their hosts.

The entertainment of the evening was the same as on the previous night, both for the soldiers and their masters. But this time, judging from the number of women at the hermitage, all wearing vermilion scarves, the festivities of the troops and their generals were duplicated by the members of the holy brotherhood.

Be that as it may, the cavalcade was off again early the next morning, for the third day of the journey, to Oropesa where they had lunch overlooking the beautiful valley of the Tiétar River. Then on they rode, past huge fields of growing tobacco, to Navalmoral de la Mata, where they were put up for the night at the vacant house of a member of the family of the Duque de Frías—"friends of mine," Roberto explained, saying that the family lived at Oropesa but had these tobacco plantations at Navalmoral. Their food that evening was simple but plentiful, nor was there any dearth of amusement that night for the three generals and their troops.

The next morning, they left the main highway, which went southwest to Badajoz and Lisboa, and took the road to the north, past the village of Talayuela, and across the Campo Arañuelo and the fertile La Vera Valley. They crossed the Tiétar River over a Roman bridge, reconstructed by the Moors, and climbed up a winding road to Jarandilla de la Vera in the foothills of the Sierra de Gredos, where they stopped for lunch.

"We have decided not to cross the Sierra," Gonzalo announced. "It is a hard trip, and dangerous for the wagons, not only because of the rough road, but because of marauding bands of semi-savage shepherds who might be strong enough to overpower our teamsters. And we don't want any trouble for ourselves, in spite of the fact that Jorge said he would like to try out his new sword. So, instead of going straight north to Béjar, we'll go out of our way to Plasencia, and on to Béjar for the following night."

"It's not the shepherds I'm afraid of," said Marilú. "It's the shepherdesses. I understand that hardly a man gets by the pass over the Sierra without being raped by a half a dozen of those wild shepherdesses."

"They're strong enough to do it," agreed Jorge laughing.

So on they rode, through the foothills, past the village of Jaraíz to Plasencia with its great Roman aqueduct whose fifty-three high arches spanned the valley and brought fresh water from the Sierra to the city. Many wealthy families lived in Plasencia—the Zúñigas, the Trujillos, and others. They put up for the night at the mansion of the Carvajal family, and were graciously attended to and dined by the majordomo and servants in their master's absence.

Fortunately, the walls in the Carvajal house were thick and solid, else Nardjis, Marilú and Zoraya might have been surprised by the groans and shrieks issuing from a neighboring room, where Jorge and Conchita spent themselves time and again in rapturous passion.

The next morning Conchita's countenance was so radiant with joy that Nardjis, Marilú and Zoraya knew that there was something in the wind, but it was not until lunch-time that they had an inkling of what had happened.

Northward the cavalcade galloped, across the Plasencia valley, past the Roman ruins at Oliva de Plasencia in Tras-la-Sierra, beyond Abadía at the end of the Jarilla plains, to Hervas, a summer resort with a magnificent panoramic view over the mountains and valleys, and a Jewish quarter—a ghetto that was far from being a ghetto, with its spacious and elegant summer houses on the hillside. They stopped for lunch just outside the town, and Marilú, sensing that

Conchita was just bursting to tell them something, suggested that Gonzalo, Roberto and Jorge leave them alone again to gossip.

As soon as the men were gone, Conchita flung her arms around Zoraya's neck, and cried, "Oh, Zoraya darling, I love you so! It happened! It happened! And it was so wonderful, so unbelievably wonderful. I'm so happy, and you're all so good to me. I'm a *kabbázah*."

And with that, Conchita burst into tears as though her heart would break.

"You don't seem very happy, my little cousin," Marilú smiled, as she took Conchita in her arms and comforted her as she used to do when Conchita was five and she was ten.

"Oh, but I am. I am," Conchita cried through her tears. "I've never been so happy in all my life. And it's all due to you three—and to Jorgito, of course. He says I smell better than any shepherdess."

"Well, that's something, after all," laughed Nardjis. "For our sake, I'm glad you do. And I think you're nicer than a shepherdess in other ways too, my darling. If ever I marry again, and have a daughter, I hope she looks like you, and is just as sweet."

They ate their lunch quickly, and then rejoined their waiting husbands.

"It's not far now," Gonzalo was saying. "Only fifteen or sixteen leagues to Béjar, but it will be the hardest part of our trip thus far, and our horses will have to do most of it at a walk. Let's go."

Some two leagues further on, climbing ever higher into the foothills, they came to another village in a valley, also obviously a resort area—Estremadura.

"Those are the Roman baths of Montemayor over there," said Jorge, pointing to a large building on the right, where a line of people wandered in and out. That smell in the air is sulphur, and the water comes out of a spring hotter than you could stand it. Yet some people do get used to the heat gradually, and bathe in the spring for a half hour or more, with the water smoking and steaming. They also drink it straight from the spring—it's supposed to be good for what ails you—ugh!"

The road now rose steeply, with many dangerous bends and turns, a deep canyon on one side, a high cliff on the other, until they came to the Béjar pass, more than three thousand feet above sea level. From the pass, they could see the valleys of Batuecas and Hurdes and, nestled in the hills, the picturesque, fortified town of Béjar. It was only two leagues away, but the road twisted and turned, and the descent from the pass was even more perilous than the ascent had been. A false step, the horse and rider would be hurtled to certain death at the bottom of the precipice.

The road had been built by the Romans centuries ago and had been kept in perfect condition. At Cantagallo they passed a Roman fort, well-preserved and still used as an army post by the Christian forces as it had been by the Moorish troops only a few years earlier. At Béjar itself, the fortifications were Moorish, and the walls and towers showed signs of decay, although the fortress itself was still in use. It was there that they lodged for the night, as guests of the colonel, an old friend of Gonzalo's and of his comrades. The dinner that night was gay and convivial, with a dozen army officers, and as many women, as their hosts. The fare was simple but abundant, and the wine good. All in all, it was the merriest party that the seven travelers had attended since they left Medina al-Zahra.

And by eight o'clock the next morning, the travelers were again *en route*, headed north on the road to Salamanca. Down the steep, winding road they went, past Vallejera de Ríofrío nestled in the foothills of the Sierra de Gredos, their horses carefully picking their footsteps along the perilous path between precipice and mountainside. Then on to the Valley of the Tormes following the borders of the long lake and swampland between Guijuelo and Fresno Alhándiga, from which Salamanca drew its water supply, to Arapiles and Tormes on the left bank of the Tormes River.

They crossed the Tormes over the ancient Roman bridge, with its twenty-six great arches, that had been rebuilt by the Emperor Trajan and again by the Emperor Hadrian. The horses traversed the thirteen hundred foot length of the bridge at a slow walk, it being forbidden to trot or gallop across any of the bridges of Spain for fear of damaging their foundations. From the bridge, the travelers had a splendid view of Salamanca on the northern bank.

Much of the old city had been destroyed by the Caliph Modhafer during the civil war between Christians and Moslems, but reconstruction was going on everywhere, masons, architects and workmen busy on every side with their great engines for lifting the heavy blocks of ochre-colored limestone into place.

The lovely Romanesque Cathedral, just across from the bridge, was still under construction, but its outside shell had been completed, and capped by the octagonal tower known as the Torre del Gallo, from the weathercock at its summit. Workmen were still busy constructing the hollow square of arches that would in time become the cloisters, but one side had already been completed with twenty little cubicles that would eventually house the priests and monks attached to the Cathedral. It was there that the seven travelers lodged for the night, comfortably enough, for the Archbishop had supplied four of the cells with beds and furniture from his own palace, which was still too far from completion to house his guests.

The Archbishop himself, however, was there to greet the travelers and to invite them to dine with him that evening in his palace. He showed them around the Cathedral and pointed out its beauties—those than had already been installed; and the places where other architectural wonders would be constructed over the next century, according to the plans of the builders. A group of students and their professors were engaged in deep discussion in the crypt of the Cathedral. The Archbishop explained that it was planned to erect a great university in the square to the north of the Cathedral but that, meanwhile, classes were being held within the confines of the Cathedral itself, and, in fine weather, among the trees lining the square—in the "Grove of Academe," the Archbishop declared with a smile.

The supply wagon and soldiers were encamped in the center of what was to be the cloisters, but the rectangle was so large that this did not disturb the privacy of the four cubicles assigned to the generals and the four ladies. Which was just as well, for the soldiers lost no time in finding a group of town ladies with whom to share the pleasures of their mess and beguile the hours of the night.

As it was still early, Roberto suggested that they take a walk around the city, which they did, stopping to watch the construction work on the churches of San Martín and Santo Tomás Cantuariense, the former almost completed, the latter nothing but an unroofed crypt.

Dinner that night in the palace of the Archbishop was a feast of Trimalchio in the abundance, variety and quality of the viands, wines and liqueurs—fresh fish and shrimp from the Tormes, roast pheasant and suckling pig, asparagus, eggplant, endives, pastries, cheese, strawberries, and many other delicacies.

There were only eight at table, and the Archbishop spent most of the evening engaged in conversation with Lady Nardjis, expatiating on the merits and virtues of Christianity, and particularly on the minuteness of the adjustments in her beliefs that his prospective proselyte would have to make to convert to Catholicism which, after all, was by definition the universal religion.

But all things—even a Trimalchian feast and a theological discourse—must come to an end, and, by the tenth hour, the seven travelers had bid goodnight to their host and to each other, and were installed in the four little cubicles to which they had been assigned.

"I feel like a monk in this little cell," Roberto commented, as he looked around at the four bare, white walls, the wash basin and huge pitcher of water, and the two chairs, table, and bed that comprised the furnishings of the room. There were two large candles in silver candlesticks on the table, and an oil lamp whose tiny flame would suffice for a night-light the whole night through.

And yet the night passed pleasurably enough in three of the four walls of the cloisters as well as in the tents at the far side of the supply wagons.

It was a short and easy trip north from Salamanca to Zamora, but the travelers left early and pressed their horses at a gallop, for they planned to reach Bragança that night on what would be by far the longest leg of their journey. As they left Salamanca, and cornfields gave way to a series of hills covered with evergreen oaks, they passed the Convento de Valparaíso, birthplace of San Fernando, then rode up the rocky, vine-covered terraces known as Tierra del Vino from which they had a splendid view of the

Duero River and the city of Zamora on its further bank.

The travelers lunched on the rocks under the shade of a large holm oak, and again the three generals left their ladies to gossip by themselves. Luncheon over, the cortege descended the steep incline to the bank of the Duero, crossed the river by the old Roman bridge, and did not stop to see the many attractions of Zamora. But Gonzalo had told them that the city had been a frontier between Christians and Moors since the beginning of the Moorish occupation, that it had been destroyed by al-Mansur a hundred years ago and rebuilt by King Fernando who gave it to his daughter, Urraca. That Urraca was forced to defend it against her brother don Sancho, and that Urraca's partisans had slain King Sancho; that Alfonso had then been acknowledged as the successor of Sancho, had captured his other brother, King García, and thus became Emperor of Spain.

They left this historic spot and proceeded eastward, crossing the Esla River at Muelas del Pan, just north of its junction with the Duero, over a stone bridge so narrow that there was barely room for the supply wagons to pass. Then on to Alcañices and over the *sierra* to the Province of Trasos-Montes. The Valley of the Douro that they now entered offered a fantastic vista, the pasture land parched from the broiling sun. Despite the heat, the cattle they saw seemed well-kept—strange beasts, with horns each three feet long menacing the travelers as they galloped by. On either side were steep cliffs, terraced tier after tier, with retaining walls of rocks piled unevenly, without mortar—the work of generation after generation of hard labor. These terraces, Gonzalo told his companions, represented the wealth of the province, covered as they were with ancient vines, laden with grapes that would soon be picked to make the rich Port wine that was the principal product of the region. A number of men, carrying long sticks to help them climb the steep hillside from one terrace to the other, were patiently tending their vineyards, tying the heavier bunches to the vine, or cultivating between the rows.

"Those men are *borracheiros*," Gonzales said.

"*Borrachos*?" Zoraya asked. Are they drunk?"

"No," Gonzalo laughed. "Not *borrachos—borracheiros*. The language they talk in Tras-os-Montes, and from here to Oporto and Lisboa, is not the *Romance* you speak in Andalucía. The *borracheiros* are the harvesters, and when those grapes are ripe you can see the men climbing down these same cliffs with a sack on their back and a hundred and fifty pounds of grapes in each sack. The hills are too steep for *burros* or carts. And they will need their long sticks to prevent a fall. Hard work, but the harvest is the merriest time of the year in Tras-os-Montes. They gather the grapes to the music of fifes and whistles, blown by the children."

They came now to Bragança, a city perched high on a hill, surrounded by walls in varying stages of disrepair, the consequence of successive invasions of Goths and Saracens and Spaniards. A number of men were at work repairing the damage, but in desultory fashion, as Bragança had always relied upon its inaccessibility and high mountains to discourage invaders, rather than upon its man-made fortifications.

In the center of the city, dominating the town and the surrounding countryside, there stood the palace-fortress of the royal family of Bragança, where they were graciously received by the majordomo and his staff of servants, with many apologies that the duke and his family were in Oporto and could not be there to welcome them.

Lady Nardjis, Zoraya and Roberto were unable to understand a word of what the majordomo said, much to the amusement of their four Galician companions, whose native dialect was close enough to the language of Lisboa and Bragança for them to understand it without difficulty. It was late by the time they finished dinner—a savory ox-tail stew, flavored with sherry—and they were excited rather than tired by their long journey. They were excited too to find themselves in so beautiful a palace, in a strange country, and surrounded by servants jabbering away in a strange dialect, but quite obviously endeavoring to make the guests feel welcome.

Next morning the cavalcade got under way shortly after eight, and within less than an hour, had left the Province of Tras-os-Montes, and crossed the Sierra de la Culebra, arriving at Puebla de Sanabria a half hour later. Zoraya had already told her plans to Roberto, who heartily approved, beaming at the thought that he might be a father in the spring. Boy or girl, he didn't care, so infatuated was he with the idea of having a baby by Zoraya whom he adored. And Roberto and Zoraya together galloped up to where Gonzalo and Jorge were cantering along the road, and explained that the two of them, with their baby would be visiting Iria Flana in the spring, God willing.

So, although the parting was a tearful one, it was not as painful as it might have been. They had dismounted at the juncture of the Castro and the Tera, two small streams that joined at Puebla de Sanabria, and, after many an *abrazo* and many a kiss, Roberto and Zoraya mounted their horses and took the road to the right, followed by two of the wagons and one squad of soldiers. The others, including Abdullah and Rosa in one of the wagons, took the road to the left, together with the other squad of soldiers and the other four wagons, and they soon disappeared beyond a bend in the road.

"We shall take the old Roman road to Lugo," said Gonzalo to his companions. "Some day they will build roads to Orense and from there we could go to Iria Flavia, which would be much shorter, but there are only mountain paths between here and Orense now, and the wagons could never make it. So we still have a long ride ahead of us."

It was a sharp climb from the valley up to the Pedernelo pass, four thousand feet above sea-level, in the foothills of the Sierra Segundeira, and the winds were cold and bleak in the mountain country. Then down again to the valley at Lubián, and a steep, winding road up to the Canda pass, the highest they had yet reached. They galloped past the Romanesque church of San Pedro at Pereiro in the next valley, then slowly wound their way up to La Gudiña, arriving late in the evening at the little hill town of Viana del Bollo, whose winding streets and arched passageways and steps twisted up and down the hillsides like a grapevine on a trellis.

They headed for the castle keep, a tall tower surrounded by fortifications that enclosed an inner courtyard in which the soldiers and teamsters tethered the horses and stowed the wagons, while Jorge escorted the three ladies into the castle. There they were ushered into their apartments by a gray-bearded captain who was in charge of the fort.

Gonzalo remained below to give instructions to his sergeant. "With the six teamsters and your squad, you have fourteen men here, fifteen, including yourself. As you know, this is the wildest region in the *sierra,* and I want ten men here on guard at all times, in four-hour shifts. The gates must be kept shut and only opened to our own men. The four men—five with yourself—who are off duty, may go into the village, but they are not to bring any women, or anyone else, back inside the gates under any circumstances. And don't allow any of the herdsmen to enter the gates or allow their cattle to wander through, on pretext of selling us some of their milk. We shall leave at the eighth hour tomorrow as usual. It will be a strict war-time watch here, but there is only one more stop—at Lugo—and you may tell your men tonight that they will have a one-week furlough in Iria Flavia before you all head back for Alarcos."

"Very well, my general." The sergeant saluted, and Gonzalo joined the others in the castle.

"It is rather primitive in here, General, as you know," Jorge remarked, "but the captain has given us a good supply of heavy woolen *mantas* to keep us warm tonight, and there are fireplaces blazing in this room which will be both our living and dining room. The captain hinted that he would like to join us for supper, and, of course, I invited him."

The old captain was a little ill at ease in such distinguished company but, warmed by a tasty rabbit stew and good red wine, he soon relaxed, and regaled his guests with many tales of the wild countryside, the feuds between the herdsmen and shepherds, and between the townsfolk and the foresters and hunters of the Imberdanegro woods, where the men were as savage as the wild boars and wolves that roam its depths.

After dinner, when the captain had left them to their own devices, Marilú spoke up: "I for one shan't need any of those heavy *mantas*. I have my love to keep me warm."

"You'll need the blankets all right" laughed Gonzalo, "and I advise you all to keep a candlestick and the oil lamp handy by your bedside. Let's pile some more logs on the fire here, and hope that some of the heat goes down the corridor. It gets pretty cold here, even now at the end of June. The winter is impossible. The captain will have more wood put on the fire by day-break. And now goodnight, and happy dreams."

What with love and the homespun blankets, the two couples managed to keep warm during the night. And Nardjis too—with a double supply of *mantas*.

But in the early morning, the five travelers came shivering out of their cold bedrooms and gathered around the blazing fireplace as breakfast was served.

A half hour later, they were on their way, traveling north from Viana del Bollo, crossing the Roman Cigarrosa bridge over the River Sil at Petín, then on to Quiroga and Monforte de Lemos, an ancient gothic town built on a steep hill overlooking the River Cabe. The river itself was little more than a rushing rocky creek, but impressive in the depth of the great gorge of Gargantas that it had cut through solid rock over centuries of spring floods, affording as wild a landscape as they had seen in all that rugged country. To their left, they could see the craggy peaks of the Sierra de San Payo in the distance.

They passed below the walls of the great stone castle of the Conde de Monforte, and the gothic Convent of San Vicente. Just beyond the convent, they stopped for lunch in a grove of trees overlooking the verdant Lemos meadow with its great vineyards extending east and west as far as the eye could see. As they looked around for a place to sit, Jorge rolled a large boulder to one side, giving them a convenient table with other rocks around it for chairs.

"Jorgito," screamed Conchita, "you'll strain yourself. That rock must weigh a couple of tons."

"I guess it does, my dear," he laughed, "but I didn't lift it. I rolled it."

"You needn't worry about Jorge, Conchita," Gonzalo said, smiling. "He's the strongest man I've ever known, perhaps the strongest man in Spain. He can roll boulders bigger than that."

"Well," Conchita giggled, beaming at the thought that her husband was the strongest man in all of Spain, "he's bolder than any man I've ever known."

"Conchita!" Marilú exclaimed. "Now that Zoraya's gone, you are trying to take her place? It must be contagious. Well, I do miss her—but won't it be wonderful when she and Roberto and little Robertito come to visit us next May?"

And all during the rest of their luncheon, they could talk of nothing but the hoped-for visit of the Ayala family the following spring.

Luncheon over, they continued north, past the vineyards, and across the barren mountains separating the valleys of the Cabe and the Sarria, then along the banks of the Sarria and past the iron mines and marble quarries and the iron-laden hot baths, *Los Baños del Incio,* in the Sierra del Oribio.

The town of Sarria itself was fascinating, the old Flavia Lambrio of the Romans, dominated by the gothic castle of the Conde de Sarria, and boasting a number of Christian edifices—the *Convento de la Merced*, an old gothic church and cloister, and the Benedictine monastery of San Julián de Samos.

They passed the village of Nadela at the juncture of another, wider highway to the east, and Jorge remarked: "That is the road that Roberto and Zoraya will take when they come from León. It is a fine Roman road all the way, and they will have an easy journey by carriage."

And, then, one league beyond, they came to Lugo, the ancient Celtic capital of Galicia. Although this was the home of their blond and blue-eyed ancestors, Marilú and Conchita had never before visited Lugo, and they and Nardjis stared with amazement at the massive Roman walls that surrounded the city, from twenty-five to fifty feet in height, depending upon the contours of the landscape. Fifty great semi-circular towers, also dating from the III Century Roman occupation, guarded strategic points along the walls.

"Let's all take a walk around the walls before suppertime," suggested Gonzalo, "and I'll tell you a little about the story of Lugo—*Lucas Augusti*, as the Romans used to call it."

They came to a fine plaza, surrounded by an arcade of Roman and gothic columns, capitals and arches, on one side of which stood a handsome house where they were welcomed by an elderly gentleman with long white hair and beard, and piercing blue eyes.

Gonzalo introduced his companions, and the old man remarked: "Yes, I am an Andrade too—probably a distant cousin from generations back. But I see you two have the Andrade eyes," he added, looking at Marilú and Conchita. "It runs in the blood. And it is an honor to have the Marqués de Clavijo and his relatives visit me here, and Princess Nardjis too, for her fame has traveled before her, and I know her great services to the Christian cause."

They all thanked their host profusely and said that they would take a walk around town and be back in time for dinner. Their rooms were simple, but adequate, and a great improvement over the quarters they had occupied in the castle at Viana del Bollo.

Gonzalo led them back to the gate, flanked on each side by the great towers they had seen from below. A stairway within one of the towers led them to the top of the wall which, to the surprise of the ladies, was from ten to fifteen feet wide on top, of great blocks of cut stone, at least what they could see of it, although Gonzalo told them that inside the rectangular blocks of granite it was undoubtedly constructed of uncut rocks tightly fitted together.

They walked around this impressive esplanade, stopping from time to time to admire the fine panorama of the city and surrounding mountains and valleys. The Miño River circled the western wall of the city and just beyond the western gate, through which they would pass on their way to Iria Flavia, they could see the bridge over the Miño, with its argival gothic arches.

The bridges they had crossed thus far in their journey all had had the usual round Roman arches, and Gonzalo explained that this bridge had probably been built after the invasion by the Suevi goths in the VI Century. The city had been captured by Musa in 714 A.D., he said, but it did not remain long in Moorish hands, for it was reconquered by Alfonso I forty years later. It was then captured by an invading army of Normans who had landed at Ribadeo on the Cantabrian coast, ten leagues to the north, and had made their way practically without opposition to the walls of Lugo. Unprepared for an attack from the north, Lugo opened its gates to the invaders who looted the town, enjoyed the favors of the beautiful blond Gallegas, and soon returned to Normandy.

"So you, Marilú, and all of us Gallegos, may have some Norman blood in our veins," Gonzalo added.

"I wouldn't worry about that," Nardjis laughed. "It makes a lovely mixture."

"Did you notice that my nice cousin Andrade promoted you to 'Princess Nardjis'?" asked Conchita. "From now on, I may call you '*Princesita*'." Turning to Gonzalo, she asked: "What's that cloud of yellow smoke over there, just beyond the bridge?"

"The *Baños Romanos*," he replied. "They are sulphur baths, and are still in use, as you can see from the people at the entrance. Would you like to try them? We still have time before dinner, if we cut short our walk around these ramparts. The walls are more than a mile and a half around."

They descended the stairs in one of the two towers flanking the western gate.

"How about some exercise?" said Jorge. "I'll race you all across the bridge." And he set off, with Conchita and the others in hot pursuit.

Gonzalo and Jorge probably did not exert themselves to the utmost, for they arrived at the Roman baths only a few paces ahead of their wives. They were met at the gate to the baths by Nardjis who had darted ahead like a gazelle and was waiting for them, smiling nonchalantly as the others arrived breatheless from their exertion.

They entered the temple-like structure and were ushered to the private bath of the Proconsul by a pleasant young woman who handed them towels and showed them their two dressing rooms beside a steaming pool. Gonzalo told the ladies that, in these Roman baths, there was a separate room for women, but that the women who frequented the baths were not exactly ladies, and that it would be safer if they all stayed together.

Afterwards, they dressed quickly and walked back to the Andrade mansion, wonderfully refreshed, and just in time for a sherry with their host before dinner.

The old gentleman graciously offered a toast, and then added somewhat lugubriously, "I hate to tell you this, but you two generals have married into the Andrade family, and you ought to know that we Andrades don't last very well. Here I am only eighty-five, and I'm already beginning to feel a bit of stiffness in my joints. Very few of us Andrades last much beyond ninety or ninety-five. So you two had better make good use of your young brides while you still have them."

It was hard to tell whether their octogenerian host was serious or joking, for never a smile crossed his face, but Gonzalo and Jorge both assured him that they would take good care of his young relatives.

Dinner was pleasant and convivial, Señor Andrade

pointing out that the quail and venison which he served came from the forests just east of León on the banks of the Esla, and that the wine was from the Lemos vineyards that they had passed that afternoon, of the vintage of '87. He excused himself after dinner, and bade them goodbye, as he said he would not be up early enough to see them the following morning.

And the next morning, the five travelers, brimming over with excitement, set out on the tenth and last leg of their journey. They left by the western gate, crossed over the bridge, passed the Roman baths, and climbed a steep hill from which they got another fine view of Lugo, and, three leagues farther along, they came to a strange dome that seemed almost buried in the ground.

"That is an underground vault," Jorge explained. "*Santa Eulalia de Bóveda.* It is full of Roman paintings from before the Christian era. The colors are still bright, and it is interesting, but we have to cover twenty leagues today and have no time to stop."

They continued along the bleak plateau of Lugo to the valley of Furelos and the little Celtic town of Mellid, and on past the church and monastery of Santa María de Mezonzo.

"The founder of that monastery," Gonzalo told them, "was Saint Peter Mezonzo, who was bishop of Compostela a hundred years ago. He wrote the *Salve Regina* that you have all heard at mass. And here, in the shadow of his church, is a good place for us to have our lunch."

They sat against the monastery wall under the shade of some weeping willows and, as they ate their simple food, the strains of the *Salve Regina* came to them from within. It was noon, the hour of the sext, and they could hear the strong voices of the monks carried to them on the breeze.

"How fortunate to have come at just this hour," said Marilú. "And God bless Saint Peter Mezonzo for having given us that lovely music."

Gonzalo sent one of the soldiers galloping on ahead to advise the people in his household that they should be arriving, God willing, between the fifth and sixth hour after noon. He knew that Marilú's parents, and Conchita's father, would have come down from Betanzos and from Puentedeume to greet them, and that there would be a banquet, and much celebration, in the Clavijo castle that night. It seemed too good to be true, after all the dangers they had come through—but only ten more leagues separated them from their families and home.

They rode on through the town of Arzúa, with cattle pasturing in the meadows on either side of the road, across the rolling countryside between the Tambre and the Ulla rivers and, by the fifth hour after noon, they could see the towers of Iria Flavia de Compostela looming before them on the hillside, less than a mile away. Never had the green fields of Galicia looked greener in the afternoon haze, never had the peaks of the Monte Pedroso and Pico Sacro looked bluer against the sky, and never had the hearts of the four returning *Gallegos* been so full of yearning and longing for their homes and families, as on that afternoon in June. Nardjis could sense the nostalgia of her friends, and kept silent, but she too was full of keen anticipation and excitement at the thought of seeing this place that was to be her future home, among friends that were the dearest to her in all the world.

CHAPTER 28

The riders crossed the River Sar and entered the city through the Holy Pilgrim Gate. They were greeted with awed respect by a squad of soldiers who guarded the city walls, but the formal greeting gave way to broad smiles and cheers when the Marqués de Clavijo addressed them familiarly in their native *Gallego.*

From there, the cortege skirted south, following the highway that circled the city within its walls, passing the market-place and the ruins of San Félix de Solovio, razed by al-Mansur over a hundred years ago. Stone masons were now beginning to restore the crypt for a new church on the same site. They passed the Fájera Gate and continued west, passing outside the walls through the Susannis Gate and on to the edge of the *barrio* known as the Pobleda de Santa Susana, after the church which, like San Félix, had been destroyed by al-Mansur but was now being rebuilt. There the cavalcade passed between two stone pylons that flanked the entrance of a steep road leading north.

At the top of that road stood the castle of the Clavijos, with its panorama of the River Sarela and the western countryside, and, looking east, its magnificent vista overlooking the whole city of Iria Flavia de Compostela.

Much of the city was in ruins, but the private houses, mansions, and shops had already been rebuilt. The churches, monasteries, schools, and other public buildings were fast being reconstructed, and the cranes and excavations in every part of the town gave evidence of the great surge of activity that was underway. Yet it would take more than a hundred years to rebuild all the walls that had been razed by the Saracens in only a fortnight.

The gates of the Clavijo castle were thrown open as the Marqués de Clavijo and his companions rode into the inner courtyard, waving to the servants, who greeted them with cheers and beaming faces. Men, women, and children poured forth from every doorway around the courtyard to welcome their master and mistress. Across the courtyard, at the entrance to the mansion, stood more than a score of members of the Andrade, Araujo and Rodríguez families, wreathed in smiles or bathed in tears.

Gonzalo, Marilú, Jorge, and Conchita sprang off their horses and rushed up the steps to greet their relatives. Lady Nardjis followed discreetly behind them, waiting only for the others to receive the warm embraces of their relatives before she herself would be introduced to them. Two little girls detached themselves excitedly from the waiting group, the older running up to her father, the younger to her mother. The children were smiling joyously, their golden locks streaming down behind them.

Gonzalo lifted the older child high in the air, and covered her with kisses. "Luisita, my darling, it's so good to see you. Aren't you glad to see *Mamita* again?"

"Yes, *Papito*, and you too. We had such a good time with grandma and grandpa in Betanzos, and I caught a fish. I can't wait to tell you everything we've done. What did you bring me from Toledo?"

"You wait and see, my precious. It's something you'll love. But you run over and give *Mamá* a kiss, and let me see Elisita."

Meanwhile, Marilú had been hugging and kissing

her younger daughter, the tears streaming down her face as she held the child in her arms.

"Why are you crying, *Mami*? Aren't you happy to be home again?"

"I'm so happy, I can't help crying, my darling. I'm just too happy for words—so terribly glad to see you and Luisita again. And *Papá* and I have brought you two a present we know you'll love. That big man over there—his name's Abdullah, and you'll like him—is carrying it up to your room with one of the soldiers. You wait and see."

By this time, Luisita was straining to replace her little sister in her mother's arms, and Marilú transferred Elisita to Gonzalo, for another round of hugging and kissing, until at last Gonzalo said: "Now you two run along to your rooms and see what *Mamá* and I have brought you."

The two children ran off, excited to see their new present.

Meanwhile, Conchita was crying in her father's arms and attempting through her tears to introduce her friend Nardjis, but too excited and tearful to manage it. No introduction was needed, however, as Lady Nardjis's fame had preceded her, and Nardjis already knew the Conde de Andrade from all that Conchita and Jorge had told her over the past seventeen days. The count was a handsome man whose tall, slim, and erect figure belied his sixty-eight years, despite his long white hair, and neatly trimmed white beard. His eyes, beneath his shaggy brows, were the Andrade blue, and his resemblance to Conchita was startling.

With one arm still around his daughter's waist, he graciously acknowledged the introduction to Lady Nardjis, and lifted her hand to his lips. He even managed to give his son-in-law, Jorge, a warm *abrazo* without relinquishing his hold around his daughter's waist.

There were other greetings too—for Marilú's parents; for Jorge's parents, brothers and sisters; for Gonzalo's sisters and brothers; and for more than a dozen cousins. There had not been such a scene of hugging and kissing in the Clavijo mansion since Marilú and Gonzalo returned from their honeymoon five years before.

And Lady Nardjis was introduced to everyone, impressing them all with her charm, intelligence, and beauty. The venerable vicar of Iria Flavia de Compostela known to all as "Dom Wicarte," was there to greet them and lend the blessings of the Church to this happy reunion.

At last, Gonzalo said: "You must allow us to get out of these dusty riding clothes and make ourselves presentable for dinner. Just give us an hour or two to freshen up and see the children again, and we'll all meet in the parlor for a glass of sherry."

He left the room with Marilú on his right arm, and Lady Nardjis on his left, followed by Jorge and Conchita who stopped to give her father another fond embrace and kiss before she left. The Count again lifted Lady Nardjis's hand to his lips, and followed them all with his eyes as they ascended the broad staircase to their apartments.

"Let's all meet in the children's room before we go downstairs," said Marilú. "But give us at least an hour and a half to get ready. I want you all to see them playing with their doll house and I want them to get to know you better, Nardjis. Aren't they adorable?"

And again the tears coursed down her cheeks as she thought of all the harrowing and wonderful events since last she had seen them.

"And let us show you your room, Nardjis. And Conchita—where has that child gone to?"

"What do you expect," laughed Gonzalo. "She knows where her room is, and she just couldn't wait to show it to Jorgito while we old folks gab around. . . . And look at that," he exclaimed as they entered the apartment that Nardjis was to occupy. "That man Abdullah is a marvel. He has put Nardjis's trunks, and all her things in her room, and it must have been Rosa who laid out her clothes on the bed. Well, we'll see you later," he added, as a smiling Rosa waited to attend Nardjis.

"Oh, Gonzalo, I'm so happy," exclaimed Marilú as they entered their apartment. And she threw her arms around her husband, and burst out sobbing as though her heart would break.

"You may leave us now, Graciela," Gonzalo nodded to the maid who stood waiting for her orders. Then, turning to Marilú as the maid left the room, he added: "You don't seem very happy, my precious. Come, my darling, let's take off these riding boots and dirty clothes, and let me tell you how wonderful it is to be home again with our two adorable little children—and with my own adorable Marilú. I do love you so, sweetest sweet, and do stop weeping. I can't bear to see you cry."

And Gonzalo soon dried Marilú's tears in the way he knew so well.

"Oh, I'm so happy, my love," he sighed. "Here in our own house again, and I love you more than ever. Now go to sleep, my precious." And he gave her a kiss on her closed eyelids.

A little more than an hour later, Gonzalo and Marilú entered the children's room arm in arm.

"Oh, *mamita*, you look so beautiful in that new dress," exclaimed Luisita as the two little girls hugged their mother and father around the knees. "And we love Nardjis who has been playing with us, and showing us how all the doors and things work in our new dolls' house. It's such a wonderful present, and I do love you so, *mami* and *papi*."

"And look at the sweet dolly I have, *mamita,*" Elisita lisped. "And the other dollies are inside the dolls' house. And I simply love Nardjis, and the presents you brought us, and I think I have the nicest *mami* and *papi* in the whole world."

Nardjis was on the floor beside the dolls' house, laughing and smiling. Gonzalo and Marilú joined her and the two children excitedly showed their parents all the wonders of their new present.

And that was how Conchita and Jorge found them just a minute later. Conchita grabbed the two children in her arms and sat down beside them on the floor. "Come on, Jorgito, and sit down here with us," she laughed. "I want to show you how everything works. I wish I'd had one of these when I was a little girl. But we weren't all millionaires then."

The dolls' house was truly a wonder—a Moorish mansion as fine as the Clavijo house in Toledo, with its tiny *hammam,* kitchen, living room, dining room, servants' quarters—everything. And even running water for the *hammam* and kitchens, flowing through minuscule brass pipes from a tank under the roof, with tiny brass taps to turn the water on and off. The doors all opened and closed, and the casement windows all worked. The whole front and back of the house opened wide, each with two hinged wings, so that the children could freely move the furniture around in every room.

Some of the furniture was already in place, but there was a large box on the floor with many other pieces, and pots and pans, and silver dishes and goblets and ornaments and lamps of every kind. And a whole family of dolls of a size to match, with children and cooks and servants, and even a couple of dogs and cats and three tiny mice—a little dream house with all its fittings, that Marilú had spotted in the market-place in Toledo.

Gonzalo and Jorge had never seen it before, and were as fascinated as the children, but at last Gonzalo said: "Well, girls, you'll have all day tomorrow and many, many days to play with the doll house, and it's time for your dinner."

"May I take a doll to have supper with me, *mami*?" asked Luisita.

"Me too?" asked Elisita, who always wanted to do everything that her older sister did.

"Of course, my darlings," Marilú laughed. "We'll leave you now, but we'll be back to tuck you into bed before we have our dinner."

And she, and all the others, kissed the little girls goodbye, and they all went downstairs to join their relatives. Gonzalo and Jorge were elegantly attired, Jorge's parents having brought some of his clothes from their home in the old Roman port of Iria Flavia on the Ulla River, just a few leagues away from the newer city of Iria Flavia de Compostela.

The three women were even more sumptuously attired in the fine dresses that Nardjis had taken for them from the palace of Medina al-Zahra. Nardjis and Conchita wore their peal necklaces and other jewels from the treasure chests of Abd ar-Rahman, while Marilú was resplendent in the gorgeous dragon necklace of al-Thuban.

"I have never seen the three of you look lovelier," Gonzalo exclaimed as they descended the staircase where all their family was waiting for them below.

The admiring glances of their relatives made it clear that they were equally impressed. The five travelers were surrounded by the Andrade, Araujo and Rodríguez relatives and plied with eager questions as to the al-Thuban dragon, the pearl necklaces, and the fine Toledo blades and scabbords that Gonzalo and Jorge carried at their side.

Marilú and Gonzalo excused themselves briefly and

ran upstairs. Luisita and Elisita were in bed—little angels with their golden hair brushed, their faces shining, and each with one of their new dolls in the bed beside them.

"No time for a story tonight," Gonzalo said. "But tomorrow night. And, instead of a story, you two can dream about the new doll house. So goodnight, my darlings. Sleep tight, and happy dreams."

He kissed them on the forehead, and then planted a tickly kiss under the chin. "Don't get them excited, Gonzalo," Marilú said, as the little girls squealed with delight at being tickled on the neck with their father's beard. "And goodnight, my babies—my little girls, I mean. Sleep with the angels."

As soon as Marilú and Gonzalo rejoined the others, two butlers passed silver trays with sherry glasses to all. The Conde de Andrade, as the oldest, proposed toasts, first to the happy newlyweds, then to the no less blissful Clavijos, and finally, "to that most gracious and lovely lady, the Lady Nardjis, without whose foresight we would not now be celebrating the return of our loved ones here tonight."

Nardjis's fame had preceded her and the Conde de Andrade could not take his eyes off her from the moment she had descended the staircase, smiling, sparkling, and as dainty and beautiful as only a Saracen princess could be.

Gonzalo responded to the triple toast with a toast to all their relatives, and to the King and Queen of Spain, then proposed that the venerable Vicar lead them in prayer before they adjourned to the dining room.

After a brief grace and prayer, the Conde de Andrade proffered his arm to Lady Nardjis with a bow. "As my daughter has abandoned me, would you allow me the pleasure of escorting you in to dinner?"

So the two of them walked into the dining hall and

chatted together throughout the meal, almost oblivious of anyone else in the room. Gonzalo and Marilú, of course, as host and hostess, occupied the center of the table, with Dom Wicarte at Marilú's right. Opposite were the newlyweds, Jorge and Conchita, with her father and Nardjis at her right, and the remainder of the Andrade, Rodríguez and Araujo clans, twenty-six people in all, were strung out on both sides of the table.

The cook, unrestrained by the guiding hand of his mistress, and proud of his Gallegan cuisine, had provided the most abundant supply of fish and shellfish ever assembled outside of the Iria Flavia fish market. There were salted sardines, dogfish, vermilion eels and conger eels, trout, tuna, crayfish, shrimp, barbels, hake, herring, shad, shad roe, dace, octopus, mussels, clams, salmon, and many others. Nor was this all, for many of these delicacies were presented in various forms—stewed, poached, fried, sautéed, grilled, cold, and in chowder. Only the youngest of those present attempted to sample something from each plate, and even the most voracious was forced to give up in despair long before attaining his goal.

"They are certainly welcoming you to Galicia with a vengeance," the Conde de Andrade whispered to Lady Nardjis at his side. And he attempted to help her select a few of the more delectable dishes from among the many that the waiters passed around.

"To Marilú's dismay, the fish courses were followed by five suckling pigs, beautifully roasted and brought in on large silver platters which she recognized as part of the treasure of Abd ar-Rahman. The butlers carved the piglets on the large buffet, while the waiters passed the platters around for each guest to select a piece to his fancy.

It was not just the table that groaned as a consequence of all this abundance, and Marilú heaved a sigh of relief when she saw that the pork was followed merely by a pannier of fruit. She smiled when the butler bent over and whispered that the cook wished to apologize, but that the huge cake he had been baking had fallen flat and that there would only be fruit for dessert—and liqueur, of course, from the Benedictine monastery of San Martín Pinario.

At last, the banquet was over and the twenty-six happy people rose from the table. The Vicar excused himself—he was old and his coach was waiting, and he would hope to see Marilú and Gonzalo at the Cathedral the following morning to discuss their munificent donation. Jorge and Conchita excused themselves—Conchita was exhausted, and she had suffered a bit from morning sickness, a happy omen that provided no end of gossip for all their relatives. Gonzalo and Marilú begged to be excused—Marilú, too, seemed to be suffering from the same welcome discomfort as her little cousin. So, with many embraces and kisses, and invitations to dine with the Rodríguez family in Padrón two nights later, the company departed, after the happiest of reunions.

Then the Conde de Andrade approached Lady Nardjis: "It is a beautiful moonlit night, and I'd like to show you Iria Flavia from the terrace. If you feel up to it, perhaps a little walk would do us good, after that abundant meal."

"I would indeed like to stretch my legs before I go to bed," Nardjis assented, "and it *is* a lovely night."

As they walked out on the terrace, her arm through the Conde's, she continued: "I've been so happy this evening. All of you have made me feel so much at home—like one of the family. And I do love you all. Conchita is just like a daughter to me. She is a darling girl—and my own children, and my husband, died nearly five years ago from the plague."

"Conchita is a darling," assented the count. "And

she seems to have grown up so in just the past two months. It is hard to believe that she is now a married woman—and apparently soon to become a mother. I am delighted that she married Jorge—a fine fellow. His family and mine have known one another for years.

"But it is of you that I wanted to talk. Conchita has undoubtedly told you all about me—and, indeed, there is very little to tell. But I do want to hear all about you—of your life in Andalucía, of the Palace of Medina al-Zahra, your escape, the ambush and the Battle of Piedrabuena, and everything." He smiled.

An hour later, they returned to the castle. The old count's lips seemed to linger a little longer than usual as he kissed the back of Nardjis's extended hand. "Goodnight, my dear, and sleep well. You are with friends, and I trust you will remain in Galicia with us."

"Goodnight, sir," Nardjis replied. "I am so happy to have met Conchita's father. I have heard so much about you, and you do remind me so of her. Until tomorrow."

And they went their separate ways, Nardjis to her apartment, the count to the small apartment he always occupied when staying with his niece and her husband.

Meanwhile, in the Clavijo apartment, the master of the house took Marilú in his arms and time after time their passionate love spent itself in the sweet rapture of love.

"We must be on our way," Gonzalo announced at breakfast the next morning to his four companions—Marilú, Nardjis, Conchita and Jorge. "We shall have to talk with Samuel Leví's cousin, Abrahám Méndez to find out when and how we are to get our money, and how you and I, Marilú, are going to turn over half your share to the Cathedral. And then we must see Dom Wicarte."

"Yes," Nardjis added, "and I would like to be back here an hour before noon. Conde de Andrade and I are having lunch on the banks of the River Ulla; he wants to show me the Galician countryside."

"*Papá* thinks you are the loveliest person he has ever met, Nardjis," said Conchita. "I saw him this morning in his apartment, and all he could talk about was Lady Nardjis this, Lady Nardjis that."

"Well, don Manuel is truly a charming man," Nardjis replied. "It is hard to believe that he is nearing seventy—so young and handsome in appearance, so active, so intelligent. Well, perhaps I shouldn't say any more, but I knew I was going to like any relative of yours, Conchita darling."

"So that's why you're wearing your riding boots, Nardjis," said Gonzalo. "We're going to take the carriage for our visit to Méndez and to the Vicar. Are we ready?"

A few minutes later, they were in the carriage, trotting down the steep road from the castle, in the opposite direction from that in which they had come the previous afternoon. They rode past well-kept orchards and vegetable gardens, down the Rúa de las Huertas, coming suddenly upon a large plaza, on the far side of which stood the Cathedral, or rather, the great stairway leading to the main entrance of what would in time be the Cathedral—the Pórtico de la Gloria. And beside the Pórtico were great piles of cut stone that would eventually form the facade of that huge structure.

The carriage took them around the Cathedral close, past the cloisters, and down an arched street, the Rúa del Villar, where they stopped before a well-kept but unpretentious stone house in the shadow of the second archway.

"The carriage will wait for us in front of the Convent of San Pelayo," Gonzalo announced. "It is only a short walk from here to the Cathedral, as you can see, and there is certainly no room for a carriage to wait in this busy street."

"Why do you call the street '*rúa*' instead of "*calle*'," Nardjis asked.

"Because you are in Galicia," Marilú smiled, "and we speak *Gallego* and not *Romance* or Castilian. And you're going to learn a lot more of our lovely language when you come with me to the marketplace."

"And if you go around the countryside with *Papá*," Conchita laughed.

A servant opened the door of the house, directed them up a narrow flight of stairs, and told them to walk up two flights and knock. "You are expected."

"This certainly doesn't look like a banker's palace," commented Jorge. "Are you sure it's the right place?"

"It must be," Gonzalo replied, "but I agree. This little cubbyhole of a house doesn't look like a place where we could hope to get our six million dinars. But, let's see what happens."

The inside door two flights up was opened by a butler who first examined the visitors through a small peephole. "Come right in, ladies and gentlemen, the master is expecting you."

"And welcome to my humble home, which is always yours," a smiling, elderly gentleman in a yellow caftan said to them, hastening to the door to greet them. "I am Abrahám Méndez at your service. My cousin, don Samuel, sent word that you were coming, and I received your message last night, my lord *Marqués*. This is my son, Salomón, who will be at your service for anything you need." He introduced a tall, gaunt young man, also wearing a yellow caftan.

Introductions were soon completed, and the banker resumed: "Let us have a sherry before we discuss business. I am sorry that I cannot offer you as splendid a reception here as don Samuel did in Toledo, but here in Galicia we Jews have learned that it is advisable not to make a display of wealth. We try to live as comfortably as we can within our houses, but avoid all ostentation without. In Andalucía they are, shall we say, more tolerant of our peculiarities and of our religion."

As they sipped their *oloroso*, don Abrahám went on: "I have your four hundred and seventeen thousand dinars here in my vaults, Lady Nardjis, and nearly half a million dinars for the rest of you—your first of twelve installments. Less, of course, the *agio* of five percent for the transfer between Toledo and Compostela. Do you realize that that makes five tons of gold? I can take you down to the vault to see it, if you wish.

"But I suppose you will wish to use only a small part of that for the present, and you may, if you like, leave the balance here, or deposit it elsewhere as you prefer. For payments in golden dinars instead of gold bars. I must deduct the King's mintage charge—the *seignorage*—but that is insignificant.

"On any amounts that you care to leave with me on deposit, you will receive whatever is the current interest rate, at present one percent a month, but it may go down to half that rate in the near future, as a great deal of money will be flowing into Galicia over the next six months—flight capital from Andalucía and Badajoz, and the King's donations to the Cathedral. You can always shop around to see whether you can get a better rate of interest elsewhere, and I advise you to do so from time to time. But let me know what you will be needing now as I do not want to keep this gold idle in my vault—not if I am going to earn enough to pay you interest on your deposits.

"Today I have the gold available, as I do not know

what your wishes may be, and the money is yours. But in future I shall have to ask you to give me fifteen days' notice before you make any large withdrawals. Up to one thousand dinars, I can always let you have the money at any time, in minted coins—barring some exceptional emergency, in which event I might have to ask for the fifteen days' grace."

"One thousand dinars!" exclaimed Jorge. "I have never spent that much in ten years. So far as I am concerned, I'd like to leave the money with you. Just give me a hundred dinars, half to Conchita, and we'll be richer than we have ever been."

"Wow!" Conchita laughed. "Fifty dinars! Goodness! Better give me some of it in silver. And thank you, sir. We're just not used to being rich."

Nardjis said that ten dinars, most of it in silver, would be all that she would expect to need for a month, but that she would let Salomón know if she changed her mind.

"We certainly shan't need more than a hundred dinars for ourselves, so far as I can see," said Gonzalo. "But you probably know that we are giving nearly two million dinars to the Cathedral, and I suppose we should turn over about one hundred and fifty thousand dinars a month to the Vicar each time we get one of our twelve installments."

"I wanted to come to that," answered don Abrahám. "The money is here for the first installment, if you wish it, and each month I can give you the next installment. But, as I am to be your banker—at least so long as that is your pleasure—may I presume to give you some financial advice?"

"I wish you would," said Gonzalo. "As you may imagine, I have never had to handle that amount of money before."

"Nor I either," don Abrahám smiled. "That is a king's ransom, and nothing like that has ever come to

Galicia before. But I do have some experience in the ways of the world and I have been thinking over this business ever since I first received word from my cousin. So let me give you some ideas, with which you may or may not agree.

"In the first place, the architects and builders of the Cathedral cannot possibly spend one hundred and fifty thousand dinars in a month—nor in a year—no matter how fast the work proceeds. And the King is going to donate an equal amount. It will take twenty years, at least, to use all that money.

"Now, Dom Wicarte is a good man—a saint. But he is not a worldly man, as you know. Would he know what to do with two million dinars if it were dumped into his hands within the course of a year? Nearly four million, if you count the King's contribution. I don't have to tell you that no new bishop has been appointed since Bishop Diego Paláez was disgraced and jailed three years ago, and that two subsequent administrators of the Church's finances proved to be scamps. Suppose the Bishop's successor should prove to be less holy than the present Vicar? As you know, there have been clerics, even of episcopal rank, who have been far from saints. You want your donation to go to the construction of the Cathedral, I presume. Would you want to entrust it to some future bishop to be spent as he sees fit?"

"Goodness, no!" exclaimed Marilú. "We just hadn't thought of that. It might all go for vestments or golden chalices or something like that."

"Or for riotous living and the priests' concubines," said Gonzalo, "if we can judge by some of the unworthy clerics I have run across in my lifetime. God forbid that the Bishop of Compostela should ever be one of those! But what do you suggest, don Abrahám?"

"Well, the King has had his agent here for the past six months or more, supervising the expenditures of the architects and builders in order to control the amount of the donations that have come from the Royal Treasury. With the much larger amounts that the King is going to contribute in the future, this control will be more necessary than ever. The agent is not an architect, but he is an honest man, and a wise one—don Diego Carvajal."

"I know him well—from Burgos. The King could not have chosen a better man for his purpose. I did not know that don Diego was still in Iria Flavia."

"Yes," the old man continued. "And I have heard from his banker,—or rather the king's banker, David de Córdova—that don Diego is going to remain here to supervise the disbursements to the Cathedral under the new donation. But you should have an architect to supervise the expenditures, an architect who has no connection with the Church and is not engaged in any Church construction, and whom you can trust to ensure that the money you give is being spent for the purposes for which it is intended, and spent economically and effectively."

"I know just the man," said Gonzalo. "My cousin Enrique Araujo. And I am sure he would accept. He is a good Catholic, of course—a friend of Dom Wicarte's—and he has contributed much of his own money to the Cathedral. But he is not engaged in any Church construction at the present time and I know he does not intend to take on any such contracts. I spoke to him last night, and he agreed to handle some remodelling we wish done at the castle—to make it more of a home and less of a fortress. But he told me that, at his age, he does not want to handle any work that he cannot complete in his lifetime—which rules out all Church contracts."

"Good," don Abrahám went on. "Well, what I would propose is that you set up a permanent board—a *junta*—to supervise the expenditures and progress in the construction work, and to make the monthly donations to cover the costs. The *junta* should consist of you, Señor Marqués, your architect, and, if you wish, my son Salomón who can act as your financial adviser and banker to attend to the disbursements. The architect should receive a fee; he will be on the job at least once a week, perhaps more often, and will be in consultation with the Cathedral architects from time to time. My son would make no charge, as it is merely a matter of a monthly payment, a normal banking service. Although I think he can be of help to Señor Araujo and the Cathedral architects in obtaining marble and other materials from abroad.

"Now, if you can get together with don Diego Carvajal, so much the better—one *junta* instead of two, or at least two *juntas* working together. He will probably have David de Córdova helping him on the financial side, and he may wish to name another architect to work with your cousin—not at cross-purposes."

"I am sure we can work that out," commented Gonzalo. "And your plan seems to me a splendid one. I'm so glad we consulted with you before we made any other arrangements. . . . I wonder if you could send a messenger with a note from me to my cousin Enrique. I'd like to have him join us here to discuss the plan, and then go with us to see the Vicar."

"Of course. It will only take a moment if Señor Araujo is home." Turning to his son, the old man said: "Salomón, would you ask Benjamín to come here?"

Gonzalo went to a secretary that don Abrahám opened for him, and, with the quill pen and Chinese ink that stood in the inkstand, he scribbled a brief message on a sheet of paper, inserted it in an envelope, sealed it with the Clavijo seal and the melted wax that Salomón gave him, and handed the letter to the messenger, Benjamín.

"While we are waiting," continued don Abrahám, "there is one more thing you will wish to decide. You know that a payment made over a twenty year period may really be worth only half as much as a lump sum payment made now. That depends on the rate of interest prevailing over that period—my cousin Samuel Leví would say 'usury,' not interest. He's more old-fashioned than I. And, of course, we don't know whether it will be twenty years, or longer or less. That depends on how fast they get on with the construction.

"Now that means that you will have to decide whether you want to give the Cathedral the approximately two million dinars as the sum total of all the payments that are made over the period—which would cost you just about half that amount, as you would be receiving interest on the balances that are not paid out. Or whether you wish to donate the full amount to the Cathedral now, but paying it out as they require it, and let the Church receive the interest—which will mean that your gift may actually be double what you have decided to give."

"Oh, we would let the Cathedral have the interest, wouldn't we Gonzalo?" said Marilú.

"Absolutely," Gonzalo agreed. "We told the King we would give half of Marilú's share of the booty, and if we kept the interest on it until it is all paid out, that *really* would be usury."

"I was sure that is what you would say," said the old banker. "It shows that we Jews and you Christians think alike when it comes to charity. If it were business, you'd find me much less generous. And now I would like you to see where I keep your money. But, as I told you, I shan't keep it here very long, now that I know you don't want it right away. I have worked hard for my money—what money I have—and

I make my money work hard for me. That is why I am able to pay you interest."

"I don't understand," Conchita queried. "How do you make money work for you?"

"The normal way," the old man explained, "is for me to lend the money at a higher rate of interest than I have to pay for it. Today, I can lend money at one and a half percent a month, and I am paying you one percent. There is risk, of course, and I have to be careful whom I lend it to. And we Jews are not in a position here in Galicia to compel a powerful nobleman to pay us back if he refuses. That is one reason why interest rates are generally lower in Sevilla or Córdoba than they are here—the Moslem judges—the *qadis*—will uphold our rights against anyone except the King.

"But today, with ibn-Tashfin's army menacing all of Andalucía and Badajoz, there are many people, say in Sevilla, who would willingly pay me one hundred ounces of gold for perhaps eighty ounces of gold paid to them here in Compostela. And there is one town—I shan't say where; that is my secret—where my connections are such that I can get the gold out at not too prohibitive a cost. And there is a city, not in Spain, where I can get one hundred ounces of gold for eighty or eighty-five ounces which I deliver here.

"There are many risks, and it costs money to maintain good connections among people of influence and power. But the profit can be high. The normal *agio* between here and Toledo, for example—the rate of exchange between the two cities—might be only five or ten percent, which would cover the cost of transportation, including a trustworthy armed guard to bring the gold from one place to another. It would be influenced too by the demand for gold here and in Toledo, and the supply of gold in each city. With all the money coming into Compostela for the construction of the Cathedral, and that brought in by the pilgrims, and flight capital from Andalucía, the *agio* is sure to go down, and interest rates too.

"I think that answers your questions, my lady. But shall we go down to the vault now?"

The old man led them to a bookcase, filled with vellum-bound volumes. He pressed a lever under one of the shelves, and the bookcase swung out into the room, disclosing a small door behind it.

"Now, if you don't mind going down in the dumbwaiter, Salomón will take down three of you, and then return for the other two and for me. The weights are set for five hundred pounds, and with that crank Salomón can easily take you down and bring you back as quickly or as slowly as you wish."

Gonzalo, Marilú and Nardjis got into the little elevator with Salomón, who released the foot brake, and their weight took them gradually down the long dark shaft. An oil lamp in the elevator provided illumination.

"We are fifteen feet below the street level," said Salomón as he put on the brake and opened the door to a large room, lit by two oil lamps, although there were a number of additional unlit lamps in sconces around the walls. "There is no other entrance to the vault," he added. "I'll be back in a moment with the others."

"This is ingenious," Gonzalo remarked, "but I don't see how you can pull yourself back up with five hundred pounds of counterweights."

"The rope goes around pulleys above and below," Salomón replied, "and with this crank I can easily lift seven hundred pounds. And when we have heavy loads, there is that other rope and crank on the other side, and two men can lift or lower twice as much. But it is not original. They used lifts like this when they built the Tower of Babel. You can turn the crank if you wish when we go up again. I'll be back in a moment."

So saying, Salomón closed the door and left them alone in the vault.

A moment later the rest of the party joined them. Don Abrahám drew aside a curtain and said: "Well, there's your million dinars of gold, most of it in bars—but those sacks there each contain one thousand golden dinars in coins. We shan't remove them, as the small amount you want today I have upstairs in my private vault, in gold and silver. Well, I guess that it's nothing new to you to see all that gold. I understand you had nearly three million dinars in golden bars from Abd ar-Rahman's treasure."

"Might I open one of the sacks?" asked Conchita. "I've never seen a thousand dinars in coins."

"Of course, milady," and Salomón opened one of the sacks.

"Wow!" exclaimed Conchita as she ran her fingers through the shiny golden coins.

They went back in the elevator as they had come down, only this time Salomón and Gonzalo turned the two cranks, as the weight of four people somewhat exceeded the deadweight on the ropes. On the second trip, Salomón and Jorge worked the cranks. When they were assembled again in the banker's living room, which doubled as his office, Salomón closed the bookcase concealing the hidden entrance to the elevator, and don Abrahám opened a small vault hidden in another wall. Salomón quickly counted out the golden dinars and silver dirhems which they wanted, and handed them receipts which Gonzalo, Jorge and Lady Nardjis signed and sealed with their signet rings.

Don Abrahám then gave the three of them parchment *escrituras* which he signed and sealed in their presence, certifying to the possession of the full amounts deposited in their names, and the conditions for withdrawal and the payment of interest.

"The accounts are in your names," the old banker said, addressing Gonzalo, Jorge and Lady Nardjis, "but you can give me a power of attorney so that your wives, or others, can withdraw the money at any time in your absence. That will be especially advisable in your case, my lord *Marqués*, to cover the disbursements to the Cathedral. And you may wish to make doña Marilú your alternate on the *junta* in your absence.

"Here are some forms of power of attorney, but I would rather you discuss them with your own *escribano*, as I believe there should be limitations on the amounts that can be withdrawn—not that there is any question of trust. But suppose your wife were abducted by thieves in your absence and forced to sign a withdrawal slip under duress. Think it over, and you can give the powers of attorney to me or to Salomón at any time."

"My, you bankers certainly do think of everything," said Jorge admiringly.

"We have to," smiled don Abrahám.

A moment later, don Enrique Araujo was announced, and shown upstairs. He was known to all of them, Nardjis having met him the night before, so introductions were dispensed with. Gonzalo acquainted his cousin with what they had in mind.

"An excellent idea," commented Enrique. "You have to have some way to control expenditures. And the Çathedral architect—I know him well, the master builder, Bernardo the Elder—will be glad to have me on the job to double check on the builders. And I'm sure that don Diego will be glad to join us. If he wants to employ another architect too, so much the better. I think I know the man he'd probably choose, as he has been consulting him on a number of things. We'll get along splendidly."

"Well, shall we be getting along to see the Vicar now," suggested Gonzalo. "And don Abrahám, I don't know how I can thank you for your advice and help. I don't know what I'd do without you. I was about to say that I don't know why I had never met you before—but, after all, I've never needed a banker before. And Salomón, please come along with us. We may need your advice. And I hereby constitute the *Junta de Supervisión* right now—Enrique, Salomón, and me with Marilú as my alternate."

As they walked over to the Cathedral together, Enrique remarked to Gonzalo: "Say, that man Abdullah you have is a marvel. He chewed my ear off last night after you introduced him to me, and I told him to come to the house this morning at eight. We've gone over some plans he has for a Moorish bath and so forth, and for the improvement of the kitchen, and he's a wonder. And he has even proposed a water ram—a pump, you know—and water tower—it will look like a Moorish watch tower—to make up for the uneven water pressure you get up on that hill of yours. I think it will work, and I'll go over the castle and the plans tomorrow."

Turning to the others, Enrique added: "I want you ladies to notice that doorway to the Cathedral as we approach it. It is called the Puerta de las Platerías, and it, and the southern transept it opens onto, are the most nearly completed parts of the Cathedral, aside from the crypt. They got a Master Mateo and a number of sculptors and craftsmen from Tolosa, the capital of the Dukedom of Langue d'oc on the other side of the Pyrenees, to work on it. Isn't it gorgeous? It's the most beautiful doorway I have ever seen, and if the rest of the Cathedral turns out as well, you can be happy with the results of your generosity, Marilú and Gonzalo. But don't expect the Cathedral to be completed during your lifetime—not unless you live as long as Matusalén.

"The Vicar's office is right down this way, in the crypt. Follow me."

He led them through the Puerta de las Platerías, down the southern transept and, just before they came to the eastern apse where the *Capilla Mayor* would be erected, they noticed a little stairway at the right.

"The crypt is the oldest part of the Cathedral," Enrique went on as they descended the stairs. "Originally, there was a small sanctuary here, built by Bishop Teodomiro in the year 813 A.D., to safeguard the tomb of Santiago the Apostle. Then Alfonso the Great replaced it with a basilica in 899 A.D., and this is the crypt of that basilica. Almanzor destroyed the basilica a hundred years later—razed it to the ground but—you know the story—he found an old monk sitting on top of the tomb who refused to move. So Almanzor left the tomb unmolested. And, of course, the crypt was underground, so it couldn't be razed, although it was damaged.

"The crypt is the only part of the Cathedral that is used today—a small chapel down there is consecrated. It will be another fifteen years at least before they can consecrate the new basilica, and I don't know how much longer it will take to complete and consecrate the whole cathedral. The Vicar, Dom Wicarte, has his office in here." And he knocked at the door.

"Come in," boomed the Vicar, in a voice remarkably deep and resonant for one so old. "I was expecting you and am delighted to see you. Would you mind if I ask one of my priests to join us? Diego Gelmírez, a remarkable man. I don't know what I'd do without him."

The Vicar spoke with a strong Frankish accent as

he was one of the many priests whom King Alfonso had brought from Cluny Abbey at the behest of Pope Gregory VII—formerly Fra Hildebrand of Cluny—in order to replace the old Visigoth ritual of Mozarabic Christian Spain with the new Roman Catholic liturgy. And when the King had Bishop Diego Peláez jailed for a conspiracy to turn Galicia over to the Norman William the Conqueror, and two subsequent administrators had been removed for maladministration, Dom Wicarte had been placed in temporary charge as Vicar under the Archbishopric of Lugo. In particular, Dom Wicarte's mission had been to proceed with the construction of the Cathedral, commenced by Diego Peláez, until a new bishop was appointed.

Ringing a bell, Dom Wicarte summoned a sacristan and instructed him to fetch *Padre* Gelmírez. Turning again to his guests, he continued: "I know you want to discuss business matters, and they are too much for my old head. But *Padre* Gelmírez is my right-hand man. I understand that he will soon be named Bishop of Iria Flavia de Compostela and have full charge of the construction of the Cathedral which is our main concern at the present time. If so, the Canon, Dom Segeredo, and I, and Abbot Dom Gundesindo will be delighted to serve under him, and so will the master builder, Benaldus Senex, who is truly a *magister mirabilis,* the designer of the whole Cathedral, and Roberto, the master mason.

"I am sure that some day *Padre* Diego Gelmírez will be an archbishop—when the city is given its rightful name of Santiago de Compostela, as King Alfonso assures me it will be when the basilica is consecrated. And," he added with a smile, "It is appropriate in the City of San Diego for our first Archbishop to be named after our patron Saint.

"*Padre* Gelmírez is one of those in whom you can trust. Too many of our clergy in Spain—I hate to admit it before a good Moslem and a good Jew—have forgotten their vows, have engaged in venality, the sale of indulgences, adultery, and other abominations. But here, in Iria Flavia de Compostela, thanks to the loyalty and devotion of *Padre* Gelmírez and others like him, our clerics are all true Christians. They have no concubines, and honest women are safe in their confessionals.

"True, many of the old Mozarabic clergy have rebelled against the new vows of celibacy introduced by Pope Grégoire of blessed memory—I knew him well at Cluny. Between ourselves I am sure that is why they cling so stubbornly to their old Gothic liturgy and refuse to accept our Roman Catholic ritual which it is my duty and that of my fellow-Cluniacs to install. True, too, we do have trouble from time to time even among the Cluniacs. One of our priests, a devout and holy man in his youth, and still a devout Catholic, became licentious in his old age and had to be dismissed from the diocese. He is now an abbot in Andulucía—I shall not mention his name nor that of his monastery. But we do not wish priests of that character here in the City of Santiago the Apostle—not with all the pilgrims coming from all over Europe to pay homage at the Tomb."

Gonzalo, Marilú and Conchita exchanged knowing glances as the vicar spoke of his scandal in the Church.

At that moment, Father Gelmírez entered the room. "You called me, my lord Vicar?"

Introductions completed, Gonzalo explained what they had in mind. Salomón Méndez and Enrique Araujo added a word from time to time, Father Gelmírez asked a few questions, and the old Vicar finally summed up: "Well, I think that everything is clear. *Padre* Gelmírez will handle all matters on my behalf. I'm afraid I can't quite grasp it all, but if ever you should wish to see me, I shall be at your service. And please just call me '*Padre*'; if I can be a good priest, it is all I ask.

"And now, if you will kneel, allow me to give you my blessing."

Nardjis knelt with the others, but Salomón hesitated, not knowing whether it would be proper for him to kneel before a cleric of an alien creed. The old vicar noted the hesitancy, and smiled: "Come, my son. I can understand that you would not wish your correligionaries to think that you had bent your knee before a priest of the Roman Catholic Church. And they would be quite right. But surely, my son, no one could object to a young man kneeling to receive an old man's blessing."

Salomón knelt, and impulsively grasped the vicar's hand and kissed his ring, tears welling in his eyes as he did so.

The good vicar blessed them all, and then spoke softly to Salomón. "You've something on your mind, my son. I saw a tear, I'm sure."

"You remind me so of a rabbi who used to teach me long ago in Córdoba, Father. You are so like him—not in looks, but in love of God. I can feel it. And I guess I still miss that rabbi, long since dead. I once asked him how God, who we were taught was just, could also be a jealous God, a God of wrath and vengeance. And he told me that, when the early books of the Bible were written, we Jews were a warring, semi-savage nation, and that we mistakenly ascribed to God the defects of our own character. He referred me to the Prophet Micah who tells us that God is compassionate and delights in mercy, and—I know the passage by heart—'What doth the Lord require of thee but to do justly, and to love mercy, and to walk humbly with thy God?'

"That is the noblest passage in the Bible, I am sure.

It is the guilding spirit of my personal faith. And, Dom Wicarte, when I saw that you were illumined by the same light that guided the rabbi of my childhood, I was moved to tears. Thank you for your blessing, Father."

"And thank you for your words, my son," answered the bishop. "Let me remind you that another Prophet, John, tells us 'God is love,' and that Jesus, a Jew, told the lawyer who questioned him: 'Thou shalt love the Lord thy God with all thy heart, and with all thy soul, and with all thy mind, and thou shalt love thy neighbor as thyself. On these three commands hangs all the law and the prophets.' That is the essence of Christianity, and it is a creed to which all men of good will—Christians, Jews or Moslems—can adhere."

At this point, Nardjis, still kneeling, asked: "May I speak, Father?"

"Of course, my dear. And don't remain on your knees. Tell me what is on your mind, and perhaps I can help you."

"Father, for many days I have found myself leaning more and more toward Catholicism. I have been so close to Marilú and Conchita and to Gonzalo and Jorge, and to two other dear Christian friends who were our companions in danger. And I have learned to love them so dearly, as, day after day, I could see that the one shining light that guided them, in all they did and thought, was love—love of God and love of their fellow human beings.

"So, little by little, I have made up my mind that I wanted to be a Christian, for I knew that, through my friends, I was seeing the meaning of true Christianity.

"I have read the Gospels, the Acts of the Apostles, the Epistles, and the Apocalypse—and, of course, all the books of the Old Testament. I read them long ago, for we Moslems are also People of the Book, as we say. So my desire to become a Christian is not based on ignorance—although I confess I still cannot fathom the meaning of the Revelation of St. John the Divine. And there are many other passages which are, and I suppose always will be, a mystery to me.

"But when you asked Salomón to receive an old man's blessing, and when you quoted the Gospel of Saint Matthew so movingly, I knew in my heart that I could wait no longer. May I be baptized, Father? Can I be received into the Church?"

"Of course, my dear. Of course you can. And I thank God that he has let me be the humble instrument of his light. Father Diego Gelmírez will give you instruction, although I think, my dear, that you are as well prepared to give us instruction as we you. None of us can fully comprehend the Apocalypse of St. John. Even Saint Dionysius, the Bishop of Alexandria, wrote that he could not understand the words of St. John, but that he knew they embodied meanings and mysteries that he revered.

"But *Padre* Gelmírez is so much better prepared than I that he will give you your catechism. I would not dare entrust your instruction to any less learned priest.

"So, Father Diego, your first and most important task will be to prepare this lovely young Saracen for admission to the Church. And your second most important task will be to proceed with the construction of the Cathedral, and to work with these kind friends in the distribution and application of their munificence. And now I must leave you all, for I have many things to do."

"Thank you, thank you, Father," said Nardjis through her tears. "Might I ask one more thing? Today is the last day of June. Could my baptismal name be 'Paula'—after Saint Paul whose day it is, not after Santa Paula, the disciple of Saint Jerome?"

"Well, of course, my dear. And now you must excuse me."

Gelmírez then turned to Lady Nardjis. "I can't tell you how grateful I am that I should be assigned to your instruction. I am sure the teacher will learn as much as the pupil. When might I see you, my lady?

"I'm going to be tied up most of the day," Nardjis replied slowly. "In fact, I should be back at the castle even now."

"Could you dine with us this evening, *Padre*?" Marilú put in. "It will just be family, and you can talk over arrangements with Nardjis after dinner. At seven? I shall send a coach for you."

"Delighted! And thank you so much," said *Padre* Gelmírez. "And now you mustn't let me detain you. I look forward to seeing you this evening."

He left the visitors, who hurried up the stairs to find their waiting coach.

"What a wonderful old man!" exclaimed Salomón. "I shall never forget this day. And it makes me happier than ever to be associated with you kind friends in the building of this Cathedral. May I call you my friends?"

"You certainly may," said Gonzalo. "And now we must leave you. Thank you so much, Salomón. And thank you, Enrique. We three—and Marilú—shall be working very closely together, and it will be as friends—not just as business associates. And, perhaps, Enrique, you could get in touch with don Diego Carvajal, and tell him what we have in mind. Bring him around to lunch or dine with us whenever you two have the time."

They parted with warm *abrazos*, and two kisses bestowed on the hands of the three fair ladies. The carriage was waiting just to the right of the Puerta de las Platerías, in front of the Convent of San Pelayo. As they rattled up the steep hill to the castle, Lady

Nardjis said: "This is one of the happiest days of my life. I shall never forget it. The beginning of a new life."

"And you'll just have time to wash those tears off your face, Nardjis darling," Conchita teased. "You'll have to look your best for that picnic with *Papá.*"

"Nardjis always looks her best," said Marilú. "And as soon as we get out of this carriage, I'm going to give her the biggest hug and kiss I've ever given her."

"Me too," said Conchita.

"And I'd like to get in on this," added Jorge. "I feel sort of—well full of emotion at Nardjis's becoming a Christian, and just through love, because we've never tried to proselytize."

"I've never had any family I've loved more than the five of us," Gonzalo concluded, "and Zoraya and Roberto too. So it makes me happier than I can say to have Nardjis—Paula—join us. And I'm going to be the first to kiss you, Paula, because I get out of the carriage first and I shall give you my hand to help you out."

Arrived at the castle, and after each had embraced Nardjis in turn, Marilú and Conchita walked back with Nardjis to her apartment, leaving the men to go about their affairs.

"This is a happy day for me, too," Conchita burbled, as Nardjis prepared for her outing with Conde Andrade. "It's Jorge's birthday. He's twenty-two years old today."

"What are you going to give him for a birthday present?" asked Marilú.

Conchita answered: "I want to give him something at dinner tonight, I've brought him six packages of *turrón* candy that I bought in Toledo—six different flavors, almond, hazel nut, walnut, pistachio, pine-nut, and fruit. He loves it, and he doesn't know I bought it. After all, you can't buy an expensive present for a millionaire—just something that you know he likes—and he loves sweets."

Nardjis then added: "I wish I had known it was Jorge's birthday, I'd have bought him something too."

"That's all right," Marilú smiled. "I have presents that we two can give him a dinner, but I shan't tell you now, as I don't want Conchita to know."

"Say, Marilú," pouted Conchita, "you're not going to try to steal my husband are you? Jorge's my private property. No trespassing!"

"Crazy!" replied Marilú. "Now you run along and tell your father that Nardjis will be ready in two shakes."

As soon as Conchita had left, running down the hall to her father's apartment, Marilú told Nardjis: "I tell you what I have for us to give Jorge—and he'll love it. When my two girls were born, various members of the family knitted sweaters and booties and blankets for them, and as some of my relatives were certain the babies were going to be boys, I have two complete sets of blue baby things. Let's each give Jorge a set, and watch him blush. As Conchita says, you never give a rich man an expensive present.... And now I guess you're ready to go out for your ride and picnic. Let me give you a kiss and I hope you enjoy your outing. I know you will. My uncle Manuel is truly a charming man."

The Conde de Andrade was waiting for Nardjis in the hall, with Conchita by his side. "I am so glad it has turned out to be such a lovely day, Lady Nardjis," he said, "because I do want to show you something of Galicia at its best. Goodbye, Conchita, dear. Goodbye, Marilú. We'll be back for dinner."

Don Manuel courteously assisted Nardjis to mount, although, to tell the truth, that was quite unnecessary.

He mounted his own horse, and they left the Clavijo castle at an easy canter, riding side by side. Marilú and Conchita waved to them until they were out of sight, and then returned indoors for lunch.

CHAPTER 29

They rode down the Paseo de Herradura and between the two pilons of León and Castilla that they had passed when first Lady Nardjis had come to the Clavijo castle. But, when they arrived at the foot of the hill, they turned west, leaving the Susannis gate behind them.

"That road goes south to Vigo," don Manuel told his companion. "But we are going almost straight west to Noya, not nearly as far—a little over seven leagues. I'd like to show you some of Galicia's wilder scenery on the way—a place where I used to play when I was a boy and we visited friends or relatives in Compostela."

The road took them through groves of pine trees, past verdant fields of grain, with here and there a mighty oak or chestnut sheltering a few cows under its spreading branches. They came to a more rugged country, and here the *conde* turned off the road to the left, up a steep narrow path and through the woods, where they could ride only in single file, Nardjis leading, with don Manuel close behind.

"Let's just turn off the path here," said don Manuel. "Better let me lead the way. And then we'll tether our horses, and climb the rest of the way on foot, if you don't mind."

"Of course not," Nardjis smiled. "I've had so little walking, and so much riding, in the past fortnight that I'd love it, and it does seem so wild and beautiful in these woods."

The *conde* came to a halt at a small clearing in the

woods. He removed the saddles and saddle blankets, then tethered the horses beside a rushing stream where the animals could forage and drink within the limit of a long rope tied to their halters.

"What are those beautiful white trees that I see in the woods?" asked Nardjis. "I don't believe I've ever seen that kind before."

"That's a birch tree. Come over here and let me show you something."

They approached one of the larger birches, and the *conde* took a sheath knife from his belt and cut off a slice of bark, about eight inches square, which he then proceeded to split into three layers, the two inner ones as thin and soft as fine silk. "We used to use this for writing paper when we were boys—parchment was too expensive for anything but legal documents and books, and paper was not available at all, at least not in Galicia."

"It's lovely, it's so soft and smooth," said Nardjis. "May I keep it?"

"Of course, my dear, it's yours. Let's just leave it here with the saddles, because we have some rough climbing ahead of us." The *conde* placed the birch bark in Nardjis's saddle bag, then removed his own saddle bag and slung it over his shoulder. "Our lunch," he said. "I'm going to let you go ahead in case you should slip or fall on the rocks, but I'll tell you the way as we go along. Just follow that path upstream along the brook."

As they climbed from rock to rock through the woods, the brook turned into a roaring torrent that cut a deep gorge through its rocky banks.

"We'll have to leave the stream here, and go through the woods—that path to the right." Don Manuel guided his companion, holding her hand or arm to steady her from time to time as the climb became steeper. "But we'll get back to it soon, at its source."

They pushed into the thick woods, the path barely discernible through the underbrush.

"Is it too much of a climb for you,?" asked the *conde* solicitously. "We don't have much further to go."

"By no means," Nardjis laughed. "I haven't had so much fun in years. I love it here in the woods." And she scrambled through the brush and over the rocks like a girl of twenty, as don Manuel followed close behind, watching her slim and supple figure with admiration.

"Turn left just past that boulder," he told her.

Nardjis did so, and there came suddenly into view a scene of wild sylvan loveliness—a wide hollow carved out in the jagged rocks, a quiet pool of crystal clear water in the center, and, at the far side and to the right, a cascade of water emerging from a cleft in the rocks, splashing on a table rock some twenty feet above their heads, and falling a further twenty feet into the pool below.

Nardjis stood there, wonderstruck with the unexpected beauty of the scene. The *conde* put his arm around her waist to steady her as she teetered precariously on a rock in the middle of the path.

"Oh, this is simply gorgeous," she exclaimed. "I'm so glad you brought me here. And I'm beginning to understand why you—and Conchita and Marilú, and Gonzalo and Jorge—speak so affectionately of Galicia. Let's just stand here a moment, while I drink it all in."

It may have been the pressure of don Manuel's arm round her waist that was in part responsible for making her want to stay there in just that position. But, in any event, she did not object to the familiarity, and both of them sensed a feeling—not exactly a thrill, but certainly a feeling of closeness and *simpatía* that had perhaps commenced when first they saw one another the evening before—or possibly even before they met, from what they had heard of one another through Conchita—"*de oídas que no de vista.*"

Nardjis heaved a sigh, and the *conde* withdrew his arm from her waist, rather surprised to find that he had put it there. "We shall picnic down there below, beside the pool," he said.

"It's strange. I haven't been here for years, not since Conchita was a little girl. It all comes back to me—the path through the woods, and everything. But I think it looks more beautiful today than it ever has before. Perhaps because I am seeing it for the first time through your eyes, Lady Nardjis. And. . . ." He checked himself, then proffered his arm to lead her down the steep rocky bank to a grassy knoll beside the pool.

They sat down upon the grass under a chestnut tree, and the *conde* removed their lunch from his saddle bag—a roasted chicken, which he split with his sheath knife and which they picked up in their fingers, accompanied by hard bread and clear, cool mountain water that don Manuel brought from the pool's edge in two metal cups.

They were in a deep gorge, lined by almost perpendicular rocky cliffs, split by the torrent of water that gushed from a cleft some forty feet above, and filled the hollow with the sound of its splashing on the table rock midway in its fall, and then into the quiet pool below. The rim of the gorge was lined with trees—chestnut, oak, and birch, with here and there a pine whose seeds had been blown by the wind into the midst of this hardwood forest.

"This is idyllic," murmured Nardjis. "But savage in a way, and rather frightening. I'm glad you're here with me. Are there any wild beasts or snakes in the woods?"

"Nothing that I can't handle with my sheath knife,"

don Manuel replied. "Would you believe that, when I was a boy, my friends and I used to climb up to that rock there, and dive head first into the pool. Again and again. I don't know how it was we never cracked our skulls. The pool is deep enough, but a miscalculation of a foot or two to either side . . . well, we were young and we had no accidents. Would you like to try it?"

"Me?" laughed Nardjis. "Certainly not! I wouldn't dare. . . . But, maybe if I were fifteen again, and you were with me, I might try it. I'd be afraid to say I was afraid. But you might show me where you used to climb up to that rock. I don't see any place where you could get a foothold."

They had finished their lunch by now, and the *conde* gave Nardjis a hand to help her rise from the ground. "Come this way," he said. "Follow me." And he held her hand as he guided her to the base of the waterfall where a faint mist rose to wet their faces with dew. "There—that's the way," and he pointed to a crevice in the rock at about the level of Nardjis's head. "Do you think you can make it? To the first rock only. It gets harder up above."

"I'd like to try," she said tentatively. "Give me a boost."

Don Manuel made a stirrup with his clasped hands, and Nardjis reached for the rock above her. Her hands slipped and she came tumbling down into her companion's arms. He lost his balance on the grass and fell flat on his back, with Nardjis on top.

Nardjis let forth a peal of laughter, in which don Manuel joined heartily, relieved to find that his companion was unhurt from the fall.

"What a lovely laugh you have," he exclaimed. "It makes me feel young again just to hear you. But not young enough, I guess, to attempt that climb."

He reluctantly released his grip around his companion's waist, although he was sorely tempted to do otherwise, while Nardjis, seeing him stretched out on his back and laughing merrily, felt like throwing her arms around his neck in careless rapture, and putting a stop to his laughter with a kiss. She felt a tremor through her body, and a responsive quiver in that of don Manuel, but she quickly recovered and, still laughing, rose to her feet.

"Oh, it is so beautiful down here, don Manuel. I'm so happy you brought me here," she sighed. "But I guess we better get back to our horses if we are to get to Noya this afternoon." She was still a bit shaken—and not solely from the fall—and she realized that, in such an idyllic spot and after their near embrace, she could hardly trust herself, or don Manuel, if they remained there much longer.

"Right you are! Let's go!" And the *conde* jumped to his feet, led Nardjis back to their picnic spot, slung his saddle bag over his shoulder again, and guided her down the path back to the horses. He preceded her this time, as it was a downhill climb, and he was forced to give her a helping hand or to catch her as she jumped from rock to rock.

When they arrived back at the glen where they had left their horses, Nardjis watched admiringly as she noted the dexterity with which don Manuel slung the blankets and saddles over the horses' withers, tightened the surcingles, and slipped the bits in their mouths and the bridles over their heads. He led the way back to the main road, where again they resumed their canter, still heading west, but this time through a very different landscape—peaceful, gently rolling meadows, verdant with grass, brilliant with wildflowers, and dotted with white, grazing sheep.

The Conde de Andrade pointed out the features peculiar to the Galician countryside—the "*medas*", or haystacks allowed to rot in the fields for winter forage, the "*cruceros,*" or stone crucifixes on stone pedestals at every crossroad, typical of the Celtic regions, whether in Galicia or in Eire. At every farmhouse, and they passed many on the way, there stood a granite corn crib—an "*hórreo*"—mounted on granite posts, roofed with slabs of granite, and with a granite cross on top at one end, a granite urn at the other. The words were Galician, and unfamiliar to Nardjis's ears, as were the sights. And, seeing and hearing through don Manuel's eyes and ears, she began to feel a deepening affection for this strange *Gallego* countryside.

The *conde* pointed to a yellow weed growing in great profusion among some rocks at the right-hand side of the road, a weed that awakened memories in Nardjis of her now dead past. "*Toxo,*" he said, then added, "let's ride across this field to the right. There are no gullies, and we can gallop safely, if you wish. I'd like to show you a very different aspect of Galicia's landscape—the rivers and the "*rías*"—the firths that cut into our coast like long fingers from the sea."

They galloped at full speed across a bright green meadow, patched with clumps of pink clover or yellow *toxo*. They rode side by side, or sometimes one or the other leading by a horse's length. And each had similar thoughts as their eyes followed the galloping figure in front: "How young and slim her figure is, and how well she rides. Surely, she can't be over forty;" and "How handsome he is—a centaur. He can't be sixty-eight."

They came to a long, quiet lake. "The Río Tambre flows in at the far end, and out again to our left. Let's turn to the left, and we'll reach the Ría de Muros."

They cantered along at a slower pace, following the bank of the river, coming to a bridge with ogival, gothic arches that spanned the mouth of the river.

"We'll go back along that road later," the *conde*

said. "We've already passed Noya, which is now to our left. But let's go under the bridge, and we'll get a fine view of the *ría* from its headwaters, looking out toward the ocean."

He tethered the horses to a pine growing under the bridge, loosened the surcingles, but did not bother to remove the saddles, blankets or bits. There was only a narrow ledge between the arches of the bridge and the edge of the rocky slopes that led down to the quiet waters below.

"How peaceful it is here! How lovely!" Nardjis exclaimed, as they sat down on a rock side by side to contemplate the view.

There below them stretched the Ría de Muros, a long, narrow body of water, tranquil as a lake, that stretched out for miles into the distant, misty horizon—like a Norwegian *fjord* in appearance, although the *fjords,* of course, were formed by glacial action, whereas the *rías* were the result of the gradual sinking of mountainous land beneath the sea, the *rías* being the valleys.

Gently rolling meadows sloped down to the banks on both sides as far as the eye could see, a few sheep or cattle pasturing on the green fields, a farm house here and there, a farmer or farmer's wife attending to their chores, children doing what country children do the world over, chickens, ducks, and geese wandering around in search of food—as peaceful and bucolic a landscape as one could find anywhere in the world.

Down at the water's edge were fishermen and fishermen's cottages, some of the women and older men engaged in the never-ending task of repairing nets, others, up to their knees in water or in small boats off shore, pulling in the nets live with squirming, wriggling fish. On the left bank, on the Noya side, a number of children, women, and men were busy digging for clams or raking for oysters, their trousers or skirts pulled up above their knees.

"Those strange-looking vessels out in the middle of the river," don Manuel remarked, "are mussel barges—*mejilloneros.* The barges underneath are small, but the platforms on top are forty feet long, and perhaps half as wide, as you can see. There are hundreds of ropes suspended from the platforms, and the mussels attach themselves to those ropes—look, you can see one of the mussel men pulling in a rope now."

Sure enough, as he drew in the rope, Nardjis could see, even at that distance—and it was half a mile from where they sat—that the rope was covered with a black mass of mollusks dripping with strands of seaweed.

"The little mussels are about three years old—they're the ones I like the best. But they let them grow bigger, four or five years old, for their '*caldeira*'—a Galician seafood stew. The barges remain out there, of course, year after year, and the men go back and forth in the rowboats you see moored to them. For some reason or other, mussels are not considered a very stylish dish, and rich people prefer the shrimp and lobsters and other spiny shellfish, like the *cigalas* that you sampled last night. But mussels are the staple diet of the poor, and I find them delicious, steamed in wine and garlic and parsley. Some day, you must let me take you to a place where we can have a dish of them, with a fine, dry sherry to wash them down."

"I'd love to," said Nardjis. "But let's just sit here. I find it so restful, so peaceful and beautiful. I'd like to sit here forever. Somehow or other, this place seems like home, although I've never seen a place like this before, and it is nothing like any place I have ever called home. It just makes me feel so nostalgic, if one can be nostalgic for something one has never known. What is it you call that feeling—'*morriña*'?" And again Nardjis felt a reawakening of memories from her dead past.

"Yes, '*morriña*' is the word. Marilú must have taught it to you, for Conchita is too young to know the meaning of *morriña*. But tell me, which scene do you love the most—this *ría*, or the waterfall we saw back in the woods?"

Nardjis reflected a moment. "Well, the waterfall was beautiful. I loved it, and I want to go back there again some time. I think that, if you had asked me that question when I was younger—fifteen or twenty—I would certainly have said the waterfall was more beautiful. But now—I am well over forty, you know—I find this place so tranquil, so peaceful. I'd be content to spend the rest of my life in a place like this. So, give me the *ría*, don Manuel, for all time, but let me know that there is always a wild and splashing cascade somewhere in the woods where I can find it when I want to."

"I am glad you said that, Nardjis—may I call you Nardjis?" She nodded her assent, and don Manuel continued. "I too used to love the waterfall, the wild splashing of the torrent as it crashed down upon the rocks, the danger of climbing and diving, and just the reckless abandon of being young and enjoying every minute of it. But now that I'm only two years removed from three score years and ten, I too like the tranquillity of these Galician *rías*. Although, like you, I still thrill to the wild cascades in the woods, and the still wilder pounding of the ocean against the rocks that line the Galician coast. Some day, I hope, you will let me show you the quiet waters and the wild cascades at my home in Puentedeume, and the ocean beaches and rocks still further north.

"And that, really, is why I asked you here, Nardjis.

You must forgive me for being so forward. I've only known you since yesterday. But at my age, life is too short for the waiting game. You must know now, if you did not know last night, that I am in love with you. I knew it as soon as I saw you—yes, and even before, for I had heard all about you from Conchita, and knew what a lovely, wonderful person you are.

"So, if you don't mind looking forward to a life and a love as tranquil as this quiet *ría*, my dearest Nardjis, I would like you to marry me. We cannot recapture the past. We never can know again the wild and carefree rapture of our youth. But we can enjoy together the love and peace of quiet companionship and affection. And, from time to time, I think I can assure you,"—he smiled fondly at his companion—"we shall also know the pleasures of the roaring torrents and the stormy waves of love. Will you marry me, Nardjis dear?"

He turned around to face her. Impetuously, Nardjis flung her arms round his neck, and through her sobs she sighed, "I will, Don Manuel. I love you too, but I didn't dare tell you. And you've made me so happy." Again she burst into tears as he pressed his lips to hers and held her tight to his bosom.

"Oh, my love, my dearest Nardjis," he whispered. "It is you who have made me happy. Life is so beautiful, my love, with you beside me. And I never have told you how beautiful you are. But you are beautiful! And more than beautiful—you are the most wonderful woman in all the world!"

He raised her to her feet, and again they embraced, more closely, more passionately. And, as their tongues explored the delights of their new-found loves, and as don Manuel held Lady Nardjis tight within his arms, they both could feel, from the pressures below their waists, that their love would not be entirely one of quiet and tranquil *rías*, but that crashing cascades of careless rapture would also be theirs—at least from time to time.

Their arms round each other's waists, and gazing at one another as fondly as any teen-age couple, they walked back to their horses. Don Manuel tightened the horses' girths, helped Nardjis to mount again, and exclaimed joyfully: "This is your Galicia now, my love. Look at the mountains on the far side of the *ría*. That is the Sierra de Outes. We shall go there together some day. And now, we shall go to Noya and then back to Iria Flavia as fast as we can. I can't wait to tell Conchita. I know she'll be happy. And all the others. Let's get married tomorrow, my darling. Time is fleeting. And I want you to be the Condesa de Andrade. Immediately!"

They were soon cantering along the road to Noya, and Nardjis was trying to collect her thoughts, bewildered, excited, and radiantly happy. "Can we get married that soon, my love? I hope we can." She told don Manuel of her visit to the vicar that morning with Marilú and Conchita, of her decision to be baptized, and of the prospective visit of Father Diego Gelmírez that evening. "I'll ask *Padre* Gelmírez if I can be baptized and if we can get married tomorrow. I don't want to wait either, Manuel, my darling. Let's surprise them all with the news tonight at dinner."

They entered Noya, a charming seaport and fishing city, but don Manuel suggested that they ride straight through, for they could see it at their leisure some other time. "But I want to stop off for a moment at this house," he added, drawing up before a small but handsome stone house on the main street. "Just wait here; I shan't be a minute."

And he sprang off his horse, passing his bridle to Nardjis who wondered what this was all about. A moment later, don Manuel emerged from the house, smiling from ear to ear, and accompanied by a man at least ten years his senior. "My *fiancée*," he smiled, "and this, Nardjis, is my good friend, don Belarmino Barbanza, a doctor of letters and the most eminent citizen of Noya. And he is going to do me a favor—a tremendous favor. But I'll tell you about it some other time. And now we must be going."

He gave don Belarmino an *abrazo*, and the old gentleman kissed Lady Nardjis's hand, giving her a charming smile as he did so. "My friend, don Manuel, has excellent taste, I can see. And he is a very lucky man. I do hope to see you again, my lady, when you return to Noya."

With that, the two riders turned their horses back on the road to Compostela, waving goodbye to the old gentleman at the curbstone. The part of the road they now traversed was new to Lady Nardjis, as they had cut across the meadow on their way down. It was beautiful, rolling countryside, green and colorful. On either side of the road, there were charming manor houses, large and sprawling places, shaded by oak and chestnut trees, and surrounded by the farms and pasture lands that quite evidently formed part of the manor.

"We call those manors '*pazos*,' and they are typical of Galicia," don Manuel remarked.

"They are charming," exclaimed Nardjis. "And look at that one there—the most beautiful of all, with all those flowers and chestnut trees. How lovely!"

"I'm glad you like it, my love," Manuel smiled. "Because that's the *pazo* of don Belarmino Barbanza, and—I just can't keep the secret from you—that's where we're going to stay on our honeymoon, my darling. Just you and I together—and the servants of course. Don Belarmino lives in his town house now. Oh, I do hope we can get married tomorrow! And no one—absolutely no one but don Belarmino—will know where we are."

"I hope so too, my love, and I can't wait to get back and surprise Conchita and all the others. Do you think she'll like having me as a stepmother? I do hope so. I'm so fond of her."

"Like it? She'll love it. I can't tell you all the nice things she's said about you. And do you know, my sweet, I really believe she planned it all the time. She's such a darling. . . . But let's get going."

They reached the Clavijo castle at the sixth hour after noon, dismounted, and handed the reins to a groom who greeted them with a smile. They walked side by side up the stairs, but not hand in hand, as they wished to reserve their surprise for later. Marilú and Conchita met them at the door.

Conchita rushed up to her father, threw her arms around him, and sobbed: "I'm so happy for you, *Papá.* It's just what I hoped for. And I'm so happy for you too, Nardjis dear. So terribly happy." And again she burst into tears.

Marilú too embraced Nardjis and her uncle almost simultaneously, and expressed her joy at the happy news.

"But how in the world did you know?" asked don Manuel, puzzled. "We were going to keep it a secret until tonight," he added ruefully, as Conchita screamed out: "Jorge, Gonzalo, come quickly. *Papá* and Nardjis are going to get married."

Marilú smiled: "Uncle Manuel, you darling you. Your faces gave you away. I wish you could see yourselves. As soon as Conchita and I spied you from the window, we knew it had happened, and we're both so happy. I couldn't have a nicer aunt—nor uncle, either."

"And I couldn't have a nicer stepmother," burbled Conchita. "Oh, Nardjis, I do love you so."

By that time, Gonzalo and Jorge had entered the room, and there were *abrazos* and kisses all around.

And Marilú and Gonzalo reassured Nardjis—of course they would be delighted to act as godparents at her baptism, and they felt sure the happy couple could be wed tomorrow. They would ask *Padre* Gelmírez tonight. And much better a quick marriage than a long engagement. It would be such a happy event—the only thing that could equal the joy of their homecoming the previous day.

At last they allowed the happy pair to get away to their respective apartments so that they could slip out of their dusty clothes and take a *siesta* in preparation for the events of the evening—the celebration of Jorge's birthday, which he himself had forgotten, and the formal pledging of the troth between Lady Nardjis and don Manuel with a glass of wine, and in the presence of a priest.

Dinner time came at last, *Padre* Diego arriving punctually and being immediately apprised of the happy tidings by an effervescent Conchita. Little Luisita and Elisita were allowed to come downstairs in their nightgowns to take a sip of sherry in a toast to their beloved great uncle Manuel and his betrothed, both of whom looked radiant and at least twenty years younger.

"But I always knew Aunt Nardjis was my aunt," Luisita declared. "She played with us and our doll house last night."

"I knew it too," lisped Elisita, determined not to be outdone.

"Well, off to bed, children," Gonzalo smiled, as he and Marilú carried the two upstairs, trailed by their nurse, and by Nardjis who also wanted to give them a good-night kiss.

They were met at the top of the stairs by a smiling Rosa who embraced Lady Nardjis, and an equally happy Abdullah who kissed her hand, and wished her happiness.

"I've already told you your bedtime story, darlings," said Gonzalo, kissing them both. "So, goodnight, sleep tight, and happy dreams."

Marilú and Nardjis each gave them a goodnight kiss, and then all three hastened downstairs to join the others, the two ladies with packages under their arms, tied with blue bows.

Conchita also had a package, tied with red ribbon, and as Nardjis and Marilú came down the staircase, she threw her arms around her husband, and cried out: "Happy Birthday!"

He opened the package. "Just what I wanted, you darling," he exclaimed, giving Conchita a great hug and a kiss.

Jorge then opened the two packages from Marilú and Nardjis, which they told him were from Gonzalo and don Manuel as well. He blushed red as a beet when he saw what was inside, but he kissed them both, and assured them that their gifts were a harbinger of what he wanted more than anything else in the world. The men all shook his hand, and wished him many happy years to come, while *Padre* Gelmírez expressed his pleasure at being allowed to join such a happy family gathering.

"I see what you mean, Lady Nardjis," he added. "You are very fortunate to be on your way to becoming a member of such a loving family, and they are very lucky to have you join them."

"Do you think I can be baptised right away, Father?" Nardjis asked. "And do you think that Manuel and I can be married tomorrow? The Marqués and Marquesa de Clavijo say they will be my sponsors."

"There's no reason why you can't be baptised immediately," answered *Padre* Diego, "but I think it would be better if you would come to the chapel tomorrow morning, say at eight o'clock, and ask Dom Wicarte to baptise you in person. I'll speak to him tonight, and ask him if he will be willing to forego the banns. A vicar, as the acting bishop, has many powers that we simple priests do not possess, and I feel sure he will consent. But I think he will like it if you ask him tomorrow at the baptism. Let me talk with you, and your prospective sponsors after dinner tonight about the meaning of baptism, and of the marriage sacrament, and then we'll see what we should do."

"I know what we should do right now," smiled Marilú, as the butler came to announce that dinner was served. She took Father Diego's arm and placed it around her right arm as Gonzalo let her slip her other arm into his, and the three of them led the way into the dining room. Jorge and don Manuel followed with Conchita and Nardjis on their arms.

"Would you say grace, Father?" Marilú asked as they sat down at table. After grace and a prayer for the happiness of the betrothed couple, Gonzalo raised his glass in a toast, first to them, and then to Jorge and Conchita. And they proceeded to dine on what was a delicious dinner, accompanied by the finest wines of the region. But what they ate and what they drank, it is improbable that any of those at the table knew, so happy were they in such joyful company and with such glad tidings of things to come.

Dinner over, Father Diego asked if he might be allowed to talk with Lady Nardjis and her proposed bridegroom and godparents in private. Excusing themselves, Gonzalo and Marilú left their guests and led Father Gelmírez into the library followed by Conchita, Lady Nardjis and the Conde de Andrade.

Marilú looked at the young priest in some amazement. He had told her at table that he was only twenty-three years of age—a special dispensation, as in Spain the minimum age for ordination of priests was thirty, and elsewhere thirty-five. Yet his appearance was that of a man in his mid-thirties—beardless, tonsured, self-assured, extraordinarily intelligent and quick, and according to Dom Wicarte an outstanding administrator. She could readily believe that he might indeed some day be made a bishop and even an archbishop, as the old vicar had predicted. Instinctively, however, she preferred her old friend, Dom Wicarte—a saint if ever there was one—but she knew that the Church had need of men possessing the energy, ambition and ability of Father Gelmírez, especially for such a major task as the construction of the Cathedral of Santiago de Compostela.

She listened intently as *Padre* Gelmírez reviewed the essentials of the baptismal service—the renunciation of the devil and all his works, the acceptance of the creed, the desire to be baptised, and the willingness to keep God's commandments and to walk in the way of the Lord. As Marilú had a Missal book that contained not only the Order of the Mass but the rites of the Ministration of Holy Baptism and of the Solemnization of Matrimony, Father Diego went over these with the five of them, and suggested that they read them over that evening.

He then questioned Nardjis to determine her knowledge of the articles of faith of the Roman Catholic Church, the books of the old, as well as of the new testament, and her belief in God, the Virgin Mary and Jesus Christ. *Padre* Gelmírez was one of the most learned young theologians of his time, and was well able to explain certain matters that Nardjis raised but, when his brief catechism was over, he exclaimed: "It is to be regretted, my dear Lady Nardjis, that there are many of our priests who are less well versed in scripture and in creed than you."

And he concluded that Lady Nardjis was certainly amply prepared for baptism and for marriage, but suggested that she should study the Offices of Instruction and the Order of Confirmation, and assured her that as an adult, she could be confirmed immediately after baptism.

"And now," he concluded, "I know you only by the name of Lady Nardjis, and I understand that you wish your baptismal name to be Paula. That will be the name the bishop will use in the marriage service. But I must tell him your father's surname and the name of your late husband—that is, your maiden name and your previous married name—for our marriage records."

"My father," Nardjis replied, "was the Caliph Hisham III, the last Caliph of Spain. He was known as al-Mu'tadd. Of course he had many names and titles, but the family name was Omayya, so I suppose that, if you translated my name according to the Spanish Christian custom—which, of course, Moslems do not do—it might be Nardjis Omayya. My husband was Omar ibn-Ishaq al-Farabi. I was known as Lady Nardjis, the wife of al-Farabi."

"Well, I suppose we would call you, in Spanish style, Paula Omayya, widow of Farabi," suggested the priest. "And, after your marriage, you will be Paula Omayya de Andrade, or simply the Condesa de Andrade. Will that be all right?"

"But then you really are a Princess," Conchita burst in.

"Yes, my dear, but I could never use the title. You see, my father was overthrown by the rebel leaders of the community of Córdoba. The rebels threw him into a dungeon, without light, without food, and he died there with me in his arms. I was only an infant, so I remember nothing of that. And then the widow of the previous Caliph, my cousin, rescued me from the dungeon, and later I became the companion and lady in waiting of her daughter, the Princess Walladah. And after that, the nurse of Walladah's son, who became the Grand Vizier ben Zaydun, and, later, I was lady in waiting of ben Zaydun's wife.

"But, of course, I never dared to use the title of Princess, even after the King of Córdoba welcomed ben Zaydun to his court. Perhaps even especially then, as you could hardly expect a usurper king to recognize as a princess the daughter of the true Caliph. So I do not like to use the title.

Padre Gelmírez and the others were fascinated by Lady Nardjis's story as they all knew of the tragic death of Spain's last Caliph—how he had been shut up in a dungeon under the Great Mosque of Córdoba, and how he remained half frozen in the total darkness, almost suffocating in the fetid air. And they had heard how the doomed Caliph clasped his infant daughter—Nardjis—to his bosom to keep her warm, and how he begged for a crust of bread for his child.

Gelmírez felt sure that the rescue of the infant child was an act of God that destined her for salvation in the Christian Church. He begged to be excused, however, because it was his wish to get back to the Cathedral and speak with his vicar before the old man's bedtime. So he thanked the Clavijos for their hospitality, and for the opportunity they had given him to help bring a stranger to the welcoming arms of the Church.

"Well, Father," said Marilú, "we too must get back to our guests. Please give Don Wicarte our love, and say we shall see him tomorrow at eight. Your coach is ready whenever you wish."

So, after they had all bid the priest goodnight, the three couples went their separate ways, don Manuel and Lady Nardjis being permitted a sufficient modicum of privacy so that they could enjoy the sweet sorrow of a parting kiss until the morrow.

CHAPTER 30

Early the following morning, Lady Nardjis, accompanied by Gonzalo, Marilú, and Conchita, drove down from the Clavijo castle for their appointment with the good Vicar of Iria Flavia. They were welcomed affectionately by the old man, whom they found in his office engaged in conversation with Father Gelmírez.

"*Padre* Diego has told me of your desire to be baptized under the rites of the Roman Catholic Church, Lady Nardjis," said the Bishop, "and I see no reason why the sacrament cannot be administered this morning. Are you prepared, my dear?"

"I am, *Padre*," Nardjis replied, using the familiar form of address that the Vicar had requested. "And I suppose that Father Diego has explained that the Conde de Andrade and I wish to marry—today, if your Lordship will permit and if the publication of banns can be dispensed with. Manuel—the Conde de Andrade—says that, at his age, if it were done 'twere well it were done quickly, and I am of like mind. Would you, your Lordship?"

"*Padre*, my dear," the Vicar replied with a smile. "*Padre*, not 'your Lordship.' Yes, even for a young man such as the Conde de Andrade, time is of the essence. It is better to marry than to burn, and I see no purpose in compelling my good friend, don Manuel, and such a charming and lovely convert as you, Lady Nardjis, to burn for three weeks or more, particularly when your sponsors are so near to my heart.

"So, let us go to the chapel now where Padre Diego

Gelmírez and I shall perform the Ministration of Holy Baptism, and let me first thank you for giving me this privilege. For there is nothing that could give me greater joy than to help you to walk in the way of the Lord—unless, indeed, it be the pleasure you will afford me at noon today when you and don Manuel are joined in holy matrimony."

The baptismal and confirmation services were soon over. The Vicar gave his blessing to a tearful and grateful Nardjis—now Paula—and her companions, and they bade goodbye to the venerable priest and to his younger companion until noon.

On the way back in the coach, Nardjis suddenly remembered: "The ring—I had forgotten about the ring. Is there any place where Manuel and I can buy rings this morning."

"Paula, dear," Conchita burst in, "I just remembered. Don't you remember that when I chose rings for Jorgito and me at Medina al-Zahra, I got two extra rings so that Jorgito could choose. They are beautiful—oh, goodness, and now it just occurs to me that I stole them from King Alfonso, because when I told him about our wedding rings I forgot all about this extra pair. Can you use stolen rings? Would your marriage be legal?"

Marilú laughed: "I am sure the King would be delighted to have his property used in such a worthy cause. Although he might exact his usual tribute of a kiss. And I can hardly blame him, considering how sweet a kiss from Nardjis—Paula—would be. But, as the vicar will bless the rings, they will be quite legal. . . . Paula, my sweet, you know you mustn't see Uncle Manuel today until you see him in church, and I think you had better rest and let Conchita and me wait on you and attend to anything you may need."

So Marilú and Conchita accompanied Paula to her apartment, leaving their men completely abandoned for the rest of the morning as women often do on such occasions.

Thus, shortly before noon on that eventful day, the bride and groom and wedding guests were met at the door of the Cathedral by the venerable Dom Wicarte, resplendent in his vestments, with mitre, crozier and pectoral cross, accompanied by the youthful *Padre* Gelmírez. And all their friends and relatives, which meant practically everybody who was anybody in Iria Flavia de Compostela and the surrounding region, waited excitedly for the happy event which, in accordance with custom, would take place in the very doorway—the beautiful Puerta de las Platerías.

Never were flower girls more adorable than little Luisita and Elisita as they walked to the doorway at the head of the procession; never was bride more beautiful and radiant in her white veil than Paula, née Nardjis, as she entered on the arm of the Marqués de Clavijo; never was groom more nervous and happy than don Manuel, as he stood beside his old friend, don Belarmino Barbanza, who just as nervously felt in his pocket for the twentieth time trying to find the golden circlets that he was required to produce at the proper moment; never were matrons of honor lovelier than Marilú and Conchita, nor bridesmaids sweeter and cuter than the six blond and blue-eyed Andrade cousins who completed the wedding procession—all of whom found eager swains awaiting them at the conclusion of the ceremony; and never were more tears shed by all the women, nor more ribald repartee exchanged among the men than at the wedding of doña Paula and don Manuel, who had entered the chapel as widow and widower, and exited as husband and wife, the Conde and Condesa de Andrade.

A long line of carriages waited outside the Puerta de las Platerías of the Cathedral to take the members of the wedding and all their guests to the Castle of the Clavijos for a reception and collation, and great was the merriment, and merry the minstrelsy, and many the kisses and *abrazos* exchanged upon that gala occasion. When the time came for the bride and groom to leave, Paula stood upon the great stairway and tossed her bouquet, which was caught simultaneously by six sweet and smiling bridesmaids who were immediately embraced by six strong and stalwart swains, as each clutched her sixth share of what was once a handsome nosegay.

At Paula's insistence, Marilú and Gonzalo were persuaded to remain with their guests below while she and don Manuel went upstairs to be attended to by the everfaithful Rosa and Abdullah. A half hour later, the bride and groom, attired in riding habits, left stealthily by the back staircase, followed by Rosa and Abdullah, who were each carrying a large roll, as big as a bolster, wrapped in canvas and tied with leather straps.

"Your horses are saddled and ready, milord," whispered Abdullah. "They are tethered outside the back gate of the castle, and no one but the stable boy knows they are there. With his help, I have locked up all the other saddles and bridles in the tack room, and the key will be conveniently lost for at least three hours, so that you will not be followed by a score of celebrants waiting to annoy you on your wedding night—wherever it may be that you intend to spend that joyous occasion."

As he fastened the two large rolls of clothing and other personal effects to the cantles of the saddles, Abdullah wished the bride and groom much happiness and the blessings of Allah, while Rosa embraced her former mistress affectionately. The two waved goodbye as don Manuel and doña Paula set off at a brisk canter, behind the back wall of the Clavijo castle, and down the road to Noya that they knew so well.

"Oh, my darling," said don Manuel to his bride as they galloped down the highway side by side, "I have so looked forward to this hour, and we shall be so happy together in don Belarmino's *pazo*."

"I'm already happier than I can tell you, my love," Paula replied. "And I, too, look forward to being alone with you in that lovely *pazo*. We certainly gave them all the slip, and they probably won't even know we have left for another half hour. I can just picture Conchita—how outraged she will be that we left without kissing her goodbye. But she will understand, and be delighted at how clever her father has been. You know, my love, one of the most wonderful things about our marriage is that I am to be the mother of such a darling child."

When they drew up at the entrance to the Barbanza manor, a groom, a housekeeper and a butler were there to welcome them. The house was even lovelier than Paula had imagined from the hasty glimpse she had had of it from the road. It was a rural house, in its setting, its architecture, and its furnishings—neither a palace nor a mansion, but spacious and charming in its elegant simplicity. In preparation for the newlyweds, the housekeeper had placed vases of flowers in every room. The house was immaculate, everything fresh and polished.

"Let me show you around your new house, Mistress Andrade," don Manuel whispered affectionately.

So, arm in arm, he took doña Paula around the living room, the parlor, the music room, and the main *patio*, lush with flowering bushes, ferns and other flowers. They peeked in to the kitchen and pantry where the cook and her assistants greeted them warmly, busy in preparations for the evening meal. Then they explored the many bedrooms, arranged around a second, flower-filled *patio,* including their own spacious, sunny room, with its two adjoining dressing rooms.

"Let's explore the garden and grounds while it is still bright," suggested don Manuel. "We can get out of these riding clothes and take our *siesta* when we get back. It will be three hours before dinner."

Don Manuel did not wish to appear to be in unseemly haste to lead his bride to the privacy of the nuptial bed. Then too, he wished time to collect his thoughts and prepare himself for an experience that he had not enjoyed for nearly five long years. After all, he was no longer young....

So together, with their arms round each other's waists, they walked out on the terrace, into the loveliest of gardens, so natural in its rustic simplicity compared with the marvelous Moorish gardens that Paula had been accustomed to when she was Lady Nardjis. From there they walked to the chicken coop, the duck and goose pond, the cow sheds, the barns, stables, carriage houses, and other out-buildings of a prosperous manor house. And, from the hill on which they stood, they could see the peasants in the fields, the tidy cottages swarming with children, the wives busy at their daily chores, and all the other signs of life and bustle that betoken a well-run farm.

"Let's go back to our room, my darling," don Manuel suggested. "Do you realize that I haven't given you a proper kiss since we've been married, and my arms are aching to hold you."

"Let's," whispered doña Paula, with an affectionate smile. "It's just a lovely, lovely place, but I think we really ought to take a *siesta* after all the excitement of the day."

The housekeeper had hung their clothes in two large wardrobes, placed their other effects on their bureaus, and laid out their night clothes on the great double bed which had been turned down neatly for the night. It was amazing how many things Rosa and Abdullah had been able to pack into the clothing rolls without so much as a crease in any of the garments.

"I'd like to take off these dusty things, and just freshen up in my dressing room," said Paula. "But I'll be back for our *siesta* in just a moment."

A tender kiss before parting, even for a moment, and they both retired into their respective dressing rooms to freshen up.

When doña Paula reappeared in the bedroom, clad in a thin silk *negligée,* don Manuel was there ready to receive her in his arms, his dressing robe loosely tied around the waist. He held her in his arms tenderly, and planted a chaste kiss upon her forehead.

"My own, my beloved, my wife," he whispered. "How I have longed for this moment together. Let me embrace you, my love."

And he drew her supple body close to his, his strong arms encircling her waist. She put her arms tenderly, then passionately round his neck as he pressed his lips to hers, and she could feel his manroot rising beneath his robe, while their tongues engaged in mutual, delectable exploration.

"Come, come, my darling, come and embrace me," he panted as he opened her robe and his and laid her down gently upon the bed. His knee separated her thighs and she clasped her arms around him as she felt him enter deep within her body.

She moaned, as the pent-up passion of five long years found its outlet in the mutual writhing and churning and plunging in which they now engaged.

It was his turn to groan and gasp in rapture as Paula's strong muscles grasped him at the base and kept his stiff tumescence hard and firm, while other muscles deep inside her pulsated rapturously in a myriad of kisses along the length of that strong and virile member. Again and again a wave of ecstasy engulfed them as they struggled in fond embrace, until Paula, overcome with emotion, gasped and shrieked: "Oh, dear God, dear God, what rapture!"

Her muscles relaxed, they came almost simultaneously and, with a final desperate plunge, he sank down upon her warm body, the two of them utterly exhausted, utterly fulfilled, and utterly content. There they remained, still coupled, heaving and sighing. At sweet, long last, he tenderly withdrew, and they lay down side by side, her head upon his breast, his arm encircling her.

"Darling, darling," Paula sighed. "That was certainly not a tranquil *ría*. It was a veritable cataract of love and, oh, my dear, I loved it so."

"I loved it too, my precious," he replied. "And I have never been gripped or caressed before as you gripped me and caressed me down below when I was at the height of my passion. I have never known such rapture. And I shall love you, my darling, when we are no longer able to enjoy these cataracts of love, but only the quiet *rías* of affection."

"Oh, my husband, you must love me always, and I shall love you as dearly in the quiet *rías* as in the wild cascades.... Let us rest now, side by side. I am exhausted. And no more, darling, for this evening."

They came down to dinner that evening, fresh and relaxed. At the table, the butler helped doña Paula into her chair, at don Manuel's right, then turned to don Manuel.

"I took the liberty of asking the cook to prepare a real *Gallega* dinner for you, *Señor Conde*. A simple meal, because we are a rural household, but I know that you like seafood, and I trust that you and the *Condesa* will enjoy it.

They sipped their dry sherry in silence, toasting one another with their eyes, and holding hands beneath the table. The first course was served, a steaming hot *caldo Gallego*, a savoury broth of mussels and other seafood that was just what they needed. The *caldo* was followed by a large *empanada*—a piping hot pastry stuffed with spicy, juicy chicken chopped up with an occasional bit of green olive. It was delicious.

The butler then served them a clear white wine, and uncovered a large silver platter which he placed in front of don Manuel. "This is the *pièce de résistance*, milord, so I trust you will both dine heartily on it. As you know, we live simply here in the country, and do not serve the many courses you are accustomed to in the city."

"Oh, that is beautiful," commented don Manuel, and he explained to doña Paula. "That is a *reo*—a sea trout, caught in the ocean or perhaps at the mouth of the *ría*. I am sure you will like it."

The fish, nearly two feet long, had been beautifully baked and was steaming hot. It was surrounded on the platter by fresh peas and beans and chard, undoubtedly from the manor. The fish was delectable, and the vegetables delicious. Dessert was simple—fresh fruit and cheese. But the cheese was a Galician specialty.

Dinner over, doña Paula suggested that they take a walk. "I did so love that walk with you the first night we met—and if it hadn't been for that, we wouldn't be here together now, my love. Would it be too far for us to walk down to the *ría*?" she asked shyly.

It was a beautiful, bright moonlit night so don Manuel answered: "It's not too far if you're willing to walk across the fields—a little more than a mile. If we went by the road, through Noya, it would be three miles, up hill and down."

It was pleasant walking across the soft grass meadowland, and the moon shone so brightly that they had no difficulty picking their steps to avoid the stones and higher grass and brambles. They came to the bank of the river, but did not venture down into the gorge as it was steep and rocky, and don Manuel explained that they would only have to clamber up an even steeper cliff at the head-waters of the *ría* if they wanted to see the *ría* from under the bridge as they had done the previous day.

So they walked along the edge of the *arroyo*, arm in arm, in happy silence, until they saw ahead of them the arches of the bridge linking Noya with the Sierra de Outes on the far side. They stood on the ledge under the bridge at almost the same spot on which they had first kissed in love the day before. The moonlight sparkled like a host of tiny candles on the ripples of the quiet *ría*, and shone full strength upon the mountains on the distant shore, covering their peaks with snowy whiteness. The *ría* was deserted, save for the mussel barges still at anchor, and the lights in the fishermen's cottages along the Noya shore.

The lovers' arms reached silently around one another, his round her waist and shoulders, hers round his neck. Tenderly, gently, they pressed together. Then their lips sought one another's, and their tongues brushed together with sweet, soft kisses, their arms tightening and their bodies straining passionately together in close embrace.

"Oh, my lover, my husband," Paula sighed. "This is what I wanted. To have you hold me again on just this lovely spot where you first took me in your arms. I am so happy, my love. Hold me close."

Don Manuel did not reply, but clasped his arms closely round her.

At last, reluctantly, he drew away, and whispered in Paula's ear: "I'm happy, too, my love—happier than I ever believed possible. But let's take one more look at this enchanted, moonlit spot, and then let us go back to our *pazo* where I can tell you once again how truly happy I am."

Flushed and eager, the two walked back through the fields to the manor house where once again they found happiness in one another's arms.

The next morning, neither daybreak, nor cock crow, nor the maid in her morning chores, disturbed their happy dreams, and the sun was already fairly high in its course before they stirred drowsily beneath the sheets. The unaccustomed pleasure of a bedfellow soon roused them from their sleep, and the amorous play began anew, not turbulently, but happily, leaving them deeper in love than ever.

"It must be late, my love," don Manuel whispered in his partner's ear, "you've made me so very happy in just one night. Let's just have a sip of linden tea, and then I'd like to take you for a long, long ride down to the coast. I want you to know and love Galicia as I always have."

"In Andalucía," doña Paula replied, "I would say 'with love and gladness' and I think that that is the perfect answer. For I'd love to go and I'm so glad to be with you, husband mine. You've given me such happiness, my darling."

Manuel pulled the bell cord, and the maid knocked at the door, then entered smiling. Manuel gave his orders, first for the tea and toast, then for the horses. They ate their light breakfast as they donned their riding habits. In a few brief moments more, they were on their way, riding at an easy canter down the road to Noya. Again, they passed through Noya without taking time to enjoy its sights, and headed for the bridge they knew so well.

"The *sierra* and the *ría* are lovely in the morning mist," said Paula, as they walked their steeds across the bridge.

"Yes," Manuel answered, "and when the mist is still over the *ría* so late in the morning, that means it's going to be warm."

Crossing the bridge, they took a narrow road to the left, skirting the high bank overlooking the *ría,* past the walled town of Muros, and then inland through hilly verdant country where shepherds grazed their sheep, invariably with a dog, and generally with a Judas goat to help herd their flock back home. Although they rode at a brisk canter, the way was long, and it was well after noon by the time they came to the spot that Manuel knew so well, and that he wanted to show his bride.

"Here we are, my love," he smiled, as they checked their steeds, and he pointed to a matchless vista of open ocean, the waves breaking against the rocky Galician cliffs, with just a patch of pure white beach between two giant promontories.

"I've never seen anything so glorious before," exclaimed Paula. "The waves are so wild and fierce—it's even more exciting and more beautiful than the cataract you showed me in the woods. And I love the sound of those great waves breaking against the rocks. Can we picnic up here on the cliff?"

"Better than that, my love. Follow me." And don Manuel led the way, as the horses slowly picked their steps down a steep and winding path beside one of the two cliffs they had seen from above. They came out on a grassy wooded spot beside a little rill of clear water that ran out into the sea. Before them stretched the white sands and the open ocean.

"We are all alone here, my sweet," said Manuel. "We are completely hidden from the road or from the cliff, and fishermen never venture out upon this part of the sea, because of the rocks on every side. Do you swim? If not, you can just bathe with me in the ocean. You'll be safe, for I am a strong swimmer, and I shall never let you go."

"I don't know how to swim," Paula replied. "And I've never been in the ocean in all my life. Will we be safe? The waves are so high, and they sound so fierce, breaking on the beach and dashing against the rocks on the side."

"You'll be safe with me, my darling." Manuel tethered the two horses in the shade, beside the rill and next to a grassy plot where they could forage. He removed their saddles and saddle blankets, then put his arms around Paula's slim waist. "This is our dressing room, my sweet. Don't be shy. We're really all alone."

Paula blushed from head to toe as she removed her clothes, following Manuel's example, and hanging her things on the branches of a small oak tree.

"You have a lovely figure, my dear," Manuel smiled. "I don't believe you're really more than twenty. But don't let me get my mind on that—at least not right now—or we'll never get our swim."

For her part, Paula could not help admiring her husband's trim waist, broad shoulders, and wiry arms and legs. He could well have passed for a man of thirty.

Manuel grasped her hand. "Let's run down to the beach, and don't stop running—it's the only way to dash into the ocean waves. Don't be afraid, my darling. I shan't let you go."

It did feel glorious, running naked down to the beach, across the soft white sands that felt so nice and squishy between her toes—a sensation that Paula had never felt before. She hesitated just a moment as they came to the water's edge, frightened, but she held tight onto Manuel's strong hand and kept going. The water felt so cool and fresh around her ankles, then her legs, then splashing around her waist.

Manuel showed her how to turn her face away

from the waves, as they came rolling in on the beach, how to jump over the crest or, alternatively, to hold her breath and let them roll over her head.

"Oh, Manuel, it is just glorious," Paula exclaimed. "I never knew anything could be such fun. I just love the feel of the sands washing away under my feet as the waves go out, and it feels so wonderful when we let the waves lift us right off the ground. But don't let go of me, my love. I'd be so scared."

Manuel held her safely, sometimes just by the hand, sometimes with both arms round her waist as they rose with the waves or ducked under them. The water, now they were used to it, felt warm and wonderfully soothing. Paula's face was as radiant as that of a child as the water splashed it again and again.

"We better go in now, my darling," Manuel declared. "This is your first dip in the ocean, and you mustn't catch a chill." He led her by the hand toward the beach.

"You mean 'go out,' not 'go in'," she giggled, laughing with joy. "It's been such fun!"

"Let's have our picnic right on the beach, precious, and let this warm sun dry us off. Let me get you a towel before you sit down on the sand."

Manuel left her on the beach while he ran up to the glen and removed a package from his saddle bag, then returned with two cups of water from the rill, and the package of lunch, and four towels under his arms. Seated on two of the towels, they ate the cold chicken and bread the cook had put up for them, and sipped the cool water, as the sun dried their gleaming bodies.

"Let's just lie here in the sun, my sweet," Manuel whispered, and he put his arm under Paula's head as they lay on their backs side by side, with the towels beneath them.

They closed their eyes, and Paula murmured: "This feels so good, Manuel. If I were a cat, I'd purr." And she snuggled closer to him, then gave a little wiggle of sheer joy, and bent over to give him a kiss.

In a moment they were again experiencing the raptures of love, and it felt so strange to Paula, naked on the beach with the towels and soft sand so firm beneath her churning bottom and Manuel plunging, groaning and panting above and within her.

They panted happily as they lay there, completely spent but still coupled and savouring the last drop of joy in one another's arms.

"My I *am* a mess," exclaimed Paula. "My hair's full of sand, and I've never had so much sand on me before. It's everywhere—look, even my navel is full of sand, Manuel. Let's go in the water again and wash this sand off," she added.

"Good idea," he replied. "But we shall stay in only for a few minutes, and then dry ourselves, and ride back to Noya. I have another treat for you this afternoon."

So they entered the water again, and helped one another to rinse the sand, emerging clean and sparkling with the salt sea dew.

"Your hair will dry in the wind," remarked Manuel. "And, as it's short, it will soon look lovely. Not that it doesn't look lovely right now—and you, too. If I were younger, I'd love you in the sand again, you look so sweet and happy."

"Younger?" exclaimed Paula. "Thank goodness you're not any younger. I don't know what I'd do. With my old bones, once is enough. And we're going to be so happy together, Manuel. I'm so happy now—so terribly happy, and so terribly in love."

He bent over to give her a tender kiss on the forehead, and soon they were off and away, galloping back on the road to Noya. The sun was low in the heavens as they drew up in front of a little bar down by the *ría*, opposite the fish market. The market was now closed, and men were busy swabbing the stalls and floors with buckets of water and long brooms.

"Here we are," said Manuel, dismounting, and tying the two horses to a rail in front of the establishment.

"What! This tiny little place?" asked Paula, somewhat dismayed at the far from elegant atmosphere of the tavern.

Inside, in front of the bar, there were a dozen small wooden tables, most of them with two men seated facing a steaming casserole, a glass of wine or sherry beside their plates. Some of the tables were occupied by fishermen, others by townsfolk, but all were busily engaged in animated conversation and in devouring the contents of the casserole in front of them.

"There's not a lady in the place," whispered Paula, still taken aback by the motley appearance of the customers.

"There is now, my love," Manuel smiled, as he seated Paula at one of the tables by the window, and seated himself opposite. "Good evening, Pancho. A large one for two, and two *manzanillas*."

"Good evening, *Señor Conde*," their host exclaimed. "How glad I am to see you here with your bride. I've heard so much about her, and I congratulate you, *Señor Conde*, on your good taste and good fortune."

Don Manuel and doña Paula expressed their thanks, and several more of the townsfolk came over to offer their congratulations, don Manuel introducing each of them by name. Meanwhile, Pancho had given the order to the cook, and was busy drawing two glasses of pale *manzanilla* from one of the five large casks behind the bar.

"Oh, it's like sherry," Paula said. "I thought *manzanilla* was tea."

"It is tea in Andalucía," Manuel laughed, "but here in Galicia, *manzanilla* means this dry, pale wine. If you want tea, you must ask for *té de manzanilla.*"

In a few minutes, their host brought them a large casserole, filled to the brim with steaming blue-black mussels, two deep plates, two wooden spoons, two napkins, and a number of warm, hard rolls. "I brought you the two and three year olds, *Señor Conde*. I know you like the little ones," Pancho said with a smile.

"Thanks very much. I do indeed," smiled Manuel.

"Let me show you how," he said to Paula, beaming as he dished out half a dozen mussels and a large helping of the broth onto Paula's plate. He took one of the mussels in his fingers, opened the top shell and put it to his mouth, deftly extracting the succulent mollusk with his upper teeth and tongue. "And then you dip your bread into this hot broth and eat it with a spoonful of the broth."

Paula followed suit. "Why these are delicious!" she exclaimed. "The bread and broth are marvelous, and the mussels go so well with the *manzanilla*. What is your recipe, Señor Pancho?"

Their host beamed at the compliment. "It is simple—the mussels are steamed in white wine with chopped parsley and garlic until they open. The spices are my secret. I don't want your husband to set up a rival establishment here in Noya, milady."

Doña Paula laughed when don Manuel said that this was precisely what he intended to do, if he could ever learn the secret. "But you can tell me, Señor Pancho," she asked, "what you keep in those other four casks behind your bar."

"I can indeed, milady—there are two casks of sherry, *fino* and *oloroso*, and two casks of wine from the vineyard of don Belarmino, red and white. But the true connoisseurs," he added confidentially, "always ask for *manzanilla* with their mussels."

After their host had left to attend to other customers, Paula gushed: "I do like this place, Manuel. So friendly and informal. And the mussels are exquisite." She leaned closer to her husband, and whispered: "You think of so many delightful things, and I do love doing them with you. And I love Galicia too, now and forever after. And, oh, Manuel dear, I *am* so happy."

When the last tender mussel had been dislodged from its shell, the last drop of broth savoured with the hard bread, Paula and Manuel finished their *manzanillas,* bade goodbye to their friendly host and to Manuel's friends, and were soon off again to their honeymoon *pazo.*

The groom, butler, and housekeeper greeted them with even friendlier smiles than on the preceding day. And dinner that night was also simple—a roast leg of baby lamb, and a *jardinière* of fresh vegetables, with a pale red claret, all a product of the manor's garden, vineyard and meadow. Instead of a walk that evening, Paula had found a guitar in the music room, and played a Galician song that Marilú had taught her, and then several Andalucian melodies. She had learned from Marilú how to finger and pluck the strings of the small guitar and, while she was by no means as deft nor as practiced as her tutor, her sweet contralto voice was charming—and Manuel was completely charmed. She played and sang softly, almost letting the words and music come whispering into Manuel's ears, as she sat on the floor at his feet. He taught her the words and tune of another *Gallega* song and joined his own deep baritone to her contralto. For some reason or other, tears came to their eyes as they finished the song, but they were tears of happiness rather than of nostalgia.

"I guess you are a complete *Gallega,* my love," Manuel smiled. "Even to the *morriña.* I too am moved to tears—but what we feel is not really *morriña*—you will get to know the Gallega bitter sadness in all due course. These few tears are just our joy at being together, singing together, loving together—and our regret that we did not know one another, and marry one another, five long years ago."

They left the music room, and walked arm in arm along the patio corridor to their bedroom.

The next day was spent quietly, no riding, no love-making, a short walk around the manor's pasture-land and farm, and then an early supper at the city house of don Belarmino Barbanza in Noya, to which he had invited some of Manuel's old friends, including some of their sons and daughters, sons-in-law and daughters-in-law, to provide the younger element essential for family gaiety.

For entertainment, don Belarmino had procured a troupe of Galician dancers and musicians, with their *gaitas*—the small bagpipes that were typical of that Celtic region. The music was melancholy, yet the tempo was lively enough to keep pace with the *muñeira,* a dance reminiscent of an Irish jig or Highland fling, as well it might be in the light of their common Celtic heritage. The dancers—two young girls and two young men in their late teens—were truly expert, the girls sweet and bonnie with their blond hair and blue eyes, the young men braw and bony, and of a like complexion. The dance and the music ended with a shrill cry, uttered by the dancers and musicians alike, that brought a startled "*Dios mío*" from Paula, to the amusement of the entire company.

It was late by the time Manuel and Paula bade their friends good-night. "I've had a lovely evening," Paula said, and it was clear that she really meant it as she kissed don Belarmino squarely on the cheek, much to his astonishment and delight, and to Manuel's amusement.

"You better call me 'Uncle Belarmino' if you're going to kiss me like that," the old man laughed. "We're not used to more than a hand-kiss here in Galicia."

"Nor in Andulucía either," Paula admitted. "But I'd love to call you uncle, for that's just how I feel. And it is so good of you to let us use your lovely *pazo*. You've made me feel so much at home, and I'm so happy in your beloved—my beloved Galicia."

It was another clear moonlit night for the brief ride back to the manor house, and they both felt so happy, so much in love that it was not long before they were again locked in amorous embrace. And then, once more, to happy dreams, and the sweet comforts of a marriage bed.

And so it went for three more days, their love sometimes as thrilling as the tempestuous mountain cataract or the wild beating of the ocean waves upon the rocks, but more often as tranquil and as lovely as the ripples on the quiet *ría*. And at last they headed back to Iria Flavia de Compostela, to Conchita and Marilú and all their other relatives and friends who had not the faintest idea where the wandering honeymooners had been.

Conchita and Marilú met them at the door, Conchita flying to her father's arms: "I am so glad to see you, *Papá*—and I have never seen you look so happy." And she transferred her embrace to Paula who was already being hugged ecstatically by Marilú. Marilú put her arms around her uncle, and bussed him on both cheeks, as Conchita screamed out: "Jorge, Gonzalo—they are home again."

This called for more fond *abrazos* and more affectionate kisses as Gonzalo and Jorge joined the group. They all trouped into the house together, laughing and talking, their arms around each other's waists—six people as happy as one could find in all of Spain, Moslem or Christian, or for that matter, anywhere in the whole wide world.